Praise for *To Kill a Common Loon* by Mitch Luckett

"Anyone with a taste for bizarre fiction will find plenty to feast
  on in these pages."
        — Portland *Tribune*

"Mitch Luckett writes with rare humanity and a quirky,
  disheveled grace. This is a marvelous, quixotic, funny book.
  There is no hero's story I would rather read."
        — Geri Doran, recipient of Academy of American Poets'
          Walt Whitman Award for *Resin*

"*To Kill a Common Loon* reads like a cross between Carl
  Hiaason and Edward Abbey. Mitch Luckett has invented
  crazy but convincing characters, both human and animal, in a
  magically, realistic whodunit."
        — Mick Houck, writer and Executive Director at Urban
          Greenspaces Institute, Oregon.

Praise for *The Man in the Loon* by Mitch Luckett

"Toss together a banjo-playing, recovering alcoholic with an
acrylic plate in his head, a hideous mental demon dubbed
Elpenor, a three-legged dog with the moniker Medusa, a
beautiful young woman named April Old Wolf, a pampered
potbelly pig called Barbie Jane and an assortment of large
diving waterbirds known as common loons and you have a
fantastical mystery that steals your heart. Somehow, Mitch
Luckett brings this ragtag crew and their story into coherence
and winds up with a captivating novel. His love for animals,
little boys and suffering humans shines through."
    — Marjorie Reynolds

"Author Mitch Luckett does it again… a big dollop of humor
along with passages of wildlife, plant life, and a brooding
mystery."
    — Martha P. Miller

HOLY ROLLER HEART

Holy Roller Heart *is dedicated to Alma,
my dear Mama, who was keen to inform
anyone within earshot: "I got my false
teeth the same day Mitchie was born,
and my teeth ain't never caused me a bit
of trouble."*

B&H Bennett &
Hastings Publishing

Bennett & Hastings titles may be ordered through
booksellers or by contacting:
bennetthastings@yahoo.com.

Author photo: Russ Stamp (stampphotography.com)
Editor: Adam Finley (adamabroad@gmail.com)
Map: Janet Anthony
Layout and cover: AgioPublishing.com

Contact Mitch at mluckett43@gmail.com or
visit www.mitchluckett.com.

Holy Roller Heart
ISBN 978-1-934733-91-2 (print)
ISBN 978-1-934733-92-9 (ebook)

10 9 8 7 6 5 4 3 2 1

HOLY ROLLER HEART

MITCH LUCKETT

B&H Bennett & Hastings Publishing

PART I

Book of Conjuration

And beheld among the simple ones,
I discerned among the youths,
a young man void of understanding.

— Proverbs 7:7

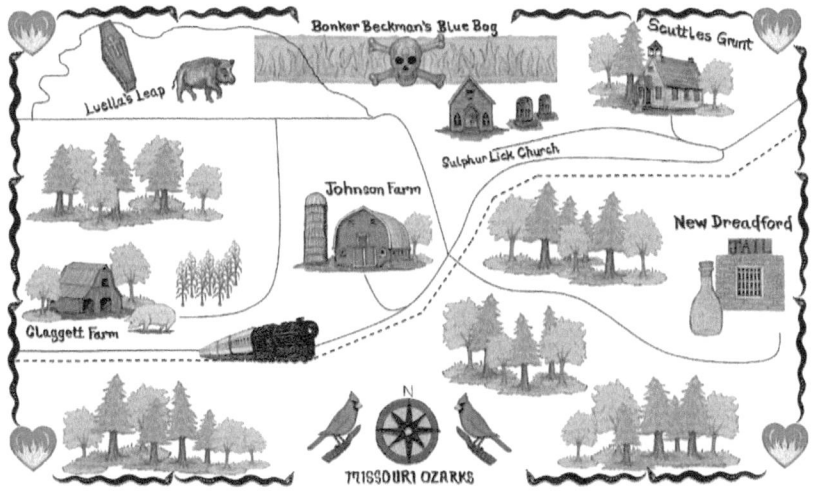

CHAPTER 1

Delicate Polarity and Warts'n All

First time I saw the two-headed preacher, the two-headed preacher only had one head. And one mouth. First time I heard that one mouth was at Mama's wedding to Freeman Joe Claggett in the year of our Lord, 1954, and that one mouth was a'shouting hell and damnation you could call home about.

'Cept you'd get no answer. We never had no telephone. No 'lectricity neither. Mama made sure of that before she conjured Freeman Joe into marrying her. She'd never take us seven kids to live in any place that had 'lectricity. She couldn't abide powerful, invisible current she didn't control. Said it put a stitch in her polarity.

Mama's delicate polarity was the main reason she married the craziest man in Sulphur Lick Valley, maybe the craziest man in the whole Ozark Mountains of Missouri.

Mama, the morning before her wedding, sat us seven kids in a circle on the plank floor of our cabin. 'Cepting for having Mama's hazel eyes and droopy nose, none of my five older sisters looked alike on account of having different fathers. But me, the only boy, and Millie Faye were twins and the youngest and, of course, had the same daddy, who Mama called 'the sonsabitch' every time his name was mentioned.

Mama lit beeswax candles around the room and crouched in the middle of our circle. She had her mortar and pestle in her lap and ground foul smelling orange and black roots, dog bane and felonwart.

She sniffed the aromatic mixture, smiled and told us that Freeman Joe's wild energy was what she needed to balance hers.

"'Sides being touched in the head in a good way," Mama said, "Freeman Joe and his brother Harman Cornelius own a farm with a big farmhouse. You girls will split two bedrooms, and Mo Grady—well, he's getting of an age he needs a room of his own."

She gave me one of her knowing looks. My flesh burned in the thumb and finger bruise pattern on my left shoulder put there by my soon-to-be step-Uncle Harm.

"Can me and Mo Grady have a dog?" Millie Faye said. "Don't matter how good a farm it is, it ain't worth a tinker's damn without a working dog to protect us from the beasts of the Blue Bog."

"No, you can't have a dog. Ain't I got enough mouths to feed?" Mama said, pointing her pestle at my wee twin. "And watch your goddamn foul mouth, Millie Faye. You wasn't raised that way."

Mama banged the pestle against the stone bowl, attacking the flora with ferocity. I knew she'd use that stinky concoction to shore up her sanctification spell to cleanse the shack we were leaving.

"You're gonna be around God-fearing righteous folks all afternoon," Mama said. "I swear, you twins been nothing but trouble and heartache."

Mama didn't mean it about us twins being trouble and heartache.

Well ... Millie Faye's condition. She hadn't grown nary an inch since she was six. And that missin' heart gave Mama no end of grief—me, too. Doc Abernathy called it an arrhythmic ticker. Been that way since she almost upt'n died of the rheumatic fever. Mama says I have to spend all my waking time watching out for her so she don't get so excited her heart starts missing a tock as well as the tick.

What Millie Faye lacked in size, she made up for in mouth. Had herself a bon-a-fide preacher's mouth, loud and carrying, with a bad habit of telling the truth about folks to their face. That's why people thought she was retarded.

Truth-telling ain't highly regarded 'mongst holy roller folks in Sulphur Lick Valley. Ain't exactly sought out 'mongst conjure folks neither.

But me, a normal thirteen-year-old boy, didn't cause Mama no grief a'tall. Well, not much. I did have this little problem with homing in on things. Mostly new things. I never had nothing new. That sugary smell of newness near to drove me nuts. "You're like an ol' hound dog gnawing on a fresh jawbone," Millie Faye says. "Can't let it go once you sink your teeth into it. One of these days, you're gonna grab a'hold of some unholy demon that'll bite back hard and drag you kicking and screaming through the gates of hell. And don't expect me to save your sinning hide. All I got time for is fixin' on how to persuade Mama to let us have a dog of our own."

That mouth. That running mouth.

Mama poured the herbal powder in an earthenware bowl. "Now I want y'all to pack what things you're taking and put on your clean Sunday-go-to-meeting clothes for the wedding. Then wait in the yard while I get this old shack ready for the next poor sinners. Ain't much, with the leaky roof and copperhead nest under the porch, but it's been a sanctified home to raise young'ns in."

Me and Millie Faye went around the back of the house. I hoisted her up on my unbruised shoulder, and we watched Mama through the one window in the cabin.

"Mama sure is a powerful cleanser," Millie Faye said, hanging on to my hair with her baby hands. "When I grow up I'm gonna be a con-jurer just like her."

"You're never gonna grow up," I said.

She bit my ear.

I howled.

Mama shook her pestle at us. "You two trouble-makers get away from that window, or I'll turn you into horny-toads."

We ran off holding hands, giggling into the woods. Mama had threatened to turn us into toads for years and hadn't done nary so, yet. 'Sides, we liked toads, warts'n all.

CHAPTER 2

Dazzling Ankles
and the Swallow Dance

Mama's wedding took place in a tent pitched at the bottom of Cemetery Hill. The day was so muggy even the dragonflies saved energy by hovering in place, fanning themselves. Their red and green wings decorated the space around the tent. Underneath them came a girl about my age. Long ruby curls bounced behind her. She wore a one-piece blue dress that didn't cover her ankles like the Holiness Christian girls.

I homed in.

The skin on her ankles dazzled in the hot sun.

My head congested.

"That's the Johnson's granddaughter," Millie Faye said, nudging me in the ribs. "Loveda. She's ugly'ern a butter churn in pig flop, ain't she?"

My throat was too tight to talk.

Loveda breezed past me. Her blue, fall chicory bloom eyes looked at me and widened to the size of silver dollars. A faint scent of jimson weed and lilacs tickled my nostrils. I hurried and took a seat where I could watch her.

I don't remember much about Mama's wedding. My mind blazed with red and green wings, lilac perfume and sunlit ankles.

I do know the Reverend Jesse James Waywater—Millie Faye and me hadn't yet started calling him the two-headed preacher 'cause he still only had one head—came all the way to Sulphur Lick Valley to marry Mama and Freeman Joe Claggett on account of the groom was brother-in-law, to be, to the reverend.

Freeman Joe's sister, Bertha Sue—the Reverend's wife—and his older brother, Harman Cornelius, stood with him at the altar. The Claggetts were a large-boned family. Mama looked dwarfed standing with them.

Harman Cornelius was the least crazy one in his family. Everyone in Sulphur Lick Valley agreed. But, being uninsane gave him a touch of meanness.

Bertha Sue was just as big and twice as mean as Harman Cornelius and, folks said, filled to the brim with brittle sanity and righteous ambition. Proof being, she was hitched to the preacher and everyone knows preacher men, being ambassadors of the Lord, have a divine fix on reason and righteousness.

Bertha Sue held wilting flowers and swatted at flies.

Freeman Joe didn't really say the "I do's" when the one-headed preacher asked if he'd take Mildred Garnet Witt as his lawful wedded wife, on account of him being stuck in tongues. So, Harman Cornelius said the "I do's" for him.

Freeman Joe was apt to get stuck in tongues. Before he met Mama, whenever he got stuck, his brother took him up to Springfield to the nut hospital for shock treatment. Mama couldn't abide doing that. She, on their wedding night, hooked his ear lobes up to the negative and positive side of the deep-cycle, 12-volt grain-grinder battery, had me pull-start the gas generator, and we zapped Freeman Joe with Mr. Edison's invisible juice.

"This ol' grinder," Mama said, "is a whole lot less trouble than a drive clear up to Springfield. And, you get some hog feed ground in the bargain."

Mama, although steeped in the backwoods art of wildcrafting, was not against using advanced technology as a sort of do-it-yourself-in-home-mental-health curative. She had nothing against 'lectricity as long as she directed it.

Freeman Joe, jolted, halted in mid-jabber. His eyeballs rolled around. Tongue slowed to a halt. He flung his arms and legs—a bull-frog impaled on a gig.

Mama glanced at me. "And I seed that look in your eyes, Moses Grady Witt. Don't you dare be trying this on Millie Faye when she has one of her dead cockroach fits."

I wiped the smile off my face and scratched that itchy place behind my knee, wondering how Mama knowed the workings of my undisciplined mind.

Their wedding night, Mama fed Freeman Joe a love potion and led him, grinning like a barn cat drunk on catnip, into the bunkhouse. She put up a sign:

DO NOT DISTURB UPON PENALTY OF HADRAS' WRATH

Mama was not opposed to sicing pagan witches on us when she wanted us to mind.

"All 'n all," Mama said, emerging two days later, skin flushed from concentrated honeymooning, "I should've got married years ago." She looked plum tuckered out, eyes sparkling with wheat flakes in the morning light. Freeman Joe's catnip grin was gone, replaced by a frozen hound-dog smile. His bushy, black eyebrows, crooked and flat.

The next day, Mama, all five-foot nothin' of her, stood in a white purification robe and blessed and spelt the Claggett brothers' red clay, Ozark hog farm. Her long black hair smelled like rosemary and angelica.

She made us seven kids stand, hands joined, in a circle around an old oak stump. Using the stump as a table, she laid out herbs while we chanted: "Praise Jesus, we is blessed, hallelujah, we is blessed." Our feet, in spite of it being against the Lord's teachings, couldn't keep from dancing this way and that.

Mama ground three herbs: fumitory, mugwort and vervain. She poured the mixture into a square cloth and tied it with a red thread. Facing north, she placed the tip of her magic knife against the sachet and said, "May this, which I have fashioned today, serve as guardian of this house and all who reside within, especially them that need it the most, Mo Grady and Millie Faye."

She hung the sachet over the front door and peered around. Closed her eyes and listened to the evil east wind whispering. All east winds, being against the natural rotation of the earth, were negative influences to Mama.

I listened to the wind, too, setting up a lot of ruckus and rattle around that old farmhouse.

Mama gathered her robe up and sent my five older sisters inside. They knew she was in one of her spell-spinning moods and things could get ugly. Millie Faye, who sore loved gruesome ceremonies, screamed and fell on her back, stick arms and legs straight up in the air—her famous dead cockroach fit.

Mama, not wanting her conjury jinxed, let her stay.

"We need meat for supper, Mo Grady," Mama said, "and I need to do extra purification. This old farm is nigh to burstin' with negative energy. Not a good woman's set foot on it in years. You run out to the barnyard and get me a young rooster. And hurry, I don't like the looks of those clouds pussel-bunching up over Luella's Leap."

I picked up a smooth pebble and ran around the barnyard, scattering chickens, ducks and pigs. I spotted that violet-green feathered banty rooster with a red top-knot that attacked Millie Faye when she got near the hen house. I wound up and let fly my Bob Feller fastball. Caught the rooster square in the chest. Feathers flew and he dropped. I grabbed him and ran back to Mama. My hands held him on Mama's sticky chopping block while she murmured:

"Beware the oak, it draws the stroke.
Avoid the ash, it courts the flash.
Creep under the thorn, it will save you from harm.
None for the rooster, one for the crow.
One to rot, one to grow."

That rooster woke as Mama's knife chopped off its crested head in mid-cluck. The abruptest sound in the world is the thunk of a knife cutting the core off a scared cluck. Mama caught the flopping body and dribbled its blood around the outside of the farmhouse.

Keep Satan out. Keep safe in.

Mama came back around the house, her white robe red splotched and the rooster bled dry. She pointed the bloody neck at me. "Don't you ever cast a spell like this, Mo Grady, until you get old enough to understand the responsibility. A spell can go bad in a full-moon minute without the proper ritual. The Conjurer's Law of Three says bad spells come back to haunt the goomer three times over."

Mama, a goomer—some say yarb—doctor, practiced a blend of witchcraft and holy roller Christianity handed down from her mama and her mama's mama who was half-Celtic and half-Cherokee. Mama wanted us kids, 'specially me and Millie Faye, to have balance and polarity to fill the spiritual void when conjure folks become extinct.

The rooster's red crest faded to dull pink next to the chopping block. The eye opened and closed, getting milkier until it finally stayed open and fully milked over. A crow atop the barn flew down and pecked it out, escaping with its pearly delicacy before Jubal Jen, my 600-pound pet sow, lumbered up for her red meat treat.

Mama's purification ceremony took all the dancing and chanting and praising heaven right out of me. Suppertime came, but I wasn't hungry. Goomering can sure put a stitch in your gut polarity.

My new stepdad, after Mama's marathon honeymooning, floated around the barnyard, shoulders back, head tilted up, watching barn swallows fly. He made like a scarecrow, mesmerized, I think, by the beauty and wisdom of the swallows.

Some landed on his outstretched arms, peeping a message in the language of birds. Some pooped on his arms. He poked a glistening glob and grinned like he'd nudged a gold nugget.

I took a feather, held it up, let it drop. A swallow careened down and nabbed it mid-air. Freeman Joe giggled, flapped his arms and pumped his knees up and down.

He tried dropping a feather. Pretty soon one bird after another took feathers right out of his hand.

Maybe they kept snagging feathers for the same reason I kept finding them: it made Freeman Joe happy to dance the swallow dance. And just 'cause he, a big crazy man, looked so blissful doing it, I danced the swallow dance with him.

Flap your arms up, flap your arms down, do a head dip and wiggle all around.

Wondered what it would be like to dance the swallow dance with Loveda. See her dazzling ankles do the do-si-do. Creamy skin made my feet feather-light.

What it is, is dancing with swallows has got a lot of grace to it, is what it is.

CHAPTER 3

Warm Spit-Chaw and Red-Hot Shame

"I ain't retarded," Millie Faye said, "I'm just puny."

Kids teased Millie Faye about her size and didn't a day go by she didn't have to set them straight, which usually ended up in a fight. 'Course her foul, truth-telling mouth didn't help matters. She'd spent all of last year being sick a'bed with the rheumatic fever, honing her incendiary truth-telling skills and wrecking her heart.

Mama told me to protect her, so I spent half my school recesses rescuing her.

Me and Millie Faye, in spite of teasing and fighting, loved school though me not being much good at it. We 'specially liked when Miss Haige, our teacher, would read us stories, like about kids going down the Mississippi River in a wooden raft. The latest was about a little girl named Heidi who lived with her grandfather in a place called the Swiss Alps.

I also loved school 'cause of how the Hazeycamp sisters filled out their clothes.

One day, just before the first winter snow, I sat on a stump during recess, watching a game of girls' kickball, and some kids told me Millie Faye was at it again, this time with the Postlewaite brothers out at the edge of the Blue Bog.

I ran through Bonker Beckman's Auto Wrecking Yard where it overflows into the Blue Bog, when the smell of a black '55 Buick V8 called like a Siren from Sodom. Stopped me cold. The sweet oily fragrance, tinged with spilt gasoline, charred metal and burnt flesh sizzled in my nose. My feet detoured me over.

Millie Faye could wait.

The Buick arrived Sunday after church, its front end pulverized after losing a race with the Springfield to Fort Smith freight train at Smother's Junction. Witnesses couldn't say why the driver, a Revisionist Methodist minister from Reed Springs, tried to outrun the train. Or why, if he was trying to commit suicide, he did so with his wife and kids in the car.

I stuck my head in the driver's side. A metal object the size of a can of chewing tobaccy lay wedged under the brake pedal in a pool of copper-colored liquid. All the cramped light in that dank interior concentrated on that round silver disc. I wondered if the minister couldn't brake 'cause of it being there.

My butt squeezed between the crumpled steering wheel and front seat. I used my purple handkerchief to lift up the brake pedal and pluck the disc out of the goo. Smelled like blood and antifreeze, and felt thick and tacky.

I wiped it. Palmed it. My fingertips felt a humming. The film of dried blood vibrated off, leaving the disc as clean and rosy smelling as the belly of a newborn piglet.

I held in my hand a magnet, and a righteous one, too. So powerful, I could feel the negative and positive polarity pushing and pulling at my flesh. A tremor traveled straight up my arm to the black and blue pinch marks on my left shoulder put there by Uncle Harm during our last Temptation Training session in the billy goat stall of the barn.

Warmth coming from the magnet overrode the soreness. A magic magnet?

I had an idea. I wedged the disc underneath my green flannel shirt and overalls strap, suck side down on my shoulder. Suck out the pain and the shame.

The magnet hunkered down like an old plow sinking into new ground. The soreness quit, but the shame hit me like a kicking cloven hoof. Red hot and pulsing.

I got dizzy. I was suddenly kneeling down back in the billy goat stall, the ripe stench of animal urine and dung and rotted straw clotting my nostrils. Uncle Harm's thick thumb and trigger finger pinched my shoulder, his kerosene breath hot on my neck as he leered down at my stretched pecker in his other hand, his lantern jaw working a big chaw of Cactus Ed chew tobaccy.

"The good Lord loves you, boy," he said, "just as I love you. You're 'bout to travel that broad highway of destruction. Me and the good Lord will yank those Satan inspired thoughts about girls out of your head. Pray with me."

'Pittooee! Warm spit-chaw hit my pecker. My brain flooded with fibrous filth. Skin recoiled. My scared pecker tried to draw itself up into my scrotum and hide like male lambs do to keep from being castrated. But it was no use. Uncle Harm held my poor pecker firm in his grimy fist.

I tried with all my sinful heart to pray away nasty thoughts about girls, but the prayer got choked off somewhere between pecker and 'pittooee! My prayers reversed polarity. I prayed Uncle Harm would go away and never come back.

The Temptation Training vision was driven away by the bleats of Millie Faye and the laughter of the Postlewaite brothers in the Blue Bog.

"I ain't retarded," I heard Millie Faye scream. "I'm just puny."

"'Sides being retarded," I heard Eugene Ray, the oldest Postlewaite, say with a hound dog whine, "you're a goblin and my papa says your mama's a swamp-trash witch and we can burn you at the stake the next time we catch you spreadin' lies about us."

"Mo Grady, where are you?" she screamed. "I'm fixin' to die, I am, I am."

I squirmed out from under the mangled Buick's steering wheel and ran around a burned-out '39 Nash Roadster onto the outskirts of the Blue Bog. My twin sister stood, tied to a persimmon tree, yellow and red fall leaves piled around her. Her runty body wiggled against a rope wrapped around her wee chest and encircling her lower half down to her knees.

Eugene Ray pulled out a match beside a red tin of Prince Albert smoking tobaccy in his overalls breast pocket. His cloaked eyes flitted back and forth from me to the match. He wore a dirty T-shirt, although it was mid-December, and his biceps corded with red and blue veins.

He was in the same grade as me and Millie Faye but had flunked four years of school so he was old enough and, apparently, smart enough to get his Missouri State driver's license. The only kid in eighth grade at our one-room schoolhouse in Scuttles Grunt, Missouri, who drove to school—a black '38 Dodge coupe. Eugene Ray was always trying to get the older girls to take recess in that coupe, 'specially the Hazeycamp sisters.

Millie Faye's frog eyes spotted me. "I'm gonna tell Mama about you, Mo Grady. Mama told you to look out for me, and I'm 'bout to get burned crispy'ern a duck turd on hot iron."

Eugene Ray hiked his muscled leg up and struck the match on the back of his pants.

Two crows teased a red bird in the branches of an oak. The plucky red bird chirped, "Good cheer, good cheer, pretty, pretty, pretty."

"My mama ain't swamp-trash," I said.

My feet took off running at Eugene Ray, and in the rush to save Mama's honor and my sister's life, I forgot I had the magnet riding on my bruised shoulder. My shoulder, magnet and all, hit him chest high, right in his red tin of Prince Albert. Steel collided with tin, loud as a 4-10 shotgun blast. The tin of tobaccy poofed open and a cloud of dark brown flakes surrounded us.

Eugene Ray, me on top of him, skidded in swamp duff. The smell of match Sulphur and mildewed clothes mingled with fresh tobaccy. My bruised collarbone near to exploded with the impact.

The younger Postlewaite, Clayton Wayne, face pitted with acne and red with rage, jumped on my back, laying lumps on my ears and the back of my head with tough farm-boy fists.

My ears clanged as loud as Baptist church bells in a cave. I tried shaking off Clayton Wayne and rolling off Eugene Ray. I was wedged tight between the two raw-boned boys who both outweighed me by fifty pounds.

My ears clanged free. A tinny voice chugged through white noise.

"Mo Grady! Quit foolin' around and help me. My missin' heart is fixin' to quit and the flames are fixin' to lick my toes."

Eugene Ray kneed me in the groin. Sour-and-rotten-teeth breath in my face.

Yep, Millie's Faye's missin' heart caused me no end of trouble.

Mama blamed Millie Faye's pygmy size on our daddy, a no-account banjo picker, the sonsabitch. Mama loved the way that man picked "Day of Jubilo" and "Wind That Shakes the Barley." Trouble was, when she, after one night of rapturous coo-chi-cooing, cast a stay-at-home spell on him, it backfired. It backfired times three. First, that banjo-pickin' man went on down the road anyway. Next, nine months later along come'd me and Millie Faye, and then, adding blister to burn, along come'd my twin's diminutive size. And if'n you wanted to have some add ons; her missin' heart. And don't forget her fits.

Nobody does fits like Millie Faye does fits. She'd learned how to fake them so's she could get anything she wanted.

My chin twisted over my magic magnet and bruised collarbone enough to see leaves burning around my sister. The evil east wind swirled. Fire crackled and smoke billowed to where all I could see was tiny lace-up shoes trying to climb the persimmon tree backwards, an acorn nose wrinkling and a doll's mouth gasping for air.

This was the first time anyone tried to set Millie Faye on fire. I wondered, between fist blows to my head, what she said to piss them boys off so.

I was slipping away into darkness. All I had left was prayer: "Please Lord, let Millie Faye's missin' heart take over so's she can go into her Number 4 fit—it's the petrified mummy fit in case you forgot—so's she can go into a coma and won't feel nothin' when the flames burn her crispy'ern a duck turd on hot iron. Amen."

Now, I could get beat to a bloody pulp in peace.

But Millie Faye called out to me in her silent voice—our twins voice only she and I could hear—that voice now registering total terror. "Help me, Mo Grady! I'm fixin' to burn!"

Clayton Wayne punched me again, hitting hard steel. "What the hell?" He clutched his hand. "You broke my knuckles!"

I reached under my green flannel shirt and overalls strap, slipping the magnet off my collarbone. My hand fit perfectly into a fist around the magnet. Its heft and negative polarity gave me positive strength.

My steel fist clobbered Eugene Ray upside a fleshy ear. He yelped. Then I flung my fist backwards and struck something that crunched, like a chicken head in Jubal Jen's jaws.

Clayton Wayne grunted and sneezed. Warm liquid splattered my neck, and he rolled off me.

I rolled off Eugene Ray in the other direction and stood up. Whoa! Made my lumpy head spin, seeing triple images of bog sycamores. Six Postlewaites, three with bloody noses and three with cupped ears, rose up and started toward me. Six mouths a'cursing. Twelve feet a'clumping. Three runty twin sisters a'coughing through black leaf smoke.

I stiff-armed the magnet, set on repel, toward the army of cussing Postlewaites. "If you don't leave me alone, I'll turn you inside out with my magic magnet and you'll look like gutted squirrels."

"That's just an old chunk of steel," Eugene Ray said. "We're going to kick your booger-dog ass all over Sulphur Lick Valley."

"At least let me put out the flames before it catches Millie Faye on fire."

"What?" Eugene Ray said. Both brothers turned toward the pyre. Eyes widened.

"Dedus, Dudgend Nay, whadud ou do?" Clayton Wayne said through a broken nose. "I tot weed jus donda scor er."

"It's Mo Grady's fault," Eugene Ray said. "He knocked the match in the leaves."

My eyes quit seeing triplicate.

Something stirred in the weeds. The red can of Prince Albert jumped up out of the grass and banged upside down against my magnet. Surprised me as much as it spooked the brothers.

That magnet had some powerful goomer juice! I figured one of Mama's spells was in order, and although she'd made me promise never, never to use a spell until I had the proper training, and never, never to use a spell to do harm else vengeance times three come down on me,

I reached into my memory of Mama's Goomer Guide Book "Spelting for Everyday Use" that I secretly read when she went to town.

I pointed the magnet-can hybrid at the younger brother:

> "Oh, perfect Lughnasadh, Queen of Swine,
> bubble and boil these boys in brine,
> of mandrake, bergamot and dragon's blood,
> till their flesh and bones be thin as mud."

Clayton Wayne's chin dribbled blood, and Eugene Ray's right ear was as scarlet as the red bird singing "pretty, pretty, pretty" in the hawthorn thicket. Them boys stared at that red can of Prince Albert joined to my silver disc like it was a cottonmouth eating a bull frog.

"Dedus, Dugene Nay," Clayton Wayne said, "I dink I beshit nyself." He took off running as if he had a wet possum in the seat of his pants.

Eugene Ray's egg-pod eyes hatched sparks of vengeance, but his hatching eyes couldn't hold his frightened feet—they churned after his brother through the wrecking yard toward the schoolhouse.

My hand dropped the magnet and tobaccy can. I tied my purple handkerchief around my mouth and nose and waded into the black fog, tromping the fire, hoping it wasn't too late for Millie Faye.

When I got in the thick of the smoke, my unswelled eye saw that the burning leaves were at least a hatchet handle away from her legs. No way they'd've torched her.

"What took you so long, Mo Grady?" Millie Faye said. "You're slow as a turtle in an oil slick since you've been going up to your secret place in the barn loft, playing with your tallywacker."

She made me so damn mad, I kicked some burning leaves between her legs. "You were never in no danger from them boys, but you might be from me."

Her little shoes stamped out the flames. "Mo Grady, you cut that out right now. I'm telling Mama it was you got my lace-ups burned if you don't hurry and untie me."

I stomped out more leaves. Fished in my pants and pulled out my Old Granddad pocket knife and cut the ropes. Millie Faye jumped up and circled my neck with her spidery arms. Her brown, straw-like hair poked me. Her thin wrists hurt my collarbone, but I didn't care. It was a sweet pain. I carried her away from the smoke.

She kissed me on the neck. Ugh! Sisters! Always trying to kiss and hug you.

"You're my hero, Mo Grady. You saved my poor, missin', holy roller heart from the monster of the burning abyss."

Her sweet-talking mouth was worse than her foul-talking one.

"Holy roller heart, my ass," I said. "Where do you get that stuff?" I pried her body off me and plopped her down in the creeping buttercups.

"Be warned, Millie Faye, one of these days I might not make it on time."

"Oh, you will, Mo Grady, you will. Else Mama will have your lowdown sinner's hide. Now lean over here and let me tend to your hurts."

Wasn't much she could do. My right eye was swollen shut, and the back of my head felt welty as if stung by yellow jackets. But she spit on her handkerchief with the blue doves Mama embroidered, and she washed grit out of my cuts.

When she finished, I picked up my magic magnet laying a foot away from the tobaccy tin. I turned the magnet suck side out. The tin wiggled toward us. Turned the magnet push side out. It retreated.

I wrapped my handkerchief around the magnet and stuck it in my pocket. Muffle its energy.

Didn't take no high school graduate to figure out my touch triggered the magnet's power. Question was, how to use such power?

I looked up at a gray-ribbed sky and saw storm ogres gathering.

CHAPTER 4

Riffraff and Fornication

We slipped in the back door of the schoolroom, but Miss Haige quit reading *Heidi* and cleared her throat. "Don't bother sitting down, Mo Grady. I'm kicking you out of school. Those poor Postlewaites told me how you beat them with a Devil's walking stick. I know they tease your little sister, but that don't give you the right to …"

"Begging your pardon, Ma'am," Millie Faye said, "I'm not his little sister. I'm his older sister by five minutes. And it wasn't Mo Grady's fault. Them Postlewaite perverts called me a goblin and my mama a swamp-trash witch."

Sleepy eyes stared at me and Millie Faye. Some belonged to our older sisters: Rose Phoebe, Bonnie Jane, Nora Lee, Sherry Mae and Wilma Ann. All five may have had different fathers, but all were tattletales—anything we said would get back to Mama.

Didn't matter none. I was in for it. I'd broken the goomer's law, and the vengeance-times-three conjury curse Number 1 one was coming down fast—gettin' expelled from school.

Miss Haige put a blue slip of paper in *Heidi* and closed the book. Her brow clinched, and her lips fidgeted until they found a frown they liked and stayed put. "I declare, Mo Grady, you've got five older sisters that are the model of proper conduct, and you and Millie Faye don't go a day without some kind of hocus-pocus that upsets my classroom. Now go home, and I don't want to see you back here until you write a thousand-word essay on the importance of education to your future, and then you must stand up in front of the whole class and apologize for interrupting their education with your shenanigans."

My swollen eye leaked a tear, scorching a path down my cheek. This was gonna pole-axe Mama's polarity. I whined. "I ain't never writ nothin' 'sides answers to test questions. 'Sides, how can I write about something I don't care nothin' about?"

Miss Haige stared hard at a cache of cobwebs on the ceiling. It's a wonder that spider highway didn't unravel on the spot. "Well, you'd better start caring or you're gonna remain a piece of poor, ignorant riffraff all your life."

I looked at the ceiling cobwebs. My formal learning was at an end before I even graduated from eighth grade.

Miss Haige turned to my twin. "I'm curious, Millie Faye. Just what did you say to the Postlewaite boys that caused them to treat you so shabbily?"

"They didn't treat me shabbily," my twin said. "They tied me to a tree and set me on fire." She hopped up on Miss Haige's desk and lifted her skirt, revealing her lace-ups. "See? Them shoes are still a'smokin'. Mo Grady done rescued me, I tell you. Now, can he stay in school so's we can hear more about sweet little Heidi? We've taken a liking to her, and I don't mind saying, she kinda reminds me of me."

The whole student body groaned, including my sisters.

Miss Haige gazed up at Millie Faye. "And what, pray tell, could you possibly have said to make the Postlewaite boys tie you to a tree and try to set you on fire?"

Millie Faye jumped down, and her warty eyes looked at me for help.

I whispered, my tongue thick as woody nightshade, "Go ahead and tell, Millie Faye. Just don't cuss. Mama says we wasn't raised that way."

Her hair crackled like dried black-cap mushrooms. "I just told 'em why nobody buys eggs from them anymore."

Miss Haige squeezed her forehead. "What has buyin' eggs got to do with them taking such extreme measures?"

"I don't know nothing about extreme measures," Millie Faye said, "but I reckon it was the way I told them."

"And how was that?" Miss Haige said.

Every student scooted closer to the edge of their seats.

"I told them if they want decent folks to buy eggs from them again," Millie Faye said, wetting her pale lips with a tiny pink tongue, "they'd have to quit fornicating with the laying hens."

The only sound in the room was a wood rat scurrying for cover under the plank floor.

Miss Haige's rodent eyes found mine. "Mo Grady, you take your foul-mouthed sister home with you. I don't want to see either of you back here till you have that essay and an apology."

I reckon my sister gettin' expelled from school was vengeance conjury curse Number 2. Mama was gonna be more pissed off than ever. She believed in education. Probably 'cause she didn't have much. Now I failed her—twice. Mama told me to take care of Millie Faye and here I got her kicked out of school, and me to boot.

"I doubt, Miss Haige," I said, grabbing Millie Faye's wee hand, "you'll be seein' much of me anymore. I ain't no essay writer—a thousand words or ten. No one can read my writing anyways."

"What about me?" Millie Faye said. 'I can 'pologize just as good as Mo Grady, probably better, and I already know the importance of getting an education—so's I can become a movie star when I grow up."

It was the Detweilder boy that snickered first. Set the whole room off into peals of laughter. Miss Haige laid her head down on her desk so's Millie Faye wouldn't see her sideways snigger.

The Henderson boy, through thin, scaly lips, said, "The only star she's gotta chance of being is a circus star."

Millie Faye looked up at me. "What's he mean 'bout being a circus star?"

Miss Haige raised her head off the desk and let out a sigh big enough to erase chalk on the blackboard. "Shut up, Henry Henderson!" She faced my twin. "Millie Faye Witt, I don't think a person of your size and personality needs much of an education, anyway. You may be better off staying home. However, if Mo Grady does his assignment,

I'm willing to let you back, too, provided you leave your foul mouth at the door."

I wondered what the third vengeance conjury curse was gonna be. And did I have any control over thwarting it?

If my magnet could cause Clayton Wayne to beshit himself, what else could it do? Make Uncle Harm quit his Temptation Training? If that goddamn training was so righteous and holy, how come I felt so angry? 'Sides which, it didn't work. Wasn't stopping my nasty thoughts about girls and didn't stop me from wantin' new things.

Millie Faye leaned into me. Didn't weight no more than a feather pillow. I looked down at her straw hair, her shadowed eyes, pale skin. I reckoned my sister, due to her delicate condition, had not taken well to farm life.

I reached in my pocket, wrapped my fingers around my magic magnet, letting its goomer power pulse into my veins. My other hand burned where it held my sister's. Energy rippled, riding my blood, between Millie Faye and my magnet, until hitting against a brick wall. Something behind that mental wall she didn't want me to know about. I released my magnet and her hand.

I reckoned if I really wanted to help her, I could get started on that thousand-word essay. No hurry, though. First, after Mama's punishment, I was gonna enjoy my freedom a spell. Hunt rabbits, skate on the pond, fish for bass and study me ways to get a dog.

"Now that I got plenty of time," Millie Faye said, as I dragged her out the schoolhouse door. "Maybe I can start by practicing on Jubal Jen."

"Practicing for what?"

"Standing on her back so's I can work up to horses so's I can become a circus star like Lizard Lips said. You know, like those beautiful girls riding white horses we saw when the circus came through town?"

"That's not the kind of circus star he was talkin' about," I said, but then clamped my mouth shut. How could I tell her that Henry meant she could star in a circus freak-show, like the fat lady or the alligator man? "Mama's gonna be mad, us getting kicked out of school. Don't you make it worse by tellin' her 'bout me putting a curse on them Postlewaites. Only reason I did it was to save your miserable hide."

"You won't think my hide is so miserable when I become a circus star," she said. "I just might let you groom my white stallions, if you mind your crappy manners." Millie Faye stopped next to the two-seater outhouse and looked back at the one-room school.

I detected a wee sigh.

"Does this mean," she said, "we ain't never gonna find out what happens to my sister under the skin—sweet little Heidi?"

CHAPTER 5

Unholy Growth and Uncured Mind

"Mo Grady," Mama said, "You're gonna sleep in the barn until you write that school paper." The wheat flecks in her hazel eyes turned to flint.

We were in the kitchen, and she grabbed her magic knife and whacked the gourd neck off a butternut squash. My heart dropped into my shoes. Writing that essay scared me worse than being attacked by Ol' Slasher, the Blue Bog's thousand-pound hog from hell.

"I reckon I'll be out there in the cold and lonesome all winter long," I said, trying to make her feel guilty. But I secretly liked sleeping out in the barn 'mongst all the critters—critters being a lot more interesting than sisters.

"Yeah, well don't get too comfortable," Mama said. "I know you don't mind being off school—but Millie Faye needs schooling. So you get to writing and practicing your stand-up apology tomorrow morning."

Sometimes it seemed like Millie Faye was no twin a'tall, but a toxic tumor. She would've had to sleep in the barn, too, had it not been for her delicate condition.

I put on an extra pair of long johns, wrapped my blue scarf around my neck—the one Mama knitted me last Christmas—grabbed my red bird quilt and made my bed in the barn's hay loft that night. Even with my magic magnet hugged between my thighs, with temperatures dropping below freezing, I near to froze my balls off. I got up, shivering, when I heard some clunking in the barnyard. I bundled my quilt around me and shuffled over to the loft bay door for a look.

The night was black as the rear end of a manure spreader, the air moist and still. Something moved down there. My ears picked up heavy breathing and an occasional snort. Couldn't a been Jubal Jen. She was in her pen inside the barn, all tucked in.

Probably Ol' Slasher. If it was, I wasn't about to mess with him in the middle of the night, even if I had my rifle.

I threw hay bales below to the barn floor and climbed down from the loft over the rabbit cages. I used cutters to snip the bale wires and spread out the hay. Made me a soft bed beside Jubal Jen. Despite her bodacious farts, creatures of the night seemed tolerable with a warm 600-pound sow between them and me.

A whole month went by with me out in the barn listening to things go bump in the night, pondering my wicked ways. Didn't nary a day go by Mama and Millie Faye asked me about my paper. I swear, I started that essay a thousand times in my mind, but not once did I sit down to write it.

Didn't have to worry about Temptation Training, neither, with Uncle Harm out of town on a construction job.

Then, in January, Mama brought home a pamphlet from the Wednesday night prayer service. The coarse yellow paper crackled in my hands. Said the Reverend Jesse James Waywater and his wife, Bertha Sue, my step aunt, were coming this Sunday to the Sulphur Lick "Saved From Perdition" Holiness Christian Church to bear witness and do some righteous soul savin'. All Ozark Mountain cavorters, thieves, coveters, murderers and fornicators were invited. I figured the church would be packed.

The preacher was set to do the Lord's work in our new house of worship that the faithful had quick built out of mill-end reject lumber. No more flimsy tents for the Reverend. A grainy picture showed him with another head on his right shoulder, hidden under a black overcoat.

We'd heard rumors how the preacher nearly died from a copperhead bite on his shoulder during a snake-dancing ceremony, and how he was resurrected and reborn with that hallowed hump, now grown to the size and shape of an overripe muskmelon. My step aunt towered over her husband 'cause of a pyramid of black hair piled on her head, the size of a hornet's nest.

Millie Faye called the preacher's hump-head "the Unholy Growth."

Me, I saw the light. I needed a laying on of hands. My magic magnet and goomering had put me in the hog house. Prayer and God's forgiveness would get me out. I reckoned I was the chief thief and coveter in Sulphur Lick County and, if not cured quick, was on my way to being a low-down cavorter. Fornication, I feared, was ready to strike, like a serpent coiled around my testicles.

Murder, at that time, was not yet on my uncured mind.

I opened the barn door and saw a new snow covering the land, adding resolve to my soul's need for confession and cleansing.

Mama detoured on her way back from the outhouse beyond the chicken coop to tell me we'd suffered a night raid from Ol' Slasher. She wanted me to quick repair the damage he'd done to the grain storage building before we all piled into our '38 Ford and drove the five miles to see the preacher at the new church.

I figured I'd better get in what sinnin' I could before I sought out my salvation. When I went in the house for a clean shirt, I pulled my magic magnet from my overalls breast pocket and aimed the suck side at Millie Faye's new jacks layin' on her bureau. Snatched them up from three feet away. Sounded like ten taps of a woodpecker's beak against tin siding.

I carried them shiny silver jacks on my morning chores with me just to take a good whiff of their newness. Took them into the barn's darkness, inside my straw-bale fort in the loft, to separate them from my magnet so's I could naturally toss and sniff them proper.

I had a good view from the loft of where Ol' Slasher's six-inch tusks had ripped the grain bin open. He might've liked our good winter grain, but he liked Jubal Jen better.

I stepped onto the block-and-tackle rope outside the hayloft window and rode it down to the snow-covered ground. Jubal Jen come'd lumbering around the side of the smokehouse, plowing a furrow through the snow, as she headed toward me with that pig-satisfied look on her snout. Her thick cherry-pink hide glowed pinker with the meat scraps I fed her, like lungs, kidneys and rooster heads. She was a gentle swine, except when anything threatened her piglets or me or Millie Faye.

I let her roam at will around the barnyard during the day. She liked to rub slobber the rich brown color of sassafras roots on me the way she did her squealing piglets. It smelled like mashed acorns and had the texture of clabbered milk.

Millie Faye says nobody does slobber like Jubal Jen does slobber.

I usually let Jubal Jen rub a little on my overalls, but today I had work to do and a soul to save—mine. I reached in my pocket, took out a sack of squirrel livers and shoved them under her melon-sized whiffer. Iron jaws opened and clamped, then I shooed her away.

I stopped working on the grain bin when I saw Mama hurrying toward me in the barnyard. "Mo Grady," She said, her breath popping like a tractor, "run to the Brockman place and phone Doc Abernathy to come at once. Millie Faye's havin' one of her fits."

My wee twin had gone into her Number 4 petrified mummy fit: her skin turned ash gray, her eyes rolled up in her head and she toppled over in a coma, mouth frothing.

Doc Abernathy was the town doctor, veterinarian, dentist, coroner—and a drunk ever since his wife died. Mama paid him for house calls by putting him in touch with his dead wife, who in the afterlife was much more tolerant of Doc's vices than she'd ever been in life. Mama also gave Doc potions—sachets of herbal medicinals and little Bull Durham bags of dried Destroying Angel mushrooms.

The way my older sisters tell it, Millie Faye really laid on the dog with cryin' and carryin' on like she does when she doesn't get her way—all 'cause she couldn't find her new jacks.

It was her own damn fault. I was gonna put them jacks back right after I got saved by the two-headed preacher. How was I to know she wanted to play jacks before church?

I grabbed my .22 caliber rifle and headed for the Brockman Place, following cloven tracks in the snow, leading toward the Blue Bog. I never went anywhere near the woods without my rifle. Not just 'cause of Ol' Slasher, but a starving wild dog pack, too, with a big, one-eared,

red-bone hound—bolder than previous pack leaders. We've always had feral dogs in the valley made up of the abandoned or abused. But Mama says if a feral dog is at your throat, it's too late to worry about whether it had an unhappy puppyhood so's I always kept my rifle cocked and ready.

Dodging last year's blackened corn stalk stobs, I dreamt of my very own dog protecting me against the bog beasts. I wanted a dog to love and to love me back in spite of my sinning ways. But Mama said a pet pig'd have to do 'cause she'd had it up to her druthers with dogs in the past. Men had not only left her with a baby in her belly but a passel of hungry coon hounds to feed or find homes for.

Ol' Slasher came to live in the Blue Bog through the dark arts. Story was, old man Postlewaite, drunk on corn likker, drove his black '38 Dodge coupe fast as lightning through a Gypsy caravan on Scuttles Grunt Road. Out of the dust and screams and blood rose a giant Russian Boar. That Gypsy hog let out a squeal that rattled the windows of Duncan's hardware store two miles away and galloped into the deep woods. The Gypsies acted like the world had come to an end, like that giant Russian Boar was Lucifer's cousin. They tracked him into the Blue Bog but had no luck. Figured he got into a tar pit or pocket of quicksand and died. Hoped he did, anyways.

Everyone in Sulphur Lick Valley got a big laugh over them Gypsies and their funny notions about heaven and hell.

We quit laughing one full-moon night a couple months later.

Turkey Tom Daniels heard some commotion in his sow pen so's he picked up his double barrel 12-gauge shotgun and went for a look-see. He'd come'd upon a great, blue shape in the moonlight. Thought it was a bull pestering one of his sows. He shooed it away, but the shape turned on him, stamping the ground with hooves the size of a plow horse.

The great beast, as Turkey tells it, smelled like the three diseases of corn—rot, smut and blight—all rolled into one. Twin tusks caught the moonlight so bright they lit up like the neon tubes in the window of the New Dreadford pool hall.

Turkey blasted both barrels of buckshot into the boar's hide. All it did was slow him down enough so's Turkey could drop his shotgun and climb a mulberry tree.

That boar charged and smacked that tree hard enough to break off limbs the size of a man's thighs. Sawed at the tree with his neon tusks, leaving gashes in the trunk—that's how he got the name Ol' Slasher.

Later that week, Turkey Daniels butchered all those prize sows before they had any piglets spawned by the devil boar and then got out of the hog raisin' business altogether. His hair turned white that winter and the slashed mulberry tree withered and died next spring.

With a good hound at my side and a rifle in my hand, let Ol' Slasher try to gore me. I was a crack shot. Could take the cap off an acorn at a hundred yards. Had me a .22 rifle since I was six. Mama finagled it from a traveling Bible salesman. She was a powerful finagler, proof being she got a rifle and box of shells from a Bible salesman without purchasing nary one Bible.

I ran, jumping over Ol' Slasher's hoof prints as fast I could through a foot of snow. Halfway through the cornfield, I turned right and ran parallel to Bonker Beckman's Blue Bog. It lay the entire length of the valley beneath Wrestler's Ridge, a long shelf of limestone rock. Me and Millie Faye called the bog Bonker Beckman's 'cause his Car Wrecking Yard spilled over into it.

The bog was laced with that blue clay that sticks to everything. It gave all the swamp critters a faint blue sheen, including Bonker Beckman.

A gray morning mist rose above the Blue Bog, shrouding Luella's Leap, the highest point on the ridge. Luella's Leap is where folks go to jump into oblivion or commit murder without the body bein' found. One leap or body toss and you'd disappear into the bog below, forever. Mama says a lot of my ancestors are buried there. Don't know if they were victims of suicide or murder—maybe both.

On clear days, I could see Luella's Leap from most places in town. Old timers say there's a logging road leading away from Luella's Leap that cuts through the mountains and Mark Twain National Forest and joins up with US Highway 70 near Bolivar, where, once you get on it, you can go anywhere in these United States. Even places on the other side of the world, like Kansas.

I figured, before I grew up and left Sulphur Lick Valley for good, I'd have to pay a visit up there. Look down on the whole valley and the bones of my kin. Take care my bones don't end up there.

I arrived at Brockman's farm out of breath. Called Doc Abernathy and told him Millie Faye was in her number four coma and a'fixin to die.

Jewel Brockman gave me a steamin' cup of Ovaltine to warm my innards before I made my trip back home. Said she heard from the Widow Johnson, who heard over the party line, that my rich step uncle, Harman Cornelius Claggett, was driving in Scuttles Grunt in a bran'-spankin'-new, red '55 Chevrolet.

I stepped out of the Brockman's house and glimpsed Luella's Leap through the mist. Old timers also say they've seen Ol' Blue Satan peeking out of that mist up there.

I sighed. Couldn't imagine what a bran'-spankin'-new, red '55 Chevrolet was like. I suspected, though, it bein' new, and since I hadn't yet been purified by the two-headed preacher, I'd like it a lot. What I didn't know was that me and that red Chevrolet was on a head-on collision course with the devil himself.

CHAPTER 6

Old Gooseberry and the Witt Curse

I could see Doc Abernathy's wreck of a beige '48 Pontiac already parked crossways in our driveway. Looked like it skidded in the snow to avoid smacking our old Ford. I jumped over the fence and back-tracked Doc's zig-zaggy footprints to his car.

I tipped up the bill of my Allis Chalmers ball cap. A weak light fell out of a low sky. Luella's Leap was outlined gray and chunky.

Jubal Jen waddled up from her favorite place near the smokehouse and lay down in the skid marks of Doc's car, slobbery snout against my leg.

Even with the windows closed, Doc's car smelled like cigar smoke, cracked leather and rotgut booze. The back seat brimmed with Plaster of Paris boxes, Camel cigarette wrappers, a wooden leg with the words "Old Gooseberry Lives"—Satan's nickname—on it in red crayon, empty liquor bottles, a meat saw and Marian Lee Mitchell's gray skull with a neat bullet hole in his right temple.

Marian Lee Mitchell lost his head in a poker game, during what Doc called "the best five-dollar bet I ever made." Doc's four threes beat Marian Lee's full house, aces over sevens, so Doc made him sign a paper willing his head for scientific purposes.

A few months later, when Marian Lee peeked out the door of Cap Smith's chicken house, the old sea captain ricocheted a .45 caliber bullet in and around the woebegone gambler's brain.

Doc paid his respects at the funeral service, waiting with his #10 meat saw and a woven basket to collect Marian Lee's head before they lowered the body into the ground.

He carried the skull around, he claimed, to demonstrate dental problems, but I think he did it so's folks'd sit tighter in his chair while he probed them with instruments of torture. Worked for my sisters.

I opened the back door of Doc's Pontiac, stuck my little finger through the bullet hole in Marian Lee's temple and brought his skull closer. His head seemed smaller than I remembered. Smelled better, too, a scrubbed talcum odor.

We stared at each other. The wind whistled a lonesome tune through his nose and snowflakes skittered, like white flies, in and out of his eye sockets.

"Howdy do, Marian Lee?" I said. "Ain't you kinda cold going out in this weather without nothin' on your head?" I put my Allis Chalmers cap on him. "What's it like being dead?"

I stuck a finger behind his molar and worked his jaws. *"Why thank you, Mo Grady,"* Marian Lee said. *"Been awhile since anyone inquired about ol' Marian's well-being. I'm doing just fine, I am. I reckon I'm the only one stayin' warm this winter, if you get my meaning, ha ha."* He laughed through an overbite, his lipless teeth clacking.

"Tell me, Marian Lee," I said, "will I be saved from perdition?"

"Can't tell you that, but I do see a blue ball of fire in your future, consuming all in its path, including your immortal soul. Woe to you, you'll wicked see, beware the snake that kisses thee."

My hair coiled in tight knots, pinching my scalp. I didn't remember Marian Lee as being given to spoutin' poetry while living.

"'Scuse me, Marian Lee," I said, "I don't suppose you'd know if my puny twin sister is faking her fit or not?"

"I 'spect your sister is always playing footsies with the tobac-cy-spittin' monster of the burning abyss. Why don't you give a listen to the good doctor and your mama? Redeem yourself before you end up like me."

Marian Lee's crooked teeth grinned. For a split second, I glimpsed a forked tongue flick behind those teeth. My fingers jerked out. I tore my cap off his head and tossed him back into the Pontiac. He rolled to a rest beside the wooden leg.

I slammed the door, rattling bottles of Four Roses Whiskey in a case in the front seat.

I turned around and saw shadows pass across the high kitchen window. Mama's shook like she was blubbering. She cried a lot 'cause Millie Faye died a lot.

I began to wonder, with the way things was goin' today, if I might never get to see the two-headed preacher for my sorely needed soul cleansing. Millie Faye once went into her petrified mummy coma for three days after my praying mantis collection ended up in her undies drawer.

I reckon she didn't fake that fit. You'd think being twins, I'd know. And I do know, sometimes. But we're as opposite as you can get. 'Sides her being a girl and me a boy, she was left-handed, I was right-handed, she was fragile as a fruit fly, I was healthy as a plow horse, she was afflicted with truth-telling, I was afflicted with … well, you get the idea.

No matter how much we fought, there was this link between us. We'd look at each other across the supper table or church pews and bust out laughing at the closeness of being together in each other's head, like we were still intertwined in Mama's womb.

I scratched Jubal Jen's ears as I looked at the kitchen window. It was too high. Couldn't see or hear much.

Jubal Jen's muffler-sized nostrils snorted snow across my shoes and steamed my ankles. Warm ankles make you think. I brushed snow off her back and sat on her, bronco style. Her tough bristles prickled my crotch. Jubal Jen gaacked once and then cooed. Happy to please.

I grabbed hold of her floppy ears, guiding her over to the window. I stood up, feeling my toes grab bristles through the thin soles of my shoes.

First thing I saw was Mama's wildcrafting quart and pint jars of bloodroot, sour dock, castor bean and blue vervain lining the kitchen walls. The pint jar closest had little dirty white bits, shriveled and sharp, like goblin's teeth. Too far away to read the label, but I knew what it said: Destroying Angel. Of all the mushrooms and herbs we kids gathered for Mama, Destroying Angel was the worst.

I'd asked Mama why gather something so poison?

"What can kill, can also cure." That's the way Mama talked —mysterious.

Mama and Doc huddled at the kitchen table, an Aladdin lamp's glow between them, making shadow circles on the red checkered tablecloth. Doc's face looked waxed and dried tight, squeezing his long ears flat against his balding head. His wide chin and cheeks had whisker stubble thick as Jubal Jen's bristles. A cigar stub grew out of his mouth, and a nose hung between his spectacled eyes with such a red tip, you'd a thought he was eating a pickled beet. He wore a rumpled white shirt, black suspenders and creased trousers. A bulge in his back pocket told me where he kept his whiskey flask. A black doctor's bag sat next to his chair.

Mama wiped her eyes with her favorite apron, the one with kissing white doves. The shadows brought out deep lines in her forehead. Her long black hair frizzed around her head like leaves of wild ginger. Her voice gurgled, a thistle burr caught sideways. "She's a little fooler, Doc. Can't tell sometimes if she's true passed out or not. What'd I do so terrible that the good Lord is testing me in such a way?"

Doc reached big, brown-splotched hands across the table and patted Mama's small, lean ones. "For starters, Mildred Garnet," he said, "you got seven kids with six different fathers. If you wasn't a goomer doctor, I doubt if these holiness Christian folks would put up with such promiscuous behavior."

"You never seemed to mind my 'promiscuous behavior' before," Mama said.

Doc looked up at the row of pint jars. Craned his head to peek behind the wood cookstove. "I don't reckon we ought to talk about that now that Imogene is dead. Her spirit might be listening in."

"Don't have to listen in," Mama said. "First time I conjured up your wife's spirit, I told her all about all the years you stopped by my house for medicinal and carnal fortification."

Doc pushed his chair back and staggered to his feet. His silver flask popped out of his pocket and clattered to the floor. "Good Lord, woman, what'd you do that for?"

"Don't get your stethoscope in a twist. Imogene said she knew all along and appreciated my sacrifice. 'Course, weren't no sacrifice to me. None a'tall. No, none a'tall."

My feet shuffled on Jubal Jen. Carnal fortification?

Doc picked up his flask, put it to his mouth, took a long pull and wiped his lips. "I always suspected Imogene didn't much care for my affections." He stared at a quart jar of Mama's love potion. "You don't reckon, after these troubles with the twins is over, that you and me can …"

Mama held up her hand. "No, I don't reckon, Thaddeus Albert Abernathy. I'm a proper married woman now."

Doc hurrumphed, coughed and farted in rapid order, like they were a package deal. "Now, getting back to Millie Faye, ain't a damn thing you done to cause her condition. And you got to quit being so crit'cle of yourself. Got to look at it like she's not a burden—she's a gift. Appreciate her while you got her."

"I dunno," Mama reached her hands up over her head toward the Pearly Gates. "I sometimes think Mo Grady, being so strapping healthy and passing strange, from the minute they's born, sucked the energy right out of his twin."

"I should have told you sooner," Doc said. "I sent off to the University of Missouri there in St. Louie and told them about your little girl. They sent back several similar cases." He fixed his eyes on the lamp's harsh glow. Waves of red checks washed across the table, while whiskey sweat rolled down his neck. "It's a form of growth problem called 'midget,' and combined with her heart affliction, I don't see her living past eighteen. You got to prepare yourself, Mildred Garnet. I'd advise making her feel special—treat her like a rare piece of china."

"Eighteen!" I nearly fell off Jubal Jen.

Mama cradled her head in her arms on the table and wept. "That settles it then," she said to the tablecloth. "We know which twin the Witt curse is on."

"Don't talk rot," Doc said. "I don't want to hear nothing about a Witt curse. Ain't no such thing."

"You know there is. Been twins in every other Witt generation since 1747, and ain't but one of them lived past eighteen. Died horrible deaths, too."

"Even if there is a curse," Doc said, talking around a cigar stub in his mouth and a pint of Four Roses in his gut, "don't be so sure it won't get to the boy first. Way he's got trouble written all over him, he could go before your midget."

Mama sobbed harder.

My feet shifted again. First I heard of a Witt curse. Well not exactly. I knew some of my murdering ancestors had died in strange ways and had their bodies tossed over Luella's Leap into the Blue Bog, but didn't figure it had anything to do with me.

Two crows lit in the pecan tree and cawed at me and Jubal Jen. They dumped snow on my pet sow's head. She didn't like those black birds. Every chance they got, crows stole her meat scraps. Every chance my pet sow got, she stole a crow.

Something barked behind us. A human bark. I knew that mouth. Jubal Jen turned fast and faced the porch stoop. Almost gave me whiplash.

Millie Faye stood there, no longer a petrified mummy, trussed up in a hand-me-down coat. The coat had patches from old overalls, a fire-damaged bear claw quilt and one of Mama's old aprons of singing orioles. Singing orioles looked out of place on my midget twin. Her head was covered with a red scarf, nickel-sized ears lost in pink muffs. Her right arm cradled her broken left wrist mending in Mama's homemade plaster cast. Millie Faye said she broke it on Christmas day trying to climb on top of the rabbit cages to get to my secret place in the barn loft.

She gave me her goblin look.

I was glad she was over her Number 4 fit but unhappy about that look—worse thing being, I deserved it.

Jubal Jen waddled to the stoop, me teetering on top.

"I neared to kill myself runnin' past the Blue Bog to get you help," I said. "I thought you was dying."

"I thought so, too," Millie Faye said, "and then I remembered who it was I last played jacks with, and how much the turd-face admired them, and how weird he's been lately looking at girls' tits in church and sneaking up to the barn loft doing Lord knows what."

That mouth. That damn tiny, truth-telling, foul mouth.

My magic magnet burned against my sinner's heart. My armpits stank of fried turnips. The loft was the only private place on the farm ever since I wrecked the ladder. Until now, nobody else, far as I knew, could climb up on the rabbit cages, then jump and grab the edge of the loft floor and pull themselves up. Even then, for double privacy protection, I built a fort wall of hay bales six feet high.

My hideaway was the fitting and proper place to admire stolen treasure, eat a bologna sandwich or masturbate. Only thing could possibly see me was the Archbishop of Canterbury—my semi-tame barn owl. Archie owed me his life after I freed him from chicken wire and fed him dead mice until he could fly and hunt on his own. Archie wouldn't betray me to Millie Faye, who he didn't give two hoots for anyway.

She held out the bare hand of her good arm and cupped it. "Gimme my jacks, Turd Face."

I reached into my pocket, pulled them out and handed them down to her. "I wasn't stealing 'em. Just thought I'd take 'em to the grinder and polish 'em a bit for you."

She folded her hand around her precious treasure and held the jacks under her nose. Closed her eyes and inhaled. Her eyelids flew open. Marble eyeballs cracked. Knocked me backwards off Jubal Jen onto my butt in the snow.

Just as me and my twin can feel a pull of closeness, we can also feel the push of awayness. Being in negative polarity with Millie Faye was the loneliest feeling in the world. Felt like I was curled up in a ball all alone on a chunk of ice in the middle of the Blue Bog.

"Ugh," Millie Faye said. "They smell like Ol' Slasher's rolled on 'em in rutting season." Held them out to me in her good hand. "Smell."

I leaned over and sniffed. No more newness. I had them jacks only three hours and the new was gone.

"How would you know how Ol' Slasher smells when you ain't never even seen him?" I said, glad for the shift in conversation.

Her eyes looked past me toward Luella's Leap. "Oh, I seen him, Mo Grady. I seen him in a dream whilst in my coma. Smelt his rotten breath, too. I was holdin' onto his six-inch tusks trying to save your worthless hide."

"You're talking nonsense," I said. "Let's wipe the snow off the stoop and play a game of jacks before church. I have a feeling it's your lucky day."

She flung her good right arm over her shoulder and threw half the jacks against the pecan tree. They bounced into a snowdrift.

A crow dived and snatched one, then lit on the mangled lightning-rod rooster on the barn roof.

Millie Faye flung the rest at the snowdrift, but one slipped out, catching in her straw hair for a second, then tumbling down, twirling and landing on the porch before bouncing into the snow.

Jubal Jen's dreamy eyes followed it. Her great snout plowed the snow, found the jack and crunched it, easy as a chicken head.

Millie Faye's tiny head turned. "What's Jubal Jen eating?"

"Nothing," I said. "Just some old bones I saved for her from last night's rabbit stew."

"You treat that ol' hog better'n your own twin."

"Yeah, well she's easier to get along with. And she don't get me into all kinds of trouble."

"One of these days you're gonna go too far, Mo Grady, and you're gonna get me killed. And when that happens, you're gonna sore miss me."

"I'd like to give missing you a try but come to find out whenever I get used to the idea, you're just playing possum."

I'd no sooner said it than I thought about her not living past eighteen. I looked at her straw hair, her ash color and her patchy, too-big coat and wondered what she had in common with a rare piece of china.

Even knowing she was gonna die, I wasn't cured from getting mad at her.

Or losing my immortal soul to a blue fireball. Prayer was the plan. Salvation, the answer. Getting saved by the two-headed preacher would be the climax of my guilt-ridding goal.

CHAPTER 7

Aunt Big Tits and Turds to Tumble

As I was planning how righteous and holy and pure my life was going to be after today's church service—treating Millie Faye like rare china, not playing with my pecker and not wanting new stuff—I saw a speck of red stirring up snow on Scuttles Grunt Road. Everything was gray-black and white except for that red speck—a pack of devil dogs with two flame-yellow eyeballs, each big as a hunter's moon.

The speck growed and slowed and pulled into our driveway.

Sweet Jesus! The red Chevrolet! It was lust at first sight. I'd never set eyes on nothing so pretty, never heard nothing so lovely, never smelled nothing so new. My skin sizzled, hot enough to evaporate and float above Luella's Leap.

The car of my dreams stopped right beside Doc Abernathy's Pontiac.

When I stole Millie Faye's new jacks, I understood what God's tenth commandment meant by not coveting thy neighbor's goods. But the red Chevrolet drove me beyond coveting. This was the lust of the damned. I lusted after my Uncle Harm's red Chevrolet with all my heart and soul. And, with all my body.

Harman Cornelius Claggett leaned a beefy arm out the window. Grime stained his hands from years of working his diesel Caterpillar tractor—the only one in Sulphur Lick Valley. A white Madonna and Child ring hugged his pinky finger. His bottom lip a spread adder's head, all puffy like, and his mouth spit tobaccy venom, making a neat black hole in the snow.

"Just thought I'd drop by," he said, "and show you little bastards my bran'-spankin'-new '55 Chevrolet. She is beauteous, ain't she? See what minding the Lord does for you, Mo Grady?"

Behind his back, I called him 'Uncle Harm.' 'Cause that's what he did. Millie Faye called him 'Uncle Hurt.'

He had a lantern-shaped face, red as crab apples, and his black hair was parted an inch above his left ear, clinging to his head like a rubber mat. His eyes, steely as gray ice, sliced through me from the driver's seat. Next to him was his sister, Bertha Sue.

I called her 'Aunt Big Bertha.' Ever since Mama's wedding, you could tell by the way her eyes turned to chunks of coal and her lips puckered, she didn't like us kids.

Millie Faye called her 'Aunt Big Tits' or 'Aunt Big Butt,' depending on whether my step aunt was coming or going.

Me and my twin agreed on staying out of Aunt Big Bertha's and Uncle Harm's way. Which was not always easy, them being so big and determined to save our immortal souls. Uncle Harm, whenever he came for a visit, hunted us down like a red-bone bloodhound.

Mama said we should be grateful, said Uncle Harm had taken a likin' to us—but we knew it was the kind of taken a likin' to we didn't like to be taken to.

Uncle Harm spit in the snow again.

"You get that rifle there all cleaned and oiled good tonight," he said, his breath coarse as singed goose feathers. "We'll go shoot us some hogs with cholera. Can't let disease and pestilence spread throughout the valley. Then we'll see about you getting a ride in this here car."

"Thank you, sir," I said, nice and polite the way Mama told us to do. My gut polarity turned inside out. "I'd much admire to go for a ride in your red Chevrolet."

Uncle Harm's forehead shone slick, his thick eyebrows bobbed with righteousness over his broken nose. Spiny pieces of barbed-wire hair grew out of each nostril. His voice was clotted with the Spirit, and he liked nothing better than saving errant souls.

"Christ hisself came to me in a dream," he said, "and told me you little bastards were a result of demon seed, on the verge of stupendous wickedness, and it was my God-given duty to head you away from the abyss."

He leaned his burnt breath closer. "You look a little pale. Like you may be hiding somethin'. You ain't got a pet dog, have you? I won't abide dogs on any farm of mine." His eyes roamed the barnyard. "That's one thing me and your whoring Mama got in common."

"No sir," I said. "I don't have me a dog but one of these days I'd sure admire to have one."

"Well, give it up," he said. He tapped the vent window with his Madonna and Child ring. "Or, better yet, maybe you could go live with them wild dogs? They'd enjoy a tender little boy to gnaw on." He spit a tobaccy wad with some arc and distance to it.

He looked past me at Millie Faye and Jubal Jen. "My, if you two don't look a sight. A wee girl and a giant hog. You better keep that hog penned up or it's liable to end up bacon for my breakfast."

"Jubal Jen's my pet hog," I said, "and always throws good piglets. Mama says she ain't to be butchered."

"She ain't no pet nor your hog as long as she's eatin' my grain on my farm," he said.

The unhallowed scent of Uncle Harm's tobaccy juice and his pink mouth making talk about owning my hog made me wonder, who'd get that bran'-spankin'-new, '55 red Chevrolet if he was to up and die? Just up and die? Jus' like that. Up and die?

A sunless shadow flew over my head. Crows lit on the barn, and I couldn't stop that thought from ricocheting around my brain like a bullet. Echoes of Marian Lee.

Uncle Harm backed out of the driveway. A red bird scratched in snow on our old Ford. I picked up my rifle and aimed. Had that bird dead in my sights and pulled the trigger. Gun clicked. Mama taught me never to put a shell in the chamber 'less I was ready to kill.

Millie Faye tromped behind me, stood on tiptoes and whispered in my ear. "Well, I can see right now, Mo Grady, I won't have to worry about my new thangs no more. I seed the way your eyes popped when that red Chevrolet pulled in. You got bigger turds to tumble."

CHAPTER 8

Jerusalem Orchids and Sweet Chariot

I spent the whole twisting trip to church fixin' on sitting behind the wheel of that bran'-spankin'-new, red '55 Chevrolet at least once before I had temptation taken from me by the two-headed preacher.

Me and Millie Faye ran up the hill behind the church to the cemetery. The plumes of gray clouds looked like they'd been scraped out of a coal mine. A cold wind blew snow, hard as broken glass, against my cheeks. I ducked my head down into my blue scarf.

We sat on the Bledsoe boys' knee-high tombstone—the boys who'd tried swimming last year in a snake-infested pool in the Blue Bog. Millie Faye's oversized galoshes dangled right above the words: "Died 1954."

This part of the cemetery, with a panoramic view of Sulphur Lick Valley, was the resting place for the innocent and the holy. Nary a Witt buried anywhere near it.

Sulphur Lick is what the early pioneers—some bein' my homicidal ancestors—named the valley. Underground sulphur deposits bubbled all around, and if you happened to hit one digging a well, you had to start over somewhere else if you sought pure water. Some folks like the Jones family put up with the sulphur taste even though it turned their skin the color of old sweet potatoes and made their sweat smell like rotten Guinea eggs.

Our new wood church sat on a plateau below the cemetery. Sulphur burped out of the ground on the side of the building nearest the Blue

Bog. I heard Deacon Jones explain: "We built on sacrilegious ground as an almighty challenge to Satan himself. Why, we're gonna worship so hard and deep, won't be long till them sulphur fumaroles dry up, and we'll be planting Jerusalem Orchids in 'em."

Deacon Jones was so skinny he could've hid behind a stork leg, and bald enough for his head to be mistaken for birch bark. He shook a righteous fist at the fumaroles.

A toxic tonic belched back.

I didn't understand the "valley" part of Sulphur Lick Valley. Just a bunch of rolling hills with bigger hills all around. Railroad tracks ran the length of the dry side of the valley. Scuttles Grunt Road, named after the town of 251 people, snaked through those rolling hills. Claggett Creek ran alongside the road and fed clear water into the Blue Bog, where it turned into a murky paste.

Gray-blue steam rose from the bog. Quicksand and tar pits bubbled there, and summer cottonwoods, cypress and willow trees grew so huge their weeping limbs could hide a whole community of cottonmouth water moccasins.

Along the seam where the Blue Bog and bluff met, hidden from view by thick summer foliage or roiling winter vapor, was a series of deep caves with no exit. That's why Ol' Slasher had lasted so long. He disappeared into them caves after escaping from them gypsies and woe be unto he that follows. Ain't no one went in them caves since the Skinner boy and his hounds. He was never heard of again, and only one hound out of four, limping and bloodied, ever came out.

Black clouds hung over Wrestler's Ridge. Purple flashes braided the clouds, releasing the smell of dry winter lightning. Muffled thunder rumbled between sky and earth. Pretty soon, them angry clouds would break loose and rush straight toward us, unleashing another blizzard.

Over in the late farmer Johnson's field, three cows huddled, their unmilked udders dragging in the snow next to Uncle Harm's tractor. The smell of oil and diesel fuel mingled with the sweet milky odor of oozing udders. I knew the tractor was there to dig the trench for the hog killing tomorrow. A mass grave. Didn't seem quite right for it to be within sight of the church.

Beyond the tractor, smoke poured out of the Johnson's farmhouse chimney a half-mile away. When his hogs got sick, Farmer Johnson had stuck a double barrel twelve-gauge shotgun in his mouth and pulled both triggers. Uncle Harm said Widow Johnson would sell the farm and go live in Springfield. My heart wilted. I reckoned I'd never see Loveda, their beautiful strawberry-curled granddaughter again.

I reached under my overalls and got my magic magnet off my collarbone where it had ridden on the drive to church. Magnet did its job good. Sucked the pinched soreness right out. I put my magnet in my pants pocket.

Uncle Harm pulled into the parking lot.

I couldn't keep my mind from floating over to where bundled up worshipers milled around the red Chevrolet. It sparkled brighter than the fresh, falling snow. I could smell a spicy, faraway fragrance tinged with leaded gasoline. My feet tromped up and down in place. Hand worked my magnet.

Millie Faye threw snow on the back of my neck. "I see you lookin' over there. Can't fool me, Mo Grady. You done car struck. Uncle Hurt's new Chevrolet's got a hold on you tighter'n an alligator turtle on a piece of rotten pork rind. Turtle won't let go lessen you cut off his head."

I brushed snow off my neck and pulled down my cap over my eyes so's I could only see snowflakes falling on my knees and my go-to-meeting shoes with the holes in the soles. A wisp of sulphur tickled my nose.

"Mama says you're not supposed to call him Uncle Hurt," I said.

Millie Faye kicked Danny Bledsoe's death date with galoshes too big for her tiny shoes. "How about Uncle Spit? I seed what he did to you out in the barn t'uther day. In the goat stall. Heard him saying he's gonna cure you from temptation like his daddy done him."

My neck flushed. It spread to my bruised collarbone. Uncle Harm's tobaccy breath sallied up my nostrils. Could feel my heart beat in my shriveled pecker.

"Uncle Harm's helping me," I said. "He says he's teaching me how to control my heathen urges. You let me worry about what he does, and stop calling him names. You wasn't raised that way. If Mama catches you talking him down, she'll tan your ..."

Millie Faye kicked the tombstone to coincide with her tinny voice, left foot sounding louder than the right. "Uncle Pinch, Uncle Hate, Uncle Touch, Uncle Evil, Uncle Spank, Uncle Feel, Uncle Turd, Uncle ..."

I put my cold hand over her running mouth. Boy! At Sunday meeting, too. Righteous folks millin' about. Deacon Jones turning his birch bark head toward us.

I took my hand away. Millie Faye teetered on her tombstone, then tried to catch snowflakes on a tongue thin as dried cottontail jerky. Caught one so big it turned the tip of her tongue white. She whispered, her mouth full of white fluff. "Uncle Pinch caught me out in the barn alone. He prayed to save my immortal soul from perdition."

My fingernails scraped up the tombstone. "Did he spit chewing tobaccy on your ... ah ... your ..."

"My pud? Is that what you're trying to say?" she said. "No, he didn't. I fooled him. I did a dead possum number on him. Scared him away, I guess. Anyways, when I woked up he was gone."

"Did you tell Mama?"

"What's to tell?" She rubbed her cast. Kept her frog eyes on the ground. Her small body shrunk inside her coat.

Plastic flowers rattled on a grave behind us. Uncle Harm had no need to save Millie Faye's soul. 'Sides her foul mouth, she hadn't committed any sins. It made me angry thinking about him being alone with her. Made me angrier than it did me being alone with him.

"Wanna hear a little song I made up whilst in my coma?" she said.

"No. If you was in a real coma, how could you make up a song?"

She sang:

> *"Oh, Freeman Joe, please say I do,*
> *before the dog is dead,*
> *Oh, Freeman Joe, if you say I do,*
> *we'll screw back on your head."*

"Your songs never make any sense. We ain't got no dog and not likely to have one as long as we live on Uncle Harm's farm."

"Didn't have to make it up," she said. "Come to me in a dream when I seen you holding a puppy. He was a wee thing and about as close to dead as you can get without being in the grave." She slipped sideways on her perch. "Come to think of it, he was in a grave and you in there with him."

"I swear, Millie Faye, you got about as much talent predicting the future as Jubal Jen has of pouncing over the moon."

Millie Faye's slide ended with her butt in a snowdrift between tombstones. She looked up at me. "I got more talent in a coma than you got awake and tryin' to pick out a tune on that banjo our real daddy left us, the ..." She looked up at me sideways in that special comic way. Our eyes met and we shouted, "The sonsabitch!"

I leaned over and we clung to each other, her good arm around my calves, my arms around her straw hair, our bodies racking with laughter.

Millie Faye's laugh was thin and reedy, like a marsh wren calling from deep in a cattail thicket. Her laughter turned into choking. She turned around and leaned her back against Dinky's tombstone. I made to turn aside to give her more room, but she grabbed my legs and held them against her head. Her choking quit and we sat quiet, listening to snowflakes and ghosts gossip.

"I hate my missin' heart," she said. Her breathing sounded rough and ragged, like the well pump wanting more water for a prime. "If you go down for a laying on of hands by the two-headed preacher, Mo Grady, could I follow along behind you and ask him for my heart back the way it was before the fever?"

I wadded up snow into a ball. Threw it at a bluebird nest hole in the Johnson's fence post. Hit it square center. "You stay seated in church, 'cause there's liable to be low-down sinners rolling around and thawed out serpents crawling about," I said. "If I go down, I'll ask the two-headed preacher for your heart."

"You got rat bowels for brains," she said. "That's not how a laying-on-of-hands works."

We heard a shout from the congregation in the parking lot. Fingers pointed up the road. A green '51 Studebaker come down the lane, around the mulberry tree black with crows. Three heads filled the car.

The passenger side head nearest the door was Aunt Big Bertha's, barrel hair piled on it.

My wee twin leaned forward, shielding her eyes. "My, my, did you ever see such admirable hair?" Millie Faye hated her own uncontrollable straw hair.

The reverend's head, topped with a black hat, took up the driver's side.

The middle head looked like a baby cloaked in a blanket riding on his daddy's shoulder—that newborn's cold-blooded mother, a copperhead pit viper.

The good reverend had a passion for dancing with poisonous snakes. And just naturally, some serpents don't care to dance. No, don't care to dance no matter your status on the chart of righteousness nor how politely you ask permission.

Some snakes couldn't carry a tune in a tote sack. And neither could some reverends. Some of those arrhythmic reverends lay under tombstones in the cemetery, spending eternity in the shadowed section with a view of the Blue Bog.

Where, I wondered, were the righteous biters after "a blasphemy" occurred? Was the ceremonial reptile bludgeoned to death by the congregation or did it slither away to escape in a dark hole?

Some elders say, in the mass hysteria and to escape from divine retribution, the snake would take over the body and soul of one of the churchgoers. A sinner so smitten with sin, they was primed and ready to be taken over. Thereafter, the possessed sinner's soul wandered forever, lost in eternal damnation.

Millie Faye half believed that bull-pucky. I, being bigger and wiser, knew it was nonsense.

Just in case though, I planned to seat myself in the back of church, as far away from that pulpit as possible 'cause if there was any takin' over of sinners to be done by Satan I was bound to be looked at with interest.

Folks say that after Mama's wedding last May, while Reverend Waywater still had one head, he drove over Night Hawk Mountain and disappeared down the other side into the black bottom fog, down to New Dreadford where, according to Uncle Harm, the Jezebels and Sodomites cavort with ravens and goats and serpents under a blood-red moon.

I didn't know what a Sodomite or Jezebel was, but cavorting under a blood red moon sounded like damn good fun to me.

Would be even more fun if I could do it all in the red Chevrolet.

I expected, though, that after the two-headed preacher's laying on of hands, such cavorting would seem like Satan's handiwork.

Millie Faye scratched her wrist raw where the cast quit and skin began, snowflakes falling on the red ring of exposed flesh.

"Quit scratching your wrist," I said. "You'll only make it itch worse."

She scratched harder. "It hurts, Mo Grady. It hurts something awful." A strand of dull blonde hair hung down her face. She quit scratching long enough to tuck it back under her red scarf. Her mouth drug down.

I pulled out my magic magnet and handed it to her. "Here, rub this back and forth over your cast. It'll draw out the pain."

She took the magnet in her red mitten. It filled her whole hand. She turned it over and over. "Which way is suck?"

I placed it on her cast. Made a sound like a swallow hitting a window.

The Studebaker pulled into the parking lot. White fluff choked headlight beams. The engine screamed before the two-headed preacher shut it off.

Folks gathered around it, but my eyes fixed on the red Chevrolet.

Millie Faye's face changed from ash gray to crabapple blossom pink, and her mouth lost its downward tilt. She slapped her galoshes together, buckles flapping, and tapped me on the shoulder with my magnet clutched over her chest. "Hey, Mo Grady, your magnet really works. The soreness in my broken bones stopped."

"You're supposed to keep it on your arm," I said.

"I already cured the hurt in my bones. I'm workin' on my heart."

I twisted the magnet out of her scrawny fingers. Didn't trust it with her ticker. On our monthly trip to Scuttles Grunt, Mr. Mincy's son, Pee-eye, had made fun of my magnet so's I put it against the Grandfather's clock at Mincy's Mercantile. Stopped that clock cold. Ain't squeezed out nary a tick-tock since.

Having a heart missin' a tick is better'n having a heart with no tock a'tall.

Millie Faye's rosy color faded. Made me squirm to look at her. I returned my attention to the red Chevrolet. Now was my chance before lust was taken from me. I turned the suck side of my magnet out. Aimed it at that sweet chariot.

Damn if that car didn't suck me right off Dinky's grave! Pulled my heavy legs slipping down the hill, caroming off tombstones, slogging through snow like a puppy on a leash.

Millie Faye hollered, "Where you goin', Mo Grady? Wait for me!"

I figured whilst no one was looking, I could stroke the silver eagle hood ornament. Maybe open the door and sniff the leather insides. Kiss the steering wheel.

Millie Faye caught up and tugged at my blue scarf. "I don't like what I'm feeling from you. Your mind is black as a Russian boar's butt."

She yelled for Mama.

Mama's got special antennae for hearing Millie Faye. I saw her break from the crowd toward me, and just as I reached out to lay a hand on the car's red satin surface, she grabbed my wrist. "Stay your hand, Mo Grady, and come away from that vehicle. Only way the likes of us would ever have a car like that is if some misfortune happens to your uncle and leaves it to Freeman Joe. And that's not likely to happen."

Mama's hummingbird shawl clung to her head. Her nose reddened from the north wind and brown bags hung under her eyes. Her breath came in short bursts, and her gloveless hand was pale blue and firm on my arm. Firm except for her index finger, swollen and blackened, damaged building the new church in service to the Holy Ghost.

So near my heart's desire, my mind filled with red heat from that red car. Who did Mama think she was, stopping me? I grabbed a'hold of her hurt finger and twisted.

She winced. Her eyes, wheat kernels flying hither and yon, calmed my mind. Hummingbirds hummed, probing my ears with their silky beaks, soothing me.

My hand folded Mama's sore finger back alongside her others. I bowed my head in shame.

Mama grabbed my ear.

"Ouch!" Drug me toward the church. She motioned with her head for Millie Faye. My puny sister's galoshes clumped, and together we three entered the church.

CHAPTER 9

Bucking Stove and Spun Spit

The church was empty 'cept for Freeman Joe building a fire of dry mill ends, loaded with combustible pitch, in a thirty gallon tin barrel stove. Mama let go of my ear and went to help him. The stick-built church, being the only non-tent one most Holiness Christians in Sulphur Lick Valley had ever attended, needed special care.

The stove was donated by Widow Atkins. Its barrel top had been cut off and a flat piece of metal welded to fit, for sitting things on like clothes irons and tea kettles. The stove crouched on short, splayed legs. Its burn belly almost dragged the ground like an old, gaseous hog that'd gotten into fermented winter sorghum silage.

At the far end, a podium stood beside a crude plywood stage and a small wooden table. Eight rows of hand-hewed pews were bisected by an aisle down the middle. Behind the stage and up next to where rafters joined at the apex, a window let the Lord's light shine down. Thick gray wood smoke billowed past the window, making the light roll like waves of dirty dishwater across the stage.

Millie Faye cupped her cast in her good arm. Her breathing came in little grunts, like she was climbing stairs. "Are you gonna ask the two-headed preacher for forgiveness for being car struck, Mo Grady?"

"Yes, and don't you sass me," I said.

"I'm not thinkin' any such thing. I'm worried about you is all. Lately, you seem like a stranger. You climb up in the barn loft and hide from me. You jerk your magnet out of my hand after sayin' I can hold it to fix my hurt. You twist Mama's mashed finger, and you walk around all the time with such an angry look in your eyes, would make Ol' Slasher look like a teddy bear."

Millie Faye saying I looked angry all the time made me mad. "Yeah, well, you'd be angry too if all the time you had to watch out for a retarded sister with a running mouth."

"You know I'm just puny," Millie Faye said. "Without me telling you what to do, Mo Grady Witt, you'd be lost."

"I'd sure like to give that kind of being lost a try."

"Oh, unless you change your ways, Mo Grady," she said, "I 'spect you got lots of kinds of being lost in you."

God, I hated her honesty. She was right about me being lost. Time I was found before it was too late. I clutched my magnet in my pitching hand, feeling positive polarity pulsing through my sinner's veins.

The church stage, bathed in divine dishwater light, seemed a long ways away.

Other folks started pushing from behind.

"Let's sit over there in the corner by that window," Millie Faye said, pointing to the last pew as if I might even get lost in our new church.

I followed her. My five older sisters and Mama sat a few rows in front of us. Uncle Harm, with big workman's boots, stomped down the aisle, pushed Freeman Joe out of the way and dumped a tote sack of coal in the stove. His unblinking eyes searched the pews.

Me and Millie Faye ducked down too late.

His boots sounded louder and louder and stopped beside our pew. His butt squeezed between me and my sister. Fingers laid on my shoulder, right over my bruised collarbone. My skin burned. Uncle Harm grinned at me, the corners of his thick lips spread back to show a big empty mouth and lots of pink gums. Millie Faye said it's a wonder how he can chew burnt pork steak without any teeth.

Thick eyebrows knotted up in the middle of his glassy forehead, like his thoughts crept through his skull, all twisted and hard. He pointed out the window. "Look out there in the Widow Johnson's field and you can see my Caterpillar. Ain't she a Lulu? You mind the Lord, boy, and I'll let you sit on the fender tomorrow when I dig the hog trench."

"Seems really strange Mr. Johnson's hogs got cholera in the winter time," I said. "Maybe they's dying of something else."

"Jebediah Johnson had old folk's disease, boy," he said. "Kept all three hundred of them hogs in a tiny heated shed. Some disease was bound to touch 'em."

I knew disease and pestilence needed to be stamped out, but I wanted no part of it. I looked out the window, but my eyes got no further than the bran'-spankin'-new, red '55 Chevrolet. That car, sitting apart from the others, nearly blinded me. The wax polish reflected a red light onto a bed of soft white snow, creating kind of an upside-down neon halo. Cream-colored leather looked snug and inviting.

The sides of the tin stove glowed pink, like the flushed faces of the faithful.

Widow Atkins sat in front of us, wearing a yellow hat filled with false fruit, and nodded her head at the Arnold brothers sitting in the pew in front of her. "I'm fit to be tied with excitement," she said, "just a'knowin' I'm to worship with a preacher who'd come back from the dead with two heads!"

The Arnold brothers showed no excitement until the Hazeycamp sisters, holy and righteous, walked by their pew and seated themselves in the front row.

Diesel odor clung to Uncle Harm. His coat, a dirty charcoal color, was made of coarse material that scratched and burned when he rubbed up against you.

Millie Faye leaned away from him. She clutched the back of the next pew so hard, her measly knuckles turned white.

I felt like a calf cut off from the herd, stalked for branding.

The back door of the church opened and in walked the two-headed preacher.

Talking stopped.

Behind Reverend Waywater came Aunt Big Bertha carrying a rectangular glass cage with a red towel draped over it. She was a head taller than her husband and stout as an Angus bull with a ripe-to-burstin' pumpkin butt. Atop her thick body sat a face stern as the crags on Wrestler's Ridge. Her eyes in comparison with the rest of her looked newtish. Astraddle that sanctified head rode the hunk of hair, coiled in an iron knot, the size of a blacksmith forge and just as black. She took up a whole pew for herself and her glass cage.

The pew groaned under her bulk. Pew sitters behind her moved aside so's to see around that forged hair.

Reverend Waywater removed his hat, shaking the snow off, and hung it on a hook beside the door. Red hair, matted with sweat, clung to his small head.

He undid the big black buttons on his overcoat. We leaned forward.

The reverend shrugged his shoulders and his overcoat fell off. A collective gasp came from the congregation. Rumors did not do that Unholy Growth justice. He still had on a black coat, but the bulge underneath on his shoulder stretched the coat's arm to above his wrist. Now, the thing was, the good reverend had a little head to start with, so the Unholy Growth was near on a level with it.

He didn't let us stare long. He strode to the edge of the plywood podium, balancing on the middle of his polished black shoes, rocking back and forth, and pointed a thin finger at the bulge on his shoulder.

"You see this!" he shouted. "You see this! This is Satan-ah's work-ah."

We all snapped to attention.

"I went down into the belly of the whale-ah," he said. "Down into darkness and rot-ah. Down so far, I ran into Lucifer-ah. And you know what I did-ah?"

That was our signal.

"No!" half the congregation shouted.

"You know what I did-ah?"

"No!" Response talkers warmed up, putting some steam behind their shout.

"You know what I did-ah?"

"NO!" screamed the whole congregation, me and Millie Faye included.

"I spit in Satan's-ah eye-ah!"

"Yes!"

"I spit in Satan's-ah eye-ah."

"Yes! Yes!"

"I spit in Satan's-ah eye-ah!"

"Yes! Hallelujah! Yes!"

My crotch burned. I crossed my legs. "I spit in Satan's eye" was what Uncle Harm said when he had me penned in the billy goat stall.

Joshua Tuckett hopped out of his seat and did a little three-legged circular jig in the aisle, his hand-carved hickory cane with the raven's head pounding the wood floor.

Hats and scarves and coats peeled off bodies warming up from the inside out.

Reverend Waywater, a slight, sloped-forehead man, with blue eyes like high beams on a speeding snowplow, traipsed up and down the stage in a canted gait, favoring his humped shoulder. His strong, musical voice filled the church, punctuating the last syllable of words like an upright bass fiddle, beating the crowd into a rhythmic frenzy. Agitated sinners jumped and jerked in time with the preacher's voice.

The stove, hopping and puffing with excess heat, provided percussive backup.

The crowd hushed as Aunt Big Bertha got up. She brought forth the cage, placing it on the table next to the podium, then wiped her hands on her hips and sat back down quick.

Reverend Waywater whipped the towel off the cage, rolled up one end and snapped it. Widow Atkins' dead-fruit hat leaped a foot in the air. The bottom of the glass cage moved. All eyes strained to see.

A flat, blue head raised up—high-set eyes and sharp cheekbones, like flint arrowheads. The head stretched elastic jaws and darted a cobalt forked tongue. I saw two fangs and a mouth full of white, bright as a newborn lamb in a spring squall.

Moonshiners and fornicators gasped. Only me and Millie Faye strained to get a better look. It was the real thing all right—a cottonmouth water moccasin, big, old and wise in the ways of swamps and bogs but no doubt confused by the ways of churchgoers.

The flesh under my toenails turned to juice.

An odor of cut cucumbers tickled my nostrils.

The two-headed preacher swayed backwards, like he might be having second thoughts about dancing with that big fella. The cotton-mouth swayed forwards, like he might be having first thoughts about biting that abomination.

Uncle Harm moaned and clutched my thigh with his rough paw. "I hate snakes," he said. A jolt of fear slithered from his hand up my leg and coiled in my chest. The stink of nicotine and diesel came out of Uncle Harm's pores.

I tried worming away from him, but he locked onto me like a Leghorn rooster locked onto a night crawler. I wanted to be the first in line to be healed when the laying on of hands began. Prove my penitence to God. Couldn't do that clutched in Uncle Harm's iron grip.

A chant arose from the congregation:

"SAAAATAN! SAAAATAN!"

Clump, clump, clump went the pews. Clink, clink, clink the stove door joined right in there. Coal burns ten times hotter than wood. The sides of the stove turned from orange to red.

The serpent head swiveled in slow motion, scarlet eyes narrowing. The skin had a faint blue tinge like on the creatures found down at Bonker Beckman's Blue Bog, Bonker Beckman included.

I figured that cold-blooded reptile didn't like being yanked out of his snug bog hole during his long winter's nap.

A boiled eggs smell seeped in from cracks in the floorboard of the Sulphur Lick Holiness Church. My leg burned, feet thawed, toes tapped.

Ol' Blue Satan didn't budge, 'cept for his tongue darting out and up to lick one red eye. Then he reared back. Shook his scaly head. Swiveled. Crimson eyes seeking a target.

"Look at me, SATAN-AH!" the reverend shouted.

Uncle Harm jumped, pinched my thigh harder. Then his hand relaxed. Squeezed. Relaxed. Squeezed. Tuned in to the rhythm of the burning stove.

"Look at me, SATAN-AH!" That lopsided, two-headed preacher said again, sweat congealing in the deep grooves of his forehead. He danced a disjointed offbeat boogie behind the snake's cage. The stage swayed and groaned.

The snake turned toward the preacher. Stopped when he beheld the stove bucking and swaying to an invisible flute player.

Ol' Blue Satan got the rhythm, swayed back and forth. Mouth opened in a sticky yawn. Fangs glistened with spun spit.

Reverend Waywater stamped his heels on the plywood stage. Circled the glass cage, summoning God's own courageous hand. "That's right, SATAN-AH, you've met your match today-yah."

Uncle Harm released his grip on my leg, threw a muscled arm around me and hugged hard. My neck bones popped. He leaned behind me, breath like kerosene, fear in his voice, "Get thee behind me, Satan!"

A red bird lit on the outside sill of the high window and, feathers flapping, tried holding on. Giant shadowy wings swept over the congregation.

"The Archangel has come to deliver us," Widow Atkins cried, flapping her ancient arms, plastic oranges and grapes clacking and dust a'flying from her hat. "We is blessed. We is blessed."

I slipped my magnet under my right shoe.

Uncle Harm shifted his foot over on top of mine, his big boot dwarfing my shoe.

I turned to pull away and saw again that new, red Chevrolet beckoning me in white snow. Body lines so clean and elegant. My fingertips ached to touch.

Uncle Harm's hot breath singed the back of my neck. "You mind the Lord, Mo Grady. The Lord will set you free."

Millie Faye entered my mind. My fear mingled with hers and doubled whilst my magnet scorched a channel up through a hole in the sole of my shoe to my brain.

"Hallelujah," shouted the congregation. "Hallelujah! He hath come!"

The temptation tango had begun. Two dancers on stage. The preacher had that cottonmouth water moccasin in his Satan-smiting hand—the same hand that was attached to his humpy shoulder, the same shoulder that jerked and gyrated in time with the reverend's arrhythmic dance, the same dance designed to subdue the savage beast.

Good and evil, eyeball to eyeball. Push and pull. Suck and shove. Negative and positive. That blue-tinted devil was caught, embraced tight by the power of the Lord.

Then Ol' Blue Satan shifted like a Missouri twister and coiled thick and quick around the red-faced reverend's stout forearm.

Embracee became embracer.

CHAPTER 10

Tongue Talkers and Hot Little Hooves

"Hallelujah! Hallelujah! He has risen!" Freeman Joe leaped out of his seat like he'd been sitting on fire ants. He stood on tiptoes and flapped his long arms, swallow wings taking him closer to the Almighty, air waves folding the goose feathers on Rose Phoebe's hat. His head tilted back, wild black hair neared to cover his sun-baked neck. His great beak of a nose jabbed at the high window where the red bird had found secure footing and now cocked a crested head at the crazy bird man.

My new daddy's cracked lips worked over words like a meat grinder—not a noun, not a syllable, not a vowel slipped past sounding anything like English. Talking in tongues, he was, speaking a language only God could understand. One-fourth of the congregation, taken with tongue-talk themselves, yelled in encouragement.

It was time I had a laying on of hands by the two-headed preacher. Forgive me my sins. Deliver me from evil.

The barrel stove, still dancing and snorting in the corner, flushed an ornery red. Heat waves blurred the stage act—the tangoing duo. The Hazeycamp sisters burst out of their pew, screeching "I'm heading for the Pearly Gates." They peeled off their winter wrappings and stripped down to matching white blouses and ankle-length wool skirts.

The youngest clawed at her pinned auburn hair until it fell in rolls down to her waist, thick as a good second-hand store army blanket. She shook that blanket like a hound tosses a king snake. She collapsed to her knees, making a thump you could feel in the back pews, then lay down and rolled into a corner behind the stove, hair wrapping around her body.

The eldest sister leaned backwards so's the whole congregation had to look at the preacher's Unholy Growth around her abundant breasts, hump upon hump upon hump. I was hoping she'd claw them free like her sister did her hair, but instead, she beat 'em with her fists until she drove herself backwards to the floor. She, too, set off rolling behind the stove.

The Arnold brothers bounded out of their seats, bodies pulsating with celestial energy. They hopped over ol' lady Bryant's body writhing in the aisle and wasted no time gravitating over to the Hazeycamp sisters' corner, whereupon, overcome with piety, they collapsed in a pile upon the good sisters. All four penitents just naturally wedged together in that hot corner, smelling of moist hair and hallelujahs.

The aisles of the little church filled up fast with supplicators, proners and groaners. Coal cinder and sweaty armpit stink mingled with sulphur fumes licking up from the floorboards.

The hopping stove turned blue-orange. A cast iron lid lifter popped up in the air before plunging to the floor a serpent's length away from the Arnold brothers and Hazeycamp sisters.

My neck and cheek were on fire, rubbed raw by Uncle Harm's coat. His arms around me, held firm. I closed my eyes. Could see myself driving that red Chevrolet, my butt on Mama's portable chopping block so's I could see over the dash. Steering down a twisted highway, dodging potholes, weaving over the centerline, pulling back to miss slamming head on into oncoming cars.

Uncle Harm chanted in my ear. Congregation 'amening' and 'hallelujahing' and 'praising the Lord' in one voice.

My sisters, all except Millie Faye, had joined in the babble.

In the midst of many, I was on my own.

The two-headed preacher, sweat gushing off his chin, oily red hair clinging to a possum-shaped forehead, lips talkin' Jesus-talk to Ol' Blue Satan coiled thick around his arm, ripped off three quarters of his black coat and, sure enough, through a cut in his shirt, up reared his other head—a vibrating, melon-sized pustule.

That Unholy Growth, I swear, had a mind of its own, shedding its outer skin even as the congregation watched. Underneath the flakes of gray, the flesh puffed tight, raw and pinkish with purple veins like the Widow Atkins' calves when she wades Claggett Creek.

Ol' Blue Satan's high-set eyes edged higher. That old swamp devil had probably never laid eyes on anything so cold-toes ugly. He jerked around again to peer at the rodeo stove, which, allowing for size, would've given a Brahma bull tit-for-tat in a bucking contest.

I couldn't take it anymore. I had sinned. I had to find salvation. The next time Uncle Harm rocked back, I gathered my strength. When he rocked forward, I shot to my feet, ripping my sweaty body from his grasp.

My muscles unscrunched, shoulders stretched. I reached down and plucked my magnet from under my shoe and stuffed it in my pants pocket. I sprinted down the aisle, jumping over a hip here, a head there, dodging fat butts and skinny necks.

I kneeled in front of the stage, five feet from the preacher and Ol' Blue Satan. I willed Reverend Waywater to lay his hands on my head. "Oh please, heal me!" I said, swallowing dry spit. "Bless me! Save me! For I have grievously sinned." My wretched voice sounded muffled.

Ol' Blue Satan turned, floated closer, leading the preacher's captive arm in my direction.

Good Lord! The magnet, set on suck, was pulling that serpent straight to me. Too late to turn over the magnet. Caught crossways in the magnetic field. Negative polarity switched on high.

I stared into Ol' Blue Satan's brimstone eyes and went stiff as a smokehouse plank. I reviewed my whole thirteen years of sinning in ten seconds: playing with my pecker, cussing at Millie Faye, lusting after Loveda's ankles, coveting the red Chevrolet. There was lots more, but I didn't have time to account for everything, not with a snake snout inching closer, preacher's grotesque other head bobbing behind.

The reverend's voice cut through my rapturous haze, "You been called down here for a reason, boy. He's challenging you, boy. Show him you're not afraid. Touch his scaly skin, boy. Smell his fetid odor, boy. Kiss his rotted flesh, boy. You've stepped into a world where few others have ever gone. Show Satan your lack of fear. Show him how much you love sweet Jesus."

I reached up and petted the serpent's throat with my knuckles. Skin, not rough and rotted. Pearly smooth. Serpent leaned into my hand, liking my warm touch, pushing still closer. His breath smelled clean and fresh. Bog humus. Wild cucumber. Blue clay on a summer day.

I didn't know my sore shoulder was twitching till it stopped. Pain gone. A chattering in my mouth quit, too. Throat filled with swamp pox. Eyeball to eyeball with Ol' Blue Satan, and I was not afraid. I was not afraid 'cause Ol' Blue Satan loved me. Ol' Blue Satan forgave me.

Ol' Blue Satan pushed my hand aside with his porcelain-like skull. Reached out and kissed my nose with a long, cobalt tongue.

My first kiss. I was not afraid.

Felt like wet satin.

He licked again and lingered.

My first smooch. I was not afraid.

Ol' Blue Satan hissed inside my head, "Pray to me, Mo Grady Witt, your soul to keep. Pray to me that I might be your savior. Pray to me that I might show you the true path and you will get your heart's desire—that red Chevrolet."

His tongue, slick, caressed my eyelid.

My first true love. I was not afraid.

"All you have to do," Ol' Blue Satan said, "is kill your mean old Uncle Harm. Kill your Uncle Harm and in no time, you'll be driving that red Chevrolet to Luella's Leap and beyond. Maybe even Kansas."

I was afraid.

Millie Faye, way back in the church, wailed in my head, "Get outta there, Mo Grady! Run! The fires of hell are breathin' on your ass! Run for your life!"

My ears unclogged. Mama screamed. The babble of the congregation rushed back into my brain. A pollen cloud, yellow and gold, drifted between me and the serpent. I squeezed my eyes shut, palmed my magic magnet and inwardly prayed: "Ol' Blue Satan, deliver me from evil. Crawl with me through the Sulphur Lick Valley of the shadow of death. Stop the Unholy Growth from possessing me. I will know no fear, sittin' behind the velvet wheel of the red Chevrolet and driving, driving, driving my proud sinner's heart away."

The whole congregation gasped. My eyes opened, and I beheld a cottonmouth water moccasin's fangs imbedded to the hilt in the two-headed preacher's second head. The reverend's glassy eyes were big as brass ball bearings. His mouth widened, round and dark, a muskrat den with no escape tunnel.

Feet stompers froze. Aisle rollers flattened. Tongue-talkers tongue-tied.

Hot coals shifted as the stove let out a long, low-pitched whistle, cutting the abrupt silence. Round lids on the stovetop rattled. I turned to see cast-iron legs fan out and the tin barrel's bottom burn through. Hot orange coals flooded onto the wood floor, like eggs lain from a fiery succubus. A pencil-thin line of orange flame crawled out from the fire-egg pile.

But the crowd had eyes only for that hypnotizing snake dance.

The stricken preacher gaped, unbelieving, at those fangs married to his flesh and commenced shouting, summoning the Lord in language most foul. He pranced around the stage with a sense of rhythm never before demonstrated and began to fleck me and the worshippers in the front pew with snakebite spittle, which stung my flesh like wasps and caused the front pew's faithful to feel they'd been anointed by the baptismal water of Jesus Christ hisself. Just when the preacher's dancing reached a drumming crescendo, he fell backwards, his body spasming, his mouth frothing yellow slaver.

That old cottonmouth uncoiled hisself from the holy man's thickening wrist, waddled past me off the stage and climbed right on top of those hot coals like he was gonna hatch 'em. He turned black as Uncle Harm's boot and blew a ten-foot blast of blue flame between bared fangs, setting the Sulphur Lick "Saved From Perdition" Holiness Christian Church on fire.

Aunt Big Bertha jumped up, pointed at me and screamed, "Abomination!"

Millie Faye shouted, "You gone and done it now, Mo Grady!"

Mama said, "Wake up, Mo Grady! You come away from there and take care of your sister. Chillun! Get your asses in gear and get to gittin'."

I uncoiled myself. Stood up. Rolled my head around. Eyes watery. Skin feeling like broken eggshells.

Millie Faye a statue, face white as the Madonna. Mama in motion, gathering her brood, kicking bodies out of the aisle. Fuzzy flames, stoked with hell-fire venom, caterpillared along the floor and peeked over the stage at the writhing two-headed preacher.

I sensed Sunday Services were over.

I pulled my magic magnet from my pocket, suck side out, and, clutching it to my thudding chest, ran up the aisle. I slithered away from Uncle Harm's grasping paw, pried Millie Faye's white knuckles off the back of the pew, threw her protesting body over my shoulder, and we hit the door as fast as my hot little hooves could trot.

CHAPTER 11

From Rapture to Rotten

Sleet mixed with soft snowflakes. I shut my eyes against the little shards of ice. When I opened them, there, big as death, beckoned that bran'-spankin'-new, red '55 Chevrolet, radiant in the fading light. It tugged at me like a four ton, suck-sided magnet.

I flung down Millie Faye, heard the burning crackle of the "Saved From Perdition" Holiness Christian Church and ran to the car. I cuddled behind it in the canted, driven snow, my shoulder against a frozen steel hubcap. I cupped my magic magnet in my hands, tilted my nose into my covetous palms, breathed in blue clay on a summer day and watched the reflection of flames, orange and jagged, frolic back and forth between hubcaps and snow drifts.

I never knew fire and snow and car could be so compatible.

Millie Faye's big frog eyes stared at me. "Stop watching the fireworks, Mo Grady," she said. Gulp, gulp. "We've got to help Mama!" She always gulped her breath when she got overexcited. She clubbed me with her wrist cast.

I dropped my magnet in the snow. It slid under the car.

My mood went from rapture to rotten.

Damn her! I wanted to choke her chicken neck. It'd be so easy. She was just one big aggravation anyway. Tagging after me. Tattling on me. If I didn't have to watch out for her, I could roll in the aisles with the Hazeycamp sisters, get behind the wheel of my red Chevrolet and drive down to New Dreadford and do me some serious cavorting.

I picked up my magnet, stuck it back in my overalls pocket and stood up, dusting off snow. Screams and shouts came from inside the church. Smoke pushed out past tarpaper. Thin tongues of fire licked through pinholes in the black paper. The air smelled of melted snake fat.

Uncle Harm roared out of the church, arms across his barrel chest, hugging himself. Mama, packing a bundle of coats and scarves, hustled my five older sisters out next. Pew sitters followed in a rush. Widow Atkins hobbled out, clutching her melting false-fruit hat.

The Hazeycamp sisters and Arnold brothers stumbled out, breathing hard. All four toted articles of clothing on account of them stripping half nekked to be closer to the everlasting truth.

Explosions sounded from inside the crackling place of worship—which we found out later was caused by jugs of moonshine Widow Atkins had stashed under the stage. Smoke cleared and flames stuck hungry fingers through the mill-end walls, creeping up toward the rooftop.

Deacon Jones ran around, scooping and throwing snow on the siding, waving others to join. But nobody helped. After a few scoops, he took a step back, and then another, and another till his scoops didn't even hit the building. He put his hands in his pockets and, head bowed, walked away from his first, and likely last, genuine wooden church.

Widow Atkins, steam curling off a broiled pear, glanced over the crowd. "Folk's a'missin'," she said.

The two-headed preacher and Aunt Big Bertha and who else? Millie Faye hit my hip with her cast and pointed. Someone was still in there, waving his arms and jabbing his finger in the air. Freeman Joe. Probably discussing the price of hogs in Havana.

I wasn't about to give up my first and only live-in daddy. I ran up the church steps, took a deep breath at the open doorway and swam through thick smoke. Skin on my face swelled.

My feet panicked, and I ran smack into Freeman Joe sputtering in a foreign language. I threw my arms around him and hugged, a gesture uncommon to our religion between two males over four years old. And, wonder of wonders, Freeman Joe put his big, crazy arms around me and hugged back. He lifted me off the floor in a twirl, my head in the smoke clouds. Squeezed me so hard, the only thing that kept my bones from breaking was my heart swelling to fill the cavity inside my rib cage.

No matter the blistering heat, Freeman Joe's chest felt safe and solid, a chest you could pound with a number nine sledgehammer and do no harm. I molded my face against his starched Sunday shirt, closed my stinging eyes. The smell of Mama's homemade lye soap lodged sweet and hot in my lungs, letting me know that was my last clean breath in this church.

So safe did I feel, I could've stayed like that for hours. Until I remembered I was the one doing the rescuing. I flared my arms, breaking Freeman Joe's grip.

He jabbered, still determined to keep lines of communication open with a phantom listener, but his coughs came a lot faster than the jabs. He was choking. And I'd be, too, if I had to take another breath of that tar-tasting fume.

I found his overalls strap and tugged. Like pulling a Jack mule mired in mud. I hated to do it, but I cuffed him alongside the temple. Hit the off switch on the grain grinder. He quit in mid-jabber. I tugged again.

Freeman Joe wrapped his fingers around my wrist. His skin felt rough and cool. Smoke cleared around his face. His eyes looked red and sunken, and his lips moved. His voice boomed from the bottom of a milk can.

"All spirits are enslaved which serve things evil. I saw the serpent kiss thee, Moses Grady. He knows thee, craves thee. Your destiny and the destiny of your family will be decided this deadliest of winters."

Freeman Joe, or whatever or whoever was talking through Freeman Joe, paused.

The light behind his eyes faded. His voice faded.

I stood on tiptoes and hollered in his ear, "Sssswaaalllooows!"

"Swallows!" he said. His feet moved up and down in the swallow feather dance. I danced, too. Grabbed his hands, raised his arm and waltzed toward the light. Left, one-two, right, one-two, swing and do-si-do. Bird dancing out the door to safety.

Mama, eyes wet, met me and I felt her hands pulling me to her. Her chest, under a thick winter coat, pounded my forehead. Her musky sweat and the crisp Ozark air filled my lungs. Sweet life.

She handed me my coat and wrapped my blue scarf around my neck.

The whole congregation stared at me like I'd let a big fart. I'd just enticed Freeman Joe out of the burning church, and they looked like they wanted to throw me back.

Behind me and Mama, Millie Faye said, "I swear, Mo Grady, first you kiss a snake, then you come dancin' outta church with flames licking your ass. Folks are gonna wonder whose side you on."

Freeman Joe, covered with smoke and soot, was unfazed. He struck out over the drifts, floating like a 200-pound glider, cleared the late Farmer Johnson's barbed-wire fence by six inches, sat in the snow Buddha style and commenced milking a Jersey cow.

"Do not despair, bovine sister," he said, "your agony will soon be over." White milk sprayed from a swollen teat on white snow. Looked pure and regenerating. Only time in my life I wanted to be a barn cat sitting under a cow udder with my maw open.

Widow Atkins was still counting. "There's some yet missin'," she said in the same voice she used to lead graveside prayers.

Reject wood fueled the fire. Sulphur and black-tar smoke make a sticky, bitter smell. The side door flew open and here come'd Aunt Big Bertha's pumpkin hips backing out, her high-bunned hair smoking like tractor engine exhaust. She dragged her venom-filled husband feet first behind her, now with two and a half heads bouncing down the church steps like rubber balls.

Once clear of the burning house of worship, her log-sized legs gave out and she fell to her knees. Her smoldering hair burst into flames.

Uncle Harm reached his sister first, grabbed her flaming head and shoved it in the snow. It hissed, breath coming through Ol' Blue Satan's nose pits.

She then rocked up on her knees, head bald as a seedling peach pit and reflecting gyrating light from the burning church.

The congregation gasped. Did a collective backstep.

Aunt Big Bertha's hair lay blackened and battered in the snow. A spiral of charcoal smoke blew westward from it, carrying an acrid odor of shampoo and shellac.

She stopped rocking. Her granite eyes searched the crowd. Found me. Her lips moved in a silent curse.

My toes felt like someone had lit matches between them.

Millie Faye tugged at my sleeve. Pointed at the smoking append-age. "What is it?"

"What they call a wig," I said.

Her eyes lit up and her little tongue darted out like it does when there's bread pudding and fresh cream for breakfast.

She stroked her straw hair, stepped forward and stretched to get a better look at the smoldering mane, as did the congregation. They'd had quite a day of sinning: a poisonous snakebite, dancing in church and now false hair, the sin of vanity by the fallen preacher's wife.

"Has the Lord forsaken us?" Someone said from the milling crowd.

"I bet there's still some good hair left on that wig," I said. "A clever person might fix it right up. Have themselves some mighty pretty store-bought hair."

While everyone was distracted by the burning church and smoking wig, my feet once again delivered me to the red Chevrolet. I caressed my cheek against its refined red paint. Cold and delicious. I stroked the sleek eagle hood ornament, then stuck my nose in the seam between the body and the door. Smelled the tantalizing newness inside. I toyed with the latch of the back door on the driver's side. It made a snapping, metallic connection and swung open. I was washed in the blood of the car, seduced by its untarnished perfume, propelled by the promise of big city sorcery. I hesitated, sensed blessed torment beyond anything a thirteen-year-old's world should contain.

"Don't you go in there, Mo Grady Witt," I heard my wee twin warn. "You'll live to regret it."

Shockwaves shot through me, and I nearly hit my head on the car door. "Jeez, Millie Faye, don't sneak up on me like that!"

She gave me one of her 'I'm onto you' looks, but her olive eyes kept glancing over at the wig. "Don't change the subject. I'm telling you, there's something not right about that car. It stinks."

"It's new," I said. "You ain't never smelled nothing so powerful new before."

"If that's the way new smells, then new stinks. You go in there, I'm not gonna be responsible for what happens to you." She skittered through the crowd in a beeline toward the preacher's wife's false hair.

Alone again.

The red Chevrolet muttered in the voice of Ol' Blue Satan. "Come on in, Mo Grady. You deserve me. Why, me and you belong together. That ol' nasty step uncle of your'n just borrowing me until you and I can be together forever. Climb on in here, ol' son. Don't be afraid. Get a taste of newness. Get a taste of your future."

I looked around. Nobody saw. Nobody heard. Nobody cared. They all stood watching their cheap church burn to the ground, their preacher convulsing in the snow.

No one hurried to call an ambulance for the stricken reverend or offered to haul his spasming body the forty miles to the New Dreadford hospital. Serpent handlers have an unspoken agreement with their congregation. You get bit, you're on your own. No messing with the Lord's divine plan.

I stroked the corded seam around the car seat. Put one knee on the carpeted floorboard. The pain in my thigh from Uncle Harm's hand oozed into plush fabric, thick and buttery tapioca pudding. My shoulder brushed a silver ashtray on the back of the driver's seat. My breath warmed the metal. I lay my tongue on it, tracing around the edge. Tasted like big city breath. I opened the ashtray. Unused.

I stuck my magic magnet inside. Made a joyous clink. Metal colliding with metal and liking it. Suck side toward the driver's seat. A perfect fit. I grabbed onto a handhold and climbed all the way into the car, newness swallowing me. Pulled the door closed. All outside noise ceased, shapes blurred.

I sucked in great gulps of anointed air, letting it fill my lungs, my brain, my soul. Pried my magic magnet out of the ashtray and lay down on my back on the pliant leather seat. Cool red flames, reflected from the burning church, danced around the cream interior. I reached a hand up and pulled the flames down, folding them into my magic magnet on my chest. Felt its power penetrating my heart.

The car spoke again. "It's all up to you, Mo Grady. You can have me if you want. All you have to do is kill your nasty old Uncle Harm. Have me forever."

I jerked up. "No! I won't do it. I can't."

"Touch me, taste me, smell me, Mo Grady. Am I not divine-ah?"

"Yes, yes, you are divine."

"Am I not exquisite-ah?"

"Yes, yes you are exquisite."

"Am I not irresistible-ah?"

"Yes, yes you are irresistible."

"Then do what I say and kill your Uncle Harm-ah."

"No, I can't."

"Oh, you will, Mo Grady, you will. You cannot resist."

I covered my ears. Silence. I lay back down. Under my layers of clothing, I swam in sweat. The leather seat wrapped around me, soft and seductive as my feather bed mattress.

CHAPTER 12

Hellfire Words and Simple Air

Mama opened the car door. The wrinkles in her forehead like plowed furrows in rich bottomland soil. Her cheeks rosy as ripe peaches. "Come on, son. We're takin' Reverend Waywater home with us. It's undignified to bear witness to so much agony."

Mama hustled me over to the disgraced preacher. The right side of his upper torso looked like someone had inflated it with a tire pump. His left half appeared drained and white as the snow, as if the swollen side sucked all the oxygen out of the good side. All two-and-a-half heads nodded to me—those spawned by the serpent, dry as ping-pong balls.

The preacher's right eye swelled shut. He opened his good eye, and his lopsided mouth moved. A shriveled arm floated up, and a finger pointed straight at me. "I saw Lucifer kiss you, boy. Taste you with his foul tongue. Repent!" His unblinking eye rolled around to the death-watchers.

The crowd stepped back.

"This boy's been summoned by Satan. He's been cursed. You have an unbeliever amongst you. Unwashed in the blood. The armies of the Lord will strip ye putrid flesh and fling ye bleached bones down to Hades to burn in everlasting agony. Repent! Repent!"

His hellfire words hung in the frigid air for all to hear.

The crowd backed away some more.

Sleet bounced off Aunt Big Bertha's baldhead. "The boy is a plague upon us. Best he be banished from the order."

Widow Atkins waved her melted fruit hat in the air. "A sinner like you, Bertha Sue, wearing false hair, has got no call to be banishing anyone. But she's right. In all my born days I never seed a serpent kiss a soul before."

"Leave off my boy—all of you. The reverend's raving," Mama said. She looked straight up into the sleet, her silver-black hair blowing across her face. "He's got snakebite fever. Somebody help me pick him up. I'm takin' him with me. If the poison don't get him, he'll catch his death of pneumonia laying here."

Nobody moved a God-fearing muscle. Crows cawed from the nekked branches of a sweetgum tree. Cows chewed. Church crackled.

Mama drilled Uncle Harm with a conjure folk dark look. "Harman Cornelius, you get your coon dawg bones over here and latch onto your brother-in-law's legs. That new car of your'n probably got a good heater in it."

"Leave him lay. He's touched by the devil," said Uncle Harm. "He ain't ridin' in my new Chevrolet. I didn't spend hard earned money on it just to have a death curse put on it."

"Amen," said his bald-headed sister. "My husband knew the consequences of flirting with the devil. Let the Lord decide his fate."

A cow leaning on barbed wire mooed, low and mournful.

"He ain't dead yet," Mama said. "Besides, this man's snakebit, not cursed. Any poison a snake can put in him, I can pull out." Icy pellets ricocheted off her shoulders. "We'll put him in our Ford. You Arnold boys get over here and tote the reverend. Mo Grady, you get in the back and hold the reverend's head and keep him from swallowing his own tongue. Harman Cornelius, you take the girls home in your Chevrolet."

The Arnold brothers hesitated, torn between the wrath of God and the anger of Mama. The Hazeycamp sisters prodded them. Mama was said to have the ability to visitate bad luck on people thick enough to cross her. Put a bona fide hex on 'em.

I cut through the snow and climbed in the back seat of our car. Millie Faye followed, holding the burnt wig. She stuck it out the open window and squeezed out the wet.

"Drop it, Millie Faye, and get in the car with your uncle." Mama said.

"No," she said, grinning like a banty hen eating June bugs. "I want it. I ain't never had me a fine, store-bought wig before. And I ain't gettin' in that spooky red car with Uncle Hurt. I wanna be with Mo Grady."

There's no getting away from Millie Faye. She sticks to me like pig lard.

Sleet ticked on the Ford's roof and blew on my lap through the broken-out window. Years of tobaccy smoke from previous owners settled into the upholstery. Smelled dank and deplorable. Made me yearn for the newness of the red Chevrolet.

The church roof collapsed. Startled cows and humans alike. Bovines waddled under the upright bucket of Uncle Harm's diesel tractor. Humans, seeing their snakebit spectacle leaving and roads icing up, muddled away, heads ducked against a relentless east wind.

Freeman Joe left off milking the Johnson's Jersey cow, climbed over the barbed-wire fence and into the front seat of our car. Crazy eyes shone from a face blackened by smoke.

The Arnold brothers lugged Reverend Waywater to our Ford and flung him in the back seat, two and a half heads bouncing on my lap.

Millie Faye scrunched in the floorboard between my knees, facing me. "Smells like our outhouse." She lowered her voice and made exaggerated mouth movements. "He's beshit himself."

"You watch your tongue, young lady," said Mama, covering up the preacher with a gray blanket then sliding in behind the wheel. Just the top of her hair stuck up above the back seat. She looked even smaller seated next to Freeman Joe.

Millie Faye was right. The preacher did smell like our old two-seater. First time I was glad for the broken-out windows.

"He's full of poison, Mo Grady," Millie Faye said. "What if he dies in your lap?"

"Mama won't let him die," I said. But I had my doubts. The preacher's skin had the gray-blue tint of an unscraped rabbit pelt. I touched his sweating forehead, like sticking your hand on a skillet of sizzlin' hog fat. Thin crimson lines led from two tiny fang marks, and his infant head oozed a gravy-like goo.

Mama hit a bump and Reverend Waywater's good eye flew open. Found my face and spoke, "Repent, sinner! Repent! You've eaten of the apple. Sucked on the Devil's cock. The armies of the Lord will march over you, stomping your lustful flesh to dust."

Only me and Millie Faye heard.

"What's he mean …'sucked on the Devil's cock'?" she said.

Between the sleet and wind buffeting me through the broken window, I could barely hear Freeman Joe's blatherings. Mama hunched over the steering wheel, staying on a road fast becoming a tunnel of ice and snow.

The preacher's good eye went blank, and he quit breathing.

"He's upped and died on you, Mo Grady," Millie Faye said. She flattened herself against the back of the front seat, away from the preacher.

Mama, without slowing, turned around in her seat. "Blow in his mouth, Mo Grady. Then push on his chest."

I looked at that mouth. Boy! That hell and damnation mouth! Lips like blue clay. I looked at Millie Faye for help. She shrugged.

Mama said, "Do it."

I took a deep breath and pressed my lips against his. Felt spongy. My breath churned down his throat. I drew back and pushed on that half-swelled chest, adding my magic magnet, suck side down. I pushed and blew and pushed and blew. Trying to jumpstart his heart. I don't know how long I rammed that magnet into that preacher's breastplate, it pulsing and hot under my hands.

I then held the magnet down on the snakebite, willing it to draw out the poison. My mouth whispered the words spontaneously jumping into my brain:

> *"Oh, Litha of night, devoid of light,*
> *empty this wound of toxic blight,*
> *from Ol' Gooseberry his soul to spare,*
> *and fill his lungs with simple air."*

Blue-orange veins flowed toward the magnet. Noxious liquid bubbled and gurgled out of the puncture wounds and disappeared into the magnet. Reverend Waywater's chest wrenched. Sucked air unto himself.

It worked! I plucked the two-headed preacher from the Grim Reaper's harvest. Sucked doom into a metal puck. Locked death in a wedge of hard steel.

I held the key. I swooned with the weight of it. I remembered folks saying, "Mo Grady 's got the goomer's dodge like his mama." And Mama replying, "The goomering he got from me. Whatever dodge he's got come'd from his no-account daddy—the sonsabitch." I never even knew my daddy so's I don't know how any of his "dodge" could've rubbed off on me.

Mama jerked the steering wheel, and the Ford fishtailed whilst sleet blew horizontal across the hood.

A howling sound, blown in from outside, filled the car. Could've been the clever east wind bringing the baying of the wild dog pack.

"Did you hear that?" Millie Faye said. "Sounded like it came from hell. Satan's mad at someone today."

"No," I said, "that's just the wind blowing through the Blue Bog."

The magic magnet seethed energy into my hand. I was prepared to dodge my goomering destiny and toss the magnet out the window. Freeze death for good. Let the blizzard bury it. But my fingers had other ideas. They folded around the vibrating disc, stuck like a warm tongue on a frozen smokehouse hinge.

Reverend Waywater's body spasmed, good eye staring at me, terrified. Wet lips moved, "I saw the light, boy. We hung on a precipice with nothing below but steam and muck. He was coming for you down a path of hot coals. Oh, you'd better be ready 'cause Ol' Gooseberry is coming for you." His eye closed.

Mama's voice came from far away. "Hold the reverend down before he ruptures somethin'."

Millie Faye grabbed his legs, and I grabbed his chest and heads. We hung on for dear life, riding that stinking soul home, snatched from oblivion, over Bones Pass, like two feathers tethered together riding the evil east wind.

CHAPTER 13

Manly Chores and the Conqueror Hog

Seemed like yesterday's church burning changed the temperature of the whole valley. Sleet quit as I started my chores, and when I came out of the barn carrying pails of fresh milk, a warm boiled-egg breeze hit my face. Snow melted, and underneath, mottled ice lay on the branches of trees, nekked and bleached opaque. The sun, small and feverish, hung low to the Ozark hills, a coyote stalking quail.

Me and Millie Faye usually waved at the kids on the morning school bus, but today school had let out for the hog shoot. All men and boys in and around Scuttles Grunt were expected to join in the festivities. I might even get to see Loveda, Widow Johnson's granddaughter. Maybe glimpse those scrubbed alabaster ankles.

"Get your rifle and bullets," Mama said at breakfast. "Be sharp, Mo Grady. You're the man of the house now that Freeman Joe is makin' like a scarecrow in the barnyard. Don't shame us."

Mama had three motivational statements: One, if she wanted me to do something I didn't want to do, she'd say, "You're the man in the family. I kept having little babies till I had me a boy child just so's we'd have someone to do manly chores." Two, if Mama wanted me to stop doin' something I did want to do, she'd say, "You're gonna wind up just like your papa, the sonsabitch. A good man taken by hard liquor, pool halls and banjo music." And three, when staring at humiliation and defeat, Mama'd say, "Never you mind. One of these days you'll get yours, Mo Grady."

Up until yesterday, I 'spected mine was a long ways down the road, and if it did come at all, it'd do so with a whole passel of trouble and heartache. But today, trouble and heartache be damned! I was gonna get mine. And mine was that damn fine red Chevrolet.

After breakfast, I chopped wood for the cook stove and started the grain-grinder engine so's Mama could zap Freeman Joe's brain. Chores done, I sat on the farmhouse back stoop, watching Millie Faye astride Jubal Jen. My sister wore galoshes, red scarf and mittens, a wool coat with a white collar, and on top of her tiny head sat the preacher's wife's big black wig. She'd stayed up last night washing and shaping the piece until it lost some of its acrid smell and sizzled look.

Millie Faye's little legs were too weak for a good clamp around the hog's plump belly. She gripped one of Jubal Jen's ears with the hand coming out of her cast. With the other, she hung on to a stout willow branch. Her chin jutted out in princess attitude, and she leaned the staff in my direction. I smelled the green, wood fiber.

"Don't go to the hog shoot, Hercules. Run away and hide in your hay-bale hidey cave," she said. "You must obey me. I am Queen Bathsheba of the circus on my white steed." She stamped her scepter in the snow. Her white steed belched corn mash.

A screaming-curse came out of the bunkhouse where last night we'd dragged Reverend Waywater—him fighting the snakebite fever.

Mama'd packed a senega, red puccoon and snakeroot poultice over the new swelling on his second head. When I went in the springhouse earlier to get more milk, I noticed Mama's bottle of snakebite venom was missing and the Destroying Angel pint jar was also gone from the kitchen. I reckoned Mama must've goomered a potent antidote. Fight poison with poison. What can kill can also cure.

Reverend Waywater wailed all night long. The wind howled and sleet hammered against tin roofs and siding. Chickens got so fidgety, they refused to lay. Cassandra, my favorite breeder rabbit, 'bout ready to birth kits, hid in her nest box. Even Gweneviere, my gentlest milk cow, kicked over the milk bucket. Mama said the reverend's Merchant Marine background was showing and to pay it no-nevermind.

Mama's potion by late morning had done its work. The reverend settled down, and Rose Phoebe and Bonnie Joe took turns in the bunk-house tending to him.

We kids called the fourteen-by-fourteen shed 'the bunkhouse' 'cause it sounded important. It had a tin stove with a gray ash pail and stacked wood beside it. A wall-mounted shelf between the stove and door held hand tools and a ball of binder-twine. Ten-penny nails driven into the wall on either side of the door served as clothes hooks. The reverend occupied a bed that, at the foot, had a window overseeing the barnyard. Two wooden chairs and a table with my initials M G W—carved on the surface with my Old Granddad pocketknife—made up the only other pieces of furniture.

Mama said Reverend Waywater was going to live but "snakebites so close to the brain was sure to addle you some. 'Specially if you had a good shove in that direction in the first place."

"Oh, great Queen Bathsheba," I said to my sister, "I've got to go on this crusade. I promise I won't shoot any infidels—meaning hogs. I'll aim high."

Millie Faye's big-bellied steed gaacked.

"Mama says not to waste bullets," my twin said. "'Sides, folks know you're too good a shot to miss what you aim for."

I gave Jubal Jen's big floppy ear a pull. She snorted, spraying my pant legs with acorn slaver.

Millie Faye adjusted her salvaged hairpiece, her frog eyes swell-ing. "If you go, you'll be forced to shoot. You'll kill Jubal Jen's cousins for no other reason than one single pig tested diseased. The men and boys'll make fun of you if you don't."

I picked up my short-barrel .22, break-away, single shot rifle and aimed it at the lightning rod atop the barn. The rod used to be a roost-er, but too many high-voltage hits twisted its polarity into a grotesque gnome. I aimed at it but never shot. "I promise I'll aim high, Millie Faye. There'll be so many people around, nobody'll notice whether I actually shoot any hogs or not."

Jubal Jen quit rooting snow and laid her massive head in my lap. From the time she was a piglet snuffling in the muck, she had a fine sense of sympathy. She knew letting me scratch her hide calmed me.

Her eyes searched mine—gentle porcine orbs probing me for signs of mercy.

I sat down the gun and ran my fingertips over her long forehead. Stroked from forehead to neck, her fine mat of flat hair. So soft and even. Folks who've never touched it think it's tough and bristly. But a hog's head hair lays one way, smooth. Got a grain to it, same as a piece of hickory. It's only when you rub it the wrong way you're in trouble.

My sister cocked her soot hairpiece at me. "You just want to ride in Uncle Hurt's new car, and you'd shoot hogs to do it. That's a low-down thing to do."

"You're gonna get in trouble calling him that. And besides a little pinch, he ain't never hurt you. You got nothing to complain about."

Millie Faye's cheeks turned red. She was keeping secrets from me. But what she said about the car was true. I ached to ride in that red Chevrolet. Whatever I'd expected from a laying on of hands by the two-headed preacher didn't turn out a'tall. I swear, that short time I'd spent in the bosom of the red Chevrolet was the best time of my life. Even when it spoke to me in Ol' Blue Satan's voice.

That scaly devil voice scorched an inroad into my heart, even though I couldn't possibly kill Uncle Harm—murder being the most unpardonable sin. I'd be in hell with the likes of the Sheriff of Nottingham and Brutus. Spend eternity fiddling around with Nero, playing "Ol' Jawbone" and "Off to California."

With the new church burned to the ground, spilling pig blood was all the folks of Scuttles Grunt had to look forward to. I'd be surrounded all day by gun shots and good cheer. Men and boys talking guns. Hogs screaming. Men and boys drinking moonshine. Hogs bleeding. Men and boys smoking roll-your-own cigarettes. Hogs dying.

A festive occasion for all. 'Cept the hogs.

And poor Widow Johnson. First, losing her husband, and now, her hogs.

Widow Johnson could get along without her husband, Mama said, but she'd have to sell the farm. Uncle Harm would be the buyer since he's the only one in the whole valley's got enough money. And he done bought up every other farm that come'd on the market in the last few years.

Jubal Jen nudged the stock of my .22 and coughed.

I pulled out my magic magnet and laid it against the rifle. Click. Magnet felt hot. Not from capturing death, but from bein' left a little too long this morning in the cook stove oven. Blistered my palm when I picked it up. Like it was trying to tell me not to go to the hog shoot.

Millie Faye grabbed the box of rifle shells. "I'll just hold onto these, and if Jubal Jen knowed what you were thinking of doin' today, she'd never have anything to do with you again." The box disappeared in her coat pocket. "I saw that cottonmouth lick you. You're goin' to hell for sure." She patted her fake hair pile. Blonde strands of her own hair stuck out from under the wig, like a crown of thorns.

"Mind your own damn business. He didn't lick me. He just laid his tongue on my nose. Just a touch."

"You know what that means? In my circus kingdom, anyone kissed by a snake turns into a snake. 'Specially those who hog the holy roller stage so Queen Bathsheba can't get her broken heart fixed."

"I ain't turning into a snake. And we ain't in your circus kingdom." I did my best to deflect the guilt she was hurtling at me.

"Yes, we are. Only way you can be saved and turned back into an innocent boy, is to be kissed by a virgin."

I was fixin' to say I sure as hell wasn't getting kissed by no girl, but the red Chevrolet turned down our driveway. No sound. Our old Ford, you could hear comin' way before you saw it.

My butt raised off the stoop. The Chevrolet's chrome grill, set close to the ground, flashed silver sparks back and forth with road ice. Drawing closer, I heard it purr. My thumb toyed with the gun cock of my rifle.

Cocking and releasing. Cocking and releasing.

The car glided, smooth as a diving chicken hawk, and stopped in front of us.

Uncle Harm got out. Aunt Big Bertha sat in the shotgun seat. She wore a raven-feathered hat and looked out from under those black feathers with eyes like spent coals. She zeroed in on Millie Faye wearing her wig.

She screeched and flew out of the car, legs slipping every which way on the ice, and snatched that wig off my sister's head.

Jubal Jen gaacked.

"That's mine, you little bastard," Aunt Big Bertha said. She turned her back and stuck the hair mop, now snipped to fit a much smaller head, under her hat. Pounded the hat down so that it fit like a tight lid on a garbage can.

Uncle Harm moved a wad of chewin' tobaccy from one side of his toothless jaw to the other. "Now, Sister Bertha, I told you them little bastards was little bastards in strictest confidence."

Millie Faye may be puny, but when angry she's got volcanic fire in her missin' heart, lava traveling through her veins and flames shooting out her eyes. I reached for her too late. Before you could say "Joshua clobbered the walls of Jericho," she come'd off Jubal Jen a'spitting and a'snorting, sprang from the porch and pounced on our step aunt's back.

"It's mine!" Millie Faye screamed, clawing at the feathered garbage can lid. "I stole it fair and square!"

Aunt Big Bertha stumbled forward, spouting cuss words that would straighten a steel knot. She draped herself over the hood of the Chevrolet, and Millie Faye commenced shredding our step aunt's raven hat, squawking like a blue jay protecting her nest.

Millie Faye, with her arrhythmic heart, shouldn't even be riding on no gentle 600-pound sow let alone an agitated 300-pound preacher's wife.

Uncle Harm reached to grab Millie Faye.

Jubal Jen let out a tree-splitting squawl like I'd only heard her do one time before, when a wild dog snatched one of her newborn piglets. That wild dog didn't know what hit him. Only bits of fur and paws and eyeballs remained in her wake.

Everyone 'cept me froze, knowing what that squall foretold.

"No! No!" I rolled off that stoop onto Jubal Jen's bristled back, steer-wrestling style, and grabbed onto her ears as she charged Uncle Harm. I managed to throw her aim off, and she missed his ankle by an axe blade, smacking into the car's chrome rear bumper, causing it to shift and creak. Jubal Jen turned on a dime, squealing the porcine equivalent of bloody murder. I hung on like a flea on a terrier.

Millie Faye, with Aunt Big Bertha's hair prize in hand, bounded over the car onto the melting snow and skidded to a stop, hollering, "Jubal Jen! Nuts! Jubal Jen! Nuts!"

Jubal Jen stopped, turned to look at Millie Faye and gumped in her direction, anger forgotten, ready for a special nut treat.

Uncle Harm leaned backwards over the Chevrolet's trunk and, before righting himself, kicked my 600-pound pet in the snout. "Goddamn sow, shouldn't be running around loose like she is."

Jubal Jen absorbed the kick and, quick as a pneumatic punch, grabbed Uncle Harm's number twelve-size black boot in her number fourteen-size jaws. Crunch.

Uncle Harm hollered, tobaccy spittle flying to nigh and yonder.

Jubal Jen pulled the hollering man onto the ice and waddled astraddle of him. The conqueror hog gumped again, fanned her legs out and lay down. Pinned Uncle Harm good. Breathed cabbage breath and possum guts in his red face.

Uncle Harm's face turned the color and consistency of head cheese. "Get this goddamn sausage off me! If you don't, I'll ..." Jubal Jen lay down harder, pushing any talking breath out of Uncle Harm. His face turned apple red, eyes bugged bigger.

I grabbed my pet sow's ear and pulled. No go. Jubal Jen, having a tough hide but a tender personality, didn't like to be called a sausage. Uncle Harm's lips moved, but only a sucking sound came out. I whispered in Jubal Jen's ear, "Kidneys and guts and heads," I said. "Yum! Yum!"

Jubal Jen's ears shot straight up. She gathered her four cloven hooves together and rose, hind-end first, mashing her slavering nose and mouth into Uncle Harm's face.

I went around in front of her and pushed her backwards. Shooed her over to Millie Faye who took the big sow by the ear and towed her toward the barnyard.

Mine and my sister's eyes met. We knew Jubal Jen was in trouble.

Better get her out of sight before Uncle Harm re-inflates his lungs and self-esteem.

He looked like a penny run over by a locomotive. His overalls lay flat against his barrel chest. Strap buckles dug into his flesh. He sucked in a chest full of air, skin returned to its natural mottled redness.

I helped him to his feet. He wiped hog drool off his forehead with a dirty handkerchief. He grabbed my rifle. "I'll teach that oversized cob roller to throw me."

"Millie Faye's got the shells," I said.

"Go get them shells and bring that retarded sister of your'n, too. I've got a belt strap for her backside."

Mama came out the side door, kissing doves apron around her waist. "What are you doing with my boy's rifle, Harman Cornelius?"

"I'm gonna shoot that fat sow and whup your uppity daughter. She's well enough to snatch Bertha Sue bald, she's well enough to take a switching."

"You lay a hand on my daughter, and by all that's holy and unholy I'll make you wish you hadn't. 'Sides, who's got time to butcher a 600-pound hog today? You and your wiggy sister?"

I reckoned Uncle Harm's main concern was Mama's spell casting talents versus hog butchering. Mama had a reputation.

"Well, mark my words, Mildred Garnet," Uncle Harm said, "come May I'm takin' that sow to market with my load of shoats. Look what she did to my boot. Gnawed on my ankle, too."

Mama's leaned her head down. "I'm disappointed in Jubal Jen. Thought she had better taste. You may own half interest in this farm Harman Cornelius, but that sow belongs to Mo Grady."

"You're wrong about that, woman. I own fifty-one percent. By law, everything on this property belongs to me. You might've thought you married into money when you suckered my loony brother into gettin' hitched, but I own you. I own everythang. I mean everythang, and most everythang in this valley. If I want to whup one of your bastard chillun, I'll do it, by God. And if I want to kill a hog, you can bet I'll do that, too."

He leaned over and rubbed his ankle. Peered up at Mama from that position. "And don't think I'm afraid of your spells. I've got the Lord looking after me. I'm only giving you some leeway 'cause you taking care of my crazy brother."

"You ain't foolin' me, Harman Cornelius," Mama said. "You're more'n glad to be rid of Freeman Joe. Now you got someone to watch over him and tend the farm and make it pay for a change."

She wiped her forehead with a white dove. Her voice turned to honey, like when she talked to Bible salesmen or wandering banjo players. "Now, Harman Cornelius, I got some fresh baked bread and fresh churned butter and a pint of rhubarb-blackberry preserves so sweet, it'll make your tongue play hop-scotch with itself. Bring yourself in for a slice whilst we get ready."

A line of cuss words, blue enough to make crow beaks curdle, streamed from the bunkhouse.

Mama's lips threw a fresh churned buttery smile at Sister Bertha Sue. "I'm sure you'll want to see your lawful husband, encourage him on in his battle with the devil?"

Aunt Big Bertha leaned down and wiped Jubal Jen's nose print off the chrome bumper of the red Chevrolet. "You tell that bastard dwarf of yours, she can have that burnt wig, but she'll have to pay for it in the long run." She opened the back door, got in and slammed it. Rolled down the window. Said loud enough for the Brockmans two miles away to hear, "Any man gets snakebit twice is playing in the devil's barnyard. Anybody that aids him is doing the devil's work, too, and will get no help from me."

She settled her pumpkin butt back in the seat. Rapped her knuckles on the silver ashtray. "Brother, tell this witch she better not try any of her boogering on me, either. I'll do better than calling on the Lord for help. I'll burn down the farm like her bastard boy burned down the Sulphur Lick Church."

"Now, Bertha Sue," Uncle Harm said, "there'll be no more talk of spells and burning this morning. We've got the Lord's work to do." He tried putting on a friendly smile. Tight fit. Like me climbing into last year's overalls. "If you want to go to the shooting, Mildred Garnet, get yourself ready. I can smell them fresh baked loaves of bread out here."

"I'll get the bread," I said, and ran into the house and out the back door. Found Millie Faye and Jubal Jen in the barn next to Cassandra's rabbit cage.

Jubal Jen cracked black walnuts with her massive jaws. Millie Faye picked out the meat, then fed some to the hog and some through the wire mesh to Cassandra.

The wig was back in place, canted and mussed. Her eyes looked sunken, and the skin around her nose was the scuffed gray color of our kitchen linoleum.

"You need a lay down," I said. I hopped up on Cassandra's cage, jumped for the loft, caught a plank and pulled myself up. My feet kicked a fresh bale of straw down. I jumped on top of it and tore it in half. It smelled of summer sun a long ways away.

I brought the straw to the stall and made a bed.

"I'm afraid, Mo Grady," she said, gulping. "Don't go to the hog shoot with Uncle Hurt and Aunt Big Butt."

She lay down, and I scattered straw on top of her.

"I'll be fine," I said. "You just take a little nap." I turned to my pet sow, "Here, Jubal Jen. Lie down right here." I patted my hand beside my sister. "Keep Millie Faye warm."

Jubal Jen buckled her front legs and lay down, careful not to crush her human piglet. The rich meaty aroma of sow mingled with the scent of homemade soap from Millie Faye.

My sister giggled, putting her arms halfway around the hog's back. "Jubal Jen's as hot as Aunt Big Bertha was when I stole her wig. You reckon we're gonna catch on fire, Mo Grady?"

"You're just unnatural cold and excited." I could almost hear her tiny chest thumping off a beat. "You shouldn't get yourself all worked up."

"I feel better knowin' I got me a store-bought hairpiece. And I got your bullets so's you can't shoot anything shouldn't be shot. Somebody's got to look after you, Mo Grady. Keep you from traveling the road to ruin."

Her eyes closed. She snored, a sound no bigger'n a mosquito's buzz. Her lips dream-spoke, breath fluttering an errant wheat straw:

"Don't leave me before Uncle Hurt gets gone, Mo Grady. Peek under my dress and see if my butterflies on my panties are flying right? Last time Uncle Hunch showed me the Lord's way, I woke up with 'em flying backwards with broken wings."

My heart skipped a beat like Millie Faye's. My trigger finger slid her dress over her pale calves, knobby knees, and broom handle thighs. Her butt was the size of a Ford taillight. A baby butt.

My eyes focused on the top of her panties to check the label. There it was. On the outside. Her panties were inside out.

I pulled her dress back down over her pencil legs, all the time furious about how her butterflies had gotten turned around backwards.

Aunt Big Bertha's wig, in spite of all Millie Faye's cleaning and preening, still had a rancid Claggett smell. I took that wig off Millie Faye's head and beat it against a support beam until I was out of breath.

I lay next to Millie Faye, her eyes still closed. I brushed straw off her white forehead. "I'm mighty proud to have a big sister taken an interest in my well-being. Sleep tight, Millie Faye. I'm not gonna let anyone hurt you ever again."

I reached in my sister's coat pocket and tugged out the box of rifle shells. It seemed heavier. I opened it and counted. Thirty pieces of silver and brass. I put the box in my left pocket and, in my right, shoved my magic magnet.

My polarity shifted into high gear.

I left the barn, got Mama's bread out of the kitchen and marched, as befits a snake prince of noble birth, toward that red Chevrolet, off to do battle in the crusades against infidels.

Claim me the golden fleece.

Rid the earth of pestilence.

And get kissed by a virgin.

CHAPTER 14

Creamy Thigh and Pearly Gates

Uncle Harm, driving us to the hog shoot, stopped the red Chevrolet alongside Widow Johnson's field to admire his trenching work. He'd been busy with his Caterpillar tractor earlier in the morning. Behind a mountain of brown, steaming dirt was a trench the size of twenty automobiles across and deep as our two-story farmhouse.

Two cows with bloated udders huddled under his tractor's bucket. A third one lay on her side, not moving.

"Mo Grady," Uncle Harm said, "herd them cows into the Widow Johnson's barn and see they get fed."

"Yes," Mama said, seated beside me in the back, "and, for Christ's sake, milk 'em and put dry straw in their stalls."

"That one there on the ground, if she's still alive, blow in her ear," Uncle Harm said. "Might get her on her feet. If she doesn't, put a bullet in her head."

"Rub her nose real hard and fast before you do that," Mama said.

I'd slipped my magic magnet in the driver's side back seat ash-tray for safekeeping. Couldn't rescue it with all eyes looking at me. I opened the door and let my fingers trace along an inside seam. I closed the door. Got my rifle out of the trunk. Stuck my tracing finger in my mouth and sucked the last drop of new car flavor. I stopped sucking when I needed my hand to climb over the barbed-wire fence between the church parking lot and hog killing field.

The red Chevrolet pulled away.

The mid-morning sun, hard as an old penny, hung at an angle over Wrestler's Ridge. Mist fragmented above the Blue Bog. Luella's Leap flashed in and out of the coarse light. I was drawn to that place but didn't know why any more than a moth knows why it's drawn to a flame.

My shoes kicked last year's corn stobs that were throwing broken shadows in the melting snow as I trudged toward the cows. The stobs, wounded children of the harvest, made corn-cricklin' sounds.

A red bird, crest raised, perched on the black muffler on the hood of Uncle Harm's tractor. Like a preacher cloaked in a scarlet robe at the pulpit, the bird called out, "What, what, what, more cheer, more cheer" and "Pretty, pretty, pretty."

Red birds got no sense of proper fun nor beauty.

I broke off a piece of corn stalk and slung it sideways, my Bob Feller curve ball, at the red-robed preacher. He flew up to miss it, bobbed his head and hopped down to land on the fallen cow.

The other two cows watched me coming, thick lips flaccid, eyes flat and dull.

I gave the downed cow a kick in the butt. She grunted. If I could get her on her feet, I wouldn't have to kill her. Before I blew in her ear, I started to pray for her, then stopped. I didn't know who to pray to.

The red bird hopped onto the metal tread of the Cat. His beak opened and closed, chirping, "Pretty, pretty, pray to me, Mo Grady. Your soul to keep. More cheer, more cheer."

"Leave me alone," I said. "There's nothin' to be cheerful about."

I saw small footprints on the other side of the cow, leading around the tractor. My nostrils caught a faint trail of lilacs. Red and green dragonfly wings danced in my head. The skin on my thighs tightened.

"Hello," I said. "Don't be afraid. I know you're there. You're Loveda Johnson, ain't you?"

"I'm not afraid," a soft voice said, and a thrill traveled my backside from my heel to my head.

She stood up from behind the folded seat of the Cat. An angel anointing a mechanical beast. "Who were you talking to?" she said.

"Just trying to talk myself out of having to shoot this downed cow."

She spotted the rifle in my hand. "You're that bunch of bog riff-raff, aren't you, come to kill my poor grannie's hogs? And now you want to shoot one of her cows, too."

Loveda's voice fluffed my earmuffs like a summer breeze. I leaned my .22 short shot against the Cat.

Loveda wasn't wearing Holiness Christian girl's clothes—brown and gray frocks covering the body from neck to toes. She was a vision in full Technicolor: purple suede slip-on shoes below shapely ankles in green socks. A purple pleated skirt and an open light green coat bright against snowdrifts. A chestnut brown cotton shawl slung loosely around her. And a long ponytail, the color of rich bottom loam, cascaded in curls down her back.

"I'm not gonna shoot any hogs, and I won't shoot this cow if we can get her on her feet." I sounded tight and nasal. "Just brought my rifle so I could pretend to shoot."

"You can't shoot sick hogs? Are you chicken?" She pointed her freckled strawberry chin straight at me. "And don't think we can't take care of our own milk cow."

My first encounter alone with a snow goddess and my thoughts were tied up in knots. Loveda, I surmised, was complicated as religion—no matter what you did, you were damned. And yet, there she was like forbidden fruit, ripe for the picking.

I wanted a bite.

Then it hit me: Red hair. Red car. Loveda and the red Chevrolet together, ecstasy beyond anything imaginable. Going down that open highway, red curls tickling my shoulder, rolling down my nekked arm. Never was there a prettier thought.

That obnoxious red bird on the exhaust pipe echoed, "Pretty, pretty, pretty."

"What's the matter?" Loveda said. "Some skanky old barn cat got your tongue?" She hopped down on the tractor's steel treads and crouched there.

I caught a flash of creamy thigh above long green stockings. My throat commenced a fit of dry swallowing.

"Well?" she said. "Aren't you going to catch me?"

Head, an empty soap bubble, legs, fence posts a-dragging, I sidled over to the tractor. Didn't know how to go about catching her, but if it meant touching her, I was willing to give it a try.

"Hold out your arms," she said.

My arms started up and here she come'd, her butt landing perfect between them, thighs on one arm, back on the other, her arm gripping around my shoulder right over my bruised collarbone.

My mouth let out a "yike," but I cut it off quick. Ain't never had nothin' hurt so good.

Her face buried in my neck, red curls caressing my cheeks, breath warming my skin from ear lobe to big toe. My fingers naturally folded into her, the better to keep her from bouncing out of my arms into the burning abyss.

Aside from sitting in the red Chevrolet whilst the Holiness Christian Church was on fire, this was the best moment of my thirteen-year-old life.

My second-best moment lasted as long as the first.

Loveda squealed and rolled out of my arms, landing on her feet like a cat. "You tried to cop a feel from me, didn't you? I'm going to tell my grandmother."

Her breath smelled like creamed gooseberries.

My throat sprouted cacti, thorns shooting out my mouth. "No, no, I didn't do no such thing." In truth, I didn't know what "cop a feel" meant, but I figured it was nasty, evil or both.

"If you'd a'been Nathanial, my Baptist boyfriend in Springfield, you would have copped a feel, and I might've let you. Nathanial's so handsome, and he's old enough to drive his daddy's V-8 Packard."

Usually, it takes me awhile to hate someone, but not this high-falutin', car-drivin' heathen from Springfield. "Nathanial?" I said. I didn't like the way it sounded, just a bunch of flat syllables crammed together. Hate controlled my stutter. "I'm gonna have a car of my own pretty soon."

She twitched her perfect nose at me. "Where's a swamp trash boy like you going to get a car? My grandmother says …"

A bell rang from the distant farmhouse.

"Oh, that's Mother," Loveda said. "We're going back to Springfield today. Mother says the hog shoot is barbaric."

The bell rang again, and we both looked in its direction.

Loveda brushed a red curl out of her green eyes. "Speaking of barbaric," she said, "here comes Mr. Claggett."

Uncle Harm walked toward us.

"He isn't barbaric," I said. "Just powerful righteous."

"Righteous, smighteous. Mother says that's why your church burned down. A clear case of excess righteousness."

She put a cool hand to my hot cheek. Liked to jerk me out of my lace-ups. "I hope, when the time comes," she said, "you won't let righteousness get in the way of doing what your heart knows to be true."

She tugged my blue scarf three times and took off running for the farmhouse.

I sat down on the nearest available seat, a shoulder of the poor, buckled cow. Her lungs ushered a weak sigh.

Uncle Harm, his head on backwards, watched Loveda's legs kick up slush, flesh glimmering between socks and knees. He then sat down—collapsed more like it—on the cow's hip.

She farted. Digested hay merged with my step uncle's whiskey and garlic breath.

"Oh me, oh my, my burstin' boy," he said. "There's temptation and then there's temptation. That girl's a wanton bushel of it. Looks like I'm gonna have to increase your lessons before temptation yanks ye under. But don't you fret none, I'll guide you through them Pearly Gates."

The red bird lit on the tractor tread. "Pretty, pretty, pretty time to kill your nasty old Uncle Harm. All alone. Nobody to see. Good cheer, good cheer."

Ol' Blue Satan inside an innocent bird. My ears sizzled like overcrisp bacon. Hands shook. I might never again get such an opportunity. I looked around for my rifle leaning against the tractor.

The cow kicked a front and back leg. Gaseous emissions came from fore and aft. She raised her head to glare at me with an eye like a new moon reflecting in an outhouse window.

Uncle Harm gripped my rifle in his hands. He cocked it open, looked inside. Did he hear the red bird's song of murder? Decide to strike first?

He walked with my rifle around to the cow's head. I moved to intercept, my fingers wrapping the cold gun barrel. "Let me blow in her ear and rub her nose awhile," I said. "She's still got a lot of life in 'er."

Here I was, plotting a human's murder on one hand and trying to save a cow's life on the other.

"Hold on, boy. I can tell by her farts this cow ain't froze. Et something she shouldn't've. She's a prize milker." He let loose of the rifle, and I almost dropped it in the snowmelt.

He hopped aboard the tractor and started it up. The two cows under the bucket moved away. "I'll scoop up the cow and take her into the barn. She can warm up there and walk it off."

Hills beyond the Johnson's field rippled with waves of violet-green and red sunshine. Globs of melting snow tugged apart thousands of last fall's spider webs as cars pulled into the driveway.

Hog killers a'coming.

Uncle Harm became a block of gray, his head and torso silhouetted against dissolving webs. An easy target.

Here was my chance! One well-placed bullet, and I'd get that bran'-spankin'-new, red '55 Chevrolet. Mama would get her farm, a home already purified to raise us kids in. Millie Faye would never again get her butterflies on backwards. And me, I wouldn't have my pecker stretched to nigh and yonder and spit upon.

Car doors slammed in the distance. I had to be quick about it. Gun in hand, I stood unmoving, feeling my feet sink into squishy ground. I would tell folks: "It all happened so quick. I was gonna put the cow down, and I stumbled and the gun went off accidental, and I heard Uncle Harm cry out."

My feet dragged over next to the cow's head. I raised the rifle to my good shoulder. Only had seconds to set up.

I took aim.

Uncle Harm was within my sights, seated in the tractor cab, playing with the dials, lowering the bucket, oblivious.

Noxious cow farts hit me again. Damn cow! Would've been easier to put a bullet in Uncle Harm's temple if he would've put one in the cow's ear.

Uncle Harm glanced up. Saw the barrel of my rifle looking him straight in the eye. His ruddy cheeks turned the color of maggots on chicken guts. He had time to duck behind a fender but didn't.

We froze, caught in a sort of slow-motion standoff.

I saw through the black exhaust smoke Marian Lee Mitchell's skull bobbing above Uncle Harm's head. Heard his bony jaw clacking crooked teeth: "On this day, you'll wicked be. Beware the lure of eternity."

I blinked and lowered my rifle. Cow farts and ghost talk weakened my resolve.

Color came back to Uncle Harm's cheeks, and he fixed me with a gummy grin. Wagged a knowing finger at me.

Yep, the old skanky barn cat was out of the bag. But worse yet, Uncle Harm knew of my cowardice. That wagging finger promised tobaccy-spittin' retribution.

The tractor engine blasted the winter silence. My step uncle scooped up the bloated cow with the bucket and treaded toward the barn, the two cows following their sister in distress. Uncle Harm spun around in his seat and watched me till he was out of range.

My knees turned to slush. I sat in the wet snow next to Loveda's retreating footprints.

Mama's words rang out loud and clear in my head, like the Johnson's farmhouse bell. "Never point your gun at somethin' you don't aim to kill. 'Cause if you don't kill it, it may turn around and kill you."

CHAPTER 15

The Last Supper
and Temptation Training

I don't know how long I sat there, my butt getting damp and cold, my mind a nest of snakes crawlin' round and round themselves. How come I couldn't pull the trigger? I had every right to. Had hate and greed and vengeance on my side. Ol' Blue Satan in my corner.

I prayed for another chance before the hog shoot was over.

My ears heard chaos coming before my eyes saw it. Excited cries and gleeful shouts. Teenage boys and dogs driving the herd of hogs from their pens, slogging our way. Old pigs, young pigs, big pigs, small pigs. Grunting, scuffling, crunching corn thrown to them by toddlers—everyone was encouraged to participate in the festivities. Pigs not panicked yet, ignorant of coming carnage, happy to get out of their pens, taking a stroll in the sunshine, praising their masters for giving them such a treat.

One young pig, about 75 pounds, skipped in front. He had a black splotch on a pale forehead, resembling a five-pointed star. Starface broke from the pack and trotted over to examine me. He must not have known he was riddled with disease 'cause he had a goofy pig-grin on his snout and a bounce to his step.

Curious, considering he had cholera. Too much life in 'em for being sickly and now about to die.

Starface rooted at the stock of my rifle, liking the smell of cordite. He stirred me out of my murderer's paralysis. Numb feet kicked at him.

I did not want to get too friendly with a corpse. He squealed, gave me a no-never-mind grin and pranced over to join the rest of the condemned entering the gaping earth.

The trench had ramps on both ends leading down to the main channel. The two Postlewaite boys dropped a heavy makeshift gate, sealing the back exit. Eugene Ray and Clayton Wayne then picked up their rifles and hurried to sit with their feet hanging over the edge of the trench, a ringside seat.

I waddled over to my side of the trench across from them Postlewaites, who made lewd gestures at me with their fingers—letting me know they hadn't forgotten the stake burning incident with Millie Faye.

I looked down in the pit. Corn. The pigs were munching ears of corn. Uncle Harm had dumped bushels into the pit. The pigs' equivalent of the Last Supper.

Two men came alongside me, and I heard one say, "Damn waste of good corn, if you ask me. We should just shoot 'em and get it over with. I've got a plow to mend before spring."

Hearing munched corn, all outside hogs galloped into the trench for the feast. Stuffed full, the trench was, emitting an overwhelming odor of ammonia, cob slaver and corn shuck. The front gate dropped and two 4 X 4 slanted braces locked into place. Uncle Harm in his diesel tractor chugged back from the barn, and he secured the tractor bucket hard against the back gate.

Uncle Harm killed the engine and leaned his wide shoulders against the seat. Took his oily cap off and wiped his face. He put the cap back on and motioned for me to join him in the tractor cab.

My feet dragging, I climbed up. Tried to leave my rifle leaning against the metal treads, but Uncle Harm motioned for me to bring it.

No way out of it. Barbaric behavior was comin' down the chute.

He closed the door behind me. I was walled in up to my chest. Anything went on below that was concealed from God-fearing folks on the ground.

Uncle Harm's coal ash eyes watched me fidget and sweat. My

gonads clinched, sending a faint squirt of bile all the way up to the underside of my tongue.

Uncle Harm opened his can of Cactus Ed. He stretched his bottom lip like an old inner tube with a trigger finger and deposited a chunk of chewing tobaccy, big as a Chrysler hood ornament, between gum and lip. Snugged his chew down with thumb and finger, the same talented pair that matched the black 'n blue marks on my shoulder.

He offered the can to me.

I shook my head.

He insisted, his eyebrows waving like a wing-shot goose. Scooted to the edge of the metal seat, Madonna and Child ring—a grease smear covering the Baby Jesus—resting on his knee. Garlic-whiskey breath puffed in my face. "Go on, now, Mo Grady. Tobaccy is one of the Lord's graces for the righteous and holy. Stimulates the mind and relaxes the body."

I scooped a wad 'bout as big as a rabbit turd into my mouth. Had a tart taste and spongy bite. I put my hand over my mouth to hold in the sickening mess.

Three hundred happy jaws crunched dried corn in the trench. The sound roared in my ears. Men and boys talked, laughed and smoked. Adjusted rifle sights.

Uncle Harm scooted closer. The Madonna and greasy Child lifted off his knee, floated up to rest on my sore shoulder. Squeezed. "Boy, you been huntin' for years, you know not to point your rifle at folks even if it's not loaded."

So! He didn't know I'd had a bullet in my gun with his name on it.

"Yessir, I know not to point an unloaded gun," I blurted, tobaccy wad twisting my tongue. "My gun was loaded when I aimed it at you."

"Can't understand a word you're saying"—he shook his head—"with that chaw in your mouth. Why don't you load your rifle and get ready. An opportunity like this comes once in a lifetime."

The crunching stopped. So did the talking and laughing. Even the crows stopped cawing. Only the red bird chirped, "Good cheer, good cheer, pretty, pretty, pretty."

I turned around, kneeled down and supported the barrel of my rifle on the metal front casing. Pulled back the bolt and checked the shell. Aimed the barrel through the wooden fence toward the center of the herd. Raised it to point at the opposite bank. Concentrated on the big right toe of Eugene Ray Postlewaite.

Starface spotted me again and broke from the crunch of pigs, trotted over and stuck his curious snout through the wood slats. His belly had a cobby roundness. Gave me a couple of recognition gaacks.

I shooed Starface with my hand and a command under my breath. "Get out of here, pig. Last thing I want to do is see you die in front of me."

Starface scratched his corn-fed gut against the fence and gaacked some more, glad of the attention.

Uncle Harm stood up on the tractor and clapped his hands three times. "Listen up, brethren! What we're doing here is the work of the Lord. We're here to save this valley. Deliver it from disease and pestilence."

A murmur of amens sounded. "Now, there's a right way and a wrong way to do this. Soon as the first shot's fired, pandemonium will erupt. There's fifteen tons of hog meat in there. We don't do it right, they'll come through these gates like ball bearings thrown through a spider web. And I reckon we got enough wild hogs—and dogs—in the valley as it is."

A great shout of AMENS erupted from the shooters.

"Now, I want the men to take the sows down first. Take the one closest to you. Start at the bigger pigs first and work your way down. Those that ain't never done this, be prepared for sounds and smells most dreadful. But you can't stop and run away. You can't quit until the last hog dies. May the good Lord bless and keep you. Now, I want to pause a moment in silent prayer."

Uncle Harm's trigger finger and thumb found my sore collarbone. He pinched as he bowed his head and prayed. Pain worked its way down my left side to settle in my crotch. Made me forget the sickening taste of the tobaccy, feeling like a wad of pig flop in my mouth. Uncle Harm didn't pray for long.

While the others bowed, he whispered in my ear, "I'm praying for you, Mo Grady. You're gonna be lost in immoral civilization unless I speed up your training. My daddy cured me of temptation and his daddy cured him. By the time you're a grown man, you won't give nary a nasty thought to Jezebels, like that red-headed girl."

His pinchers on my shoulder tightened. "But you have to pray to be cured, can't cure you without your help."

I tried pulling away but those pinchers paralyzed me with pain.

His other hand fumbled for the pee-hole buttons of my overalls. His jaws commenced gumming the hell out of his huge chaw into spitting consistency. "You just keep lookin' straight ahead, Mo Grady. You know, you're a mighty pretty boy. But your prettiness is going to get you into a bushel of trouble if I don't head it off. Pray with me, boy."

I prayed my head off. I prayed to be cured of lust. I prayed to be cured of pain. I prayed to be cured of shame. I prayed for my magic magnet to get me out of this fix. I wished I hadn't left it in the ashtray of the red Chevrolet.

I prayed to have the strength to turn my rifle around and put a bullet through Uncle Harm's heart. But my arms betrayed me. They didn't move.

Uncle Harm quit gumming. His lips parted and a fine tobaccy spray covered my face. He raised his chin toward the shooters, sucked air up his clotted nostrils. "Amen, brothers. On the count of three start shootin'," he said. "One"—his fingers broke through the buttons of my overalls—"two"—his rough hand rasped my retreating pecker—"three!"—he yanked it out of my pants and pulled.

Forty rifles fired, followed instantly by the sledgehammer thud of bullets hitting thick foreheads. Thirty-nine pigs grunted and died. One was not so lucky. Emmanuel Simmons had a 30-aught-6 rifle that he'd forgot pulled a little to the left, and he hit a sow square in the right eye. She bucked straight up on her stout hind legs, wailed like the north wind whistling through a knot hole and snorted blood high enough to sprinkle the boots of rim shooters and wide enough to shower several other pigs.

Pigs know about blood.

It took the remaining 260 hogs about three seconds to figure out they were on the receiving end of a slaughter. They shrieked as one, a bleat so loud and engorged with terror, bark curled on the rough-cut wooden gate.

My hair roots vibrated, and I forgot for an instant the stabbing pain in my shoulder and my pecker, and felt the universal dirge of helplessness, a fat, dirty worm stuck in a valve of my heart.

Had all 260 pigs hit the same gate the same time, they would've shattered it. But mass murder is messy. Hogs tried climbing mud walls, rooting under the fence, and some pounced up over the backs of others as if they'd sprouted wings.

The thick smell of blood, cordite and raw earth hovered like a pall over the trench.

The shooters fired at moving targets, no clean or silent kills now. Injuries were loud and liquid.

The Simmons boy backed away from the trench, turned and up-chucked buttermilk biscuits, chunks of sugar-cured ham and four eggs over easy. Eugene Ray and Clayton Wayne, who started at a nonchalant, steady pace, became hurried and random, firing haphazardly into the mass of squealing, quivering flesh.

"You're not firing, Mo Grady," Uncle Harm's voice smacked more gummy than usual.

"You're hurting me so bad my eyes are watering. I can't see to aim," I said. My eyes were gushing tears alright, but not from pain. My pecker was stretching beyond hurting, hardly felt it at all, numb and flat like it'd been laid on blacktop and backed over by a spreader ball.

Uncle Harm leaned his head over, hurrumphed deep in his throat and spit a hot wad of phlegm and tobaccy juice on my pecker. Worked it around my retreating gonads, squeezing and lathering, with his rough hand. His other hand pinched my collarbone so hard, I neared to keeled over. Little blips of black splotched my vision, shadows of backwards flying butterflies.

Ol' Blue Satan coiled out of my rifle barrel and sat on my forearm. His porcelain eyes scanned my face. His satin tongue licked moisture from my eyes. Blue clay, bog breath dried my damp cheeks. "This is your chance, Mo Grady. You got about thirty seconds before the shooting is over. Plenty of time to shoot him through his black heart."

The din broke through the shadows. Shooters and hogs in a final death frenzy. Fading back into consciousness and stroked by Uncle Harm's Madonna and Child hand, I felt my bladder swelling nigh to bursting.

"Stop! Stop! Stop!" I cried.

Uncle Harm slobbered black juice all down his chin, his eyes white as the lining of Ol' Blue Satan's cotton mouth. "Shoot, boy, shoot! This is your birthright. Shoot before it's too late."

Starface ran up to the makeshift gate, oinking like a stuck throttle and poked his orange snout through a hole at me, beady eyes rimmed with a pink film of terror. One ear had been blown to smithereens and blood leeched down his forehead, turning his black star crimson.

"Shoot him! " Uncle Harm said. "Shoot the damn thang!" Pittooee. "Oh, please, dear God, shoot the damn thang!" Pittooee.

His left hand released my pecker. It felt helium light, like an iron glove had been lifted. Still, his right hand kept the pain coming to my shoulder. I heard the tobaccy spit now hitting on something else and a rapid sloshing sound, like bubbles breaking after a pond turtle splashes off a log. I knew, I just knew, in the split second, if I turned around to shoot Uncle Harm, I'd see him in the full throes of masturbation.

I froze. My mind, in that moment, opened another door of escape. It was so simple really, I had to laugh. Ha. Ha. The Farmer Johnson way out. Stick the barrel of my .22 in my mouth and blow out my brains.

I cocked my rifle and stuck it under my chin. It felt cold and hard. I adjusted my hand to where my thumb fit the trigger. Closed my eyes.

Starface squealed louder. My eyes flew open. Another bullet had crushed his jaw bone, but still his eyes pleaded with me. I couldn't stand it.

I aimed. I squeezed. I shot. Put a bullet right between the damned thing's beady, pleady eyes. A quick, clean, merciful kill. Stop the sickness, the disease, the pestilence from spreading.

I let go and pissed all over Uncle Harm's pant leg and shoe, and if my pecker would've pointed skyward, I swear my powerful stream would've knocked that red bird surveying the carnage and shouting, "Pretty, pretty, pretty" off its damn perch.

Uncle Harm, in spite of, or maybe 'cause of, me pissing all over his shoe and pant leg, let out a half groan, half squeal, followed by a dozen sharp intakes of breath. I smelled tobaccy, cordite, blood and piss, mixed with my step uncle's semen. The Bible calls it seed. Harman Cornelius Claggett had cast his seed upon his Caterpillar tractor.

My numbed brain wondered: did Uncle Harm masturbate in the barn before he put Millie Faye's butterfly panties on backwards?

My pecker shrank to the size of that white worm taking root in my heart. My hand found my handkerchief in my back pocket, and I wiped tobaccy juice off my pecker and balls and buttoned my pants. Didn't think I'd ever get clean again. I bowed my head over my rifle butt and swallowed sobs so wrenching, it felt like chunks of my lungs broke off and came out my nose.

The shooting and squealing faded, then stopped altogether. One more squeal, one more shot. Then, the loudest silence I've ever heard.

Uncle Harm let out a long sigh and released my shoulder. Blood rushed to my shoulder, bringing pain so fast it jolted my head.

I heard the Postlewaites and a few others boys firing again into the pile of bodies. Target practice.

I fumbled in my pocket for another bullet. Pulled one out and broke my rifle open. Tried shoving the bullet in the chamber, but my shaking hands dropped it. It pinged off the metal fender, hit the chassis and disappeared in the snow. I reached for another.

Uncle Harm's tobaccy-stained hand caught my arm. "Forget it, boy. It's over. What you need to do now is get yourself prepared for company. Looks like in your excitement you pissed all over my leg. Anyone asks, I'll say I spilled coffee on myself."

He buttoned up his pants. "Folks might not understand the righteous temptation cure I'm passin' down to you. You just keep it our little secret." He smacked his gums and winked. "One day you'll thank me, Mo Grady, for saving you a passel of heartache and trouble."

I couldn't fire off my rifle, but I could fire off my mouth. "You're a perverted sonsabitch," I said. "I hate you, and the good Lord hates you. When I pointed my gun at you, I knew it was loaded. From now on you leave me and Millie Faye alone, or one day I'll point my gun at you and pull the trigger."

He couldn't have looked more surprised had I clouted him between the eyes with my rifle stock. His eyes then narrowed, and he hissed, "You ain't got the grit for murder, you little bastard. The Lord has commissioned me to lead you and your little sister. And the sooner you learn to like Temptation Training, the happier you'll both be. And don't even think about talking to your goomering whore of a mama, or I'll jerk the farm right out from under you and your whole swamp trash family."

I stood up on legs of straw. Opened the half door of Uncle Harm's tractor and eased myself down to the ground.

Uncle Harm started the tractor and scooped dirt over the slaughtered pigs. Men and boys stood aside, watching, smoking and drinking whiskey.

I sat under a black walnut tree on a dry spot, my rifle cradled in my lap. The cold ground felt good seeping up into my crotch. I spit out the last of my tobaccy chaw on the tree roots. Even my mouth felt dirty.

Wood smoke from Widow Johnson's cook stove blackened the gray sky, and her farmhouse in the distance grew harder to see. She was cooking a lunch for the shooters.

My stomach felt like I'd never eat again.

Uncle Harm was right. It just wasn't in me to kill a person with a gun. A good swine, yes. A bad man, no. I had to find another way.

Maybe my magic magnet! Hadn't it saved the two-headed preacher's life? Mama had said, "What can kill, can also cure." I wondered if the opposite was true.

When we piled in the red Chevrolet to go home, I sat behind Uncle Harm, who was in the driver's seat. His lacquered hair and bald spot mocked me. I waited until Mama and Aunt Big Bertha dozed. My shaky fingers unclasped the ashtray, took out my magic magnet, turned it around, suck side facing Uncle Harm, then put it back and closed the ashtray. Leaned my forehead against the magnet's compartment and cast a spell:

"I plead thee, Ol' Blue Satan,
If I truly have the conjure folks dodge,
To heed my words,
Only the wicked shall catch this spell,
Suck out the soul and cast down to hell."

A great tiredness came over me, and I sank back in the plush leather seat and waited, hoping when the magnet took hold Uncle Harm wouldn't wreck the red Chevrolet and kill us all.

I braced myself and watched. Only thing happened was my step uncle slowed down. Drove more careful. The nearer we got to the farm the more my jaw twitched.

Red birds chirped around every bend: "The harm you cause, comes back to thee, times three, pretty, pretty, times three."

When we pulled in our driveway, Uncle Harm slumped over the steering wheel. My heart near to climbed out of my chest.

He raised up his head, hair oil beading on his red neck. "Whew! Shootin' hogs is hard work. I'm dog tired. Reckon I'll stay in the bunkhouse tonight. Need to have me a private talk with the Lord. Find out where I stand with Him." He looked at Aunt Big Bertha. "You can either stay here with your afflicted husband or drive my car home."

"My God-fearing husband hasn't performed his husbandly duties since he was first snakebit last summer," she said. "I reckon with two bites, he'll never take up his conjugal obligations again."

Wasn't no hesitation in her mind or body. She almost knocked Uncle Harm out the car door when she scooted her pumpkin butt over and shoved her tits against the steering wheel. A tight fit.

I felt betrayed by my not-so-magic magnet, and I thought about leaving the silver disc in the ashtray. But maybe I'd said the wrong spell? Was inept at conjury? I was, after all, a rank amateur compared to Mama.

Mama stared at me. "I don't know why I didn't notice it before, Mo Grady, but there's something amiss with your polarity. Have you got that goddamn magnet in your pocket?"

"No, Ma'am," I said. "I'm plumb tuckered out, too. Thought I'd do my night chores and go to bed."

"With you still not havin' enough gumption to write a little school paper, don't forget, it's the barn again for you. With Harman Cornelius in the bunkhouse, we'll put Reverend Waywater in your nice, warm room."

I quick pried open the ashtray when Mama wasn't looking. The metal was hot. I took my purple handkerchief, wrapped my fingers, and pulled out my magnet.

I swear it sparked with energy every which way.

My eyes, looking through the car window, caught blood red clouds a'massing in the eastern sky.

CHAPTER 16

Barnyard Popsicles and Brotherly Hug

Next morning, I crept out of the farmhouse, a lantern in one hand and a bucket of table scraps for the pigs in the other. I was bundled tighter'n a smokehouse ham. The temperature on a gauge tacked up on a fence post showed three below zero. A fresh round of snow had fallen overnight. Ice coated tree branches and the barnyard was like a skating rink.

I'd snuck in the house last night and slept beside the wood stove 'cause Uncle Harm's shouting to the Lord from the bunkhouse kept me awake.

Crisp air filled my lungs, and I let it out long and slow. It was a fine morning to be alive—to be alive and not be a murderer. I was glad I hadn't pulled the trigger to kill Uncle Harm. Glad my magnet hadn't sucked the living soul out of him.

My life as a murderer was over before it began. No road trip. No escape to Luella's Leap and beyond with Loveda by my side. No possibility of rotting in prison or playing poker with Marion Lee Mitchell in hell for eternity.

Still, Uncle Harm promised to turn up the heat on his temptation training. And I could only imagine what else he might do to Millie Faye. I didn't really think my death threat to him and follow up spell were gonna stop him, which left only one thing for me to do: tell Mama after morning chores, I'm gonna tell Mama. Risk losing my new step daddy, risk losing the farm. Risk me and Millie Faye never being able to show our faces again in school, even if I did get up the gumption to write that 1000-word essay.

Risk it all.

A snowdrift erupted beside the house. Jubal Jen shook off chunks of snow and plowed to greet me. I sat down the lantern and scraps bucket and gave her great head a hug. "Please forgive me for killin' one of your kin, Jubal Jen. I had to put Starface out of his misery."

She gaacked absolution. Hogs may not forget, but they do forgive.

I coaxed Jubal Jen to cut a trail through the drifts, my lantern lighting her back end like a taillight. Her massive rump parting the white fluff comforted me.

I looked around the barnyard, taking in drifts against fences and buildings. Our Plymouth Rock rooster, Bejesus, uttered a feeble cock-a-doodle-don't. Guinea fowls, roosting hidden in a cedar tree, shrieked a reply. The golden glow of sunrise shuddered against a broken combine. In the dead calm of the frozen morning, surrounded by familiar objects, I exhaled a deep, foggy breath of gratitude.

I sat the lantern and bucket down again and tackled Jubal Jen. She gaacked and fell over. We tumbled and rolled. I scooped snow on her, and she nudged snow on me with her great snout. She chased me 'round the corner of the bunkhouse, both of us grunting and snorting. I made a sharp turn and ran my face smack into a pair of bare-nekked feet—feet sticking out the bunkhouse window.

Big, pale feet. Blue-white toes. Froze solid. Drifted snow, between two ankles, formed a pyramid. I took my red mitten and swiped off the top.

An errant east wind found holes in my clothing and whistled up my long johns, chilling the gladness in my heart.

Jubal Jen grunted and tilted her pink snout up to sniff those feet. Food is where you find it.

I pushed her nose away. Pulled her by the ear as I backtracked my footprints so's to get my lantern on the other side of the bunkhouse.

A crow perched on the lip of the bucket, pecking at scraps. Jubal Jen squealed and the bird flew to the roof and leaned over the edge, watching us.

"Jubal Jen, stay here and help yourself to breakfast." I kicked the bucket over on its side, then hurried back around to those frozen feet. Held up the lantern for a better look. Ice had formed webbing between Uncle Harm's toes.

The window glass was opaque, but I looked through the open crack. Uncle Harm was asleep in bed, snoring and smiling. His eyebrows relaxed, and the hard lines around his mouth and eyes were gone. With all his ranting and ravings last night, he must've made peace with the Lord.

I thumped a big toe. Ice crackled. Uncle Harm didn't move. Frostbite. I'd been convinced my spell hadn't worked. Had it? My heart sunk. Maybe I was a murderer after all—without knowing it—and the conjurer's curse would be comin' hard and fast for me in three. No knowing what that would mean.

But what can kill can also cure.

Maybe my magic magnet could thaw those frozen feet.

I ran to the barn. Up in the loft my magnet still sparked from yesterday's goomer work. I grabbed it and hurried back to the bunkhouse.

I pressed the warm disc suck side against the bottom of one foot. It hissed. The foot thawed to release a stinky odor as water dripped to the snow below, making a black hole the size of a .22 caliber bullet.

Uncle Harm didn't twitch. I rubbed the warm magnet over stiff toes and ankles and calves. Rubbed at first soft, but then hard. The magnet sounded scratchy—metal skates on the mill pond. More water dripped, creating a dark foot-like pattern on the snow.

A dawn red bird called: "Pretty, pretty, pretty."

I pocketed my magnet and slogged around to the bunkhouse door. I scooped and kicked drifted snow out of the way.

Cold inside as outside. I lifted my lantern. Snow sat piled against the foot of the bed. I'd left plenty of wood in the bunkhouse for last night, but Uncle Harm didn't bank the fire in the wood stove.

The unlit kerosene lamp on the table had a blackened chimney. Must've run out of fuel and burned weak. An empty bottle of Old Crow whiskey sat next to an overturned drinking glass, a half-empty pack of

Camel cigarettes, a big copper ashtray full of ashes and empty butts, and a stubby pencil.

I set my lantern on the table.

Stale cigarette smoke clung to the green army blankets covering Uncle Harm from neck to knees. A dog-eared Bible lay open across his chest, moving up and down with his breathing. Not dead. Not yet, at least.

His lower legs, blanketed with snow, disappeared through the up-raised opaque window.

I tugged the window open wide enough for Uncle Harm's froze feet to pass through. That rooftop crow left his post and landed on my step uncle's left ankle and then homed in on Uncle Harm's toes. Barnyard popsicles. A Missouri crow is not picky.

He cawed and pecked a big toe. I stuck an arm out the window and shooed the bird away. A bloodless nick marked Uncle Harm's toe. Still, my step uncle did not stir nor stop smiling.

I shivered. Put one red mitten under his knees, bent over and reached out as far as I could and wrapped my arm around the bottoms of his feet. They felt hard as hog hide. Cold as creek rocks. Heavy as cast iron.

I lifted his knees and pulled his feet at the same time. Nothing moved. I pulled harder. My back creaked. Then, up went his knees and in came his feet.

Inside, Uncle Harm's feet looked uglier than outside. I pulled the blankets over them. Tucked them in. Hid them from my eyes so I could think better.

The Bible on his chest slid off. I caught it. Noticed some lines underlined in pencil. I read in the dim lantern light: *Mark 16:17-18:* "And these signs shall follow them that believe; In My name shall they cast out devils; they shall speak with new tongues; they shall take up serpents; and if they drink any deadly thing, it shall not hurt them."

I closed the Bible, placing it on the end table beside the empty Old Crow bottle. I cranked open the wood stove door and rolled and twist-ed a Sears Roebuck catalog for a starter, put a hickory 'pitch' stick on the paper, then some more kindling. Plan being to get a good fire roaring, then go get an audience for when Uncle Harm waked up.

Didn't want to be alone with him when he confronted his feet.

I scratched a match on the stovetop and lit the paper. Burned a red gash around the damp edge. I leaned over and blew. The gash smoked and flared, and the pitch wood popped and cackled.

One of the twists of paper coiled and turned blue-orange and curled around a color photo of a model in a black bathing suit. The end of the coil closest to me grew a flat, scaly head with high cheeks and marble eyes. Ol' Blue Satan's mouth opened, baring yellow fangs and white cotton: "You did good, Mo Grady, real good. I see your plan clearly now. Oh, you got a future, boy, in service to me. You're as natural born a sinner as ever came down the chute."

My eyebrow singed.

"Ain't got no plan. You're crazy'ern Freeman Joe," I said. But he was right on one thing: I did seem to have a knack for sinning. Maybe I was born with it, like Mama says I was born with the conjuring dodge.

"Don't mention that name in my presence. He's a dangerous man. The two-headed preacher's wife is the one you should look to for guidance now."

A cobalt tongue, forked and ribbon thin, reached out to touch my face. I fell over backwards, slamming the stove door. A chunk of snow slid off the bunkhouse's tin roof, shaking the bunkhouse frame.

Behind me the bedsprings squeaked. Uncle Harm's hoarse whiskey voice filled the room. "Why thank you for building me a fire. I don't think there's ever been such a freeze on the land. But the good Lord's got a plan, boy. I had this heavenly dream, and the good Lord told me there ain't much time; told me to make peace with my adversaries. Love thine enemy. We're put on this earth, and we ain't got much time to do the things as necessary to please the Lord."

Hearing his voice sickened me to the core. I was still glad I hadn't killed him but at the same time wasn't much glad to know he was alive.

"You stuck your feet out the window," I said, my voice steely. The glow of dawn slanted through the glass, erasing the dark.

He looked at his feet under the army blanket. Then up at the window.

"That was in my dream, too, Mo Grady. Show the Lord my righteousness. Could you throw another stick on that fire, my pretty boy? I've got a chill in my bones."

He clutched the covers around his neck. A big toe, the color of a dead, milky eye, peeked out the other end.

"Weren't no dream," I said. "And I ain't your pretty boy."

Uncle Harm reached a hand out of the cover and picked up the whiskey bottle.

"Told me to bury the hatchet with you, the Lord did." He shook the empty bottle and sat it back down. "He said, 'Give that pretty bastard boy a brotherly hug. Show him there's no hate in your heart for him tryin' to kill you.' So, come here, boy, give your Uncle Harman a big hug."

He extended his arms and tried sitting up.

I took a step back. Pious or not, I'd rather embrace a wolverine than Uncle Harm. My stomach knotted up. I thought about turning tail and fleeing. Let someone else tell him, be the bearer of the truth.

"Weren't no dream," I said, again. "You stuck your feet out the window and fell asleep."

"What'd you lay on them, Mo Grady? A sack of hog feed? You're playing tricks on me."

"Ain't no trick. Your feet froze." I fingered my magnet in my pocket. Didn't say nothin' 'bout nobody casting a spell.

He whipped the covers off his feet. Face went white as a poached goose egg. "This can't be—wasn't in my dream—wasn't in the plan. I looked the Good Book over and over, bless Jesus, from Genesis to Revelations and Revelations back down to Genesis. The Word was upon me. The Word insisted I do something to test God's love."

"Well, I think you done something to piss Him off." I palmed my magnet, more'n happy to pass the blame to the Almighty, more'n happy to give a little lip to my tormentor.

"Reverend Waywater said it was okay for me to test God's love," he said.

"Reverend Waywater ain't exactly the best example of God's love with two snakebites to the same shoulder. I'm gonna get Mama." I moved toward the door.

"No, don't leave me. Maybe my legs just need circulation. Here, Mo Grady, help me to my feet. I'll walk it off." He reached out to me.

I took another step back. "I don't think so."

His eyes filled with tears. "Please, Mo Grady. Please help me." Workman's grimy fingers grasped at me.

I took a deep breath and moved within reach. He grabbed my shoulders and pulled himself to a sitting position. I stiffened. He threw his covers off, and I saw his long johns shoved above his knees. An overripe fetid smell swamped my nostrils.

Uncle Harm slid his legs off the bed. His feet collided with the floor. Sounded like the time Mama dropped the clothes iron. Bunkhouse planks vibrated.

I couldn't take my eyes off those chunks of frozen flesh. Uncle Harm reached down and slapped his ankles. A sob ripped from his throat. "My God, Mo Grady, I got no feeling in my legs a'tall. The Lord asked me to prove my love for Him, and now I got no feeling in my legs."

He clasped my collarbone harder. "Come on, boy, help me to stand up."

He braced himself on my shoulders and pushed up. I turned into him and grabbed under his arms and shoved, too. He balanced on his feet, unclinched my collar, and swiped a sleeve over his wet eyes. Tried a Glory Hallelujah grin on for size.

"There, Mo Grady, see. I'm gonna be okay. The Resurrection is a'comin', praise Jesus. The good Lord's gonna guide me through this, praise Jesus."

"Praise Jesus," I said.

Uncle Harm did a header. Before he could get his arms out to catch himself, his forehead smacked the floor. Happened so fast, I just stood there. He bounced and tried dragging his feet. He jerked and pulled and hollered, but it weren't no use.

I never in my life expected to feel sorry for Uncle Harm. Only yesterday I'd spelt him dead. Seeing him flail like a spiked frog, a welling in my chest surged up my throat. I squeezed my eyelids to stall tears.

Fire raged in the wood stove, and my whole body poured sweat under my layers of clothes. I had a flash of summer, the sun shining, lilacs in the air, me and Loveda sitting in that red Chevrolet. But we didn't look happy. A tornado a mile wide and reaching into the black clouds was coming straight at us down the road.

A cold claw clamped around my ankle.

Uncle Harm had shifted around and reached a grimy hand out to snag me. He peered up at me with a look of pain and pure hatred. "You did this, boy. You tempted me. Last night I argued with the Lord. Told Him how I wanted to possess you and your tiny sister. I thought he gave me permission. But he didn't. He gave Satan permission to punish me through you, a fallen angel boy."

Spittle ran out of his blue-gray lips. He pulled me toward him. I dug in with the other foot. I was near enough the wood stove to grab the iron poker wedged in a top plate. "I ain't a fallen angel boy," I said, all pity gone. "I'm just a boy. And I ain't gonna let you whup me."

I brandished the poker in front of his eyes.

He didn't see that foot-long piece of iron—he saw vengeance. "I should've done this months ago when my crazy brother married your whorin' Mama. I was too nice to you little chillun."

"Let me go, Uncle Harm, or I'll smack you."

"Vengeance is mine, sayeth the Lord." He twisted my ankle.

A jolt of pain shot through my leg, and I swung that poker down across his wrist. Steel on bone, a bullet hitting a hog skull. He grunted and his hand flung open like I'd stepped on the release spring of a leghold mink trap.

He stared at his quivering hand. "You broke my hand. First you broke my heart, then you froze my feet, and now my hand. What foul beast has Satan released upon the land?"

"I'm not a foul beast, nor no fallen angel. I'm goin' to get Mama."
I ran outside and stumbled into Jubal Jen. I hugged her stout neck. My

tears flowed onto her floppy ears. "You believe me, don't you? I didn't want to hurt Uncle Harm. I'm not evil."

Jubal Jen gaacked and shook her massive head up and down, knowing in the way animals do that our childish game of rough and tumble in the pure, driven snow was over forever.

CHAPTER 17

Lispy Prayers and Turtle Poop

Doc Abernathy arrived two days later, drunk.

Uncle Harm's vomiting, shits and stomach cramps had quit. Mama, to cover the smell and banish evil spirits, lit black beeswax candles all around the bunkhouse room. She ground cedar gum and pawpaw bark for incense.

We all took turns tending and cleaning Uncle Harm, even Millie Faye and Freeman Joe. The two-headed preacher, back from the dead once again and still our guest, spent hours praying over his brother-in-law. The preacher's right shoulder and part of his mouth were partially paralyzed from the second snakebite, so his somber, lispy prayers sometimes overlapped with Mama's joyous pagan incantations. She often chanted in a sing-song soprano, sending a mixed spiritual and musical message to anyone within hearing distance.

Uncle Harm's legs stank like the root cellar when sauerkraut brine was bubblin' ripe. After two days of thawing, them upstanding toes, nails blackened, had wilted, laying down this way and that, like blighted corn stalks.

Mama had wrapped a poultice around Uncle Harm's shins. An herb paste of crushed cedar wood chips, dried red carnation petals, rosemary leaves and Mama's special ingredient, boiled bird feathers mixed with purified sunflower oil to bind everything together.

Doc unwound the wrap and thumped around on Uncle Harm's feet and toes. "Leg needs amputated immediately," he said, "or he ain't got nary a chance in hell of survivin'." He took a black crayon and made marks on Uncle Harm's legs about four inches below the knees, took a long swig from a whiskey flask and passed out cold at the foot of the bed.

Mama and me shoved him in the corner out of the way.

Mama scrubbed her hands in a dishpan filled with saffron water. "My choppin' block's next to the cook stove, Mo Grady. Go fetch it, and tell Millie Faye to get water a'boiling in a big pot."

I returned and Mama had put on her white purification robe and her favorite apron with mourning doves cuddling, strings tied in a double hard knot 'round her thin waist. She breathed hard. A look came into her eyes, like she was trying to hold on to a hot skillet with a greased handle.

She lifted Uncle Harm's right leg, and I scooted the block underneath. My fingers skimmed over hatchet nicks in the hard hickory.

Mama placed Uncle Harm's leg on the block, wiggled it for fit. "Get the tools from the smokehouse, son. Stick 'em in the boiling water and put the branding iron in the cook stove fire box till it's red hot."

I entered the farmhouse kitchen where Millie Faye stood on a footstool in front of the cook stove. I handed them to her and one by one, and she slid the cold cutting tools into a pot of boiling water.

I lifted a round lid on the stovetop and stuck the branding iron in the fire-pit of the stove.

"Ask Mama if I can come watch," Millie Faye said, her mouth twisted into that barbed-wire shape. "I wanna see Uncle Hurt suffer."

"No," I said. "Ain't no place for someone with a missin' heart. And what makes you think he's gonna suffer? Mama's saving his life."

I had my hands on a potholder, made from my old overalls, around the iron, but my bare fingers felt cold. Matched my insides. The iron glowed red hot within a few inches of its handle.

Millie Faye rattled the metal tools in the pot. "I know you put a curse on Uncle Pinch with your magic magnet, Mo Grady. Oh, he's gonna suffer alright, praise Jesus, and I want to watch."

"I thought you didn't believe in my magic magnet."

"That was before you cast a spell with it, a spell that I wanted to work with all my missin' heart." Millie Faye took the tongs and fished Mama's magic knife out of the boiling pot. She waved it in a clockwise pattern. "And now it has."

"If a spell can be done," I said, prying her little fingers from around the knife and waving it in a counterclockwise pattern, "a spell can also be undone."

"Sometimes you got turtle poop for brains, Mo Grady. Don't you understand, it's either him or us. You let the curse stay put."

I grabbed the tongs from her and fished for the rest of the tools. "I got my everlasting soul to consider."

Seeing my sister on that stool, stirring the bubbling pot, one arm still in a dirty cast, I had some sympathy for the Postlewaite brothers—she did look like a little goblin. A monster in miniature. Still, she was my sister, and if I'd looked after her better, maybe Uncle Harm would've never hurt her.

I returned to the bunkhouse, cutting tools trailing steam. The room was lit by black candles and an Aladdin lamp sitting on the table.

Uncle Harm lay in bed, eyes closed, blanket from chin to knees. Black hair covered calves the color of goat-cream gravy. Mama's green, yellow and feather brown poultice makings blotched his skin like some kind of swamp pox, traveling down to his ruined toes.

My magic magnet shifted in my pocket. Maybe I could use it again, this time for righteous reasons instead of Ol' Blue Satan's handiwork. Somehow undo what was done. I said a silent prayer over my step uncle's blighted toes: "Blessed Savior, lead and guide me. Please get Mama out of the bunkhouse so's I can be alone with Uncle Harm. Please!"

Mama turned up the lamp flame. Shadows swam over the room. Mama dowsed a rag in a basin of soapy bleach water and cleaned the block and Uncle Harm's right ankle and calf, her small fingers firm against his puffy skin and size 12 foot. She ripped a strip off the bottom of her apron and tied it in a tourniquet around Uncle Harm's upper calf.

Her mouth puckered like she was making spit. "Fetch me my knife."

I turned to the table where I'd laid Mama's magic knife next to the meat saw. My hand reached out and stuck to the knife handle. "Mama, I don't feel so good. Can't we wait for Doc to wake up?"

"We're the only chance Harman Cornelius has got now. You've got to help me. I can't do the ether and cut, too."

"Rose Phoebe's the oldest. Why can't she do it?"

"Girls ain't made for this kind of work, son."

"You're a girl," I said.

"I don't remember ever being a girl, Mo Grady." Mama slid her hand down her face, and her fingers closed around her throat. "I'm a mother and seems like I been a mother all of my born days."

"I'm afraid, Mama."

"What are you afraid of, Mo Grady? You've seen lots of blood before."

I rubbed both hands hard on my pants legs. "I'm afraid I'm goin' to hell."

Mama reached her right hand toward me. "I don't understand you. Ain't no evil in helping me save a life. Now, hand me the knife."

I passed it to her, wooden handle first. I saw myself in the steel blade. My head was long and flat, neck cocked to one side, eyes dazed, like a wren that had flown into a window.

Mama passed me an orange can with a cone tip and a damp rag. "Hold the rag easy-like over his nose and mouth. Drop a few drips from the can on the rag every time he stirs."

I took the can and rag and joined Uncle Harm's face in the shadows. My hand cupped around his hawk nose, fingers straddling nostrils blowing hot air. I put a few drops of ether on the rag over his mouth. I caught a whiff and saw swallows swimming in sauerkraut brine.

"Back away," Mama said.

I did, and the birds flew out the closed window into the morning snow flurry. I stretched my arm and dumped several more drops on the rag. Uncle Harm's uneven breathing got smooth.

Mama held the knife up to the light and looked down the flesh-cutting edge. She flicked it crosswise with her thumb and listened. The skin on her cheeks stretched tighter. Sweat splotches appeared around her breasts on her white robe. She lay the knife blade on the mark made on Uncle Harm's leg by Doc Abernathy. Drew back and scored the skin. A necklace of blood beaded.

Something landed in the snow on the tin roof. Death was a'knockin'. It shook the Aladdin lamp. Shadows bounced.

I palmed my magic magnet. "Please, sweet Jesus, give me a few minutes alone with him."

CHAPTER 18

Hacksaw Blade and Blessing Frenzy

"My damn nervous bladder," Mama said. "I got to pee, Mo Grady. You hold off with that ether till I get back." She moved toward the door, feet pounding hollow on the wood floor. The door opened, letting in swirling snowflakes, then closed.

I left the rag on Uncle Harm's face and set the ether can on the floor beside his bed. I fished in my pocket and pulled out my magic magnet. Felt hot.

The bunkhouse door burst open, letting in flakes of snow. Tiny feet tread on wood, light as a lizard on sawdust.

Millie Faye stood beside me, bundled up in her coat. "If he's fixin' to die, let him. Don't be messin' up the natural order of things with that old magnet of yours."

I pulled the rag off Uncle Harm's face. Placed my magic magnet over his heart, suck side down.

Millie Faye laid her tiny hand on mine and pulled, a fledgling robin tugging on a sack of spuds. Her ivory wrist, sticking out of the cast, was as thin as the handle on Mama's magic knife.

I leaned my mouth close to my step uncle's ear. "Please forgive me, Uncle Harm. I didn't mean to cause you no suffering, didn't mean to put a death curse on you. Please forgive me."

I didn't mean for him to come awake.

His big, Bible-clutching hand grabbed my blue scarf. Twisted.

Stout pinching fingers felt for my collarbone. His thumb and trigger finger found their target. Brought tears to my eyes.

His eyelids opened. Eyes rimmed with orange light. He raised up his head and his chapped lips opened. Breath, after three days of fever, still reeked of Old Crow.

"Look, Mo Grady," Millie Faye pointed. "His lips got a green glow to 'em. Like he was kissed by Lucifer or the Frog Prince, himself."

"I heard the Word, Mo Grady," green lips said. "Genesis on down to Revelations and back again. And the Word said that ye have been planted a demon seed, and ye have grown into a degenerate weed bright with illicit flower."

I sputtered like Uncle Harm's diesel tractor, "Help me get loose, Millie Faye."

She leaned over and took her barbed-wire mouth and bit Uncle Harm's thumb. He grunted and released my collarbone. He lay his head back down. Eyes lost the orange light. Lips lost their green glow.

My hands still clutched the magnet over his heart.

"I take what I said back, Uncle Harm," I said. "I don't want your soul to rot in hell. Glory to God, I take it all back."

His cracked lips moved, "You and your retarded sister won't be able to hide, Mo Grady. The Word will seek you out. You'll search and you'll search, but there'll be no hiding place."

The east wind howled outside.

Millie Faye pecked me on the ear, lips hard as plier grips. "Tell that sonsabitch I ain't retarded, I'm just puny." She ran out, leaving the door open.

Mama came in seconds later. She shook snow off her head and shoulders.

I slipped my magnet under the metal frame of the bed, suck side up, aimed at Uncle Harm's body. I then resumed my post with the rag and can of ether.

Mama gave a final twist on the dove tourniquet. Picked up the skinning knife. Our eyes met over the blade. She nodded. I added the ether. She turned and made a round cut down to the tibia bone—the same motion she used to de-wing a dead duck. Black blood bubbled up.

"He's twitching," Mama said. "Use more ether and then drape yourself across his thighs."

I tilted the can and poured. Heard it splashing onto the rag and Uncle Harm's hot breath soaking through. I sat the can down and slumped over his thighs.

Mama turned to the table and set down her knife. She picked up the meat saw—a number 10—two-foot hacksaw blade in a heavy metal frame. She laid it on the open wound and made a forward cut.

Blue jays make that same rasping noise when they raid robin nests. The back draw made a different sound, a hammer claw scraping over limestone. Jay, claw. Jay, claw. Jay, claw. Jay—

I could feel the beat from the meat saw in my chest. Uncle Harm's thighs bucked. Remined me of when he masturbated at the hog shoot. I covered my ears, closed my eyes, dug my elbows into the army blanket and box springs.

Mama's voice called to me. "This one's done, Mo Grady. Open your eyes. I need your help."

Mama held Uncle Harm's severed leg up by the big toe. "Take this thing out and shove it deep in the snow. We can bury it with the other one, proper like. Don't tarry and don't let your sister see this thing."

Uncle Harm's cheeks, the color of coal ashes minutes before, turned as yellow-green as summer squash.

Mama stuck her hands in soapy water. "I swear, I didn't know freezing and thawing gave a person's skin such a jaundiced pallor. Only time I ever seen skin color like that was when the Leavenworth family ate poison mushrooms."

My warm, sticky hands floated up to receive the leg from Mama. The stub smelled of bubbling sauerkraut and felt slick and heavy as a cooked goose.

My iron feet carried me out the door. My head full of mush. Millie Faye was waiting with outstretched arms. "Let me have the foot, Mo Grady," she whispered.

"No."

"Let me have it."

My brain was too numb to argue. I laid the fat leg in her stick arms.

Her knees bent with the weight. "Mama says to shove it in the snow till we can proper bury it."

Millie Faye's thin lips smiled over the jaundiced leg, and her face shimmered pink with hard light. "You get on back in there, Mo Grady, and I'll take care of Uncle Pain's foot. Me and the two-headed preacher are doin' your chores. Starting with the rabbits, he's blessing every animal we got. You might say he's in a blessing frenzy."

I should have seen it then, but I didn't. Even the Postlewaite brothers would've noticed something peculiar about a midget with a missin' heart in a winter storm toting a missin' leg, grinning like she just became a circus star.

CHAPTER 19

Cock-a-doodle Dirge
and the Angel of Death

I trudged back inside and found Mama pulling the branding iron out of the wood stove. She wrapped a piece of her apron around the warm end and stuck the fiery end against Uncle Harm's oozing stub. It hissed and discharged a purplish black smoke. Burning blood and flesh smelled like a church barbeque. Mama applied the branding iron three times to seal the stump.

When she pulled off the iron the third time, Uncle Harm sat up. The ether rag fell off. His yellow eyes opened and found me. Tiny red lines surrounded his pupils. "Thou art traveling a degenerate road, Mo Grady. Ye have spake with the tongue of a serpent, and …" his hairy nostril sniffed the air, eye waved over his leg, "thee and thy whoring mama have amputated me to death."

He lay back down, let out a clotted lung full of whiskey breath, and failed to draw any air back in.

Candle flames dimmed. The east wind flapped tin on the barn roof. Bejesus crowed a weak cock-a-doodle dirge. My magic magnet, under the bed, clattered onto the floor.

"What was that?" Mama said.

I reached under the bed. "I'm sorry, Mama. I know you don't care for my magnet, but maybe we can save Uncle Harm's life by putting it on his chest and sucking away death."

"Leave him be, son. Harman Cornelius has been paid a visit by the Angel of Death. Ain't no magic strong enough to overcome that."

I felt a tightness in my chest. So my spell had worked. This is what being Mo Grady Witt, murderer, felt like.

Mama wiped her sweaty face with the back of one hand. "But that magnet of your'n been messin' up my polarity. Take it outside and lose it. But first bring me your step uncle's leg. We'll stitch him back together. The less people know about what went on here the better."

Millie Faye met me in the barnyard.

"Uncle Harm died," I said. "Where's his leg?"

"Why?" She twirled a circle in the snow. "If he's dead he won't be needing it no more."

"The least you could do is not be too overjoyed," I said. "Now give it so's we can get this over with."

"I ain't got it."

"What do you mean, you ain't got it?"

Her tongue licked her upper lip. "Jubal Jen was looking a mite piqued. I threw it in with her meat scraps." She did another twirl.

Millie Faye ain't retarded. She ain't all that damned puny either.

Jubal Jen don't pick over her food. She's a gulper. By the time I got to her feeding trough, all the flesh was stripped off Uncle Harm's leg. She had the foot stuck straight up between her cloven hooves, the nekked leg bone gleaming white in the soft light.

I heard little clicking sounds as Jubal Jen bit toes off. I ran and latched onto the leg bone, pulling it away. She bellowed and belched.

I leaped on a bale of straw and onto Cassandra's rabbit hutch. I threw the remains in the loft and pulled myself up. I scooped out a bale of straw and buried the bones and magnet together. My plan was to keep them in a safe place until I could figure out the best way to get rid of 'em. In my reborn status as a murderer, I knew they was prime evidence.

For the first time ever, when I came back from the barn into the farmhouse kitchen, Mama, seated at the table, looked like a witch. A worn-down witch with her sniveling goblin offspring in her lap.

Mama's gray-black hair frizzled around her face, her nose and chin dipping to her chest, the room full of steam from the boiling pot, still gurgling. Her smeary eyes looked up at me. "I know about Jubal Jen. We can't let other folks know, though, 'cause they'll want her kilt."

Folks in these Ozark hills believe that once a hog has eaten human flesh, they get a taste for it. Start canvassing front yards, looking for babies left untended to eat. And everyone knowed you can't eat a hog that's eaten human flesh 'cause then you become a cannibal once removed.

"What'll we do, Mama?" I said. "Folks'll see the missin' leg at the funeral."

Millie Faye giggled, her warning for going into one of her fits, her tough girl stance gone and conscience sinking in. Mama hugged my midget sister and stroked her straw hair.

"Not if we make him another one," she said. "Go out in the woodshed and find a piece of hardwood about the size of a leg. Whittle it to fit. We'll tape it on his calf, paste a shoe on it and dress him in his Sunday overalls. I'll supervise getting him in his coffin. Won't nobody never know, but us."

I should've knowed them words was like having a neon sign over your head, saying, "Guilty of murder in the first degree."

PART II

BOOK OF TARNATION

*There is no sadder sight
than a young pessimist.*

— Mark Twain

CHAPTER 20

Blood Secret and Snakeskin Boots

The day we almost buried Uncle Harm, I stood on Cemetery Hill and watched the two-headed preacher. He looked more lopsided and slanted than normal 'cause the monster swelling from the second serpent bite made his shoulder, under a large overcoat, as big and heavy as his head. In sympathy for the two-headed preacher's condition, the whole congregation leaned in the direction of the preacher's list, which just happened to be toward the snow-covered remains of the burned down Sulphur Lick Church.

The open grave and pile of brown soil was the only splash of color on ground covered by a half foot of snow. Uncle Harm's white pine casket hung from a rope and pulley tripod system over the dark hole, ready to drop into eternity when the two-headed preacher finished his eulogy.

The preacher's voice squeezed through the left side of his mouth, high pitched and whistling. "Harman Cornelius Claggett, while alive, was a fitting example of righteousnessss and ssssanity in a sssssea of ssssssinning," he said. His wide-open paralyzed eye, milkweed bloom flattened against red clay, singled me out to fix on. His other eye blinked every other second, doing double time to make up for the tainted one.

A flock of crows, cawing and gossiping, flew over and landed in the black walnut tree above Freeman Joe's head. They kicked snow on him from the branches. My swallow-dancing step daddy had gone into a howling trance after learning of his brother's death, so Mama and me tied him to the tree and covered his mouth with duct tape before the graveside services started. You could hear his muffled hound dog howls drifting across the dreary little cemetery.

Mama, dressed in black, hid her face behind a veiled hat.

Millie Faye, standing between Mama and me at graveside, spotted Sheriff Starkey, a state trooper and Aunt Big Bertha at the foot of the hill. "Look, Aunt Big Tits brung the police to put me in prison for stealing her hair, like she promised."

She lifted her hat and pried the scorched wig off her head. A whole bottle of Avon shampoo and days of scrubbing still couldn't hide its burnt smell. She stuffed it under her patchwork coat and scooted her little body behind me. Her straw hair, mashed by the wig, stuck out from under her hat like old brambleberry thorns.

Sheriff Starkey was after me for killing Uncle Harm, not Millie Faye for stealin' a stinky wig. And I did kill Uncle Harm sure as if I'd put a bullet in his head at the hog shoot.

I reached behind and found my sister's mittened hand. Her fingers seemed weaker since Doc took her cast off. We fused our fingers like we did when we had a secret to keep. A blood secret.

"You can have my .22 short rifle and my King Arthur comic books when I'm gone," I said out the side of my mouth to her. "I think I'm goin' on a long crusade."

"You're not goin' anywhere. I am," she said. "Probably to that girls reformatory Sherry Lee Detweiler went to for stealing Deacon Jones' old Nash and wrecking it."

Sheriff Starkey came up to us, boots crunching through the snow. He wheezed and his gun belt clattered like a horse harness. He held up a gloved hand. "I hate to interrupt these somber proceedings, but," wheeze, wheeze, "me and Trooper Dixon here, we want to take a look in that coffin before you lower it in the ground."

The state trooper wobbled through snow. The legs of his brown uniform slacks were stuffed into knee-high snakeskin cowboy boots made for kickin' and stompin', not grippin' and high-steppin'. The trooper, clinging to Aunt Big Bertha, came 'round the backside of the sheriff, then let go of her and stood on his own.

"Move that coffin over on firm ground. I'm going to pry it open," he said. "We've got a report of witchcraft amongst you Holiness Christians."

No one offered to swing Uncle Harm's coffin over.

Aunt Big Bertha wore another raven hat—black feathers made her wild eyes twirl like maple seeds blowing in October winds. She wagged a finger at the line of leaners. "There's who done it."

Could've been any one of a dozen people. All twelve tottered toward eternity burdened with guilt. They knew, being Holiness Christians, they was guilty of sins grievous enough to be sent to prison if only found out.

Deacon Jones straightened up. "We already nailed the coffin closed. You folks are disturbing a law-abiding consecrated burial." His voice was raspy from inhaling church smoke.

"Amen," tagged a few voices.

The trooper reached under his coat and pulled out a black wrecking bar.

A low moan floated over the cemetery.

Millie Faye pushed closer behind me. "Oh, Lordy, Mo Grady," she chirped like a baby robin. "What's he gonna do? Beat me into confession? There's no need for that, I'm ready to sing."

"No," I said. "I'm the one he wants." I squeezed her trembling hand tighter.

Aunt Big Bertha kept a rigid arm and finger pointed in our direction. "Satan is standing amongst you."

I couldn't hold the chill in my chest. It spread quicker than blood on Mama's oak chopping block. I almost toppled over in the grave. Moist brimstone perfume tugged at my nostrils. Get me on down to hell in a hurry. Throw some dirt on me, sing Amazing Grace and be done with it.

"Why's everyone leaning to the east?" Sheriff Starkey said. "There ain't no wind today."

Trooper Dixon's big brown hat had a brim sharp and shiny as Mama's meat cleaver. Dark mirrored glasses covered his eyes. He walked his three-inch heel, snakeskin boots over to the coffin, leaving indents in packed snow, and stuck the wrecking bar in a crack under the coffin lid. The coffin swayed, cradle-like, over the pit.

"If you don't want to see this, you'd better look the other way," he said.

Leaners stayed leaning.

The two-headed preacher adjusted his coat over his hidden head and tried to stand up straight. His milky eye and his blinky eye both pointed at Aunt Big Bertha.

A mummy moan came across the cemetery from Freeman Joe.

Mama lifted her black veil. "That lid's got to last Harman Cornelius a good long spell. It'll save wear and tear if you pry from the end."

"You the witch?" the trooper said.

"I'm the sister-in-law of the deceased," she said.

The lawman's teeth were little, stained brown and sharp. "I heard about you and your conjury. Don't even think about going anywhere."

Mama folded up her veil on top of her hat. She rolled her head around to take in the mourners, Freeman Joe and Farmer Johnson's red dairy barn beyond the cemetery's snow-covered parking lot. Came back to look down the row of mourners at her seven kids, stopping when she got to me and Millie Faye at the end. She winked. "I don't reckon I'd try anything with a smart fella like you. Looks like I'm stuck right here."

Her chin tucked down to her chest like our billy goat does before he rams you.

The lawman smacked the curved end of the wrecking bar with the heel of his hand, driving the tool under the coffin lid. Didn't work the coffin's end like Mama suggested.

He leaned his weight onto the bar. Hardened steel bit into soft pine. Nails screeched. Wood fiber bruised and broke. The coffin lid let out a long creak.

He adjusted the angle of the bar. Wrapped his stomach over it, making the curved end disappear in the folds of his coat, and pushed. The lid gave a series of pops, then jumped off the pine coffin, like a spring-loaded jack-in-the-box. The lid hung up on the lowering pulley, then fell into the grave.

The Hazeycamp sisters screamed.

Trooper Dixon, unbalanced, plunged toward the pit, caught himself and sat down on the slick, slanted pile of brown dirt on the grave's edge. His boots hung into the hole, rattles rattlin' like they're supposed to when danger was near.

But no one paid any attention. We were all too busy looking at Uncle Harm.

Uncle Harm snarled back at us.

No matter how much Mama pulled and shaped, she couldn't get Uncle Harm's upper lip to relax. His gum line showed, pocked and pitted from chewing red meat with no teeth. Made his pasty yellow face look like he was seein' something dreadful on the other side. Like maybe God was still a tad pissed at him.

A sweet smell of decay drifted over the mourners.

The ugliest Arnold brother turned his head and hurled.

While everyone else looked at Uncle Harm's face, me, Mama and Millie Faye looked at his substitute leg. I was right proud. With his Sunday-go-to-meeting overalls on, he looked like he was going to meet his maker a whole man.

The trooper, on his butt, slid closer toward the grave. "Somebody give me a hand," he said, plowing a furrow in the dirt, grasping with one hand, and waving the other at mourners five feet away.

His voice brung us away from Uncle Harm.

Widow Atkins clapped her gloved hands together. She hadn't cared for any uniformed, badge-totin' outlander ever since her husband's moonshine still had been shut down by revenuers in the thirties.

Aunt Big Bertha galloped around the grave, arm reaching out to catch Trooper Dixon's hand. Mama must've had the same idea, 'cause she stepped out of line, too, just as my step aunt passed in front of her. Their feet tangled, and they fell in a pile of snow, all veils and hats and feathers—and cussing. Aunt Big Bertha cussed words I never heard before.

If Sheriff Starkey hadn't stopped to listen to Aunt Big Bertha's blaspheming, he might've been in time, but the sliding trooper dropped out of sight. His meat-cleaver hat caught the edge of the grave and the upper part popped down over his eyes, dragging off those mirrored glasses. Both hat and glasses remained above ground.

The lawman's hands grabbed for the side lip of Uncle Harm's coffin.

Metal pulleys clanged, ropes hissed, tripods bucked and that white pine coffin vibrated from the strain.

Everybody held their breath, and then we exhaled all at once.

Maybe the force of all that air caused it: that white pine coffin flipped. Trooper Dixon flapped and Uncle Harm, taking his death sneer and yellow skin with him, dove headfirst into the hole after the lawman.

Two grunts and a rattle came from the grave. Then a long, stifled wail, like when you sit on your little sister with your hands over her mouth and she tries to call out "Mama!" Up come'd those hands, reaching for the hat and glasses and pulling them down in the hole. The hat raised level with the top of the hole like a mushroom sprouting.

"Couple you big fellas give me a hand up," said a tinny voice from the hole.

Aunt Big Bertha, who'd managed to get on her feet again, pointed at the grave and bellowed her favorite Christian word, "Abomination!"

Uncle Harm's upside-down body was propped up against the side of the hole, pant-legs shifted to show one hairy, yellow leg with a black, Sunday-go-to-meeting shoe on the foot and the other leg, a hand-carved hickory branch wearing a matching shoe, duct-taped and binder-twined to Uncle Harm's knee.

Mama, now upright, let out a long sigh.

It got so quiet, you could hear hearts beating and branches in the walnut tree creaking, a bass drum and ghost snares. Even Freeman Joe and the crows shut up.

Widow Atkins grabbed her birch cane from where she'd stuck it in the snow and poked the hickory leg. Clunked like a wooden mallet knocking at the door. "I didn't know Harman Cornelius had an artificial leg," she said. "And I knowed him all his life."

"You old fool," Aunt Big Bertha said, "'course he didn't have no wooden leg. It was put on after he died. That's why she killed him."

She pointed at Mama. "She needed his leg for her witches brew. Death by amputation, it was."

Mama and me hadn't told anyone 'cept Doc Abernathy about cuttin' off Uncle Harm's leg. I wondered about Millie Faye's running mouth. 'Course, in death, we didn't expect for him to be standing on his head in his grave without his coffin on.

CHAPTER 21

Stew Meat and Sleeping Monsters

"One of you bog boys give me a goddamn hand up," the voice of authority rose out of grave, "or I'll toss the whole lot of you in jail and throw away the key."

The two Arnold brothers linked hands and braced their bodies sideways in the snow and the biggest boy reached down and started pulling the trooper's hand. The trooper rose from the grave but immediately stumbled, his mirrored glasses a-tumblin' back into the grave. He cursed.

Aunt Big Bertha marched around to the other side of the grave and pointed at Uncle Harm's stick leg. "You're all fools if you can't see what the witch has done. She sawed off his leg to fix him to die. Probably boiled it up in a cauldron brew and fed it to them bastard kids."

The feathers on her raven hat stuck out in alarm. "Look at them little pagans, 'cept for the thieving dwarf, see how rosy a color their skin is? A sure sign of eating human flesh. Says so in the Good Book."

Rose Phoebe and Bonnie Sue peeked at me from under their black hats, knowing I was the source of most of the table stew meat.

"I ain't a'thieving dwarf," Millie Faye said, "I'm just a thieving puny person."

Widow Atkins turned to Mama. Her thin lips drew back, showing store-bought teeth. "If you didn't cook the leg in your witch's stew, where is it? A good fellow like Harman Cornelius ought to be buried with all his parts. Meet his maker a whole person."

Mama rose up and stepped between Millie Faye and Trooper Dixon. Her coat fluffed up like Mrs. Featherstone, our hatching-est hen when a chicken hawk shadow swept the barnyard. "Harman Cornelius had the frostbite so bad, testing out the Lord's love, I had to amputate. Doc Abernathy was there, none too sober of course."

Doc Abernathy, sleeping off a drunk, wasn't there to come to Mama's defense.

Aunt Big Bertha jockeyed for position. "How come he's dead then? The Lord loved my brother, you goomering bitch. Admit it, you killed him! If you and your bastard brats didn't eat of his flesh, then where's his leg?"

"I lost it," Mama said.

Millie Faye ran back behind me. Her breathing had a hitch in it.

Widow Atkins's skinny neck shook. Loose skin flapped under her chin. "How, Mildred Garnet, can you lose a leg?"

Trooper Dixon and Mama was havin' such a stare off, it's a wonder the snow falling between them didn't scorch.

Mama's eyes stayed steady on the lawman. "I sat the leg outside in Tuesday's blizzard, and it disappeared. We saw Ol' Slasher's tracks afterwards in the yard."

Mouths ooohed. Heads wagged. They'd heard the culprit beast came in yards and stole untended whole babies, why not untended body parts?

Widow Atkins, cane held twirling up at the gray sky, poked slow snowflakes, which didn't have a chance against her trained eye. "How come you sat it outside?"

"I had to get it out of the way," Mama said, "so's I could concentrate on cutting off the other leg."

All eyes except mine, Mama and Trooper Dixon's went to the good leg. Widow Atkins stork-walked over and poked the good leg with her cane. "It's still there," she said.

"He died before I got to the other one," Mama said. "I tried to save his life, but I was too late. The good doctor can testify it's true."

Aunt Big Bertha ripped one of her raven feathers out of her hat and waved it at Trooper Dixon. "My brother bled to death at the hands of this woman. She killed him for the farm and his red '55 Chevrolet. You can take my word for it, Freeman Joe won't be long for this world either. The witch'll find a way to do him in, too. And then she'll have the car and farm all to herself and her cannibal litter."

Trooper Dixon wiped the snow off his tin badge. "I reckon I'll take you down to the county jail for questioning," he said to Mama. "You swamp trash think just 'cause you're back here in the boonies you can get away with murder, you got another thing comin'."

I couldn't stand there and say nothing. It was all my fault Mama was getting blamed. "He didn't bleed to death from his leg," I said. "He hardly bled at all."

Trooper Dixon pulled handcuffs out of a side pocket. Dangled them in front of Mama. "Now, if you could persuade your dwarf or one of your other bastard brood to get my glasses, I'll put these back in my pocket."

Mama held out her wrists in front of her, palms up. "I ain't tellin' none of my kids to get down there with Harman Cornelius. I'm sure they had enough of him when he was alive."

I wondered, could Mama have knowed? Nah, Uncle Harm died before I could tell her about his perverted barnyard antics with me and Millie Faye. Then, of course, there weren't no reason to tell. Let sleeping monsters lie.

"See there?" Aunt Big Bertha said. "She hated him. And my poor dead brother being pure as the driven snow."

Steel snapping against steel almost burst my eardrums. Mama's face twitched once when he tightened the cuffs. Twitched again when he squeezed her hands. She pulled both hands away, reached up and unloosed her veil. "Mo Grady, you take care of the stock," she said. "Make sure you sleep out in the barn when that new ewe lambs. She looks like a breecher to me. And get to gettin' on that paper for Miss Haige. Time you got yourself and Millie Faye back in school. Rose Phoebe, you and Bonnie Sue take care of feeding your sisters and brother. There's plenty of potatoes and squash and canned tomatoes in the root cellar. Mo Grady will get meat for the stewpot. Millie Faye, you take your medicine every day and stay out from underfoot."

The black walnut tree shook, Freeman Joe wrestling with his binds. Branches clicked together, showering snow on him. Excited crows cawed and pooped.

"You all take care of your new daddy," she said. "He's the pick of the crop in these hills. The only one of the whole Claggett clan that's got any gentleness in his soul. I ain't plannin' on being gone long. Soon as we get in touch with Doc Abernathy and the real law in New Dreadford finds out what a nincompoop this state dick is, I'll be back."

Trooper Dixon's red eyes liked to burst into flames. Them boots shuffled and rattled. "I just added thirty days in the Stonecrop County jail for resisting arrest. It'll be at least that long till Judge Thurston gets here."

The black veil fluttered with Mama's breath. My lungs collapsed. I couldn't breathe. If there was a lowest step on the ladder down to hell I was on it.

"Mama didn't lose his leg," I said, "I did."

"Ain't that pretty," Widow Atkins said. "The boy is stickin' up for his Mama."

"She got them little bastards trained," Aunt Big Bertha said. "They'd lie like a dog just to save her murderin' hide, they would."

Sheriff Starkey's leather belt with all his police attachments kept sagging deeper around his hips. "Now you hold on with that name calling, Mildred Garnet Witt. And you hold on with that resisting arrest talk, Myron Lewis Dixon. And you hold on with that murdering talk, Bertha Sue Waywater, 'specially in front of God and everybody. Nobody here's guilty until a court of law says so." He worked a finger under his hat and scratched. "And as for these kids, I knowed every one of 'em since they's born. They's good kids. Not a bad bone or a liar 'mongst them."

Not a bad bone or liar 'mongst them. Those words rattled inside of me. I was already a murderer, probably full of bad bones. Least I could do is be a truth-teller. "Mama didn't kill Uncle Harm," I said. "I did."

"Them's mighty strong words, boy," Sheriff Starkey said. "Explain yourself."

Over his head, ripe, plum clouds massed around the peak of

Luella's Leap, fighting for the chance to be the first to drop another blizzard on us.

Millie Faye pressed her wig belly against my butt, hands around my waist. My feet got solid. Galoshes fit once more. "I killed him with my magic magnet I found in a '55 Buick V8 in Bonker Beckman's Wrecking Yard," I said. "I sucked the soul right out of Uncle Harm on the way back from the hog shoot."

Widow Atkins put the back of her wrist up to her forehead and let out a "Praise the Lord!"

"Amen," sounded the Hazeycamp sisters.

Confession was wonderful. Giddy words linin' up in my skull, pushing to get out. "I could feel his soul wiggling around inside my magnet trying to squirm free. But it couldn't. I got it good. So, take me instead of Mama," I said. "I'm the low-down murderer."

Trooper Dixon knocked one boot against the other. Made them rattles go off like dry gourds shaken by an angry toddler. "If this were a laughing matter, I'd bust a gut on that one. Stole his soul with a car magnet. Ha, ha. You'll have to come up with a better story than that to save your mother."

Mama put her cuffed hands together and let go a sigh.

Trooper Dixon directed red eyes at me. "I suppose you cut off his leg, too?"

"No, Mama cut off his leg with the meat saw," I said. "I held him down so's he wouldn't wiggle so much."

"That does it," the trooper said. "I'm taking this woman in for questioning in the death of Harman Cornelius Claggett. I'm also taking the body in for an autopsy by the coroner."

"But, don't you understand," I said, "I killed him. You can take the handcuffs off Mama and let her go now. Take me instead." I held out my wrists for the cuffs.

Widow Atkins took her good birch cane and pushed my arms down. "You done good lyin' for your Mama, boy. But it's over now. They takin' her away. But don't you worry, they won't 'lectrocute her till after she gets a trial fair and square."

CHAPTER 22

Grave Worms and Manacled Wrists

Trooper Dixon looked at the Arnold brothers. "A couple you boys jump down there and hoist up the body. Get my hat and glasses while you're at it."

The Arnold brothers didn't move.

"I'll get your hat and glasses if you take the cuffs off my mama," I said.

Trooper Dixon's boot rattled. "It's a deal, if you help hoist the body up, too."

The sweet death scent rose up from the pit. Uncle Harm's freshly peeled wooden leg smelled of hickory sap soaked in Old Crow and tobaccy spit. Didn't matter a'tall that Mama had cleaned his body with a homemade brick of bacon grease soap.

I balanced on the grave's edge. Uncle Harm's body from the waist down disappeared into the murky gloom. Hole looked twenty feet deep. Even a righteous fellow could break a leg jumping down into that pit. Might kill a sinner like me.

A big, gentle hand from behind rested on my bruised shoulder.

"No, Mo Grady," Freeman Joe said, "I will."

I turned and saw him smiling at me. The skin around his mouth looked all raw and puckered from the duct tape.

Mama lifted her veil, wrapped her steel-coiled wrists over my head and pulled me to her breast in a tight hug. Cut off my breath, but I didn't care. She squeezed me and moaned. "Oh, Lord, what have I done to my baby boy?"

I tilted my head back to free my mouth.

"You didn't do nothin', Mama," I said. "It was me and the magnet and Ol' Blue Satan."

Mama's eyes were wet and the pupils that crisp color of bread pudding crust first out of the oven, when there's still a few heat bubbles left. "Shussh, child. You didn't kill Harman Cornelius with that stupid magnet. He did his own self in. And, Lordy, what would a thirteen-year-old boy know of Satan?"

Above us crows pitched and swooped, cawing and scolding.

I looked around at the black walnut tree. Freeman Joe's rope lay loose around the trunk, and a red bird sat by itself on a branch.

Folks shouted and pointed at the grave, and Sheriff Starkey tried to keep people back.

I thought in the confusion about telling Mama how Uncle Harm had treated me and Millie Faye, then I figured what good would it do? No, Mama had enough worries on her mind without more upset from me about bruised collarbones and backwards butterflies and broken arms.

Uncle Harm's body rose up out of the grave, face up and floating on a mattress of air, Freeman Joe's hands between his dead brother's shoulders and butt. The mourners jumped back. Uncle Harm sank down for an instant, then came flying out of that grave to roll over and over in the snow. Came to rest at me and Mama's feet, face down, his Vitalis plastered hair still layered like tar to his head, but with clods of wiggly dirt and snow sticking to it. Grave worms.

The littlest Hazeycamp sister swooned against the ugliest Arnold brother. Several funeral goers took off for the parking lot, witchcraft and flying corpses an inspiration to their feet.

Widow Atkins prodded the body with her cane. "I reckon Harman Cornelius doesn't want to get in the cold, cold ground until he's sure the person put him there has got what's coming to her. Fess up, Mildred Garnet. Fess up so's we know you ain't never comin' back to Sulphur

Lick Valley with your witchcraft and your whorin' ways and so's we can divvy up this passel of bastard kids and get them raised proper."

Aunt Big Bertha raised her raven hat and ran her hand over her baldhead.

"I myself would take the two older girls. That new Chevrolet gonna need lots of washing and waxing."

Mama's shackled hands unhugged me and intercepted Widow Atkins' poking cane. Pulled it out of her hand, causing the old lady to stumble. Mama lifted that cane high like she was going to smack the church elder. Steel handcuffs rasped. Dry thunder rumbled over Luella's Leap.

Mama stabbed the heavens with the confiscated cane. "Listen up here, you parlor sinners," she said. "Anyone tries to separate my chillun or divvy 'em up will have me to reckon with when I get back. And I'm comin' back. Even if Doc Abernathy never wakes from his stupor to defend me. Even if I get the 'lectric chair, I'm comin' back."

Mama pointed the cane at its owner. "You understand what I'm saying, Wanda Lou? I'll make a pact in hell with your late husband Gormley Atkins. One of the meanest men I ever met alive. Being dead I suspect has only added to his meaness. We'll haunt you the rest of your born days."

Widow Atkins straightened up and backstepped a few feet, her wax fruit hat tipping away from her forehead. Her face taken on that gray, wrinkly look a crab apple gets from sitting in a dark corner of the root cellar too long.

Mama pointed the cane at Aunt Big Bertha. "Bertha Sue, far as I know Harman Cornelius left his interest in the farm to his brother, my husband, Freeman Joe. That includes the Chevrolet. You keep your paws off of it. And if you touch one hair on my Millie Faye's head, I'll sic a whole army of ringer washing machines after you."

Aunt Big Bertha clasped both hands to her head. She'd been snatched bald by the first electric wringer washer in Sulphur Lick Valley. Out of politeness, nobody ever mentioned it aloud on account she was liable to beat you to a bloody pulp if you did.

Aunt Big Bertha's mouth jerked. She let out a bellow that made the grave resonate.

A voice, deep and hollow, came from the grave. "Bertha Sue, quit your bullying and reach me a hand down here."

Aunt Big Bertha's face collapsed like snow falling off a tin roof and she fast stepped over to the grave's edge. Stuck out a big hand. A bigger hand rose to meet hers.

Sheriff Starkey reached down too and here climbed Freeman Joe up 'n out of the grave holding on to the trooper's hat and glasses. My step daddy brushed dirt and worms off his hair and powerful chest. If he was the slightest mad about Mama putting duct tape over his mouth, he didn't show it. He looked at Mama with that dreamy, goofy look in his eyes like he always did when he was havin' a short attack of sanity and she was near him.

Mama's handcuffs clicked. In the flick of time it takes a hawk's shadow to smear across the chicken coop, his dreamy look faded and his face turned into hard metal. "Who did this?" he said, pointing to the cuffs, eyes tumbling around at the mourners, searching for a target.

You'd a thought Trooper Dixon, with his starched uniform, polished badge, snakeskin boots and sparkling pistol would've stepped forward and owned up to the deed. But my step dad, sane, was a formidable enemy. If insanity struck, pure hell could break loose.

Millie Faye pointed at Trooper Dixon. "He did it. He's taking Mama down to New Dreadford to be 'lectricuted."

Trooper Dixon drew his gun, a long barrel Colt 45, and leveled it at Freeman Joe. The tip of the barrel shook. "Now you take it easy, big fellow," he said. "I'm just takin' your wife in for questioning and your brother's body in to be autopsied. Ain't no call to get your dander up."

Freeman Joe squeezed the trooper's hat and glasses. A mirrored lens popped out onto the snow.

In the blink of a frog's eye, Widow Atkins ran behind the walnut tree and everybody ran around looking for a tombstone to hide behind. Enough tombstones were hard to come by so's a whole passel of folks lined up centipede-style behind Widow Atkins.

Freeman Joe made a sound in his chest like swarmin' bees. I

knowed them bees darting around in his head wanted him to rush that pistol and die in the bargain.

I didn't see Mama move, but there she was standing between Freeman Joe and Trooper Dixon. She dropped the cane and wiped a clod of dirt off Freeman Joe's neck. Ran her hand behind that stout neck and stroked his old leathery skin. "I'm okay, Sugar," Mama said. "We just had ourselves a little disagreement here. This lawman's gonna take these handcuffs off me, and I'm gonna go to New Dreadford with him and Sheriff Starkey and answer some questions. I'll be back before you know it."

Freeman Joe's molten eyes looked down at her. He blinked three times. Thick eyebrows, like fuzzy caterpillars, touched together above his nose. Fingers spread wide apart on big callused hand that rose up and caressed Mama's crimson cheek.

The swarm of bees quit banking inside his skull. "Going away?"

"Yes, Sugar, for a little while," she said, never taking her eyes from her husband. "I need you to take care of things while I'm gone."

Mama took her hands from Freeman Joe's neck and stuck them in her coat pocket. She pulled out the keys to that bran'-spankin'-new, red '55 Chevrolet. Tucked them into Freeman Joe's overalls vest pocket.

"Now, you see the kids get home safe and sound," she said. "You understand?"

"I understand," he said.

I could tell Freeman Joe didn't understand.

"Good," Mama said. "Now I want you to pick up your brother's body and take him to Sheriff Starkey's patrol car. Can you do that, Sugar?"

Freeman Joe took her manacled wrists and pulled her over to face the lawman.

"Take these shackles off my wife now," Freeman Joe said.

Trooper Dixon holstered his gun. "I'm gonna take these cuffs off, Mrs. Claggett, but you got to give your word you'll come along peaceably." He stared at Freeman Joe.

Mama held out her hands, wrists already rubbed red under the cuffs. "You have my word," she said.

Freeman Joe never took his lead eyes off the trooper. The lawman's hands shook so bad it's a wonder he didn't jar the setting out of his Buchanan High class ring. He finally got the tiny handcuff key inserted and twisted, and the cuffs sprang open with a crisp metallic crunch.

People still remaining let out their breath.

Mama rubbed her wrists, swiveled and pulled Freeman Joe's head down. She whispered something in his ear that caused him to break out in a big coon dog grin. Then Mama went down the line and gave all her daughters a kiss and hug.

By the time she got to Millie Faye, my littlest sister was in her dead cockroach position, looking straight up with weepy eyes. "You're leaving just like our real daddy—the sonsabitch—and you ain't never comin' back," she said to the falling snowflakes, her little lips twisted.

Mama leaned over and pecked her on the forehead. "You take care of your brother and sisters."

Millie Faye's squirrely lips came unknotted. "Make Mo Grady mind me, Mama. He's an awful sinner and he's goin' straight to hell if I can't fix him."

Mama looked up at me. "Your brother's got most of his good sinning days ahead of him, child, but I'll tell him to mind you."

Mama plucked snowflakes out of Millie Faye's straw hair. "When I come back from New Dreadford, I'll bring you a new wig. I'll go in one of those places they call a Beauty Parlor—where ugly girls go in and pretty girls come out—and get you the best by-God hair-mat in the place."

Millie Faye wrapped her short arms halfway 'round Mama's waist. Sometimes, 'cause of my twin sister's big voice and pushy manner, you forgot how small she was. Only come'd up to Mama's waist. Seeing her molded into Mama, I understood, deep in my bones, that she was never going to be a fully grown-up person.

"And while you're gone Mo Grady has to mind me, right Mama?"

Mama stroked Millie Faye's hair. Mama had a way of touching Millie Faye different than how she touched the rest of us. She ran her fingers over my puny sister's coarse hair like it was the stem to a delicate Heritage Rose.

Then Mama looked up and her eyes caught me knowing what she had known about Millie Faye for a long time. "Right, honey," she said. "Now you let me go 'cause I need to tell Mo Grady something about the morning feeding."

When Mama got real close to me, her breath warmed my neck and I could smell her clean soap fragrance. I closed my eyes and drew in a big breath of Mama. Sucked it all the way down one side of my legs and toes and back up the other to my head so's Mama's fragrance could fill and keep me while she was gone.

"Now you listen carefully," she said. "Freeman Joe's liable to return to crazy any second. It's unsafe him driving. A tree might tell him to charge right through it, and he'd do it. Now soon as everybody's gone, you get the keys and you drive the girls home."

I felt like jumping in the grave.

"Mama, I can't drive," I said, my voice having trouble staying in a whisper. "I can't especially drive that red Chevrolet. I was sick to death riding in it on the way over here."

Mama rocked her elbows on my shoulders. "Shoosh, child. 'Course you can. You're my boy, ain't you? I taught you how to shepherd a team of mules, you been sitting on a tractor since you was five, and guidin' a haying truck through the fields for two years now. I'm depending on you to get my girls home safe and sound."

Mama drew back and smiled. Never was there a smile like Mama's. When she smiled at you, pearls broke off from the Pearly Gates and dropped in your overalls pocket right next to your heart.

I peeked over Mama's white-speckled shoulder. My sisters lined up holding hands tight, paper doll cut-outs. Each had a quarter-inch snow halo on her hat. Past them, Widow Atkins led the centipede line of mourners from the walnut tree and those, peeling off from behind tombstones, slogging to the parking lot. None looked back.

That red Chevrolet shone through a flurry of snow, sitting in the corner all by itself. Front bumper glared, silver teeth in a frothy mouth. Eagle hood ornament grinnin' at me like some great bloated toad.

It was no time for developing a fear of toads. Warts 'n all.

Hadn't I dreamt about driving that Chevrolet? Done it in my head a hundred times already? Didn't I know exactly how to let out the clutch when I wanted to go, shift the gears to get up speed and slam on the brakes when I wanted to stop?

Hadn't I committed an unpardonable sin so's I could drive the red Chevrolet? Reap the fruits of my labor?

Driving to hell in the red Chevrolet.

I was born to it.

CHAPTER 23

Grill Teeth and Trouble Times Five

"What are we gonna do, Millie Faye," I said, "if Mama don't ever get out of jail?"

"I already got us a plan to break her out," she said. "You and me are going on a great crusade. We'll become legends. Folks from New York will write stories about us."

Millie Faye pulled me toward the red Chevrolet. "Now come on, Mo Grady. There's a bona fide heater in Uncle Harm's car."

Her tugging wasn't much more than a baby chick pulling a sugar ant off a rotten log. Even so, it hurt my wrist down to the bone. A hot kind of hurt, igniting a steam kettle in my brain. My arms jerked up above her head, bewigged once again and smelling of bleach and burnt fiber. My fists, poised and shaking, wanting to pound her back into a dead cockroach.

"What the hell's wrong with you, Millie Faye? Mama's goin' away, maybe never comin' back, and all's you can think about is a crusade."

Millie Faye raised up her arms. "You got no call nor time to be angry at me, Mr. Man-of-the-House. Forget the crusade. You ain't never been no good at long-range planning anyway. But we ain't gonna do anybody any good standing out here freezing to death. We need to get home and get some hot rabbit stew in our bellies."

My brain cooled. I dropped my fists and pushed my head sideways back and forth. Neck bones grated and rolled.

Car doors opened and closed. The girls piled so tight into the back seat, you'd a thought they was Siamese quintuplets. They burrowed under a green army surplus blanket. Freeman Joe sat shotgun, looking straight ahead, lips moving, talking to invisible spirits. He'd helped the lawmen put his brother's body back in his coffin and hoist the pine box into the trunk of Trooper Dixon's patrol car.

The road looked much different than the way it did coming in. Like I was seeing it for the first time. A sharp curve and dip through a narrow stand of trees right out of the parking lot. Past the trees, the road swung into a black hole. Through that hole I had to plunge the red Chevrolet. And make it over Bones Pass.

"I get to shift the gears," Millie Faye said. "I know just how to do it."

She no more knew how to shift a gear than a scarecrow knew how to take a crap.

The red Chevrolet faced me. It crouched lower to the ground. A snow cat with a belly full of plump mice. Hungry grill teeth and that warped-eagle hood ornament, the size of a harpoon.

Millie Faye's tiny thumb and forefinger dangled car keys in front of my eyes. Somehow, she'd finagled them away from Freeman Joe.

"Gimme those damned keys," I said, "and get ready to shift gears."

I opened the door. The sickly smell of newness chased away Mama's clean soapy fragrance. The steering wheel and gearshift on the steering column looked bigger'n I remembered.

Millie Faye climbed in and wiggled under the steering column, reached up and petted the gearshift like it was a magic wand.

I sat beside her. My feet pumped the clutch and brake. The clutch squeaked and the brake clunked, same as on the old flatbed haying truck. I just needed to figure out how to get in granny gear and point that grinning grill toward the farm. Be home in time to feed the stock before dark.

I put the key in the ignition and twisted.

That red Chevrolet bleated and bucked like our billy goat. The back seat girls came undone, shrieking. Freeman Joe closed his eyes and smiled.

Millie Faye hung on to the gearshift with both hands. "Undo the key," she said. "Somethin' ain't right."

Well, I could see that. I reversed the key. Bucking stopped.

Freeman Joe commenced humming a spiritual song: *"When The Curtain Falls Up Yonder Will You Be On Stage."*

Untangling noises came from the back seat.

"Quit horsin' around," Rose Phoebe said, "and turn on the heat."

"It's the clutch, Millie Faye," I said. "You've got to have it in to start it up."

My left foot plunged the clutch to the floorboard. I rubbed the key between my thumb and forefinger. Said a silent prayer to the one God who'd do me any good, even though I knew I was an unforgiven sinner. Turned the key again.

The engine chug-a-chugged once, then fired up. A powerful language filled my ears. The engine spoke: "We have become one. You and me, Mo Grady. Revel in your moment in the sun. You were born for this."

Millie Faye slapped my fingers off the keys. "Don't just sit there with your mouth hangin' open, Mo Grady. Show me how to get this gear shift into back up."

"Turn on the heater," Rose Phoebe said from the rear seat.

I stretched my neck to look at the diagram someone, probably Uncle Harm, had taped on the steering buckle. L, S, H, N and R. No B for back up or G for granny gear.

"The heater!" Rose Phoebe said.

A lever stuck out under the word HEATER on the dashboard. I pushed it all the way on. A heavy noise erupted, and cold air rushed around the interior.

"The heat, not the cold!" Nora Lee said.

Millie Faye swung the lever to off. "It don't warm up till the car's going down the road. The sooner we figure this out, the sooner you warm up."

Lifting my butt off the seat and stretching my neck with my foot still holding down the clutch, I could barely see the fogged-up window over the dash. "Millie Faye, I'm gettin' a cramp in my leg. We gotta find a way to get this car out of gear so's we can study on it."

Millie Faye shoved the gearshift around. "There," she said, "try that. I put it in N."

"Why N?"

"I reckon it stands for 'Not anything else,'" she said.

Sounded reasonable to me. I eased up on the clutch. Nothing happened 'cept the motor switched to a lower growl. I sat down on the seat. Flexed my leg real quick and the cramping stopped. "I can't do it," I said. "I either got to work the pedals or see where I'm going. I can't do both."

I considered our predicament.

"Remember how we used to play train?" I said. I already had my knees pulled up, unsnapping my galoshes. "You were the locomotive, and I'd sit behind you, and we'd both pump our legs at the same time?"

I threw my rubber boots under Freeman Joe's legs. He hummed the chorus: *"I'll be playing trumpet in the Archangel's band."*

"You get to be the engine, Millie Faye," I said, "and I'll be the caboose."

My twin's mitten tightened on the gearshift. "What's an engine gotta do?" she said.

"What engines everywhere do—you make the car go and stop."

"I thought seeing and steering was the most important," she said.

"Any ox can steer. Now working the pedals takes coordination. You gotta be quick and smart. The pick of the litter."

Millie Faye peered down under the steering wheel. "I bet I can do it," she said. She sat down, unbuckled her boots, and kicked them under Freeman Joe's legs. She wiggled her toes through her red stockings, slid her butt off the seat, bounced once on the floorboard and then braced her hindpart against the seat.

The back of her neck fit between my legs, burnt wig level with my stomach. She stepped on the clutch, pushing it all the way to the floor with her left foot and stomped the gas pedal with her right. The engine liked to jumped out of the car.

Millie Faye backed off. She leaned her head back between my knees to look at me upside-down, wig punching me in the groin.

"Clickety-clack, clickety-clack, this locomotive is ready to clickety-clack down the track, Mo Grady," she said. "Put your legs over my shoulders, and I'll hold your feet. Whichever pedal you want to use, just push or let up with your feet, and I'll push or let up with my feet. If you want the middle pedal put your leg closer against my neck."

I peered over the dash and rubbed fog off the window with my handkerchief. I then switched on the wipers. The late farmer Johnson's barbed-wire fence post was a few feet in front of the bumper. It was snowin' and blowin' so hard, I couldn't see beyond that. I put one hand on the steering wheel and the other on the gearshift.

My feet test-pumped back and forth at the count of one-Missouri, two-Missouri. Pushed my left foot forward. Millie Faye shoved the clutch down. I pulled up my left foot. She released the clutch. Working like a well-oiled machine, me and Millie Faye could drive that red Chevrolet. Except for one problem. "Which of these letters—L, S, H or R—you reckon is for back up?" I said.

Millie Faye tilted her head backwards, punching me again in the groin. "I'm an engine," she said. "I don't know nothin' about gear shifting. But if I was to take a guess, I'd say the L stands for 'let's get the hell out of here' and the H stands for 'hightail it.' That means you got a choice between S and R."

"Watch your goddamn foul mouth," I said, "there's others in this vehicle ain't as backslid as you."

I glanced back and forth between S and R. Pulled the gearshift lever up toward R. Prayed to Sweet Jesus and Ol' Blue Satan at the same time. Except for the sound of rubber rubbing against metal, all went smooth.

"Okay, let's go," I said. I pulled my left leg up and pushed down my right foot. "Easy does it."

The engine got a little louder, and we inched backwards. My heart flew. I was actually driving! I turned the steering wheel to where I knew the rear end pointed toward the burned down church.

That red Chevrolet leaped backwards, wheels spinning, tires ripping through snow and grabbing gravel. We careened backwards blind as those fake feather eyes on the back of a pygmy owl's head. We hit potholes at the speed of light, and I tightened my grip on the steering wheel to keep from bouncing over the seat.

"The clutch! The brake!" I said. "Push the clutch and brake!" My knees squeezed Millie Faye's scrawny neck so hard, it's a wonder I didn't choke her to death. And such a shrieking came from the girls in the back seat, it's a wonder she could hear me. In between bounces, I pulled the gearshift into N, for 'not anything else.' The engine raced but the car stopped, and I stopped squeezing my twin's neck.

She took her foot off the gas pedal and coughed, holding her throat with both hands. "How do you expect me to think about workin' these foot-pedals right," she hacked, "with you crushing my windpipe?"

Freeman Joe's hand, steady as a dove lighting on a fence rail, switched on the heater. A fan came on. Warm air blew on my cheeks. Old dust, tobaccy smoke, and good grease smell filled the car.

Ten hands shoved over the seat to reach closer to the heated air. The fog cleared on the windshield, giving me a wider swath to see. We was pointed straight down the road. All me and Millie Faye had to do was put the car in L for 'Let's get the hell out of here,' and we could start home.

But my joy was short-lived. The weather was turning fast, from snow to storm to blizzard. Now I couldn't even see Farmer Johnson's fence posts.

Everything I did any more pointed me straight down the path to hell. Used to be disguised—a fellow had to stumble on it. Now, I spin 'round once and I'm standing smack dab in the middle, sulphur smell welling up through floorboards, spin around twice and my feet take twisty root.

Trouble times three will come back on thee.

Trouble times four will pour on more.

Yet there I was behind the wheel of the red Chevrolet. My dream come'd true. Just like Ol' Blue Satan showed me. But in Ol' Blue Satan's revelation, it wasn't snowing like bejesus. Mama wasn't in jail. His road was paved with gold bricks. His road had no slants, swamps or drop offs. And night wasn't coming on.

I found the headlights switch and turned it on.

Maybe that fit right into Ol' Blue Satan's scheme. To get one unforgiven soul, he'd kill us all.

Trouble times five will burn you alive.

Mille Faye looked up at me. "I had a dream last night I forgot about till just now, Mo Grady." Her buckteeth lit up like a pair of fireflies. "I saw you standin' up in front of Miss Haige's class, reading your 1000-word essay. All the class was giggling."

"My essay was that bad?" I said.

"No, it was funny … ha, ha."

I'd never thought about that. That might make it easier to write. Wait a minute. Maybe it would make it harder. Funny writing didn't seem to mirror anything going on in my life.

"Even Miss Haige was laughing," she said. "And so was sweet little Heidi, in the book on Miss Haige's lap."

"Your mind's not only retarded, it's twisted," I said. "And every second we tarry makes Bones Pass more difficult. Not sure we can even make it. And if we can't, I don't know what we're gonna do. So get your freckled fanny in gear."

"Hey," she said, "my fanny ain't freckled."

Rose Phoebe leaned an arm over the driver's seat. "Hurry up! I wanna go home."

Millie Faye pushed in the clutch and tapped the gas pedal. The engine purred.

"Okay, Millie Faye," I said, pulling the gearshift into L for 'let's get the hell out of here.' "Let's get the hell out of here."

CHAPTER 24

Tiny Thorns and Little Women

My feet and legs warmed up to where thousands of tiny thorns pricked my skin from my knees on down. The car chugged uphill alright, but I fought the wheel to keep us on the snowy road.

Millie Faye pinched my prickling big toe with her free hand. "It's gonna take us all night to get home at this rate. How 'bout I punch it up a little?" She pressed down on the gas pedal.

The engine revved, but we almost came to a complete stop. Millie Faye let up, the tires grabbed and we straightened and started off crawling uphill again.

"What in tarnation just happened?" she said.

The windshield wipers swished and blurred.

"I think we spun out. It's pretty slick out there."

Millie Faye hung onto my big toe like a lifeline. She leaned over backwards to look upside-down at me. Two bright sparks shone where her eyes should be. "What's going to happen when we get to Bones Pass? That's uphill for more'n a mile."

I checked the gas gauge. Almost empty. I remembered Mama saying before we left home we had just enough gas to get to the funeral and back. Didn't know how much we'd already used idling in the church parking lot. Even if we got over Bones Pass, we'd surely run out of gas before we got home. And one blanket between us.

We came to a fork in the road. To the left lay Bones Pass and five miles of bad road leading to our farm. Ruts from other cars led that way.

"We're sittin' on empty," I said. "We're going to Widow Johnson's. See if we can borrow some gas." I turned the steering wheel to the right.

Millie Fay's upside-down eyes twinkled at me. "You don't suppose your sweetie will be there?"

"Loveda ain't my sweetie."

"Then how'd you know who I was talking about?"

The engine revved, and the wheels moved. We headed into the night, steering toward Widow Johnson's, wheels crunching through the unbroken snow, a double-edged dull knife. The trees disappeared and fence posts lumbered by, then a rake and manure spreader, snow piled a foot high on the metal seats. The barn came next, and then the farmhouse with an Aladdin lamp glowing in the window.

I looked at the light so hard, I almost didn't see the car parked in the road.

"Stop!" I squeezed my knees.

She let up on the gas pedal. Going five miles per hour we rolled up to within a few feet of the car. Snow covered the back window and trunk.

I pushed the gearshift into N. Turned around and looked at the girls. All asleep. Faces flushed. Trusting me and Millie Faye to take care of 'em. Freeman Joe's head leaned against the window, mouth open, inner voices quiet.

I tied my blue scarf around my neck, opened the car door and stepped out into the snow in my bare feet. I welcomed the cold after it bein' so hot in the car. I ran to Widow Johnson's front door. Only a dozen paces or more, but by the time I got there, the cold wasn't so welcome. My fist forgot its manners and banged on the door.

The door swung open a crack. A black eye peeked through, looked at me, then took in the red Chevrolet sitting in the driveway, engine running and lights on. The eye glanced down at my feet. Then the door opened all the way.

Widow Johnson stood there, wool slippers and plain brown kitchen apron wrapped 'round a black robe. She looked dumpy as a butter churn, her hips wider than her shoulders. Behind her stood another woman, narrow hips, taller. Dressed similar but much younger.

Beside the other woman stood Loveda, her long strawberry hair flowing behind her. A closed book hung at her side with one finger stuck in it like you do to mark your spot. I angled my head to read the title of the book: *Little Women*. Slippers with pink flowers covered her feet.

I wished I'd put on my black galoshes. My feet were nekked and blue.

"Mother," Loveda said to the tall woman, pointing her book at my feet, "this swamp-urchin is in his bare feet in the dead of winter."

Mother? Urchin? I read books with words like that but nobody in the hills and bogs of Sulphur Lick Valley, Missouri, actually said them.

"My shoes are in the car," I said. I did a dance, trying to hide one exposed foot behind the other. "Didn't 'spect I'd need to put 'em on just to run up here and ask to borrow some gasoline to get home with."

Widow Johnson's silver hair sat on top of her head in a bun. "Why are you driving in this weather, child?" she said. "Where's your mother? Is she sick?"

Loveda kept looking at my feet with green eyes like spring leaves under clear water. My feet grew colder.

"No, ma'am." I said. "They taken her to jail."

"Good Lord," Widow Johnson shook her head. "Whatever for? Your mama's the kindest woman I know."

"For killin' Uncle Harm," I said.

"Oh my God, I heard he'd froze to death," Widow Johnson said. She put a pudgy finger to her chin, tilted her gray bun in thought. "Well, if she did it, they ought to give her a medal."

"Mama didn't kill him," I said. "I did. Sucked the soul out of him with my magic magnet. I didn't mean to kill him. Just wanted him to go away and leave us kids alone."

Loveda's green eyes widened. Probably didn't get to see too many low-down killers in a place where they read books and talked like she did.

A smile tempted Widow Johnson's lips. A chubby hand reached out and patted me on the head. "Dear boy, you can't suck something out of somebody they don't have in the first place."

"Mother," Loveda's mama said, "what a thing to say about someone. Everyone's got a soul."

"You never met Harman Cornelius Claggett or you might think different, Ella Mae. Guess it ain't for me to pass judgment on them that's passed. That's between Harman Cornelius and his maker now."

She pulled her black robe around her tighter. "We need to mind the living. Loveda, go upstairs in the hall closet and get as many blankets and pillows as you can carry. Bring them down to the parlor. We'll make space around the stove."

Loveda took off up the stairs with legs that came up to her shoulders. Red curls, waist length, swished.

My eyes followed her like a caterpillar watches a butterfly. On about the third step she stopped and turned her head. Twirled is more like it. She caught a strand of red hair in her pink mouth, holding it fast between white teeth whilst her green eyes looked into mine.

I shivered with something deeper than desire. My legs wobbled like the time I took a few sips of black cherry white lightning at a barn dance. I was drunk. Drunk with love, and me a murderer. A murderer in love with a long-legged, red-curled girl who talked like she lived in a fairytale.

Me, being the low-down swamp-urchin that I was, had to have her.

But why, I wondered as I was pulled into the house by Widow Johnson's chubby fingers, my head light as a sparrow's feather cradled in the wind, wouldn't anyone believe I killed Uncle Harm?

CHAPTER 25

Beautiful Feet and Homemade Biscuits

I woke to a grandfather clock striking 4:00 am.

Our stock expected to be fed on time, and I was a long ways from home, and the roads nigh to impassable. There'd be a lot of mooing and baaing and hee-hawing in the barn—animals tellin' each other what a miserable master Mo Grady Witt was.

But I could tend to Widow Johnson's stock. Probably not many feeding chores with no pigs to tend, and the least I could do for 'em with Farmer Johnson gone.

Freeman Joe lay under a patchwork quilt, his lips almost in a smile, tongue voices singing to him. The girls lay all around. Millie Faye'd crawled under my blanket during the night. Her body rolled up like a yew tree root ball, the smell of fungus and leaf pulp in her straw hair.

I rose from my pallet bed, careful not to wake her, and snatched my socks from off the drying rack behind the wood-burning parlor stove. Stiff but warm. Nothin' like warm socks to walk with into a cold morning.

A stair step squeaked. My toes twitched. Loveda. Loveda in a coat and ear muffs, strawberry curls stuffed under a hat. She got to the bottom of the stairs, sat on a stool and put on her boots. She motioned me over.

I sat on the floor beside her and started to pull on my socks. She stopped me. "Can I touch your foot?" She leaned over, chin on my shoulder, breath burning my earlobe. Before I could say 'yea' or 'nay,'

Loveda reached down and ran an index finger over the arch of my foot, down to my big toe, gave a quick tug, then traced back under my foot to my heel and up my ankle.

"You have beautiful feet," she whispered. Her other hand cupped my foot, gave a small squeeze. "I never saw a boy's naked feet before last night. They were so clean and blue in the snow. Matched your scarf."

Nothing prepared me for Loveda's touch. My foot stuck in a cocked stance, like when I kick open the silo gate. I reckon I could've stayed like that till crows come'd to choir practice.

Nothing prepared me for Loveda's words. My feet, before that, were just some old, odd things stuck onto the bottom of my legs that I walked on to get from one place to another. Who'd've thunk?

Suddenly inspiration struck: maybe I could do my whole 1000-word essay on the educational value of different kinds of feet, and why different kinds were stuck onto the legs of different animals?

In the meantime, I needed some words for wooing. "Oh, Loveda," I said, loving the way her name slipped past my lips, and paying her the cleverest compliment I could think of, "your skin is as creamy as Gweneviere's teats. She's my favoritest milk cow."

Loveda's hands released my foot fast as a metal spring recoils. She turned red as the winter red bird crying "pretty." She shushed me with one hand, her finger in front of ruby lips. "Let's slip out without Gramma hearing. She'll make us drink hot Ovaltine."

I fumbled on my socks and shoes, coat, cap and blue scarf, and followed Loveda outside. She eased the front door closed.

Blood and cordite from the hog shoot still hung in the still air. A rooster crowed. Hens clucked. A crisp layer of new snow covered everything. The red '55 Chevrolet glowed from the dawn light glancing off it. My breath bunched in front of my face.

I had to admit the white-capped car was a thing of beauty. But after what it put me through last night, it didn't have no right to any attention. I started to detour around it, heading for the barn.

Loveda crunched snow behind. "Where you going, Mo Grady? I want to sit in your car. I ain't ever had a boyfriend that drove up barefoot in a new car. It's so romantic." When she drew even with the front passenger door of the red Chevrolet, she stopped. "You may open the door for me if you've a mind to."

My brain got stuck. I hadn't ever been nobody's boyfriend before. And if I was Loveda's boyfriend, that meant she was my girlfriend. My anointed feet did an about-face and marched right over to the car.

I brushed snow off the door handle and pushed the button and pulled. Nothing happened. "It's froze shut," I said. For a second I was relieved. Deep down, I knew mixing cars and girls spelled trouble times double.

Loveda put her hand on my elbow. "Well, fix it." Her peppermint breath swept my face.

I squelched that leave-it-be voice. "Stand back," I squeaked. I lined up with the seam in the door, and punched it with the sole of my shoe. Jarred my hipbone. Metal popped and ice splattered. I tried the handle again and pulled hard, leaning my weight away. The door jumped open so fast, I had to squeeze the handle tighter to keep from getting pitched on my butt.

Loveda clapped her mittens.

She slid across the seat into the car. Like it was a practiced move. New car smell layered with Loveda's lilac-scented hair.

I waited, holding the door open, taking in the intoxicating vision of the red Chevrolet and Loveda together, like they were a package deal.

"Hurry and get in," she said, "and start the car. Warm it up in here."

I started to slam the door and go to the driver's side.

Loveda put her hand up. "That door's probably froze shut, too."

She grabbed my scarf and pulled. I sprawled on top of her, my head landed in her lap. Gamey aroma with a warm sweetness. I near to passed out. I bounced right up and fumbled for a handhold. My desperate fingers scaled valleys and hills, canyons and mountains before Loveda took a'hold of my shoulder and butt and pushed me into the driver's seat.

My butt burned where her hand touched. My hand burned from touching her.

I'd no sooner slipped under the steering wheel when Loveda slid over next to me, hip firm against mine. She reached up and petted the gearshift. "Start it up."

My hand shook as I turned the key. The red Chevrolet growled low and gave a half-hearted glug. "Come on, baby, come on. Don't fail me now. Please start." The engine glugged again. I didn't like the way it sounded. I let up on the starter.

"You can do it," Loveda blew in my ear. "I bet you know some tricks."

Ol' Blue Satan whispered in my other ear. "She's right. You know some tricks, and I'll teach you more. Slide your skinny butt off this seat and pump the gas pedal. Push it all the way to the floor and try again."

I followed his directions like a robot. The engine glugged twice and started. My chest swelled. So puffed up with pride was I, you could've popped me with a pin.

"You're racing the motor," Loveda said.

I let up and sat back on the seat. My feet hovered a couple inches above the pedals. Loveda snuggled up to me, and all thoughts of the perilous drive home shot out of my head.

Her hand reached up and turned on the radio. Lots of static. She turned another dial until an announcer said, "This is radio station H-E-double-X in Del Rio, Texas." A husky voice sang about a blue moon. Sounded like a fat Negro man with trouble breathing.

"Oh, I just love Elvis Presley," Loveda sighed. "Every time I hear him sing, I get all warm inside." She turned on the heater, clutched my right arm and laid her head on my shoulder. Put her right hand on my lower thigh and gave a gentle squeeze.

At that moment, I had no thoughts of murder or Mama. No thoughts of Jubal Jen or the other hungry livestock lookin' through slats for me bringing their morning meal. The universe was small and tight and all mine. The spell began by Ol' Blue Satan's kiss was working its black magic. And, at that moment, curse my hide, I was loving it.

Cool air from the heater quickly turned warm, but I didn't need it. My body was its own hot house. I had all the potent ingredients to conjure a lifelong romantic obsession with automobiles: a girl, music and the red Chevrolet.

The devil had got me good.

And gooder.

Loveda's lips blew in my ear again. "You may kiss me if you want."

"Dear Lucifer, lead and guide me, don't let me be shipwrecked on God's celestial shore." My body shook, remembering Ol' Blue Satan's forked tongue on my eyelid, sliding down my cheek. How soft and satiny.

I wondered, should I use my tongue?

"Oh yes," he whispered. "When in doubt, always use your tongue. I will lead and guide you to my own celestial shore."

I turned and pushed Loveda back so's our noses were inches apart. Her pink lips puckered. I parted my lips and my viper tongue uncoiled. I flicked out the end of it and licked Loveda's eyebrow, traced a crescent moon. Then down to her moist eyelid. My tongue swelled with a sweet, salty taste. I wiggled it on her eyelid like Ol' Blue Satan done on mine. Her eyelashes felt soft and pliant.

Her hand gripped my leg. She stiffened. I thought she was going to pull away. My new-found forked tongue pulled back, but when I did, she leaned her eyelid into it. I traced down her cheek. That was as far as Ol' Blue Satan had gone.

But my tongue had a mind of its own. It found her tight-lipped mouth and wedged an opening. Slipped ever so softly in and tickled her teeth till they parted. My tongue then pumped back and forth. Her mouth, behind her guardian teeth, let out waves of heat, riding on short breaths.

"There's no turning back, now," Ol' Blue Satan said.

My tongue stretched down her throat. Loveda gagged. I pulled back. She let out a moan and grabbed my tongue in her teeth and inhaled so hard, she sucked up my toes inside my kachubies. My tongue, caught in a trap of steel jaws, had misgivings, but my toes were more than grateful to make the journey from floorboard to crotch.

Our mouths locked tighter'n a worm in a robin's beak. Loveda's arms encircled me, and her neck-high legs nigh to climbed on top of me. And such moaning and crying, scared the holy hell out of me. I swear I tried to wiggle out from under her, get away from that hot box mouth, vacate that red Chevrolet and hightail it for the barn.

Barn animals, I could handle. Girls—a mystery beyond understanding.

And then there it was, my pecker, rubbed inside my overalls, pointin' toward the Pearly Gates, poking Loveda between the stomach and kneecap. It burst into song:

"Stay right where you are, my beaming boy,
Lay back and relax, don't be so coy."

Relaxation advice from a stiff pecker is like getting crochet lessons from Ol' Slasher: ain't gonna happen.

No matter, Loveda had me wedged between the seat and the steering wheel. She let go of my tongue and now her tongue was probing so deep, it pinned my head against the driver's door. Her body, and mine, was going back and forth in a rutting motion.

I was all set to go off straight to perdition or kingdom come when I heard a sharp rap on the side window

"Open the door, Mo Grady," Millie Faye's filtered voice sounded. "The car's a'shakin'. What y'all doing in there that you're steamin' up the windows so?"

Loveda tongue retreated faster'n a mouse spotting a tomcat. Our lips came unstuck. My pecker teetering on the abyss. In the scramble, Loveda's elbow hit the horn.

Millie Faye pounded the window. "You can't scare me with that old horn, Mo Grady. If you don't hurry and open this door, I'm gonna tell Mama you're doing the big naughty in there."

Mama? I had a Mama. A Mama, good and true. Who trusted and loved me. A mama who was put in jail for a murder I committed, and here I was making out in the red Chevrolet, with nary a thought to her predicament. I'd sunk lower than dingleberries on a tumblebug's ass. My elbow draped over the steering wheel, and my rushing body slowed down.

My pecker, a collapsed tire.

Loveda rustled her clothes, sat back in the passenger seat and opened the car door. Before hopping out, she turned to me, her face red as ripe raspberries, giggled and said, "Who'd a thought I would've come to these backwoods hills and caught me a new boyfriend who knows how to tongue kiss?"

She lit out for the barn and skipped a few paces. My heart cartwheeled after.

Millie Faye, arms pumping, came around the front of the car. She stuck her tiny head inside. "I heard that, Mo Grady. I'm gonna tell Mama."

"Instead of ragging me about my business," I said, "why don't you take that smart noggin' of yours and study on gettin' Mama out of jail?"

"I already done that. And I'll tell you how, if you tell me what it's like to swap spit. I got my sights set on the youngest Langnecker boy for s'perimenting."

The thought of Millie Faye kissing made me wonder if her passions were growing even though her body wasn't.

Loveda beckoned from the shadows inside the barn. Me and Loveda, in spite of Millie Faye's pestering, fed Widow Johnson's remaining stock.

The widow and her daughter gave Freeman Joe lots of sideways glances over a breakfast of homemade biscuits and fresh-churned butter, berry preserves, thick slabs of smokehouse-cured ham dripping with pork fat, home fries and pan gravy. He took a serving of every item and separated it on his plate, then mixed it in a big ol' pile and loaded his mouth to capacity, cheeks bulging.

Widow Johnson's daughter drew her mama aside in a frenzy of whispers, and then the widow waddled toward us. "I suggest y'all stay here until your mama gets out of jail." She crossed her ample arms over her apron. "I can use some help getting this place ready for selling before I move to Springfield."

Rose Phoebe, Bonnie Sue and the older girls nodded. I was so numbed with joy I near to choked on a home fry. Days and nights with Loveda. Kissing in the hayloft. Meeting after everyone else was in bed. Playing footsies under the table. My tongue grew plump with juicy possibilities.

"No thanks, ma'am," Millie Faye said. "The older girls can stay with you, but Mo Grady's got hungry stock to feed at home, and we need to take Freeman Joe there, where we can jolt him with our grain-grinder generator if he gets stuck in tongues."

I spit home fries across the room. That mouth. Trouble was, she was right.

On the way out the door, Loveda handed me a pair of ice skates. Her fingers raked my palm in the exchange. "These will help your beautiful feet reach the pedals." I sat on the driver's seat whilst she put them on for me. She did some extra stroking of my toes. My ears tingled.

The skates worked. I could reach the pedals and peek over the dash.

Loveda's mama showed Millie Faye and me how to shift gears so's my twin went from engineer to gear shifter without any complaints. You couldn't have pried her out of that car seat with a wrecking bar. Freeman Joe curled up in the back seat and went to sleep and snored like a freight train.

The road had a new coat of snow and no tracks a'tall. Going over Bones Pass I rolled down the window and nearly touched some low clouds.

"I can feel your whole body buzzing," Millie Faye said. "If that's what kissing does I'm not sure I want any part of it."

I heard her, but my head wasn't listening. I drove home in first and second in a state of euphoria. Euphoria didn't last long.

Aunt Big Bertha and the two-headed preacher were waiting for us on the front porch of the farmhouse.

CHAPTER 26

Hog Fat and Possum Lard

"Uh, oh," Millie Faye said, "I don't like the look on Aunt Big Tit's face. Maybe we should just keep driving."

Aunt Big Bertha had a switch in her hands. The two-headed preacher stood further out of range, listing to the east.

"I got stock to feed," I said. "And if Jubal Jen ain't let out of her pen soon she's liable to go right through the barn wall."

I pulled up next to our '38 Ford and the Waywater's Studebaker and cut the engine.

Aunt Big Bertha thundered down the steps, switch snapping, mouth yapping.

"Stay in the car and lock the doors, Millie Faye. I'll settle her down." I opened the door and climbed out to face my destiny.

"I don't know where you were last night, you little bastard," Aunt Big Bertha said, "but from now on, you to stay the hell away from that car. Look at you. Have to wear skates to drive it. A wonder you didn't wreck it."

"It ain't your car," I said. "Mama told me to drive it."

"Your Mama don't have no say in it anymore. She's gonna rot in jail or fry in the electric chair. I'm takin' over this car and this farm." She swished the switch at me.

I smelled willow. Willows make the best switches. Makes welts without tearing the skin.

"It's Freeman Joe and Mama's farm," Millie Faye said, sliding out of the car to stand beside me. She slipped a hand into mine. "You got no say in it."

"Not if I can help it," Aunt Big Bertha pointed the switch at me and vibrated the tip in front of my nose. Hummed like a hornet. "Now you come over here and lean over this stoop. We'll start our understanding of who's running this show outright."

"You switch me and who's gonna milk the cows and grind the grain?" I said. "You?"

"Now, Bertha Sue, the boy's right," the two-headed preacher's one mouth said. "The car's back safe and sound, and there's stock to care for. This ain't no time for a switchin'."

Aunt Big Bertha lowered the switch. I figured I had at least a two-hour period of grace.

Until Millie Faye opened her foul mouth. "Yeah, Aunt Big Butt," she said, "I'd like to see your fat ass fit on the milking stool."

The switch came back to pointing position. "I'll start with your goblin sister."

The car creaked.

Freeman Joe's big hand pushed me out of the way. He grabbed the switch from Aunt Big Bertha and jerked. It looked like he was gonna swat his big sister upside the gourd, but he twisted his wrist and commenced scratching his back.

Took off walking toward the barnyard like that, walking and scratching.

I followed, Millie Faye in tow.

Aunt Big Bertha stood stock still, her mouth agape.

A truce, of sorts, had been declared.

Freeman Joe was so melancholy with Mama being gone to jail, he took to feedin' birds full time. He stood out in the barnyard all day long—rain, snow or shine—with kernels of dried corn. He'd hold a yellow nugget in his meaty palm, at arm's length. Stand like that for hours until a bird, usually a pigeon, took the kernel. Black and white bird poop streaked his hair and face, a kind of war-paint shadowing eyes glaring over a mouth muttering incantations.

Me and Millie Faye made sure Freeman Joe had on his long johns and three pairs of wool socks. Kept his body and feet warm and dry.

We both agreed one foot amputation was enough.

Freeman Joe wasn't really no trouble. I just added him to the list of chores I had to do every morning and night, like milking the cows and slopping the pigs. We'd drag him in at night, haul him in the barn, scrub his head and face with Mama's best lye soap. We'd strip off his overalls and shirt and soak 'em in a tub of water on the barn stove for a couple hours, then scrub away the bird shit stains.

At least he didn't ask a thousand questions like some did. Questions I didn't know the answers to, like:

"Mama's been gone two weeks, when's she comin' home?"

"Are they gonna 'lectricute Mama?"

"Why aren't you in jail instead of Mama?"

"What's 'contesting Uncle Harm's will' mean?"

Mama wrote us every day.

Me and Millie Faye waited down at the mailbox for Stubby Cox to come rollin' up in his official government vehicle, a '52 Ford station wagon. Sometimes we'd fight over who got to read Mama's letter first, but most times I let my sister 'cause when I didn't, she'd cry.

Mama's letters always lifted our spirits.

One day her letter read:

> Dearly beloved children, (whichever one of us was doing the reading, we'd pause, look at the other one and smile)
>
> This Stonecrop County jail ain't so bad if you look past the negative energy. They got electricity by the flick of a wall switch and heat comes out of this metal box against the wall. It smells like frying dust clots in hog fat. I don't think this electric heat will ever catch on. Maybe they put it in the jail to remind us hardened criminals (ha ha) what's in store for us if we don't straighten up and fly right. Meaning the electric chair.
>
> Speaking of chair, there ain't a bit of privacy for bodily functions in this place. May be alright for menfolk to

do their business out in the open, but it sure gets teedjous
for me. Sheriff Starkey will turn his head when I have
to use the toilet, but I think his deputy, Pee-eye Penrod,
tries to peek at me.

I got me a defense lawyer will argue my case, but
if something bad does happen to me just remember
Freeman Joe and you kids have the farm. That's if your
step aunt doesn't steal it by some legal finagling.

Millie Faye's lips twitched. She folded the letter across her chest.
"That does it, Mo Grady," she said. "The time has come for us to go on
our great crusade and break Mama out. I can't stand the thought of her
suffering another day. We need her help to keep the farm away from
Aunt Big Tits and the two-headed preacher."

"Just how," I said, "do you figure we get Mama out of the Stonecrop
County jail?"

"I told you before, I already got me a plan that can't possibly fail.
All's you gotta do is get the red Chevrolet, Mo Grady."

CHAPTER 27

Shit Storm and Sanity Potion

Me and Millie Faye met by the cars at 2:00 am. Stars shone like ice-crystals in the clear night sky, moon a sliver of silver. Plenty of light to work by.

Something stirred in the barnyard—a scratching sound from the smokehouse. The scent of wood smoke hung heavy, mixed with Blue Bog fog over the farm.

Millie Faye shook with excitement. "Mo Grady, we'll need a box of tools, a chain and a rope."

I didn't ask what for. I put 'em in the trunk.

We pushed the red Chevrolet to the end of the driveway before hopping in. I put on my skate-feet—I'd duct taped blocks of wood on either side of the skate's metal runners. Kept me from slippin' off the gas pedal, plus I could walk on the ground. Added four more inches to my height.

That sweet honey of an engine started right up. A surge of power traveled from the bottom of my right foot, flooding all the way up to the hair follicles on my head. I crept the car onto the road, Millie Faye clinging to my right leg like butter to bread.

Snow hadn't fallen in a few days and the road was packed powder. We pointed toward New Dreadford—thirty-five miles of slick road.

Bullet holes pockmarked the tin city limits sign—some going clean through and blocking out letters:

NEW D*EADFORD

POP*LAT*ON 1101

"Would you look at all the fancy lights!" Millie Faye's doll eyes glittered.

Main Street had a Baptist and a Catholic church with pretty, lit up glass windows. No Holy Roller church though. I saw a cobbler's shop, a five and dime, and on the other side of the street sat Clifford's Tavern, The Blue Moon Tavern and Anse's Liquor Store. A large sign over the movie theatre glowed with red letters:

THE NIGHT OF THE HUNTER

ROBERT MITCHUM   SHELLY WINTERS

All the neon signs proclaimed themselves even though weren't nobody to proclaim to at six o'clock in the morning.

The town glowed as a den of negative neon. Polarity out of whack. My skin prickled. It's a wonder Mama could even breathe.

I didn't see any Jezebels, Sodomites or Gomorrahans gallivantin' with goats in the streets. Disappointed me a little, it did.

We had two hours of darkness left when we found the jail. Millie Faye had told me her plan on the way.

We found the rear of the jail and backed up under a bare mulberry tree.

Millie Faye hopped out and looked around. A few minutes later my wee sister stuck her head in the car. "Looks good, Mo Grady. Turn 'er off and help me with the chain."

I snaked the chain up over my shoulder. Hooked one end around the car's rear bumper then hoisted Millie Fay, no heavier'n a bale of dry straw, onto my shoulders. She grabbed the top of a cell's window ledge and pulled herself up to standing.

She put her ear between the window bars. "This is it," white puffs of airs flew from her mouth. "I can hear Mama's snoring."

I handed my sister the chain's other end. She lifted it, grunting like a runty piglet, and hooked it around the bars. Made a loud metallic clink.

A rooster crowed and a dog barked. Wings rustled in the mulberry tree over the car. We'd parked under a flock of roosting birds. I heard the splats before I saw the bird poop on the car's hood. More'n one. A pre-dawn drizzle ahead of a major shit storm.

Millie Faye hopped down. Little feet crunched in the snow. Breath came in short bursts. "Okay, Mo Grady, get in the car and tromp on it. Let's break Mama out."

"You better get in the car and lay down," I said. "Your missin' heart needs a rest. Besides which, I don't think this is such a good idea. Let's wake Mama up and ask her."

"Ain't you never heard of surprise? I'll rest when Mama's free," she said. "I read about this stunt in my cowboy book. I gotta be ready to unhook the chain so's we can make a fast getaway." She sat down and leaned against the trunk of the mulberry tree. Bird shadows fidgeted and shat. Droppings fell next to her.

I climbed in the car. I knew how to pull things. I'd pulled combines out of fields, jerked stumps out of fence lines and even dragged a cow out of Bonker Beckman's Blue Bog. A cow dripping blue mud and lowing melancholy.

"Well, well, ol' Son," Ol' Blue Satan said, "I can see you're having second thoughts. Now listen to me. Have I ever lied to you? You killed your Uncle Harm, and now see what you're driving. It is written that you should be a mighty Joshua and tear down that Jericho wall. Get this done, and you'll be driving down the golden road forever. Boys will be jealous, girls will want you. Loveda will love you. And maybe next time, she'll give you more than a kiss. Just pull slow and steady as she goes. Your Mama will be saved, and so happy you broke her out of jail."

The car boiled hot inside, and I stank of sweat and fear. Could also smell Loveda's animal aroma in the car.

But the new car smell was gone. Gone. New paint job scraped, new flawless chassis dinged. All gone. Layer upon layer of newness peeled off. Intoxication evaporation.

I heard the morning train heading for the station not a block away making a mighty racket.

"Let 'er rip," Millie Faye said, "whilst the train's a'passin' through."

I popped the clutch. The wheels caught and, I swear, I traveled two hundred miles an hour. For all of six feet. The chain pulled up like a junkyard dog running out his rope, and when I reached the end, everything stopped, suspended in space for a split second, then metal ripped, and I slammed on the brakes to keep from cannon-balling out into Main Street. I was afraid to look back.

I opened the door and hurried around the car. Millie Faye stood over the bumper of the red Chevrolet laying on the ground. It looked sad. As homeless as Uncle Harm's amputated leg.

Ol' Blue Satan be damned!

Mama's face came up behind the window bars. Train light reflected red in her eyes. "What's goin' on out there?" Her hands now clutched the bars. "And who's the damn fool hooked a chain to this bar?" Her voice barked, "Mo Grady … Millie Faye, come out here right now!"

Mama could go from a deep sleep to bein' real mad faster than a wild bull out of the chute.

Millie Faye jumped up and ran to jailhouse wall, hollering, "Mama! Mama! We come to carry you out of jail."

"Millie Faye Witt," Mama said, "shut your trap before you wake up Deputy Penrod."

My sister's mouth clamped. The train blew steam in the depot. Another light came on down the street. A faint glow started in the east.

"Moses Grady Witt, I know you're there, too."

"Yes, Mama."

"Pull your sister away from this wall whilst I unhook this chain."

I grabbed Millie Faye and backed away. The chain hit the ground near our feet in a fast collapsing metallic echo on the hardened snow.

"Put that bumper in the car and get rid of that chain. Park the car a couple blocks away, and then you kids come back here and come in the front door to pay me a proper visit. Go on, now. We ain't got much time."

A man's sleepy voice followed by a cough sounded inside the jail.

"Oh, nothing, deputy," Mama answered, "just greeting the morning. I feel like a little sunshine's gonna come into my life today. I been meaning to stir something up for that cough of yours, now if …" Her voice trailed off.

"I want my Mama," Millie Faye cried. I couldn't see her gorilla tears, but I felt them bleeding down her cheeks.

Streetlights brightened the alley.

"Get in the car," I said. "I'll get the chain and bumper."

Damn bumper—a chunk of pond ice and weighed a ton. I couldn't lift it into the back seat, so I dragged it over behind the mulberry tree and scooped snow over it, burying it the best I could.

We parked behind the pockmarked city limits sign. I wiped Millie Faye's face and made her blow her nose.

"Are you hungry?" I said. I'd stuffed my back pocket before we left Scuttles Grunt with some rolled-up slices from Mama's last loaf of sour dough bread. I pulled out a slice, tore off a piece and offered it to Millie Faye.

Millie Faye held the bread with mittened hands, mouse-nibbling between sniffles. We talked about how Mama's bread was the staff of life. Our breath hung stiff in the cold air, fogging up the car windows and blurring shapes outside.

A half hour passed and at sunrise, we entered the jail through the front door.

Mama sat at the front desk, reading a newspaper named *The Saint Louis Post Dispatch*, pretty as you please. Her cheeks had lost the sunken look she had on the farm. And she'd gained some weight.

Deputy Penrod lay on one of them hanging bunk bed cots in the lock up, his mouth open in sleep. Here we'd come'd to break Mama out of jail, and she could've walked out the front door anytime she wanted.

"Mama!" Millie Faye ran and buried her face in Mama's lap. I threw my arms around her neck and squeezed, burying my face in her hair smelling of a strange shampoo.

Mama stroked Millie Faye's straw hair. Patted my cheek. The hairs on the back of my neck flattened, like warm water had been poured over them.

"Okay, chillun," Mama cheeks flushed, "enough of this. We got finaglin' to do."

She pushed us away and got a white handkerchief from her pocket, wiped her eyes and blew her nose. She took my elbow and pulled me down to kneeling beside Millie Faye.

Millie Faye's lips trembled. Her mouth couldn't stay closed for long. "Mama, we need you at home. Aunt Big Butt and the two-headed preacher have taken over the farm." My sister glanced over at Deputy Penrod snoring and then at Mama taking her leisure in the sheriff's chair. "Why ain't you behind bars?"

"Don't be calling folks names," Mama said. "You wasn't raised that way. And, I ain't behind bars 'cause there ain't no decent toilet in there, and they got tired of unlocking and locking the doors—me with my nervous bladder."

"But Mama, we miss you and …"

"Shoosh, child," she put her hand over Millie Faye's mouth. "We got things to discuss. Sheriff Starkey told me your step aunt filed a court motion to have Freeman Joe put in the insane asylum for good. If she does that, he'll be declared unfit to inherit the farm and it'll automatically go to her. So will the new Chevrolet."

"Ain't so new anymore," I said.

"No matter," Mama said. "They're gonna bring Freeman Joe before a judge tomorrow afternoon, and then they'll whisk him off to the nut house, and he and you kids'll be out of your rightful inheritance. What we have to do is make your new daddy presentable for the judge. Make him look sane."

"How we gonna do that?" Millie Faye said. "He's crazy'rn a stray cat with an ear tick."

"Not all the time," I said. "After we shock him, he turns kinda sane for a while."

"Kinda sane ain't what we're after," Mama said. "He has to be all the way sane, or we're lost."

Millie Faye's lips scissored, a snail chewing swamp grass.

Deputy Penrod's cot chains rattled, his snoring so loud it's a wonder the concrete walls didn't crumble.

"Maybe we can stay with Widow Johnson," I said, "till she sells her place?"

Millie Faye gave me a rotten look.

"No," Mama said, "I've got a way to make Freeman Joe uncrazy for a while."

"Well, Mama," Millie Faye said, "If you could do that, why'n you do it all the time? Then me and Mo Grady wouldn't be having to take care of him."

"I don't mind seein' after Freeman Joe," I said. "But I don't understand, Mama, why you ain't did it before this."

Mama adjusted my sister's weight in her lap. "I've had my fill of so-called normal men 'round these parts. And it's mighty slim pickin's, let me tell you. Most of the time I like Freeman Joe crazy. He's sweet. Brings me feathers in bed." Mama paused. Her eyes misted. "So maybe he talks in tongues. Men and women in these hills speak a different tongue anyways."

Mama stretched her neck. "The second reason is the real hang up. It ain't exactly easy getting' the ingredients for a long-term sanity potion."

"It don't matter none," Millie Faye said. "Mo Grady's strong and I'm smart. Whatever they is, we'll get it."

"There's only one concoction I ain't got in stock, that might be a titch difficult," Mama said. She spread the list on Sheriff Starkey's desk. It read:

SANITY POTION
1. Pinch dried Destroying Angel Mushrooms
2. 1/2 goblet Stinging Nettle tea
3. Pinch of Sow Thistle weed
4. Root of Devil's Walking Stick
5. Hysopp
6. Catnip
7. Bloodroot
8. Bugbane
9. Blue Cohosh
10. Bowl of Paw Paw bark
11. Two Devil's Snuffbox Mushrooms (In the root cellar under the dried Horsetail)
12. Beggar's Lice

13. Two tablespoons of powdered wild boar's tusk (no more than 24 hours old)

Millie Faye keyed in on the difficulty straightaway. "What's this about wild boar tusk?" she said.

Mama's hand edged up and her trigger finger scratched a brown mole the size of a deer tic on her temple. A drop of blood oozed out.

"You heard right. And in this case, it has to be fresh," Mama said. "You can't take it off a dead boar. Loses its kick." She looked us both in the eyes. "Now this ain't gon' be easy, but only one wild boar that I know of lives in Sulphur Lick Valley. You gotta find a way to capture Ol' Slasher and cut off a chunk his tusk. Grind it up and mix it with the other fixin's and get Freeman Joe to eat it. Then see that he gets to court on time."

Millie Faye slumped against the desk. "That's not fresh, that's suicide. And how we gonna get Ol' Slasher to hold still whilst we hack off his tusk?"

"You're not," Mama said. "Mo Grady is. He's the man of the house." Mama reached up and gave my blue scarf a quick tug.

Was the Conjurer's Law of Three comin' to call on me again? Or was this Ol' Blue Satan's way of wreaking revenge on me for questioning him? Surely, I was going to be kilt one way or the other, 'cause there weren't no way I could hold Ol' Slasher down and cut off his tusk.

Mama handed me the recipe. "Don't lose this."

Millie Faye tried to jerk the recipe out of my hands. I held on tight and it ripped in two.

Mama cuffed us both behind the ears. "Stop it," she said. "You can both take your piece of it and put 'em together when you get home."

Deputy Penrod sputtered.

"Everything you need 'cept courage is written down there. Now give me a kiss and get to gettin'."

CHAPTER 28

Outhouse Fidget and Shadowy Things

The snowy road out of town lay vast and empty. The wheels of the red Chevrolet rolled along in the tire ruts. A bitter east wind blew white flakes everywhere. Roads signs stood cloaked in white, hiding their directions.

Halfway home Millie Faye started fidgeting. Her got-to-go-to-the-outhouse fidget. "We have to stop," she said.

"You'll have to hold it till we get home. Time's a'wasting."

"I can't wait. It's number two. Feels like a knot in my lower stomach is gonna explode if I don't let it out."

I spotted a grove of trees, exhaled hard and skidded to a stop. "I'll go with so's you don't get in no trouble."

Millie Faye puffed up like a Devil's Snuffbox mushroom. "You'll do no such a thing, Mo Grady Witt. I reckon I can poop in the woods without you holding my hand, thank you." She got out, slammed the door and trudged toward the trees.

I pulled out my half of Mama's Sanity Potion recipe, which ended with "Bloodroot." Mama taught me this herb was from the poppy family and good for curing skin tags and moles. I was mystified as to how it worked with powdered boar's tusk to cure insanity.

I watched Millie Faye disappear into the dark forest. Her tracks weren't much bigger'n a rabbit's.

A disease last August rendered rabbits scarce. I wondered what the wild dogs roaming the countryside ate. My mind twisted around to my wee twin out there by herself like a little cottontail ready to be pounced on. Oh me, oh my! Mama would break my head if wild dogs ate Millie Faye. But she'd be too late. I'd break my own head first.

I opened the car door to go to her rescue, when here she come'd trudging up, face shining like a pear in July. The wind blew so hard, she leaned sideways, her mittened hand held up so's to keep slanting snowflakes out of her eyes.

"Now I can think proper, Mo Grady," she said, climbing in. "I swear, sometimes I think you're just like all the other sonsabitchin' folks. Just 'cause I'm a little person, you think I'm retarded."

"Not retarded," I said, "just foul mouthed and puny."

I pulled back on the road, and we drove a couple miles in silence. "I'm sorry," I said, "I'm just crossways 'cause I want to get home as fast as I can to get started on a way to trap Ol' Slasher."

Millie Faye drummed on the dash. "Sorries accepted. But trapping Ol' Slasher ain't gonna be easy. Just how you fixin' to do it?"

"Very carefully." I handed her my half of the Sanity Potion recipe. "Here. Put this with your half and tell me what Mama says to do."

Millie Faye fumbled in her coat, reaching in this pocket and then that.

"Gettin' a piece of that boar's tusk is gonna be well nigh impossible. Whatever are we …" She quit talking and stared, then let out a scream. "Stop the car! Stop the car! We have to go back!"

I braked. "What are you talking about?"

Millie Faye sat hiding her head, sobbing buckets from a well. "Oh, Mo Grady," she said to the passenger door, "I done lost the farm and condemned Mama to the 'lectric chair. I can't find my half of the recipe."

"It can't have gone anywhere," I said. "Scoot over here and let me help you search."

"It did too go somewhere. I done … I done wiped my fanny with it and left it back in the woods."

"You used your half of the recipe on your butt? Are you crazy?"

"Well, I didn't do it on purpose. My fanny was so cold, and I heard somethin' breathin' in the woods, and I got scared and used whatever was in my pockets."

I groaned and turned around in a wide place in the road. Driving got harder facing into the wind. I could see my white-knuckled fingers on the steering wheel fittin' real firm around Millie Faye's wee neck. I did nothing a good brother might do to ease her sobbing. "Look for your poop trees," I said. My gas pedal toes ached from my reinforced skates.

Millie Faye put her little nose on the window, eyes fixed on the forest. "All the trees look alike to me."

We rounded a sharp curve that looked familiar, and just past it, I turned around again. Crept along, watching the road and the woods. Didn't help none that Millie Faye huddled, whimpering, next to the passenger door.

I saw my face in the rearview mirror. The skin on my cheeks looked stretched and gray, my eyes sunken with tiny red lines exploding out of my pupils.

The car jerked, and I tore my attention away from the miserable wraith in the mirror. I refocused on the trees.

My sister was right. They all looked alike. I switched to watching the snowy ground, looking for a tiny rabbit-like trail. But that blowing snow blanketed even our most recent tire tracks.

My eyes were so riveted watching the ditch, I didn't hear the oil truck behind us. It passed by so close, if the window would've been open, I could've licked it with my tongue. A horn blast nearly sent us through the roof.

I yelled and accidentally tromped the foot pedal. For the space of a short barnyard, we fishtailed all over that snowy, blowy road. Millie Faye cussed, eyes big as ketchup bottle caps.

My foot came off the gas pedal, and we coasted to a stop. Stomach acid climbed my throat. I threw open the car door, rolled out on all fours and upchucked. Steam rose from my vomit hole in the snow. My head hung, nostrils dripped, eyes closed.

Millie Faye's little hand patted me on the back. "Well, I swear, Mo Grady, you done found my tracks. Look."

She pointed to a series of shallow depressions leading from the road to the woods. They wound between a black walnut tree and a crooked woodpecker snag.

"You're right," I said. "Now, go get the paper. And wash it off in the snow so's you don't stink up the car."

Millie Faye didn't move. "Something's in them woods, Mo Grady. Maybe Ol' Slasher. Maybe he already knows we're fixin' to come after him and he's going to fix us first."

"You big chicken," I said, "nothing's out there. Ol' Slasher is miles from here."

"Get your rifle out of the trunk," she said.

"I didn't bring it."

"You been addled and careless since the hog shoot, and it only got worse since kissing that Loveda."

Millie Faye mentioning Loveda riled me. I was suddenly crossways again. Nonetheless, we needed that Sanity Potion recipe, rifle or no rifle.

"Come on," I said. "You go first. Only you know where you squatted."

She shuffled ahead. It'd stopped snowing, but snow covered everything.

"Right there," she pointed to a tiny white mound between two trees. "And, lookie, I told you somethin' was out there with me."

Fresh tracks led up to the mound. Big tracks. Wild animals—dogs or coyotes.

Coyotes didn't scare me. Never knowed one to hurt a soul. Mama said coyotes knowed how to forage for the good earth's bounty. Wild dogs is different. They lost the instinct to survive in the wild. They're desperate. And Mama said desperate dogs, like desperate people, do unnatural things.

I started to scoop snow off the mound with my hands.

Millie Faye shoved me away. "I'll do it, Mo Grady. It ain't proper you seein' it."

"Yeah, you're the picture of proper," I said. "Just hurry."

With no rifle, I needed a stick to defend us. My eyes swept over hickory and black walnut trees. My hands brushed over limbs until one felt just right—rough bark for a non-slip hand-hold, straight and no knots.

I leaned on it. The crisp snap echoed through the frozen woods. I had me a good, stout staff, five feet long. I jabbed the cold wind and smacked a tree and got doused with snow in the bargain.

Shadowy things moved in the frigid forest just outside my line of vision. I heard my sister rooting in the snow behind me. "Hurry up, Millie Faye, I don't like these woods."

I waited. And waited.

Millie Faye started sobbing again. "It's gone, Mo Grady," she said. "Something's ate Mama's recipe."

"Better the recipe than us," I said.

Millie Faye screamed.

The woods growled.

CHAPTER 29

Skate-Feet and Heavy Breathing

I turned my skate-feet too quick and fell face first in the snow. Millie Faye, backing up, fell over me. I bucked her off, swiped snow out of my eyes and stared into the crazed eyes of a red bone hound gone to bad, less than a barn door away.

His dirty coat looked like a rusted straw doormat. One ear was gnawed down to a rippled nub on his head. Every rib showed. His lips curled back and his eyes shone like the black buttons Mama sewed on Millie Faye's Raggedy Ann doll.

Small hardwood eyes set deep in One Ear's sockets catalogued my every move. My eyes locked onto his, hands felt around for my stick in the snow.

Something told me to stand up quick.

Three other wild curs joined One Ear, all doing the slink of starvation. The weaker ones wouldn't last the winter unless they found some prey lame or stupid enough to get caught defenseless out in the woods.

A pregnant dun-colored terrier mix, tail between her legs, sidled up to One Ear, whimpering and licking him under the chin. Rows of teats swelled over her bloated belly. She wore the ragged look of abandonment and betrayal.

I recognized her. Lila. One of Delilah's litter, the Atkins' terrier bitch.

I called out, "Lila, come here girl."

She came toward me with lips curled back in a doggy smile, tail wagging. One Ear cut her off, nipped her neck and barked her back.

My fingers closed around my stick. Using it as a prop, I rose up slow. "Millie Faye, I'm gonna yell and rush the dogs. You lite out for the car when I do."

Her heart thumped. "I ain't leavin' you here to fight them dogs by yourself."

A snowball, sailing past my ear, hit a white dog with a gray scar across his right front shoulder down to his stomach.

Scarbelly yelped.

One Ear crouched in attack stance, his sunken eyes leveled at my wee sister.

"It's you they want, Millie Faye," I said.

I vowed then and there to never let my puny sister poop alone in the woods again. Hold her hand if I had to. Wipe her baby butt if that's what it took. If the wild dogs would've found her taking a poop, she'd be gristle and bone by now.

Might still be if I didn't think of something, soon.

"Get out of here before they surround us." I shook my stick, wielding it like a sword.

One Ear came out of his crouch and barked. The dogs spread out.

Millie Faye let out a whoop and her feet crunched quick in the snow, sound trailing away. I shouted, did a sideways dance and swung at the pack with my stick. A car door opened and closed, signaling my sister was safe and I could make a dash for it on my skate-feet.

Scarbelly and a short-tailed hound-boxer broke away and headed in the direction of the woodpecker snag. One Ear turned sideways toward the other dogs, the wind rippling his fur, showing pus-pocked purple skin.

I glanced behind me toward the car. Millie Faye's tracks had gone to the car, but she wasn't inside and, dammit, a new set of tiny tracks trailed back into the woods.

My heart liked to leaped out of my chest.

"Mo Grady! Over here!" Her voice sounded high off the ground. I backed up and saw her up in the woodpecker snag, legs wrapped tight around it. She held onto a rotten branch with one hand and waved something in the other.

Short Tail sniffed around the snag's bottom, and Scarbelly propped up on the trunk of the tree, front paws inches from Millie Faye's feet.

"Look, Mo Grady! The other half of Mama's recipe," she said. "I saw it hung up on this ol' snag. The wind must've blew it. So's you can quit your worrying. Mama and the farm will be saved now!"

I wasn't worried about the farm, nor even Mama right then. I skate-walked fast backwards toward the snag. No easy feat on four-inch skate-stilts on packed snow over uneven ground.

One Ear followed, lips curled, fangs showing, his mangy head an inch off the snow-covered ground.

Lila trotted behind, wagging her skinny tail.

When I got to the snag, I turned and hit Scarbelly's rump with my stick. He yiked, and both dogs backed off a few feet.

"Mo Grady, you got no more sense than a terrapin." She stuffed the recipe in her coat pocket. "Climb up here a'fore them hounds get brave. Somebody'll come along on the road and rescue us."

"Nobody except a fuel truck's drivin' in this weather and it already went by."

I could've probably waded through the dogs by myself and left Millie Faye up in the tree whilst I went for help. But even if she didn't get too cold and fall out of the tree, she was liable to jump down and follow me. No, I couldn't leave her. Mama would never forgive me. I would never forgive me.

"Listen, Millie Faye. One time Mama told me, 'If you meet a feral dog, stand as tall as you can and look 'em square in the eye. They fear tall people.' I sidled up against the snag, under my sister's feet. "Come stand on my shoulders."

"This is no time for kid's games. We're fixin' to get et."

"I'm gonna hand you the stick. Step on my shoulders, I'll hold your feet, then let loose of the tree limbs and wave the stick around and shout, 'Get thee gone, booger dogs!'"

"You're crazy," she said.

The gnarly pack leader took a step closer, showing a mouth full of teeth and yellow slaver. He bit the snow. Mouth lined with white fluff.

A midget foot landed on my right shoulder. I clasped it. Handed the stick up and felt Millie Faye grab it. Her other foot now pressed on my left shoulder. I clasped it with my other hand. Both feet felt hesitant. "Let go of the limbs," I said. "I'm gonna start walking."

"I hope you know what you're doin'."

"If I fall," I said, "you hit the ground runnin'."

She swung the stick around, coming within a possum hair of whacking my nose. "Back away, booger dogs, go away!" she shouted.

They backed up a few feet. Lila shivered and panted, her taut belly undulating.

I took a baby step. Another baby step. I inched us forward, slow as cold beeswax, following our trail back to the red Chevrolet whilst the pack followed us.

Millie Faye chanted, "Booger dog, booger dog, go back to your booger bog."

I hobbled with my stick-wielding other half. The red Chevrolet reared up in the snow. I fell against it, my cheek leaning on its icy side.

Millie Faye dropped the stick, jumped on the roof and hollered, "We did it, Mo Grady!"

I grabbed the stick. "We're not safe yet." I turned around, wound up with my good pitching arm and threw a twirling stick-ball at the wild canines. Scattered 'em long enough so's I could open the car door.

One Ear raised up and howled.

I held out my arms for Millie Faye to jump. For once she gave me no argument. I tossed her in the car, jumped in behind and slammed the door.

One Ear nipped Lila on the butt and disappeared through the trees. Scarbelly and Short Tail followed. Ribbed phantoms. Zombie hounds.

Lila stopped at the forest's edge, turned and slinked back to the car and sat on her haunches.

Me and her soft brown eyes met.

We both knowed what was in store for her pups if she followed the pack into those woods. First good meal the pack would've had in a while. Maybe she'd be a meal, too. Either way, I'd lay odds a thousand to one, Lila wouldn't last the winter.

I started the engine and we rolled to start. I glanced in the side mirror to see Lila running in a disheveled lope alongside the car, her tongue dragging in snowdrifts.

My foot pressed down. The car pulled ahead.

"Time to shift gears," Millie Faye said. "Push in the clutch."

Another glance in the mirror, and Lila was still there, starting to fall behind, struggling to keep up. Her eyes looked wild. I let up on the gas pedal, pushed on the brake.

We stopped.

I glanced all around. No sign of the wild pack. I got out, opened the back door and said, "Get in, Lila."

"What kind of stunt are you pullin'?" Millie Faye said. "That dog ain't about to get in this car. Let's go."

Lila looked back toward the woods and whined. Tail stopped wagging. Back at me with those soft knowing eyes. Studying me. Tormented. Craving safety and affection. Direction. Gauging the gap between self-survival and loyalty to her pack.

Her tail channeled her thoughts, wagging like a windsock in a storm. She let out a crisp bark and charged.

Millie Faye eeked.

The wild dog leaped.

Lila landed in the back seat. Turned around three times and rolled over on her back, slapping the soft leather with her tail.

I laid a hand on her mangy balloon belly, traced my finger up to her neck and scratched behind her ears. Took a couple marble-sized pieces of the sour dough bread out of my back pocket and fed them to her. She wolfed them down, then near to peeled the skin off my hand licking it so hard.

I closed the door and got back behind the steering wheel. Millie Faye peeked over the seat. "You know Mama won't let us have a dog. 'Sides, she smells like rotting squirrel guts. Gonna get our new Chevrolet all stinky."

"Mama's in jail. She don't have no say in it." I sniffed in my twin's direction. "And who are you to talk about smelling? That poop paper don't smell like roses. Put it in the glove compartment till we can get home and clean it off."

"I hate you," my sister said. "And if you tell the girls about this I'll hate you all my born days." She put the paper away, then scrunched herself into a ball in the far corner.

Lila put her paws on the back seat and licked Millie Faye's left ear. My sister giggled and hunched her shoulders. Lila licked again, stronger. More giggles and hunching. Licked again. No hunching. Millie Faye climbed into the back seat, petting and cooing. Girl and dog sighs for the next few minutes whilst I kept my eyes on the road as the odometer ticked off the miles. Then heavy breathing. I glanced in the rearview mirror and saw Millie Faye and Lila snuggled up, asleep.

Been a hard day.

The car hit a slick spot, and we skidded toward the ditch. I pulled back in the middle of the road and slowed. The back seat duo never stirred.

What in the hell possessed me to think I could ever drive down the road in my new, red Chevrolet—me, proud and happy, with not a care in the world? Ol' Blue Satan, that's who. He lied to me. The more I drove the car of my dreams, the more nightmares I encountered.

The Conjurer's Law had come down on me with a vengeance. And I still didn't know how I was gonna coax a 1000-pound Russian boar to saunter up and donate me a chunk of tusk.

PART III

BOOK OF JUBILATION

When the gods want to punish us,
they answer our prayers.

— Oscar Wilde

CHAPTER 30

Bumperless and Bumkiddled

I stopped the red Chevrolet behind our barn so's no one could see us from the farmhouse. The early morning sky looked the color of a fox squirrel's tail and was filled with high clouds and low hills. Rancid dog stink blended with air smelling like early maple sap. I let out Millie Faye and Lila next to a hole in the fence.

My sister said nary a word as she and the dog crawled through the opening. They trudged through knee high snow, Lila leaping around Millie Faye, and then they went in the back door of the barn.

Aunt Big Bertha, standing on the front stoop, was waiting for me. She barreled down the steps, her massive udders bouncing up and down. She honed in on that spot of the car where the bumper used to be. Didn't even ask where Millie Faye was.

I untied my skate-feet, slung them over my arm and got out of the car. I stood barefooted, braced my back against the car, preparing for cannon fire.

"What in the Sam Hill did you do to my new car?" she said. "Didn't I tell you to stay the hell away from it?"

"Ain't your car."

"Will be in a couple days," she said. "And where'd you get all the bird poop on it?" Her mouth twisted inside out. "Get away from that car. Every time you get near it for a minute, it ages a year. You're a walking blight, you are."

Aunt Big Bertha wore a new wig big as a military gas can. The huge lacquered hairpiece veered off in one direction and then the other when she wiggled her head.

I kept a leg cocked and ready to run. "Bumper caught on a tree root and ripped off," I said. "It's in a snowdrift behind the Stonecrop County jail. If you want it, you better get to it before somebody else does. Bein' new and all, it'd probably bring top dollar from Bonker Beckman."

Aunt Big Bertha's wig shook. Purple and gold flashes of light flew. She circled the car. "What were you doin' in New Dreadford? Seein' your jailbird mama?" Her eyes weaseled into slits. "When I get back with that bumper, you got some 'plaining to do, boy."

Just then, Lila barked in the barn.

Aunt Big Bertha cocked an ear. Her eyes glowed with a strange light—a light all shadowy and thick as beech gum. The same light that'd come into Uncle Harm's eyes when he was filled with the Word. "Did you bring a dog on my farm? And where's your retarded sister?"

"Ain't your farm," I said, "and Millie Faye ain't retarded."

Aunt Big Bertha hollered at the house, "Reverend Waywater, you keep these kids here to home while I'm gone. After we get Freeman Joe committed, we'll have us a vermin dog roundup."

He appeared on the front stoop, his right arm in a sling, and hollered back, "Alright, Bertha Sue."

Aunt Big Bertha had taken him back as a husband now that surviving two snakebites elevated him to a higher plane of holiness in Sulphur Lick Valley. Twice bitten and still above ground was the closest thing to the Second Coming folks'd ever seen 'round these parts. And, of course, being Holiness Christians, God got the healing credit and not Mama.

Aunt Big Bertha drove away in the bumperless, bird-poop-spattered Chevrolet.

The two-headed preacher, letting off a sickly sugary smell, followed me around while I did chores. Although he had two heads, he only had one leaky eye that worked between them. He took some gettin' used to, but it's not like I hadn't had practice with crazies.

He asked a ton of questions. "How do you squeeze a cow's teat to get the milk? Why do billy goats smell funny? What's in that rabbit box looks like a big furry brain?"

"Cassandra just had her a litter of kits," I said. "She used her own fur to make 'em a baby blanket."

I reached in the cage, petted my rabbit, slid my hand into the warm fur and hauled out a young'in—pink, blind and hairless. It squealed, little mouth smacking, searching for a teat. "Here, Reverend. You can hold one."

The preacher brought the wee kit up to his good eye. "Looks like a mouse and smells like a newborn human child."

Whilst the preacher sniffed, Millie Faye motioned me over behind a stall. "I figured out how we can get some fresh boar tusk. We'll find Ol' Slasher when he's asleep and get some big ropes and ..."

"And how long you think he'll stay asleep when I go to hackin' on his tusk?"

"Well, you tie him up first, you dummy—"

I shook my head and puffed up with pride. I'd been thinking on this while chorin' with the Reverend. "I got a better idea. I'm gonna dig a pit and trap him in it."

"You can't dig Ol' Slasher's pit fast enough by yourself," she whispered.

I opened my mouth, but nothing came out. She was right, damn her.

"Why not get the preacher to help?" she asked.

The problem and solution, all in one go. Damn her smarts.

Soapsuds clung to her clothes up to her shoulders.

"Why are you covered in suds?" I said.

"I'm givin' Lila a bath a'fore she pups. If the life she led didn't kill her babies, the stink could when they's born."

My nose puckered. "That stink hopped off the dog and onto you. You better get in the tub with her."

Millie Faye kicked me in the shin. "Never you mind about my business. You want to get Mama out of jail, you get the two-headed preacher to help you dig."

"And just how do you reckon I do that?"

"I don't," she said. "But I reckon a smart boy who's heard Miss Haige read about a boy trickin' other boys into paintin' a fence for him, could figure it out."

She flicked soapsuds on me and scooted out the back way.

My shin smarted. Millie Faye could be a little finagler when she had a mind to.

I went to the tool shed and got a pick, a two-bladed axe and two shovels. The preacher followed, gimping along, his right foot dragging, his Cyclops eye taking me in. "What'cha gonna dig, boy?"

I handed him a shovel. "Me and you got to dig a pit and catch Ol' Slasher. Keep him from destroying our winter silage."

"Why not get Freeman Joe to help?"

"Freeman Joe's not much good for nothin' since Mama's been gone."

"Now hold on here," the two-headed preacher said. "The good Lord called me to preach the gospel, not do manual labor. 'Sides, my right arm ain't fit for diggin'."

"You can work a shovel," I said. "I'll work the pick-axe."

I dug with the pick for a half an hour, through a foot of snow, loosening frozen top soil for a six-by-ten-foot pit. I then axed through two thick red oak roots that I pretended were the heads of the Postlewaite brothers. Sweat steamed under my long johns.

The two-headed preacher, unlike me, stood shivering, hugging the shovel handle to his chest. His extra head pulsed up and down, two pistons pumping.

I put down the axe and wiped sweat off my forehead with my purple handkerchief. "My, this is warm work." I picked up my shovel.

The preacher removed his arm sling. "We'll be out here all day in the freezin' cold at the pokey rate you're a'goin'." Icy vapor poured from his lopsided mouth.

Took him a few minutes to get the shovel positioned right between his shoulder and arm, but he got to where he scooped loose dirt fine. He just couldn't wait till I got the entire outline of the hole loosened up with the pick, so's he jumped right in. I didn't have to pick up my shovel a'tall. He had the dirt out as fast as I could break it up. The more he worked, the more his snakebite swelling went down.

After a couple hours, we climbed out for a break. Our feet dangling over the hole, we sat and sipped water. The preacher's eye seemed to have straightened a bit.

Then we set back to our task. When the pit got too deep for me to climb out, I got a ladder and set it near the hole. The preacher and I got to giving each other a hand up out of the hole, sometimes forgetting our situation—pitted against each other as ordained by Aunt Big Bertha—and we'd grin at one another whilst pulling past roots and rocks.

I think that preacher would've dug all the way to Hades if I hadn't hollered stop. We sat again with our legs dangling over the sides of our hole. Two weary workers sharing a moment of rest.

"Why do y'all want to kick us off the farm?" I said.

He rubbed his second head. "Well, boy, I was sitting here thinking the same thing. I reckon we're gonna need someone to take care of this farm. I'm not much of a farmer. I can dig holes, but when it comes to puttin' seeds in the ground or plowin' a straight furrow or butcherin' stock, I'm afraid I'm not much good—the sight of blood makes me faint, plus I'm partly crippled. If you was to shape up and quit taxin' your Aunt Bertha Sue's patience, I might persuade her to let you chillun stay on here as share-croppers whilst me and her spread the word of the Lord."

I 'bout fell in the pit. "Thank you for the kind offer, Reverend Waywater." I couldn't take him up on it—not with Mama in jail and his wife fixin' to put Freeman Joe in the nut house.

My scheme to trap Ol' Slasher had to work, or all was lost. I resisted the urge to tell the two-headed preacher that we were plotting to keep the farm and get Mama out of jail. Resisted telling him he could stay on when we took over, but not Aunt Big Bertha. Resisted telling him he'd be better off if he got shed of her—that handling serpents in church was nothin' compared to handling her.

Sweat turned to ice on my neck. I got up, took the axe to the forest and chopped some cedar limbs. Dragged the boughs to the pit and spread them over it. The preacher got the idea and sprinkled a light pack of snow on them. We then used a bough as a broom and smoothed out snow where we'd trampled.

The preacher picked up a shovel and leaned against it, resting his gimp leg. "I hear that old razorback's got eight-inch tusks. Lem Kerpash said the old boar put a foot-long gash in his prize bull's belly, neat as a sharp knife. I'd sure admire to have those tusks when you kill him. There's some in these hills that claim drinkin' black oak stump water with ground up boar's tusk makes you a better … ah … husband." His Cyclops eye winked. "I don't mind telling you, the more I neglect my husbandly duties, the crabbier your Aunt Bertha Sue gets. If I don't quit falling short, I may be out in the cold along with you kids. Ha, ha." He looked at me. "Sorry, boy, I didn't mean to rub salt in the wound."

"No offense taken," I said. And there wasn't.

I was a farm boy and knew about animals breeding, but I didn't tell him the thought of him and Aunt Big Bertha going at it like rutting hogs was beyond my ken. 'Sides which, I reckoned preachers didn't have the same kind of urges as other men. Or boys.

And I didn't tell him I wasn't planning on killing Ol' Slasher and needed the boar's tusk for my own purposes.

"I could sure use a cup of hot tea with cream in it," I said. "Warm us up a mite."

"Reckon it would," he said, looking at me, and there was that wink again, "but, I tell you, Mo Grady, I ain't done an honest day's labor since the Lord's calling came upon me. I forgot how good it makes you feel." Grinning, he showed me the blisters on his hands.

He walked ahead of me with a new spring in his slip step. And damned if it didn't look like his snakebit second head had shrunk some.

"I gotta stop in the barn and see how Millie Faye's doing with a sick calf," I said. "You go ahead and put on some water to boil."

He waved and kept bounce-walking like he was bound for a Baptism party.

Smoke come'd pouring out of the bunkhouse chimney. I went around the barn and into the bunkhouse.

Millie Faye and Lila, both soaked, shared a blanket. Tub water was black with scum. My sister wore a crooked smile. "Boy, you never seen such a crust of dirt on a dog before."

Lila didn't look so happy. Getting scrubbed within an inch of her life was apparently something she hadn't bargained for when she took up with her human pack. Her whole body shook. Seeing me, she jumped out of the blanket, tail waving, and ran to my feet. I knelt to pet her as she licked my hand.

"I swear, Mo Grady," Millie Faye knelt, too, and laughed whilst scratching Lila's plump belly, "I do all the hard work and you get all the good licking."

Seeing my twin so happy made me want to cry. I turned my face and put more wood in the stove. Sparky devils danced in the flame. The blaze of heat dried my tears. I was the man of the house, and I had work to do.

Millie Faye looked at the door. "What'd you do with your two-headed shadow?"

"He's in the house waiting for a cup of tea," I said. "But we need to be quit of him for a while. I've gotta get Jubal Jen ready to bait Ol' Slasher."

Going back outside, the winter cold hit me. It hit Jubal Jen too, spraying bits of frost on her broad side. She gaacked and looked at me as if asking why we was outside in this weather.

Even though Jubal Jen liked to please me, a 600-pound sow won't do anything she don't want to. Like stand out at night in the winter cold, waiting for a crazed suitor with eight-inch tusks to stroll by for a cuff and a cuddle. Her large ears, like antennas, shifted around hunting for suspicious signals.

I spread straw on the ground, then drug over four bales and stacked them as a shield against the wind. I tethered her to a stake on the lee side. She watched me walk away and then followed, pulling up my puny stake without any effort a'tall.

"No, Jubal Jen!" I shook my head. "You have to stay put." I found two bigger stakes and drove them deeper into the frozen ground. Hoped it would hold this time.

I stroked her rough hide and cooed in her great floppy ears:

"Goin' up to Cripple Creek, goin' on the run,

Goin' up to Cripple Creek, have some fun—

Goin' up to Cripple Creek, goin' in a whirl,

Goin' up to Cripple Creek and see my girl..."

She grunted—her soft, floaty eyes looked at me with complete trust. The next time I walked away, she strained and keened but couldn't break free.

I didn't look back. I figured to give her a couple hours, then bring her into the warm barn.

Lila's dried coat smelled like Mama's homemade soap. Take away the ringworm around one eye, patches of missing fur, and ribs showing, and she looked like a fine lady.

I took her in my arms, "You're a good dog, Lila."

Millie Faye sat on the bunk beside me, and we both petted our new dog, getting good lickings in return—no mutt was ever more grateful for being delivered from a harsh Ozark mountain winter.

Millie Faye rubbed Lila's stomach. "She's fixin' to birth anytime now, Mo Grady. What are we gonna do? If we don't rid ourselves of Aunt Big Bertha, she'll kill 'em all." She sniffled. "And even if we do get the farm, Mama'll make us do the same. There ain't no hope for Lila or her pups."

I squirmed. No wonder the kids at school beat up on her. She talked about things other folks only thought about. "You're right. With any luck, the pups'll all be stillborn."

Tears rolled down my sister's thin cheeks. "I swear, Mo Grady. That ugly blue cottonmouth done got you bumkiddled. You got about as much feelings as a fence post."

I'd switched roles with my twin. Told the truth. Trouble was, there ain't no mileage in telling the truth to truth tellers. They're the least able to handle it.

I figured to get Millie Faye thinking about something else. "Come on, time's a'wastin'. You need to go mix up some of Mama's sleeping potion. Enough for three men. Mix some of it with fresh cream for the preacher's tea. The rest is for Ol' Slasher. Hurry!"

CHAPTER 31

Cyclops Eye and Sour Mash Farts

We sat down with the two-headed preacher to a proper alum root tea. His second stubby head twitched with excitement. A gamey, earthy smell took over that sugary smell he had before digging.

He sprayed tea all over with his partially paralyzed mouth as he talked about saving sinners as far away as Fort Smith, Arkansas and Tulsa, Oklahoma.

The preacher drank two cups of tea that Millie Faye had topped with spoonfuls of cream. Ain't nothing better'n farm-fresh cream—even laced with sleeping potion.

Wasn't long till the preacher's words slurred more than usual. His good eye's lid drooped. His words stopped. Drool dripped out the right side of his mouth. He pulled his right arm up with his left hand and laid it on the table. Made a pillow of both arms, lay his head down and commenced snoring so loud it rattled his empty teacup in its saucer.

"I gave him enough to drop one of them African bull elephants," Millie Faye said.

"I'm gonna watch our trap get sprung from the barn loft," I said. "I'll have my rifle in case things go to bad. You stay here and tend to the preacher in the warm where it's safe."

Millie Faye gave me a pre-cockroach fit look. "Ain't nary a thing in here needs my tendin'," she said. "I'm going out to minister to Lila in case she's needs help whelpin'."

I got the flashlight out of the kitchen drawer. Mama forbid us to use it 'cept in emergencies. If trapping a 1000-pound swamp monster ain't that, I don't know what is.

I lay in the barn loft watching Jubal Jen blow steamy breath in my direction by the light of a snow moon playing hide-'n-seek with the clouds.

Watching and waiting for a randy swamp devil is frigid work. An hour went by. Then two. My poor sow. With Mama gone and me in charge I could squeeze Jubal Jen through the kitchen door and warm her beside the wood stove right fast. Have her back out and staked in a half hour.

But the moment I stood up, I saw movement at the edge of the woods. A chunk of trees broke away and moved in Jubal Jen's direction. It snorted. Sure enough, Ol' Slasher. My belly did a somersault. I'd never seen the monster up close and if'n I had my druthers, I wouldn't tonight.

Jubal Jen snorted a recognition. She wasn't in season to get piglets and wasn't in any mood to get sweet-talked, let alone get mounted by the big tusker. 'Course the bog hog, with romance on his mind, didn't know that. He was headed straight for the trap.

'This is gonna be easier than I thought,' I thought.

But he stopped a few feet short. Ploughed the snow with his great tusks. Backed away.

"The sonsabitch," I whispered. "He's onto us." My great idea had failed.

I leveled my rifle. No. No way could I get a kill shot at night at that distance. It'd just piss him off.

The barn door below me flung open and here come'd a tiny figure, carrying a lantern and trouncing through the snow right toward the pit. Millie Faye. She might as well've painted a target on her tiny butt.

Ol' Slasher stopped dicing the snow. Pointed those terrible tusks at the bright light.

He charged.

I dashed to the loft's edge, took one hop to the rabbit cages and another to a bale of straw. Flashlight and rifle in hand, I ran past Lila, who exploded into barks, lunging against her rope.

I ran out of the barn. A quick glance showed Millie Faye was way ahead of me. She'd somehow got on the other side of the pit next to Jubal Jen.

Ol' Slasher was just as clever. Instead of raging across the pit, he commenced sidling around it.

Millie Faye's voice pierced the night. "Mo Grady, he's comin' to get me. You got to do somethin' fast. I'm fixin' to die."

I took aim, but it weren't no use. They were all too close together. Only thing I had left was to run and shout at the big boar. Maybe thump him on the nose with my rifle and … I stopped. When that giant hog drew up between Jubal Jen and the pit, she leaned her whole 600 hundred pounds hard against him, catching Ol' Slasher unawares.

The nudge didn't move Ol' Slasher much, him bein' almost twice Jubal Jen's size and five times as ornery, but it was enough. His feet hit the edge of the pit, dirt crumpling from his bulk. He snorted once, all anger and confusion, then toppled into the black hole.

Hugging Jubal Jen from opposite sides, me and Millie Faye stared down into the abyss.

Snorting and crashing echoed from within. My nostrils spread wide by a fetid manure smell. I hesitated a moment, poised to skedaddle. Wasn't altogether sure Ol' Slasher couldn't climb them walls.

I shined my flashlight into the pit. The air thickened with fog from the old hog's breath. My flashlight beamed purple and waxy.

Ol' Slasher attacked the purple light, tearing gouges out of the pit walls with his tusks. I scanned the beam over his body. Color of burnt copper. Spiked hair. Not an ounce of fat. Corded shoulder muscles thick as rope. Little ears on a huge head. And those tusks. My beam caught on those hooked twin impalers—sharp as Mama's skinning knife, like he sharpened them at the limestone quarry before digging roots and slicing open bull bellies. One tusk twisted. Straightened out, it would've been a foot long. Red clay covered his long snout. Blue foam flew from his nostrils with every snort.

The great beast grew tired after a spell. He stood, feet splayed, body quivering. Beady eyes looked up into the flashlight beam and seen right into my brain. I could feel Ol' Slasher's deep hate of me. Hit my face like a solid east wind. I stepped back and put my hand to my mouth to stop my clacking teeth.

Trapping the great hog was a rotten idea.

Jubal Jen grunted and moved her huge bulk to lean against me. She wasn't afraid of Ol' Slasher. She knew how to handle him—stick your butt in his face and fart. Nothing like an old sour mash fart to tempt a suitor and smooth out the communication.

Millie Faye came and put her little arm around my waist and leaned against my other hip. "You're shiverin', Mo Grady."

"Here." She tried handing me a sticky glob. "I rolled sleeping potion in sour dough batter."

"Throw it to him," I said. "I'll take Jubal Jen inside the barn and be back with the meat saw."

I leaned my rifle against a straw bale and grabbed Jubal Jen by the ear. She resisted my pulling, casting glances over her shoulder at the pit. She finally gaacked and fell in step. We passed Lila, tail stiff, jaws tensed and body shaking. She sensed somethin' wicked afoot. As soon as I walked away, she lunged against her rope, facing the pit, and growling deep in her chest.

I returned to see Millie Faye stooped down, flashlight shining into the pit. I laid the meat saw beside her.

"I threwed him the dough ball," she said, "and he et it. It better work 'cause we don't have no more ingredients."

Ol' Slasher's eyes turned from fire bright to dull and glazed. His long snout hit the ground. Butt tottered with tail upright, caked with mud balls. A last twirl of defiance, then it quit turning and the great body eased down. His nose let out a mighty snort and his eyes closed and he snored like the two-headed preacher.

His twisted tusk stuck straight up. I put the ladder in the pit, climbed down with my back against the rungs, feet pointed out, keeping my eyes on that tusk. My heart pounded against my eardrums. I hit the bottom rung with one foot, my other touched damp earth. A mud-caked butt faced me not a foot away. Smelled sour like pawpaw bark and wild garlic.

"Hurry up, Mo Grady," Millie Faye's thin voice strained through the hog-breath air.

The pit that looked so big up top looked small from the bottom. Felt cold and lonely, too. Down in that pit, staring at Ol' Slasher's clotted ass, I re-thought the pact I'd made with Ol' Blue Satan. If hell came anywhere near what it was like inside that pit, I wanted no part of it.

"Hand me down the meat saw," I said.

I tiptoed around Ol' Slasher. Fingers reached out and touched his twisted tusk. He didn't stir. I swallowed hard and choked on my own spit, let go the tusk, turned my head and coughed and coughed.

Millie Faye's faraway voice sliced through: "Stop it, Mo Grady, you'll wake him up!"

The more I tried to swallow my cough, the more I choked.

Then I heard barking right above my head.

"Shit!" Millie Faye's foul mouth yelled. "Lila's got loose."

I heard muffled wrestling. The flashlight beam flickered up and out of the hole, leaving me in the dark with the hell hog.

Lila quit barking, Millie Faye quit yelling and I quit coughing. The light came back in the hole to show Ol' Slasher still sleeping like a baby.

If he slept through that, he'd most likely sleep through anything.

I measured off a half inch of tusk—the thickness of my thumb— held the razor-sharp tooth steady with my left hand, placed the meat saw against it and pushed forward.

I might as well have blown Gabriel's horn. The rasp rang out loud- er than a blue jay squawk. The saw's back draw jangled my ears like scraping on concrete. Or cutting Uncle Harm's leg bones. Only louder. And with echoes.

Even so, a meat saw is a thing of bone-cutting genius. And I was an inspired thief. I had me a stolen tusk tip in no time.

"I've got it." I held it up for Millie Faye to see. Such a small thing that could save the farm and save Mama from the 'lectric chair. I swear it lit up in my fingers like a gold nugget.

Millie Faye got down on her knees and leaned over the pit, reaching down as far as her puny arms could. "Let me have it. And you get on up out of there before that old hog wakes up."

I reached up on my tippy toes to give it to her. When our hands touched, a snap of static electricity made me jump and that gold nugget leapt out of my hands like a bunny out of a briar patch. It danced on my fingertips.

Millie Faye, making a quick reach for it, lost her balance and come'd sliding down the hole right on top of me, screaming all the way down.

The heavy flashlight creased my ear, bounced off my left shoulder, throwing light beams topsy-turvy around the pit before hitting something with a thunk. The light went off, pitching us in total darkness.

We clunked heads, and the gold nugget escaped my grasp. I went over backwards with Millie Faye on top. I heard, between my sister's screams and Lila's barking, a grunt and a gaack, like the well pump clearing its throat before gushing dingy water.

Millie Faye quit screaming and squirming. Without a spoken word she whispered, in that special way we twins have, "I can feel him wakin' up, Mo Grady. We're fixin' to die."

"Shhh … be quiet," I whispered back. "Find the flashlight."

"I can feel his wrath in my mind, Mo Grady, and somethin' else. Pain. He's hurting somethin' terrible."

My hand felt only moist earth. Then, a new stink, like skunk musk, filled the space. Hot bog breath stirred the hairs on my hand. A bull thistle stuck crossways in my throat. Ol' Slasher's nostrils couldn't be but inches away. My hand froze.

Barking started above us again. I could hear Lila's paws circling the edges of the pit. She was just trying to protect us, but even so, at this very moment I wished I'd left her with the pack.

A loud snort made me wish I'd followed the two-headed preacher's advice and shot the beast.

I had to get Millie Faye out of there—if the hell hog didn't get her, her missin' heart might.

"I found the flashlight," she said, "but I'm scared to turn it on."

"Don't. Get up slow, and I'm gonna toss you outta here. Soon as you get up top, shine the light right in Ol' Slasher's eyes. It should hypnotize him long enough for me to climb out."

Millie Faye got up. "What if the light don't work, Mo Grady?"

Ol' Slasher's hooves pawed the ground. I prayed—to anybody listening—for a few more seconds to get my wee sister to safety.

"If it don't work," I said, "we'll go to plan B."

My hands found her waist. Her ribcage shook. "What's plan beeeeee—"

I tossed her up. Heard a thunk, then her wee voice.

"I'm fixin' to turn on the light, Mo Grady."

I flexed my knees, preparing for the rush up the ladder. My overalls squished, my body sodden with sweat.

Through the din of barking, the pit lit up. Millie Faye started spouting cuss words at the top of her voice, profanities I'd never heard her say before.

Her beam had found Ol' Slasher's beady eyes, but that wily old porker wasn't fooled a'tall. Wasn't gonna fall for looking into the light. Those twin orbs fixed straight on me, red as a poker in a firebox.

He moved his great fetid body, filling up the whole space between me and the ladder, which might as well have been a football field away.

Something 'sides me caught the old hog's attention. Them poker eyes shifted. His head cocked one way, then the other. He lined up his eyes with me and his twisted tusk, now missing a tip. That's what he was looking at. That tipless tusk.

His red eyes narrowed. Grogginess escaped, replaced by rage. His cloven hooves beat the ground, drumming up and down. The fury traveled through his thick body, fusing muscles. He stretched his great head, tossed dirt all around with his snout, stabbing imaginary boys with his one sharp tusk.

My fingers clawed the sides of the pit, grasping for a last ditch hold to pull me up.

A great gust of steam came out of Ol' Slasher's nostrils, followed quick by another. He reared back.

The whole world went quiet. I held my breath. No cussing from Millie Faye. No barking from Lila.

The great beast lunged. His spear-tusk taking the lead.

I tried to leap away and failed. Legs had no spring in 'em. Muscle weak as a strand of hair. I rolled to the wall and into a fetal ball, my arms and legs braced to take the first charge.

CHAPTER 32

Bone Against Bone
and a By-God Miracle

I braced. And I braced. My ears heard a scream, a thud and a vicious growl, a growl reaching all the way back to Lila's wolf ancestry. The pregnant dog had leaped on Ol' Slasher's back. Predator teeth ripped into thick hide.

I unfolded and saw, in the erratic beam of Millie Faye's flashlight, the hell hog buck and rear and roar like a Brahma bull at a rodeo. Lila dug into his back. I dodged hooves and tusks as best I could.

Millie Faye thwacked me on the head with a snowball. "Get out of there, Mo Grady, whilst the gettin's good."

Suddenly, with a yelp and a thud, Lila wasn't on top anymore and a 1000-pound hog had her cornered next to the ladder. I had a fleeting thought of saving her, but that's all it was. I knew it weren't no use. Just get us both killed.

My knees came to life. I ran and leaped up on the hog's rump with my left foot, pushed off and sprang onto the ladder. I climbed with my elbows to the top, and Millie Faye grabbed me, my nose pushing up snow. Wonderful, fresh snow.

Gnashing and canine cries came from the pit.

"Grab my rifle," I said. "Maybe I can save her."

The rifle was only a few paces away, but time slowed to a crawl as I waited. I put my hands over my ears. Block out the sounds of tusks against flesh, of bone against bone, and then whimpers.

Agonizing and everlasting.

My eyes watered up. My first real dog, and I'd got her kilt. Lila would've been better off if she'd stayed with One Ear and his pack. She'd a lasted longer, anyway. Poor dog—her choices put her on the wrong path anyway she turned.

I felt tainted beyond redemption. A low-down sinner who didn't deserve a dog. 'Specially a dog who'd give her life to save yours.

And she died for a stupid tusk tip that Mama and the two-headed preacher claimed had wondrous powers. Wondrous disappearing powers. Lost in the muck with a rampaging hog and a gored dog, not doing nobody no good.

Millie Faye's little feet galloped up to me. "Shoot him, Mo Grady!"

I aimed. "Shine the light in there!"

Ol' Slasher was working over Lila, his butt facing us. I could've shot him in the ass.

"Shoot him before he kills her!" Millie Faye said.

But I knew it was too late. Lila and her pups were goners. My eyes watered over again so bad, I couldn't take proper aim. Didn't want to just maim the great hog. Mean as he was, he still deserved a clean kill.

Lila kept whining.

"Hit him with a snowball," I said. "Get him away from her, so's I can get a clean shot."

Millie Faye stuck the flashlight under her arm, wadded up snow and smacked the old hog square on the butt.

The hell hog's grotesque head raised up. Millie Faye whacked him with another snowball. He turned, tusks dripping blood and guts. She hit his snout. Snout trailing entails.

I aimed at a spot between his red eyes. My trigger finger tightened. Hog grunting, red eyes staring at me. Unafraid. Unapologetic. Uncowed.

Lila whimpering.

"Shine the light on Lila," I said.

"I'm afraid." Millie Faye whimpered, too.

"Then shine the light and look away."

She shined the light, and I heard her gasp before she looked away.

I clasped her hand and steadied the light, my rifle following the beam down to a crumpled mess. Lila's body was folded in two. Folded the wrong way. Back broken. One eye gone. Not dangling, just gone, shoved up in its socket.

"Is she still alive?" Millie Faye said.

Lila's chest still moved. Mouth whining in mortal pain.

"Just barely," I said.

"Then what are you waitin' for? Shoot Ol' Slasher and let's get down there and patch her up."

I spotted a long black tube—the pup sac—in that mess of guts. Could see her heart beating, a pump of blood. Ol' Slasher's heart, a massive target.

I aimed, I squeezed.

The shot froze me and Millie Faye.

Ol' Slasher's legs shook.

Lila's whimpering did a hiccup.

Hiccupped again.

Then stopped.

"Oh, God, you killed Lila," Millie Faye said. Blows from little fists bounced about my chest and ribs.

I cast off the rifle in the snow and grabbed her fists.

"Quit hitting me and hit Ol' Slasher with more snowballs. Get his attention whilst I get Lila's pups. Hurry. They ain't got no air to breath."

Millie Faye changed directions immediately. Snowballs flew.

My feet found the top rung of the ladder. I watched Ol' Slasher to see if he saw me. The light glared weak in the pit, and I could barely see Lila's body. I climbed to the bottom rung, held onto the ladder with one hand, leaned over and stuck my other hand in Lila's guts. I felt her warm lungs, her hot liver, and then my hand closed over the pup sac.

Ol' Slasher pivoted. Saw me. Charged.

I darted back up the ladder, my hand slimy with guts and blood. Ol' Slasher hit the ladder and broke it in two. I swayed backwards and tossed the pup sac out of the pit. Millie Faye caught my flailing hand and, summoning the strength of a normal-sized teenager, pulled me to safety.

I didn't waste no time. Grabbed the pup tube and laid it out lengthwise in the snow. Four lumps no bigger'n barn mice filled the slick tubing. I took my Old Granddad pocket knife out and sliced it open. Picked up the first pup. A female. Hairless and black with one pink blotch on the back. Curled in a ball, eyes closed, not breathing. I pried her head up, took my purple handkerchief out and wiped mucus away from her nose and mouth. Clamped my mouth over her little muzzle and blew gently.

She phiffed. Clogged. Blow and suck. Push and draw. Polarity. I gave a mighty inhale. Bits of slimy parts from her nostrils slithered down my throat. I hacked them back up. Spit them out. Then puckered my lips and blew again. Her tiny chest expanded. Handed her to Millie Faye. "Keep blowing while I do the rest of 'em."

I went on with the next one. And the next, and the next. We took turns with all four.

Millie Faye started sobbing. "They ain't none"—blow, blow—"of 'em gonna live, Mo Grady. They weren't ready"—blow, blow—"to be born yet."

I felt warm tears on my cheeks. Maybe just as well. We couldn't raise a pup without a mother. Couldn't keep Aunt Big Bertha or Mama from knowing about it neither.

Millie Faye's breathing weakened. Little pants came from her throat. "I'm tired, Mo Grady. I got to quit. It ain't no use noways."

She lay her forearms on the ground and put her head between them. A mixture of wails and mumbles came from her mouth. "Dead. All dead. Lila and her pups. And for a piece of tusk no bigger'n a turkey turd."

I kept at it, blowing in one tiny nose then another, knowing, too, it weren't no use. Lila and her pups dead, and we still didn't have the tusk tip. Somehow that seemed kinda funny, to me.

Hysterical. A giggle pushed up my throat. I tried to hold it back. But that titter didn't pay no attention. It burst out right in the face of a pup, the first one—the one with the pink blotch on the back.

Another laugh got set to follow, when the pup let out a faraway keen. Her tiny nose sucked air by itself. Tiny paws kicked. Little tail flicked.

Millie Faye heard it, too. Her sobbing and gasping chopped off, and she pushed her face at mine. "She's alive! Let me hold her whilst you work on the others. Maybe they'll wake up, too."

I handed the pink-blotched pup to Millie Faye. She put her chin against the pup's neck. I worked on the others for a few more minutes, then gave up.

I was a farm boy, and knew the little one who wailed against Millie Faye's neck still had a long way to go. But my sister had a blissful look on her face.

I lay the pup's dead littermates down in a row on the snow. "Come on, Millie Faye. Pink needs milk right away or her chances of survival ain't good."

The pup's whines accented our trudge into the barn.

"She's trying to nibble my ear lobe," Millie Faye said, the flashlight zigzagging in her other hand.

"Trying to find her mama's teat," I said.

"Can't we give her some cow or goat milk, Mo Grady?"

"Cow or goat milk isn't good enough. I've tried them on baby squirrels and they died. Something's missing. And we need to find a way to get the milk to go into her mouth."

Inside the barn I stopped at the rabbit cages and studied Cassandra's nest box with what the two-headed preacher called a furry brain.

"Maybe rabbit milk'll be enough," I said.

Cassandra was a young mother, but a good one. Last summer I found a litter of orphaned wild rabbits and brung them to her. She nursed them like her own.

But rabbits and dogs are mortal enemies. Predator and prey. Extreme polarity. Still, the Bible talked about lions laying down with lambs.

"Shine the flashlight on Cassandra, Millie Faye."

The beam brightened the cage. I opened the cage door. My pet doe sniffed my hand. Nudged me for her usual ear scratch.

I scratched Cassandra's ear with one hand whilst my other hand slipped under the brown fur brain, finding the little kits. I counted seven squiggly bodies. Cassandra had eight teats. Room for one more.

My fingers closed around the plumpest bunny, hiding it from Cassandra. I brought it out real quick. "Give me Pink."

Millie Faye put both hands over the tiny pup. Took a step backwards. "Cassandra will kill her."

"I don't think so," I said. "Besides, we ain't got time for a suckling pup. It's either put Pink in the nest with Cassandra or do the merciful thing and break her neck right now."

I wouldn't have, but sometimes you have to overdo it with Millie Faye.

Her eyes filled with tears again.

"Now give it here," I said.

She kissed the puppy's nose. Pink's mouth smacked. Millie Faye handed her to me. I rubbed the baby bunny and some fur from the nest box against the pup. My hands could barely tell the difference between the two. Both were nekked, noses and feet pawing, the pup a tad bigger than the kit.

I cupped them together in my hand and slipped both under the warm, furry mass.

Cassandra watched me, then jumped in the nest and nosed around.

Me and Millie Faye held our breath.

Her head stopped. Big ears twitched. Thumped the box with her powerful hind legs. The squirming brain began bulging in places, baby bunnies recognizing mama and jockeying for a place at the supper table.

"Get Pink out of there, Mo Grady," Millie Faye said. "Cassandra's fixin' to bite her little head off."

I reached for the nest box, but Cassandra quit sniffing and lay down. Lots of ruffling under the fur brain.

Me and Millie Faye both let out a long breath together.

I petted Cassandra's head with one hand, reached in with the other and lifted the fur. Sure enough, there, third teat from the front, left side, Pink suckled away. Little paws pumping, mouth making sucking sounds, tiny tail wagging. Body glowing pink like a wild rose.

"It's a by-God miracle," my sister said.

She collapsed against me. I picked her up and took her over to some straw bales next to the rabbit cages. I sat down and held her in my lap. Rocked her. The flashlight cast a pale light at dark corners. Animals scraped against their stalls. A goat bleated.

"I've got to lay you down, Millie Faye, and then you got to mix more sleeping potion for Ol' Slasher. Settle him down so's I can either find that tusk tip or cut another one."

My wee twin stirred. She straightened up. "Mo Grady, I told you there ain't no more ingredients. But, dear brother, there's mixin' to be done, and I'm the only one can do it."

Millie Faye put her right hand in her coat pocket and pulled out the tusk tip, holding it in front of my eyes. All light in the dark barn concentrated on that tip.

"I sat on it in the pit," she said. "Tried to tell you, but things got out of hand and I plumb forgot."

"I swear, Millie Faye, you …"

"Something else I gotta tell you. You know how we sometimes get in each other's mind? Well, like I told you down in the pit I got into that monster hog's mind. And I think his got into me. And don't give me that doubting look. Only thing I know for certain is he's as bumkiddled about us as we are about him."

CHAPTER 33

Hell Hog and June Bug

She placed the tusk in my hand. Folded my fingers over it. It felt warm. I slid my thumb back and forth on the tip. Wasn't nearly as sharp as it looked when still attached to Ol' Slasher. Dull as a corncob tip. I noticed several nicks and, with my thumbnail, traced a long 'S'-shaped groove down its length. A current traveled up my thumb and arm, across my shoulder into my noggin.

My hand slipped the tip into my overall pocket farthest from my heart. No doubt about it, Mama was right, wild boar tusk fresh from the hog possessed a powerful charge.

I made my way to the barn to the sit-down grinder. It operated like a bicycle, the front wheel being a two-inch thick stone. A pyramid of metal and stone shavings lay under the grinder. I kicked them aside and spread out my purple handkerchief in their place. Pulled out the tusk, sat on the grinder seat and started. The tusk screeched against the grinder stone and sparks flew.

Every animal in the barn broke out in protest, their inner clocks knowing it wasn't 4:00 am yet. Nell the nag neighed. Gweneviere mooed. Jubal Jen grunted. Guineas, in the lower rafters, let out peels of chirps and clapped wings against hard bodies. Archie, the barn owl, landed on a stall beam above my head.

I ground down the tusk to a nubbin. Put it in my pocket. White powder lay piled on my purple handkerchief. I put the dust into a pint jar, filling it to a quarter inch. Plenty enough mixings, I hoped, to cure the craziest of persons.

Millie Faye come'd up, and I handed her the jar.

"I'll follow Mama's recipe exactly," she said, "and then I'll add some red clover honey to make it sweet tasting a'fore I put it in Freeman Joe's bowl of hot oats."

"Good idea." I grabbed a shovel. "Think you can go feed it to Freeman Joe now? I gotta get the two-headed preacher to help me get Ol' Slasher out of the pit."

Millie Faye brushed back her straw hair with her hand. "Sure, I can," she said. "Does Bonker Beckman have blue balls?"

I did a double-take. Where'd she get such a foul mouth?

I woke the two-headed preacher and told him about another digging opportunity, this time to liberate Ol' Slasher from his red-clay confines.

The preacher was so grateful to do his first physical labor in a fortnight, I could've convinced him to toss a cow over the moon.

"Why 'unt you just shoot him and bury him where he lays?" he said in a groggy voice. "Lots of folks he's terrorized in this valley be 'preciative."

"I think that old leathery hide of his is bullet proof," I said. "'Sides, I don't believe what folks say is true—that Ol' Slasher is one of Satan's minions. Jubal Jen's sweet on him. Only other hog in the whole valley big enough to be a proper suitor, and she'd never forgive me."

That seemed to satisfy the preacher. What I didn't tell him was my hog killing days, just like my people killing days, was over. I reckon one each was enough. Killing Starface at the hog shoot, same time Uncle Harm was spittin' on my pecker, sure enough drove something out of my soul, but it wasn't lust for girls. I had a break with prayer solving my problems, and it shoved me toward the goomer camp. The budding yarb doctor in me knew it was a sin to kill my brother and sister critters unless they's a danger to other folks.

Something happened to me down in that pit with Ol' Slasher. That giant beast and me—and Millie Faye—had a destiny that wasn't supposed to end in that pit.

Also, the practical side. What if Mama ever needs another tusk part from a live boar?

"If we dig a chute into the pit, he can come out on his own," I said and shoved a shovel in the preacher's hands. He gripped it and smiled. Fingers ran over the smooth oak handle. His good eye rolled heavenward. His froze eye fixed on me. "I do believe you're right, Mo Grady. A man's got to take a stand. Come on, we've got the Lord's work to do."

"Amen," I said.

He nodded, holding the shovel in front of him like a holy cross of the Crusades. He quick-stepped right out the farmhouse to that hog pit, me following with a lantern and flashlight.

"The chute needs to open out to the woods and ramp down to the pit," I said between pickaxe blows. "We can put a grate at the top end so's we can slow Ol' Slasher down once he knows he can escape. That'll give us time to get out of his way."

The two-headed preacher nodded both heads and commenced makin' dirt fly. He didn't have a whole lot of talent as a soul saver, but I do believe he'd have a good career as a gravedigger. Instead of being on the givin' side of a body, he'd be on the receivin' side.

I left the preacher and ran toward the two-seater outhouse. I'd been holding it back all morning, and it's a wonder I didn't blow the roof off when I finally did let go. Stunk to high yonder, too. I got out of there fast and ran for the barn, flashlight in hand. Took me a while, but I found an old iron gate for the exit chute.

I was a hundred feet from the pit when I heard the two-headed preacher say, "What? Oh, Jesus. Oh shit!" A shovel flew out of the chute like it had wings and up come'd the preacher, good leg and gimp leg chugging like a locomotive, his two heads pistoning up and down. His face, pale as bleached limestone.

Ol' Slasher, snout slung low, ears flat, dirt clods clinging to his tusks, broke through from the pit to the chute, letting out a sharp scream, him not more'n three feet behind that scurrying preacher who stayed a decent lick ahead of the hell hog, no sign of his previous gimp.

Then that old hog stopped, sniffed the air, turned and charged right at me, eyes glowing red cinders. I swung the old gate in front of me and stiff-armed it just as Ol' Slasher hit. Like getting slammed by a Caterpillar tractor with a bucket of concrete.

Tusks rammed through the gate, the sheer force jolting my jaw and rattling my ribcage. His sharp tusk jabbed within inches of my chin. His foul breath scorched my cheeks. Grunts clogged my ears. His front hooves tangled in the frame as he pushed me backwards.

My legs sprung me up and carried my body on top of the manure spreader in one motion.

Ol' Slasher shook free of the gate, stood back and charged the manure spreader. Smacked it till one of the bottom slats cracked and gave way. An axle creaked. The boar backed up and smacked it again. And again. And again.

Each time, the spreader sunk an inch or two. Pretty soon all that'd be between me and the hell hog was rotted slats. My only chance—I had to jump out and outrun him to the barn.

A rifle shot sounded, and the metal spreader wheel pinged a foot from my head.

"Stop shooting!" I yelled.

Ol' Slasher clumped cloven hooves around the manure spreader, making snow and dirt fly, and took off into the woods.

"Did I hit 'em?" Millie Faye said, walking toward me and waving the gun barrel all around.

"Put the gun down," I said. "He's gone."

"That's okay, I haven't got another bullet anyways," she said. "Hey, you don't sound too 'preciative toward a person that just saved your sinnin' hide."

"I don't care whether you got a bullet or not," I said. "Aim it down."

She dropped the barrel. I heard a giggle. One of her too excited giggles. "Boy, I wished I'd a been there, Mo Grady, so's I could've seen the look on the two-headed preacher's face and yours when that old hog come'd out of the pit."

I swung down from the spreader. "You calm down," I said. "We got one more thing to do."

I picked up the flashlight and the lantern and went to the edge of the pit. Millie Faye followed after, giggles bursting out like pickled hiccups.

I picked up the pup tube. Three dead pups lay curled in stiff balls beside each other. I handed it to Millie Faye. She quit giggling.

"Say goodbye," I said, "and we'll throw them down with Lila. Then we'll cover 'em with dirt to keep the scavengers away."

"We won't throw them down anywhere, Mo Grady. They're just babies. We'll walk down the chute and put them with their mama."

"I don't know if you'll want to do that, Millie Faye. That ol' hog ripped up Lila pretty bad. Not something anyone, 'specially a girl with a missin' heart, would want to see, and I ain't going back down in that hole."

"I may be a girl with a missin' heart, but I can see anything you can see," she said. "We'll hold hands."

She hugged the frozen pups to her bosom with one hand and took mine with the other. Millie Faye lay the pups with what was left of their mama. She knelt down. Made me kneel, too.

"Our Father and Mother," she said. "Blessed be thy names. Receive unto ye Lila, a good and faithful dog as there ever was, and her three innocent pups through the Golden Gate of Heaven. Amen."

We looked at each other, then scrambled out.

I shoveled dirt into the pit, but quit when awful goings-on sounded in the bunkhouse. I walked toward the commotion like I had granite weights on my feet, Millie Faye trudging behind.

We saw Freeman Joe flopping around on the bunkhouse floor, face lathered in sweat, mouth leaking pink foam and oats, eyes big and clouded as the snow moon. He fell in the snow on his back, coughing and spewing oats.

"Did you make the potion right?" I asked my sister as we ran to Freeman Joe.

"'Course I did," she said, trailing behind. "The nerve, accusin' me of mixin' up Mama's recipe."

I got to Freeman Joe, ready to leap onto his chest and hold him in place, when he suddenly sat upright. "Wide is the gate," he said, "and broad is the way that leadeth to destruction, and many there be that go in thereat. He casteth out devils through the prince of darkness. Be ye therefore wise as serpents."

Freeman Joe grinned, then he lay back down and fell asleep.

Millie Faye caught up. "What does that donkey shit mean?"

"It means he's still crazy as a goddamn June bug," I said. "And watch that foul mouth of yours."

Crazy or not, I knew Freeman Joe meant me and Ol' Blue Satan and the red Chevrolet. How everything had turned sour ever since I knelt in front of the serpent, praying to Him to stop Uncle Harm. But nothing had worked out right. Except Loveda.

I gulped hard. Did that mean Loveda would lose her shine, too?

All I knew for sure was I had to destroy the red Chevrolet. Cast out that devil before it cast out me.

CHAPTER 34

Puppy Pink and Black Smoke

I woke in the bunkhouse bed to the sound of clunking metal and whistling. A merry tune. Didn't know nobody whistled like that.

Freeman Joe stood, stoking the fire. I must of made a noise 'cause he stopped whistling. "Why there you be, Mo Grady," his voice chipper as a song sparrow in spring time. "I been waitin' for you to wake up. There's chores to be done. Songs to be sung." He wagged a finger at me, but there was no real reprimand behind it.

I swung my feet off the bed. "I been waitin' for you to get back," I said.

My step daddy cupped his chin in a big hand. "Well, it does feel like I been gone a spell, but darned if I can remember where I went."

"It don't matter," I said. "What matters is you're back."

I hardly recognized Freeman Joe. He looked square at me, instead of through me. He'd shaved himself and scrubbed his face, cheeks pink and soft. Combed his wild hair. His shoulder and arm muscles rippled with energy against a shirt free of bird shit.

"I stepped out to greet the day, Mo Grady," he said, "and it 'peers to me there's a hole needs fillin' out there near the woods. If that's true, I'd sure admire to fill it. My muscles feel tight and need stretching."

Freeman Joe looked ready for work. Maybe he needed grounding before he took off, full of uncontrollable sanity for his court hearing later today in New Dreadford.

"You go ahead," I said, "I've got other chores. Then, I'll come help you. I got a lot of things to tell you."

A soft snore came from the bed. Millie Faye lay curled in a ball, fast asleep.

I followed Freeman Joe outside.

Morning came like an egg cracked open on a frypan—sun sizzling on the snow. The first thaw in months was upon the land. Every roof in the barnyard dripped.

Somebody, probably my step daddy, had let the stock out, and chickens clucked on any surface supporting them. Jack, the mule, stood in melting snow, one ear sticking straight up, the other flat. Jubal Jen munched corn as if nothing had happened the night before.

I went in the house and checked on the two-headed preacher. He, like Millie Faye, was fast asleep.

A car going by on the road reminded me I had to hurry. Get Freeman Joe ready before the two-headed preacher woke up or, worse yet, Aunt Big Bertha came home from fetching the bumper in New Dreadford. I didn't know why it took all night. Maybe she had to wait for it to get put back on. And while she waited, she'd gone to one of those beauty parlors, like Mama said, where ugly folks go in and beautiful people come out. Now, considering Aunt Big Bertha, that would be some powerful conjury.

Millie Faye had put the remainder of the Sanity Potion in a jar and sat it in the medicine cupboard. "Never can tell when we might need it again," she said.

I went out to the barn and stopped in front of Cassandra's cage. Reached my hand into the furry brain until I found the pup. I picked her up and touched her little nose to mine and tickled her plump belly. She wiggled and squealed. I think she knew my scent. I sure knew hers. Milky sweet and puppy pink and the right kind of new. Not like the red Chevrolet a'tall. Something real and pure.

I put her back, grabbed a shovel and joined Freeman Joe at the pit. Crows and red birds pecked in the snow. He stopped between digs and threw handfuls of ground corn from his pockets to the birds. Instead of landing on him like he was a scarecrow, they kept a respectful distance.

Birds know crazy from sane.

Freeman Joe met me with a grin wide as a four-row cultivator. "I wonder, Mo Grady, could you go in the house and get Mildred Garnet and bring her out here to enjoy this grand day?"

"Mama isn't here." I filled him in, whilst we shoveled, with the story of Uncle Harm's amputation and death, then his almost funeral, then Mama gettin' hauled off to the Stonecrop County jail, then Aunt Big Bertha's plot to take over the farm, then Mama's Sanity Potion recipe, then Millie Faye and me getting Ol' Slasher's tusk, then Lila and Pink and then the big boar's escape. Told him the whole story, I did.

'Course, I left out my low-down sinnin' part and coveting the red Chevrolet. I don't know how much he understood, but somewhere along the way, a frown plowed over his cultivator smile.

Freeman Joe leaned on his shovel a full five minutes, eyes closed, pink cheeks going pale. I feared the haunts had taken him over again.

He shook his shaggy head. "We still got the black Ford?"

"It's gassed up and ready to roll," I said.

Freeman Joe left the shovel standing straight up. Headed for the car, me tailing behind. He scraped snow off the hood and windshield. Climbed behind the steering wheel. That drafty old Ford started right up, blowing a black carbon cloud out the tailpipe building up ever since the red Chevrolet rolled up in front of the farmhouse.

He leaned his shaven face out the window. "Mo Grady, I'm going to see your mama and get this all straightened out. You're a good boy. Whilst I'm gone you look after the girls and the farm." He backed out of the driveway.

The Ford coughed and belched black smoke as it disappeared 'round the bend. Occurred to me I'd never seen Freeman Joe drive before.

I didn't know how long the Sanity Potion would last. Mama didn't say nothin' about that. Didn't want to think about Freeman Joe talking in tongues halfway through the proceedings. Foaming at the mouth before the judge. Doing his swallow dance in front of a jury of his peers.

Was there such a thing as a jury of Freeman Joe's peers? He seemed like one of a kind to me.

CHAPTER 35

Booger-Dog Butt and Spider Web Cracks

Aunt Big Bertha drove up the driveway in the bran'-spankin'-new, red Chevrolet. Only there wasn't much bran'-spankin'-new about it anymore. No glow a'tall. Even the red paint had a dull edge. Little dings peppered the hood and roof. The bumper was back on, but crooked.

My step aunt parked next to the Studebaker by the farmhouse. I moved closer. A coffin stuck out the trunk. Tied down with rope. Same coffin I'd last seen Uncle Harm occupying, but now nailed shut.

I reckoned Aunt Big Bertha claimed Uncle Harm's body after the autopsy, which accounted for her being away so long—no doubt, now, fixin' on burying him.

Seeing his coffin and the red Chevrolet together made me fidget. The broken-egg sun cast dirty yellow shadows, and I couldn't tell where the car began and the pine coffin left off.

My step aunt, wearing a new wig the color of red Easter egg dye, spilled out of the car. "Where's the Ford?"

"Freeman Joe took it," I said, "to go see my mama."

She barked a laugh. "Well, if he makes it to New Dreadford, I sure hope he shows up in court this afternoon. The judge'll take one look at him and turn the farm and car over to me lock, stock and barrel. And the first thing I'm gonna do is have that human flesh-eating hog of yours taken down in the bog and shot. Then I'm kickin' your booger-dog butt and your retarded sister and all your other sisters off this place."

A snowball sailed past my head. A dead-on hit on the new wig, knocking it sideways. Millie Faye didn't have as strong a pitching arm as I did, but she was just as accurate—a female Bob Feller, pint-sized. She was liable to throw anything that wasn't nailed down, and you can't nail down snow.

Her voice behind me caught up fast. "I ain't retarded. Just puny. And who'd wanna stay on this place with the likes of you anyways." She marched right up to Aunt Big Bertha before I could stop her. "You're crazier'n a goddamned old coot in a pint jar of possum piss, and ..."

Aunt Big Bertha lashed out and slapped my midget sister. Shut off Millie Faye's foul mouth in mid-cuss. The slap sounded like a backfire from the old Ford, delivered with such force it exploded my sister's black wig into smoke and dust and pieces. All the thrashing and burning and thumping that wig took, I thought it was well nigh indestructible.

My puny twin plunked down on her butt.

A rooster crowed from the barnyard. Crows flew in and landed on a mulberry limb. Gossiping and watching.

"Had that coming, you little shit," Aunt Big Bertha said. "I sure ain't gonna miss your shriveled carcass when you're gone."

My step aunt clinched her hands in fists, hair cockeyed. She looked at me with knotted red eyes, and I froze. Something different about Aunt Big Bertha—a hardness that wasn't there last time I'd seen her. Cheeks flinty and dry like Freeman Joe's before the sanity elixir.

"As for you, you thievin' bastard," she spit as she spoke, "I'm putting these car keys on a chain 'round my neck. Just see if you can steal it now."

She marched right up to me, swerved and threw an elbow into my shoulder that near to knocked me flat. I thought about tackling her backside as she strode toward the house, but stopped to check Millie Faye.

Millie Faye usually popped right back up when she got knocked down. Didn't just sit there feeling sorry for herself, with her chin on her chest, shoulders all droopy.

"Hey," I said, "come on, get up. You're not gonna let a little slap from ol' Halloween head get you down, are you?"

Millie Faye didn't look up. In the egg-yolk light her little body near to dissolved in white fluff. Not rigid with defiance. No foul mouth spewing daggers meant one thing: she was going into one of her playing possum acts. She lay over backwards, arms clutching her chest, face so white it matched the snow.

Trouble with people playing possum is some get so carried away, they convince themselves they're dead, and their bodies don't know the difference.

I picked up Millie Faye in my arms, carried her into the bunkhouse and laid her on the bed. Tucked her in up to her toothpick neck. Her breath hardly enough to flutter a pin feather, her pulse faint as a sparrow's.

Millie Faye had gone away to one of them deep comas Doc Abernathy warned us about.

Doc told Mama to bring Millie Faye to his house if we couldn't wake her up. What's that word he used … 'fatal'? Yes, fatal—a fatal coma.

I recalled Doc saying to keep her warm. I carried her in the house and put her to bed. I stoked the stove and climbed into bed beside her. Wrapped her in my arms. I've squeezed scarecrows who had more life in 'em. I lay my ear on her chest, listening for her heartbeat. Back in the distance, I heard it.

I reckoned I needed the red Chevrolet again so's I could get her to Doc's house in Scuttles Grunt quick. But first had to get the key from around Aunt Big Bertha's fat neck.

The wind flipped the metal rooster atop the barn so fast it let out one long squeak.

Through the window, I saw the two-headed preacher, leaning into the wind, carrying a bucket of slop toward the barn. He'd perked up quite a bit since digging Ol' Slasher's pit, and darned if it didn't look like his twin head hadn't shrunk a mite more.

Maybe the cure for snakebite didn't lay in prayer but in action.

And just maybe I could interest the preacher in action of a different sort.

Last year the grain grinder backfired right next to two mating goats. They didn't even flinch. I reckoned humans and goats were alike.

I found Reverend Waywater standing in front of the rabbit cages.

"There's a pup in that rabbit nest," I pointed. "Needs blessing."

"No," the preacher's voice grew clearer, "no rabbit could welp a pup. Such a thing cannot happen."

I open the cage door, slipped my hand under the squirming fur and took out the pup. "Here," I handed her to the preacher, "her name's Pink."

The preacher took the pup. "Danged," he said. He turned her all around, checking for signs of rabbitness. "I can bless animals same as humans, so I hereby bless this hound in the name of the Father, the Son and the Holy Ghost."

He handed me the blessed pup. Our hands sparked when they touched. Made us both jump and the pup squeal. Made me wonder about the power of blessings. Wondered if a sinner boy like me could still get saved, even after taking up with Ol' Blue Satan.

I put the pup back in the cage, much to Cassandra's comfort.

Walter, my buck rabbit, watched Cassandra through the wire separating them. "I reckon Walter's ready to mate again," I said. "He used to not be able to mount Cassandra, but now he wants to all the time. I think it's that new feed I'm giving him."

The preacher's eyes grew. "I admire that. Whatever it is, I could sure use some."

"I might be able to help you out," I said.

"Well, thanks, boy, but no thanks. Alfalfa pellets ain't gonna cure what ails me."

"How about Mama's love potion with a pinch of a wild boar's tusk?" I said, knowing I still had a nubbin in my pocket. "Mama says her potion's guaranteed to make a man more manly. I reckon adding wild boar's tusk would give it even more of a kick."

"That's a fine idea, boy, but the devil himself couldn't get one of Ol' Slasher's tusks."

"I gave Ol' Slasher a sleeping potion when he was in the pit. Worked long enough to cut off this," I said, holding out the nubbin.

"You are a pure scourge and a delight, Mo Grady. I'd sure admire to have some of that potion. Had any money, I'd pay you for it."

"How about a trade? I need to take Millie Faye in the red Chevrolet to Doc Abernathy's."

He pondered a second. "I dunno, boy. Bertha Sue'd have my hide."

"I'm just askin' to borrow it," I said. "When you go in to see, ah, your wife, all's you got to do is take the key from around her neck and lay it down where I can get to it. Be back in a jiff. And Aunt Big, ah, Aunt Bertha Sue won't ever know we're in cahoots."

"You put it like that, I reckon we got a deal." He rubbed his hands together. "Now where's that love potion?"

"Mama keeps it in the kitchen on the top shelf above her other conjury ingredients."

"Come to think of it, I did see it there." His Cyclops eye fixed on me. "Just above the jar of Destroying Angel mushrooms."

"That's it. Now, go fetch it and meet me back here."

By the time I finished grinding the nubbin, the two-headed preacher showed up with Mama's love potion. I took the jar, popped the lid, added water and stirred in the last of Ol' Slasher's tusk powder.

Reverend Waywater grabbed the jar and glugged it right down. His throat rippled, and gooey chunks ran down the sides of his mouth. He wiped his face with a blue handkerchief and let out a long belch. "How long you reckon it'll take to work?"

His hump on his hump developed a twitch. Otherwise, he didn't move a nose hair.

"Don't know. Why don't you lie down on that bale of hay whilst I tend to the …"

Before I could even finish, the preacher shot out the barn door like a spring-loaded gate hinge. Headed straight for the house, stepping high, like a man going into battle with all his guns fit and functioning.

I climbed into the loft, found my magic magnet and Uncle Harm's leg bones. My magnet's polarity seemed out of whack. The bones, which I'd wrapped in a rag, smelled like rancid smokehouse meat.

I got a hammer and crow-bar, and, carrying Uncle Harm's wrapped leg, snuck out the back door to the red Chevrolet. I wedged in the crow-bar under the coffin lid and tapped with the hammer. Then wrenched.

The lid lifted up and a smell as ripe as autumn compost collided with my nostrils. My guts somersaulted. I unwrapped the severed bone and pushed it into the coffin. Almost put the magic magnet in, too, but it stuck fast to my hand. Hummed in my palm. Didn't want to go, I reckoned, into the black abyss where the monster was. I hammered back down the lid. Opened the car's rear door and put the magnet in the ashtray in a neutral position, lest it suck out any more souls.

I pulled out my Old Granddad pocket knife and stabbed the Studebaker's passenger side tires. The puncture wounds yowled like the call of coyotes in heat. I then walked around the side of the house. Placed my ear against the clapboard siding of Mama and Freeman Joe's bedroom. Springs a'springing and groans and grunts inside. Peeked through the window. Saw the two-headed preacher and Aunt Big Bertha going at it like two goats in bed. My step aunt's face lay buried in a pillow, her baldhead glistening whilst the preacher, his humps a'humpin' and his overalls around his hips, jammed smack against his wife's pumpkin butt, holding onto her hips.

The car keys lay on an end table next to the bed. I didn't know nothing about humans mating, but I knew most farm animals didn't take long. I crept into the house and crawled into the bedroom whilst Aunt Big Bertha screamed, "Ram the fear of God in me. Dear Lord, I'm comin' home." Just as she switched to "The Lord's armies are coming to carry me to Heaven," I reached out and snatched the keys.

The two-headed preacher yelled, "Oh, sweet Jesus, don't fail me now."

Backing out of the room on all fours, I reached the living room, stood up and slid out the front door. My feet bolted for the bunkhouse. I put on my skate-feet, bundled up Millie Faye in blankets and carried her to the red Chevrolet. Placed her in the front seat so's I could watch her.

I put the key in the ignition and turned. The engine growled over and over. "Come on, start!" I said.

Aunt Big Bertha's red face stared out the bedroom window. I turned the key. Engine growled again. "Please start!" I twisted the key.

The front door flew open and here come'd Aunt Big Bertha down the steps a'flying, a bald-headed, nekked cow with udders the size of ripe muskmelons, a rolling pin in her right hand.

Ol' Slasher aside, I'd never seen anything so frightening or inspiring in my life.

My foot tromped the gas pedal, and I turned the starter again. It chugga-chugged, chugga-chugged and caught. Aunt Big Bertha banged on the hood with the rolling pin. "Get your coon-dog ass out the car. I'm gonna give you the beating of your life."

I popped the clutch. Wheels spun and caught. Aunt Big Bertha clung on. Melon breasts squashed against the window. We lunged forward. To keep from running into the bunkhouse, I cut over into the yard, my step aunt pounding and hollering, the inside of the car sounded like a bass drum.

If Millie Faye could wake up, she would've. We dodged trees and shrubs, heading for the ditch between the yard and the road. I tried not to look at Aunt Big Tit's big tits and hairy crotch. I hit the ditch and the car bounced a foot in the air. Reached a hand over to steady Millie Faye. The car came down crossways in the road. I straightened 'er out and took off.

Out the side of my eye, I saw Aunt Big Bertha had bumped off. In the rearview mirror there she was sitting in the middle of the road, legs spread eagle, black bush against white snow. I couldn't take my eyes away. Ran into a shallow ditch again.

Straining the car out of the ditch, a hubcap went flying and sailed out into the woods. It banged off a tree. I liked those hubcaps, so shiny and round. Knew I should keep driving. Knew the red Chevrolet weren't new anymore, and I needed to get far away from it. But that hubcap pulled at me like my magic magnet set on suck. And I was far enough away from Aunt Big Bertha, so I stopped.

I spotted the hubcap gleaming in the snow. Pushed the door open and dashed to the hubcap. I lifted it, paused a second to admire its round beauty and steel toughness. It occurred to me, thrown flatways with some spin on it, it'd make a formidable weapon.

A great beast exploded through the trees. It bore down on me, full of grunt and tusk and hate.

CHAPTER 36

Boiled Cabbage and Baldhead

I flicked my wrist and sailed that steel hubcap as hard as I could at Ol' Slasher. Smacked him right in the snout and slowed him down enough so's I could jump up and grab a tree limb. I did a quick half back flip while Ol' Slasher passed under me, his good tusk shaving the blocks of my right skate. His hide smelled of boiled cabbage and rotted cornhusks.

My half flip completed, I let go and nailed the landing. I lit out on for the red Chevrolet.

Ol' Slasher bellowed. I felt his breath scorching my back in no time flat. He was so close, I didn't have time to open the car door. I leapt and slid over the hood. Landed on my head on the other side in a snowdrift.

Even stuffed with snow, my ears clanged as tusks smacked into metal.

The car bucked up and down like the two-headed preacher and Aunt Big Bertha in bed.

I opened the passenger side door, slammed it shut, scrambled over Millie Faye's fetal body, then scooted under the steering wheel. Something jabbed my left thigh. I reached down and wrapped my fingers around Ol' Slasher's uncut tusk, gone plumb through the driver's side door. Stuck solid.

I peeked out the window. The hog's head hugged the metal panel, both tusks buried, his huge nose squashed against the side, breath ragged. Small, beady eyes looked up at me, a pencil-length away, with all the beastly loathing in the universe.

I reckoned I wouldn't be going anywhere with 1000 pounds of stinking hog attached. I shifted away from the door and kicked them tusks with my skate-feet. Wouldn't budge.

I heard a yell through the passenger side window. "You thievin' sonsabitch, I'm gonna beat your ass bloody!"

I looked over past Millie Faye and here come'd Aunt Big Bertha propelling through a foot of snow across the Brockman's 60-acre stubbled cornfield. She still waved her rolling pin but had put on boots and overalls. Must've seen me stop—saw an opportunity, thinking I had car trouble.

And so I did—but I guess she couldn't see Ol' Slasher, wedged as he was on the other side of the car.

Steam shot from her billiard ball head, and she swung the rolling pin like it was bound for breaking all the bones in my body.

Stuck hog in the door or not, I had to get out of there. I put the car in gear, took off slow. The door creaked.

Ol' Slasher's grunts turned into ughs. The tusk tip prodded my hip. Sound of big cloven hooves doing a fast side step. The car steered hard to the left. I struggled, using both hands to keep us on the road.

Aunt Big Bertha cleared the barbed-wire fence in a leap, grabbed a'hold of the back bumper to the right of Uncle Harm's coffin and banged at the trunk.

The car lugged down. I increased speed.

Hog ughs sped up whilst shouting and trunk-pounding did likewise. Cloven hooves no longer danced but dragged. The stubby tusk let loose and the sharp tusk started spinning. A whumping noise sounded, 50-pound feed sacks unloading from a dump truck.

A quick glance revealed Ol' Slasher tumbling over and over like the grinder wheel that turned his tusk tip to powder.

A 1000-pound hog, a 300-pound coffin, and a 250-pound club-swinging crazy woman rolled down the road, tires nearly flat, the red Chevrolet practically running on rims.

My foot tromped the gas pedal. For a brief moment I thought the car might stall, but the wheels surged. The tusk ripped out the door and scraped past the rear fender. Aunt Big Bertha disappeared from the mirror. The car without the extra weight leapt forward.

I kept the gas pedal down for a good hundred yards, then stopped and checked the mirror. Did a double-take. Aunt Big Bertha sat facing me in the middle of the road like before but now clothed. Beside her lay Ol' Slasher, both dazed. Looked almost intimate, those two did, like star-crossed lovers.

I waited, wanting to see how it played out. Should I go back and warn Aunt Big Bertha? Or, fair is fair, warn Ol' Slasher?

My step aunt shook her baldhead and staggered to her feet. Ol' Slasher stirred, his hind legs rose, front legs still bent at the knees, like he was prayin' to a pagan pig god. He fell over. Tried the whole routine again. Made it up on all fours. Started lurching around and brushed up against Aunt Big Bertha.

They backed apart a few feet and had themselves a Hatfield and McCoy stare down. No doubt in my mind, both saw the scariest thing either one of 'em had ever seen.

Aunt Big Bertha blinked first. She backed away slow, her head turning this way and that, searching the ditches. She angled over and picked up her car-pounding club. Kept backing. Backed her butt up against the barbed-wire fence. Didn't seem to faze her one bit.

Ol' Slasher steadied, faced Aunt Big Bertha, pawed the ground and charged.

Aunt Big Bertha threw her club over the fence, grabbed a'hold of a fence post and sprang over that barbed-wire like a spring lamb over a bull thistle. She did a header in the snow. She propped up and took off running, slushy snow a'flying.

I reckon Ol' Slasher'd had arguments with barbed-wire before. Instead of hitting the fence head on, he found a couple loose strands and walked between them as dainty as a ballerina.

He gave chase and probably would've caught his prey but for the snow—his lean, short legs not near as efficient at plowing as Aunt Big Bertha's fat, long ones.

I lost them in a swirl of fading grunts, snow and curses.

How I wished Millie Faye could've seen that hog and human scramble. We'd a had enough merry memories to last her short lifetime.

As it was, her puny body lay curled up as laugh-less and nigh as lifeless as her Raggedy Ann doll.

CHAPTER 37

Sweet Decay and Sycamores

Cold air blew through the tusk hole in the driver's side door. The door wouldn't open so's I shoved it with my shoulder. Metal grated, and the door swung free. I got out and inspected the damage. Hinges bent out of alignment. Paint rubbed off. A raw silver crease ran from the door to back bumper. Rolling pin dents on the trunk, roof and hood. I admired my step aunt's strength. I gave the coffin a once over. The trunk, tied down over the coffin, bit into the soft pine, but other than that, the coffin suffered nary a scratch.

An east breeze blew me a whiff of sickly-sweet decay. Uncle Harm needed to be in the ground and the sooner the better. But first order of business was Millie Faye. I'd already passed the Brockman's farm. Could've called Doc Abernathy from there. But, at this point, wasn't about to turn back. I decided to stop at the Johnson's.

Course, if Loveda was there, too, I wouldn't be a bit disappointed.

The sun broke through a cloud, catching the limestone cliffs of Luella's Leap. They glowed bright—a beacon in a storm. But the leafless trees around them looked like gray and white skeletons. The Blue Bog misted over in a thick, gunmetal blue below the cliffs. Ol' Blue Satan and all his minions, biding their time there, waiting to poison young sinners. Even from a distance, I sensed his power growing, getting stronger, summoning me. I knew the only way I'd ever settle up with him would come by a sacrifice.

I got back into the Chevrolet, lifted the door and slammed as hard as I could to get it to latch.

Millie Faye moaned. First sound I'd heard from her since the big slap. Her lips were light blue and her face, a yellow duck egg, 'cept for the purple bruise on her left jaw. Neared to cover half her face.

I turned down the Johnson's driveway. I'd no sooner cut the engine in front of their farmhouse than Loveda flew out the door. Her strawberry hair flowed behind, face pink as peaches fresh-picked from the tree. I rolled down the window.

She skidded up against the car, stuck her arms through and gave my neck a hug. My nose buried in hair, drowning in lilac shampoo. She whispered and tugged on my blue scarf, "Mother and grandmother and your sisters have gone to town. Let's go for a ride."

Words I'd dreamt about hearing from Loveda's lips. My toes sprung feathers. Tickled me up through my scrotum. I wanted to do the swallow dance with her.

She let go, stepped back and frowned. "Hey, you got a hole in your door."

Millie Faye moaned again.

"I have to call Doc Abernathy," I said. "Have him take care of Millie Faye."

Loveda looked past me. "What's wrong with her?"

"She's having her Number 4 petrified mummy fit," I said, "fixin' to go into Number 5, which is bein' dead."

Loveda didn't hesitate. "The phone's on the wall inside the front door. I'll sit with her."

A heatwave swept my body as I entered the farmhouse. I unwound my blue scarf from around my neck and dropped it. Coiled like a snake by my skate-feet. Ol' Blue Satan licked my foot. I kicked at my scarf.

Had to focus. I knew Doc's number by heart. He answered on the seventh ring, and I could almost smell the stink of Four Roses through the phone.

"Doc, this is Mo Grady Witt. Millie Faye's on the verge of a Number 5 fatal fit."

"Bring her in, and hurry," his voice slurred. "But, boy, I ... I wouldn't be surprised if she dies on the way here."

I had a catch in my throat, couldn't talk.

"Your poor mother," Doc continued. "Hard to believe she would kill Harman Cornelius the way she did."

"You's the one told her his legs needed amputating, then passed out on your sodden ass before you could do it."

"Don't you get smart mouth with me, boy, the one that pulled you bloody and bawlin' from your mother's loins. I'm not talking about the amputation, I'm talking about the poison. His liver was hard and mis-shapen as a crushed carburetor. Your uncle was poisoned with mush-rooms. Destroying Angel. And your Mama's the only one in Sulphur Lick Valley has access to those mushrooms in wintertime. If I was you, I'd figure out a way to make peace with your Aunt Bertha Sue 'cause I suspect your mother's gonna be in jail a long time."

I hung up. Leaned my head against the phone, letting Doc's words sink in. My head buzzed. I couldn't believe Mama had poisoned Uncle Harm. No way. But if not Mama, who? My older sisters? No way.

Millie Faye had her butterfly panties backwards and a broken arm. Aunt Big Bertha craved the car and farm. 'Sides me, only two other folks was around then—Freeman Joe and the two-headed preacher, one down with the crazies and the other down with snakebite. Neither had a reason to kill Uncle Harm. Maybe Mama had the best reason of all: to possess the only real home we've ever had.

Course, I had a reason, too. But I didn't poison him, which meant I didn't murder him. Which meant my magnet didn't suck out his soul. Which meant I wasn't beholden to Ol' Blue Satan after all.

My knees sagged against the wall. My head near to popped.

I wanted my mama. I would go see her in New Dreadford and find Millie Faye another doctor. A sober one. One that didn't know she was fixin' to die.

I went back outside. Loveda had moved Millie Faye into the back seat where my sister could lay prone, tucked in with blankets. Loveda scooted over to the middle of the front seat when I took the driver's seat, and clasped my arm. "Come on, Mr. Mo Grady Witt, let's get on down the road. Get your sister to the doctor."

I didn't question her coming. My hands and feet took over, backed us around, and away me and Loveda went, just like in my dream—me driving down the road in my red Chevrolet.

The perfect girl and the not-so-perfect car. Perfectly imperfect in every way. 'Cause of recent events, this ol' car was near to ready for Bonker Beckman's Wrecking Yard. And, out of Ol' Blue Satan's clutches now, I didn't care.

But the girl was different. I glanced at her beside me. Vowed never to let anything happen to her.

Just then the car shimmied as we rounded a sharp curve. Melting snow presented a skating rink under the tires, and damned if I didn't hear Uncle Harm and his skeleton leg rolling about.

Loveda turned around to look. "What's in the box back there that's setting up such a clatter? Sure does stink."

"A coffin. With Uncle Harm in it," I said, shifting gears until they ground into place.

Loveda didn't exactly scoot over to the passenger door. She transferred over there in a split second. My arm felt nekked where her touch left off.

"You mean you carried me off in a car with a dead body?" Her voice sounded like it came from the inside of an outhouse.

"Seems to me you jumped in the car without me having the opportunity to say yay or nay."

I steered us ahead on the straight stretch of Scuttles Grunt Road between Turkey Creek Bridge and Jay Creek Bridge, and the sun caught a glint of metal from another car moving up ahead.

"Turn around and take me home, or stop the car and let me out right here," Loveda said. "I ain't going another foot in the same car as a dead body. I should've known better than to expect bog trash to have any manners or respect."

I stopped. The car up ahead, about a small cornfield away, stopped too. Stopped right before the wood sign that read:

LUELLA'S LEAP. TURN BACK! DANJERUS ROAD!

A hand-carved blue arrow, nailed below, pointed toward Bonker Beckman's Bog. No recent car tracks led down that road and probably for good reason.

I recognized the car—the Postlewaite's black '49 Dodge coupe. The two chicken-fornicating brothers sat inside and an enormous red head of hair loomed behind the steering wheel. Aunt Big Bertha hopped out and shouldered a double barrel shotgun at us.

"Duck!" I shouted and took my own advice.

Aunt Big Bertha let loose with both barrels. Bird shot pinged the hood, beheaded the eagle hood ornament and peppered the windshield. Too far away to break the glass. I peeked over the dash. The Postlewaite brothers hightailed it out of that Dodge and ran back up the road the other way.

Aunt Big Bertha walked toward us with the shotgun broken open, smoke coming out of the breach, reaching in the pocket of her overalls for shells. Her face fixed dark and stricken like a crazy maker.

That's when I knew my step aunt had totally snapped.

Loveda gripped the dash, her face gray and scruffy as the top of a schoolhouse desk. Her voice stuttered, "It appears… it appears there's a large lady in the road shooting at us, Mo Grady. Do something."

I knew I couldn't outrun Aunt Big Bertha driving in reverse. And there wasn't enough room to turn around. Only one option left. My hand rammed the gearshift into low and headed straight for her.

Whilst she reloaded, I kept my aim steady. I was as close as a coffin's length away when she glanced up and saw the red Chevrolet. She jumped aside and disappeared in a snow bank as I sped by.

I tromped the brakes. Came within a tusk tip of hitting the Dodge blocking the road.

Loveda spotted Aunt Big Bertha out the back window. "My God, she's comin' kill us all! Quick! Get us the fuck out of here!"

My ears stung from her unrefined mouth. My skate-feet worked the clutch and gas pedal as I steered in the direction of Luella's Leap.

A shotgun blast ticked the back of the car and Uncle Harm's coffin. A thousand more little dings in the red Chevrolet. I saw Aunt Big

Bertha in the rearview mirror, standing in the road, shaking the gun, her volcano hair canted sideways.

We plunged down the road toward the Blue Bog. Giant willows and sycamores came at us. I peered at the murky swamp through a windshield pockmarked with buckshot.

"Grandmother says there's all kinds of perverts and wild animals out in this swamp," Loveda said.

I nodded, gripping the steering wheel firmer, heading us straight into the rotten heart of Ol' Slasher territory.

CHAPTER 38

Silk Panties and Strawberry Curls

We entered the Blue Bog. Ice crackled as the wheels sloshed through deep puddles. Snow plopped and plunked around us. Giant tree limbs clawed the roof and turned the road ahead into more of a trail. Fallen branches beat the undercarriage until bigger branches scraped them off.

I saw a large furry streak cross the road ahead. And then another.

"What was that?" Loveda scooted next to me. Her skirt came up to her knees.

My throat got a crossways lump.

She brushed hair out of her eyes. "You didn't answer me. What the hell were those things?"

"Wild dogs." My hands clenched white, welded to the steering wheel. I thought of Lila lying dead in the cold ground, and Pink, alive and sucking at Cassandra's teat.

Loveda pulled her skirt down. I felt her eyes on me. "Poor things," she said. "I bet they're hungry. Too bad we don't have any food to throw 'em. It'd be the Christian thing to do." She fidgeted. "All the excitement, Mo Grady, I have to go to the bathroom."

"What?"

"You really are backwoodsy," she said. "It means I have to pee."

Soon as she said it, I did, too. My bladder felt about as big as a corn silo.

"Okay," I said, "I'm gonna find a clear spot and stop, and then you can hop out and go on your side of the car, and I'll go on mine. When we stop, don't tarry."

"Don't worry. I won't."

I drove through iced potholes another hundred yards and stopped at a high dry spot no bigger'n a tool shed.

"Okay, here we go," I said.

I shouldered open my caved-in door. Creaked somethin' awful. I scanned the deep woods on my side, fished for my pecker and got it out just in time to squirt a yellow stream five feet in front of me. The snow hissed where I pissed. I aimed at a shattered birch stump to dampen the sound and listened for Loveda's tinkle.

Didn't hear a thing. Not a tinkle, not a door opening.

"You already done, you'd better hop in the car," I said.

Nothing.

I cut off my piss in mid-stream, stuffed my pecker in my pants and ran around the car.

No Loveda. Only melting tracks leading into the Blue Bog.

What is it with girls? Whether they're from the city or country, they can't piss or poop in the woods proper.

I found her squatting behind a big sycamore tree, blue ground fog covering her from the waist down. Too late for me to backtrack—no way she could not see me. I figured she'd rip me up one side and down the other with her uppity city voice, but she didn't even look my way. Her face, dappled by sun and shadow, lit up like a white dove on the chopping block.

"Mo Grady, I'm afraid to move. He stopped growling when he heard you."

One Ear, the wild dog pack leader, crouched behind a spiny shrub not six feet from Loveda. Leaner and meaner than the last time I saw him. His eyes, like sunken lead, swept over to me. A flicker of recognition.

The soft flesh behind my knees congealed. I stooped for a stick. Nothing but broken branches. I picked up one anyway. I walked, rotten club in hand, in front of Loveda. Three other dogs appeared out of the fog. Scarbelly and Short Tail still part of the pack, and a newcomer—a rat-furred collie.

"Stand up," I said to Loveda. Hands grabbed my coat and pulled up. She pressed her front against my back. Her body trembled.

"We're gonna back toward the car. You first."

"My panties are still around my ankles."

"Leave 'em."

"These are new silk pink panties. Mama would kill me if I lost 'em."

"Your Mama'd have to get in line. These dogs are first," I said. "Okay, on the count of three then, pull 'em up and run. When you get in the car, stay put. Take care of Millie Faye. Someone'll come and find you."

One Ear, flanked by his pack, growled and moved forward. His good ear flattened against his head and slaver dripped from bared fangs. The pack moved with him.

"Wait! What'll happen to you?"

"I'll run in the other direction, lead them away from you."

"You won't have a chance by yourself." Loveda stepped beside me, stooped down and got a rotten stick of her own. Shook it at the beasts.

One Ear gave a signal deep in his belly and three dogs attacked at once. One Ear, like a general, stayed back, biding his time.

My stick broke on Scarbelly's nose.

He yelped and backed off.

Loveda yelped, too. Short Tail pulled on her coat collar and the rat-furred collie on her arm. She skidded down on her knees.

I turned and stabbed Short Tail in the ribs with my splintered stub. He let go of Loveda but grabbed my wrist hard. My thick winter coat kept my bones from breaking. I twisted to face One Ear, but Short Tail's vice-grip jaws held me tight.

The collie pushed Loveda down on all fours. I scrunched my neck, waiting for One Ear's throat-ripping pounce.

His paws smacked my back. Knocked me over the collie and Loveda.

I turned over, ready to give it my last shot.

The forest rumbled, and the dogs froze.

Something big and fast came through the bog.

"A car!" Loveda lay with her red curls in peat moss. Her voice changed in an instant. "What if it's the lady with the shotgun?"

I knew the dogs wouldn't have stopped for a car. Cars couldn't get off the road. This was more like a locomotive sent from Ol' Blue Satan hisself.

Scarbelly whined and backed up. One Ear growled, cocking his ear. Growl gave way to the signal to flee.

His order came too late.

Ol' Slasher crashed out of the blue mist at full tilt, magnificent to behold. He caught Short Tail broadside with his tusks. Ripped his powerful head upwards. The hound howled his last.

Ol' Slasher, carrying the dog impaled on his tusks, galloped right over us. One hoof stepped so close to my crotch, felt like my scrotum retreated clear up to my collarbone. His belly scraped my face, sending fetid bog stink up my nostrils.

One Ear attacked the haunches of the giant swamp hog.

"Run!" I sprang up. "Run like hell!"

"I can't! My hair's stuck."

A huge hoof print had pressed her hair in the muck. I pulled on it.

"Owww!" she said. "That hurts!"

I took out my Old Granddad pocket knife and, midst howls, growls, grunts and teeth-snapping not ten feet away, whacked off a big thatch of Loveda's strawberry curls. She didn't protest one whit.

My hand grabbed hers and we ran for the car, my skate-feet making tracks. I glanced at Millie Faye as I climbed behind the wheel. She still hadn't moved.

Another canine cry pierced the woods—then, silence.

Loveda slid inside the car next to me and slammed her door. I cranked the starter. Saw in the mirror a cloud of purple exhaust rise from the rear.

"What are you waiting for?" Loveda said. "Floor it before that thing comes for us!"

The ground pulsed. Hooves splashed, thumping through the peat.

I clutched and shifted and hit the gas pedal, driving us out through the gathering mist. I chanced one more look through the side mirror and, through a blue purple haze, saw Ol' Slasher standing defiant, crimson fluid dripping from his sharp tusk, silk pink panties dangling from his stumpy one.

CHAPTER 39

Ghostly Darkness and Blue-Gray Fog

"Check on Millie Faye," I said.

With nary a word, Loveda slipped over the seat—head first, skirt pleated over her butt cheeks. I tried not to think on her missing panties.

She came back over the seat. "She's still breathing, but feeble."

Loveda didn't hug the passenger door, but she didn't scoot over near me neither. She pulled up the hem of her skirt and wiped bog scum off her face. I glimpsed creamy freckled thighs and matching red scuff marks on her knees. She turned the rearview mirror her way and gasped. "My God, you almost cut it all off!" She reached a hand up to her hair.

I didn't mind about the mirror—too much going on in front of me to look back.

"Sorry, I didn't know what else to do," I said.

She pulled and adjusted her dirty red curls, trying to shape half a head of hair into something that looked good. She sighed. "Remind me never to go for a ride with you again. No boy in the whole of Missouri will want me now."

She was so wrong. I wanted her more than ever. Half a head of hair on her head looked twice as fetching as a whole head of hair on any other girl.

We crept along through curtains of dank moss hanging from limbs over the road. Threw the car in a ghostly darkness whilst skimming the roof and sides.

"You can't see where you're going," Loveda said. "You're liable to run us into quicksand. Stop a second." She hopped out the car. "I'll scout the road." Webbed tendrils of moss parted and closed behind her.

A girl braving the unknown, only minutes earlier cowering before wild dogs.

I suspected, at that moment, this girl would forever amaze me.

The red Chevrolet coughed and backfired. Engine sounded like Millie Faye's missin' heart.

I turned around and looked at my poor sister. Pale mucus streamed down her gray cheek from her nose. I leaned over the seat and wiped it away with my thumb. Substituted a smear of mud for mucus. Her skin felt clammy. Her nose, in the mossy light, looked smaller than ever, face thin and shrunken.

I sang her a lullaby:

Little birdie, little birdie, come and sing me your song,
Had a short time to be with you, and a long time to be gone.

The car coughed and backfired again. It, too, was dying. Its sides caved in, hood battered, bumper torn and motor shot.

A skeletal hunk of lichen, caught in the crack between the door and mainframe dripped moisture on my thigh. Smelled clean. I squinted up at the crack in the door and saw a streak of sunlight shining there.

Loveda burst through the moss, half a head of muddy red hair whipping her shoulders. She jumped in. "Let's go, turning just a smidgen to the right as you do." She grinned behind a film of dirt. "You drive, I'll direct."

She put an elbow on the dash and stared out the windshield. Her left hand reached over and covered mine on the steering wheel.

We eased through the moss, pulling the car a little to the right.

Tires pulled out of squish and squirt and caught crunch and crackle. Air grew less thick, and nekked tree branches pierced a blue sky. My eyes blinked at the light.

Could see the road, through melting snow, winding up toward Wrestlers Ridge. Blue mist from below and errant clouds from above still hid Luella's Leap.

Loveda released my hand and clapped, bouncing up and down. "We done it, Mo Grady!" she said "We made it through the swamp!"

She swept an imaginary lock of hair off her forehead, took her remaining hair and rolled it up in her hand. She examined the muddy mess. "Give me your knife," she said.

I took it from my pocket, flipped open the two-inch blade with my fingernail, and handed it to her, butt end first. She adjusted the mirror again and commenced sawing on her remaining hair.

I couldn't bear to watch.

Loveda rolled down the window. A draft of cold air chilled the back of my neck. "So long, Rumpelstiltskin." She tossed out the coiled red wad.

Just like that.

I memorized landmarks. Maybe, come spring, redbirds would weave strands of those silken scarlet locks into their nests. Oh, how wonderful that would be. To nest in Loveda's hair.

She scooted next to me, squeezed my shoulder, pressed her thigh against mine.

I peeked at her profile. Might as well have been a stranger, she looked so different. Almost boyish. Hair shorter than mine. Her lilac smell replaced by peat-moss. She even talked different. Not at all like the sweet city girl back at her grandma's farm.

I wondered if my negative 'bog trash' polarity rubbed off on her. And, if so, why did she look so radiant?

The melting road turned into a narrow ledge along a canyon wall. I took my time. Loveda's head snaked over and peered out the driver's window past me. The canyon below yawned, showing jagged boulders like mismatched goblin teeth along the edges.

"Whew! Sure is a long way down." Loveda eased back, turning her head toward me, her warm breath blowing right under my nose, kissable lips a fraction of an inch away from mine.

If I stopped now, with the engine missin' a stroke, I might not ever get goin' again. I lost sight of the road for a second, but I kept the front end cut into the bluff. Limestone scratched against the metal car body.

Uncle Harm thumped against his coffin walls.

Mama's voice rang in my head and gave me strength: You have to get to the top before you can start down the other side.

Loveda settled down beside me, her thigh pressing against me.

We stayed that way for a while, thigh to thigh, without talking, climbing along the narrow ledge. Great globs of snow fell on us from cliffs above. A pair of red-tailed hawks kept us company.

A gust of pure mountain air enveloped us with a combination of sweet rosemary and decaying step uncle. Which, strangely enough, upped the polarity.

We broke out at last into a clearing. Luella's Leap lay to the left. Our road, somewhat improved, kept going down the other side, and off to the right lay another overgrown road with a crude wooden sign that read, THIS WAY LIES ... destination, broken off.

I turned left and parked where the red Chevrolet faced downhill, overlooking Sulphur Lick Valley. I reached over Loveda's lap and pulled on the emergency brake.

The stench of Uncle Harm overtook us. Loveda's face twisted. "Hurry and hop out!"

The hog-damaged door sprang open with both of us pushing. We tumbled out in a pile on the damp snow.

Loveda jumped to her feet, grabbed my hand and pulled me up. I peeked at the back seat. Millie Faye still lay curled up like a sowbug, unawares of our plight. Maybe better she stayed a petrified mummy if our great crusade was nearing an end.

"Let's look over the edge," Loveda said. She dragged me, slipping and sliding on my skate-feet, toward the bluff.

I tugged her back from the edge. "We gotta be careful. Don't want to wind up like the girl this bluff was named after."

"Ohhhhh, what a magnificent view!" Loveda's hand fused with mine.

Like a sidewinder snake, the road to Scuttles Grunt cut through the valley floor. Railroad tracks reminded me of Doc Abernathy's stitches. The Baptist church steeple stuck up like a thorn in Heaven's eye.

"There's Grandma's farm," Loveda said, pointing to a neat white house and red barn.

I looked at the brown gash in Widow Johnson's cornfield where Uncle Harm had buried her 300 pigs. Next to that, I could make out Cemetery Hill and the dot marking Uncle Harm's unused grave.

I strained to make out our farm. Trees blocked the farmhouse, but tiny barnyard shapes shuffled about. Jubal Jen scratched her tough hide on the busted manure spreader. Reminded me that, if we got out of this fix, I needed to make one more trip to the farm to do two things: rescue Pink and take my sweet-natured pet hog down deep into the Blue Bog to keep them safe from Aunt Big Bertha.

Thick blue-gray fog roiled up from the bog. Images of giant snakes and lizards and beetles took shape. Twisted willow limbs, charred black by the winter cold, formed vaporous monster heads. An odor of stagnant water and rotting reptiles and peat moss wafted up. Ravens gronked, flying in and out of charred willows. They looked no bigger'n houseflies.

Ol' Blue Satan lay waiting down there. Waiting for a sacrifice.

I stepped back from the precipice. But Loveda clamored closer, fearless, strawberry hair stubs, now dry, blowing in an updraft. She trusted me to hold her. My heart was in my hand.

How easy it would be to take a step forward. Solve all my problems in one little leap.

CHAPTER 40

Cottonmouth Kiss
and Sacramental Wafers

Loveda, standing on the edge of the bluff, smiled at me—no inkling of my twisted thoughts.

I held on to her with all my might. Skate-feet locked in place. Loveda pulled toward me, her face pained. "Not so hard, Mo Grady, you're crushin' me."

That's what I wanted to do. Crush her against me. Keep her safe from the world. Safe from Aunt Big Bertha. Safe from Ol' Blue Satan. Safe from Mo Grady Witt.

But to do that I had to push her away. Away from my obsessive covetousness. I wanted her and yet, I knew the only way I could ever have her was to let her go.

But not while she was hanging over the abyss.

I pulled her back.

"What's the matter, Mo Grady? Your face is pale as these cliffs. Are you afraid of heights?"

"Yes," I said. "I'm afraid."

We backed away from the edge, and Loveda ran ahead of me and jumped on the front fender of the red Chevrolet. Her skirt billowed briefly. My eyes skimmed past her pantie-less parts and fixed on her hacked-off head hair. Her skirt settled over the left headlight.

Well, lack of headlight. Victim of that double barrel shotgun blast. The fender was scrunched up like an accordion, and monstrous silver claw marks gouged the passenger side. My bran'-spankin'-new, '55, red Chevrolet looked ancient.

Loveda, on the other hand, was a bran'-spankin'-new, '55 girl.

Knowing me, would she, too, end up in the scrap heap at Bonker Beckman's Wrecking Yard?

I gave that notion some powerful thought.

I heard engine noise. The Postlewaite's black '49 Dodge coupe entered the clearing. Inside, two and a half heads bobbed—Aunt Big Bertha and the two-headed preacher, his snakebit head shrunk way down. The Dodge pulled up, parking sideways, blocking our exit.

"Uh, oh," Loveda hopped off the red Chevrolet, and I noticed it rolled forward a few inches toward the bluff.

Was the emergency brake broke, too? My thoughts flew to Millie Faye inside.

I walked on my skate-feet to the passenger side rear door of the red Chevrolet and opened it. My wee twin lay on her side, legs hiked up to her chest, face with a tinge of pink—more color than the last time I'd looked. I picked her up in my arms.

Aunt Big Bertha lunged out of the shotgun seat of the Dodge, her weapon in her right hand. She clutched something with the other hand to her massive udder.

I reckoned she'd gone back to the farm in the Postlewaite's car and got her husband. That same molten lava hairpiece crowned her head, bangs down to the middle of her forehead. Cropped her face hard above her smoldering eyes. She wore under her overalls a red flannel shirt that I recognized as Uncle Harm's.

Aunt Big Bertha raised up the double barrel shotgun to rest on her shoulder and, still clutching something to her bosom, walked toward us. "Get away from the car, Mo Grady."

She stood four car lengths away, but I could see her lips brittle as bog ice, eyes ridged and rank as pig hickory nuts.

I didn't take my eyes off the shotgun.

Loveda moved between me and our car's open door. "She's madder than that old hog. What do we do?"

"If'n she points that shotgun toward us, duck behind this door. If she fires and misses, run like hell whilst she reloads."

The last time I'd seen the two-headed preacher, he was a'humping Aunt Big Bertha. He looked different now, like he had more control of his right side. He strode up behind his wife and grabbed her arm folded across her breast. "Now, Bertha Sue," he said, "put down that shotgun. Just get in the Chevrolet and be gone. The boy and girl can ride with me till you calm down. Or make them walk home. That'll be lesson enough for these youngin's."

Aunt Big Bertha pivoted and swung that shotgun over her head with one easy motion. The hard steel barrels came down hard on her husband's unholy hump.

He yelped and fell on his knees, hands clasped over his shoulder, main head twisted in pain. His mouth made quick sucking and blowing sounds. Aunt Big Bertha raised the shotgun again, and I thought she'd bring it down on his skull.

A few hours ago they'd been humpin' like goats, but now that he stood in the way of her stuff, she had no need of him. Maybe their mating had triggered some kind of black widow spider craving—she could easily take off his head with one blow.

I handed off Millie Faye to Loveda.

Loveda stepped behind the open car door.

Weak sunlight filtered through the roiling mist coming up from the bog as Aunt Big Bertha turned toward us.

"The Lord has commanded me to take possession of this Chevrolet, you little bastard," her voice bellowed, "and so's you won't be tempted to steal it again, I'm gonna fill your ass with buckshot. And since you got your little Jezebel with you, and your possum-playin' bastard sister, whose blasphemous tongue offends the Almighty, I'm gonna have to fill their asses with buckshot, too."

The red Chevrolet rolled forward a couple more inches.

"Who's she callin' a Jezebel?" Loveda said.

"Bertha Sue," the two-headed preacher said, his clubbed head spasming underneath his coat, "leave 'em be. Your brain's done gone around the bend, thinkin' you can use a shotgun on kids."

"The boy, his whore, and unholy sister are not kids." She brought up the shotgun again to her shoulder with one arm. "He's a disciple of the Devil and they follow his lead. Didn't you see the cottonmouth kiss him? You been giving snake services for ten years, and how many times you seen that happen? None, that's how many. Satan has seduced the boy's soul, and I'm gonna give Satan the boy's filthy body."

She brought her hand away from her bosom, holding a black squirming shape. "And how do you explain this?"

Aunt Big Bertha had pup-napped Pink.

I slugged the car door. The two-headed preacher must've told her about the lion laying down with the lamb.

"He was told by both his whoring mother and my dear departed brother not to keep a dog on the farm," she said, "and look what he did, hid his own hound of hell underneath the rabbit."

The shape wiggled. Mewed for its mama.

That'd be me. I breathed life into her.

Pink, not even with her eyes open yet, in the clutches of a crazy. She was born out of her mama's torn flesh by a monster, now at the mercy of another monster.

Millie Faye stirred. Tiny tongue wetted dry lips. "I was in a big circus ring, Mo Grady," she said, "and I was dressed in a frilly white skirt and dancing on the back of Ol' Slasher, who was wearing a goddamn pair of pink silk panties."

My little foul-mouthed birdie was back. She wriggled out of Loveda's arms. Sagged against the doorframe for a minute, glanced through the window. "Whoa, Mo Grady, where are we? I don't 'member Aunt Bit Tits with a shotgun … and is that our pup in her paw?"

"Just stand there and keep quiet till you finish wakin' up," I said.

"Damnation if I will!" Millie Faye's post-coma voice quavered but carried. "What's the matter with you? Do something before Aunt Big Tits hurts our dog."

"You got your retarded sister behind that car door?" Aunt Big Bertha said, "I knew she was fakin' that coma."

Millie Faye's stick-haired head leaned out from the car. "I ain't retarded." All quaver gone. "And if you hurt Pink, I'll have my mama put a curse on you will make your baldhead full of maggots."

Aunt Big Bertha laughed. "Well, if your Mama had any ability at cursing, she wouldn't be in jail a'waitin' the 'lectric chair, would she? And see this pup? It's gonna fly. Let's see if you can hex this hell hound, keep it from flying on back to Hades."

She wound up her pitching arm in a circle.

"Don't do it!" the two-headed preacher said.

On the third wind, she pitched the mewing pup in a high arc toward the edge of the bluff.

My skate-feet took off slipping and sliding, heading to intercept. I kept my eyes over my shoulder, on the twirling pup, much like I imagined the great outfielder Willie Mays would, if he were catching a dog on the fly.

My feet sensed the approaching edge. I slowed down but kept looking backwards. Here come'd Pink dropping out of a murky sky like a meteor. In that one-hundredth of a second, I could see her in every detail. My mind marveled at how she'd taken to Cassandra's milk, stomach plump and perfect, pink blotch ablaze, voice strong in her terror.

I hoped with all my holy roller heart my catching hands would be as good as my pitching arm.

My hands flew up above my head and Pink plopped in them. I fumbled. My heart missed a beat. Hands tossed her around like a hot coal then latched onto a back leg. Pink whined so hard, it's a wonder she didn't turn herself inside out. My feet skidded to a halt. The front half of my skates didn't have nothin' under them.

Ol' Blue Satan called up to me, "Come on down, Mo Grady, the water's fine. We be sittin' here, eatin' fried chicken and drinkin' red elderberry wine."

I kept Pink in one hand and threw the other out for counterbalance, waving my empty hand for a hold. But my momentum pitched me forward. I looked down into the blue jaws of the burning abyss.

I hear ya, Ol' Blue Satan. I'm a comin'.

A distant wail erupted. I wondered how Millie Faye mustered

enough strength so soon for her obnoxious whimpering. And how sorry I was I wouldn't get to hear that foul mouth ever again.

A hand caught my back pocket.

Amongst girl grunts and ripping sounds, I tilted upright and got pulled backwards to land on Loveda. Landed so hard on her stomach, she swooshed all her breath past my ear. Pink squealed.

I rolled off and got to my knees, and here come'd Millie Faye crawling, face like a death mask, to clutch Pink and climb in my arms. No vine ever hugged a tree so tight. Loveda caught her breath and got in on the cluster hug—the three … four of us clinging to life and to each other.

A gust of noxious air whistled up from under the cliff, chilling my sweaty armpits.

Aunt Big Bertha rounded the Dodge with the shotgun firmly in hand. Both barrels pointing dead at my chest. The way we kids wrapped together, we'd all be knocked over the cliff.

"You should be sayin' your prayers," Aunt Big Bertha said. "Ask the good Lord for forgiveness for your sins 'cause none of you are leaving Luella's Leap alive."

"We haven't even done any sinning," Loveda's hand flew up and brushed away phantom hair from her eyes.

"I got plenty of evil deeds," Aunt Big Bertha said, "starting with either this little bastard or his whoring mother who killed my brother."

"From what my grandmother says," Loveda said, "your brother deserved it."

Aunt Big Bertha turned the shotgun toward her.

"Bertha Sue," the two-headed preacher said, "stop this madness. Mo Grady is innocent. So is his mother." He struggled to his feet. His good head sagged on his injured head. "It was me gave Harman Cornelius the Destroying Angel mushrooms."

Aunt Big Bertha's shotgun barrel shook.

My heart beat faster.

Gravel crunched under the red Chevrolet's tires as it lurched forward yet another few inches. Stopped. A clunk came from the ashtray on the back seat. My magic magnet was in there.

Savvy crows, well out of shotgun range, clustered together and cawed. Wind ceased, leaving a sour odor of swamp muck and decaying body hanging in the thick air. Aunt Big Bertha ran a hand over her red wig.

The twin killer eyes of the shotgun turned toward the two-headed preacher, then swung back to my chest. "You're just sayin' that to save these pagans," she said to her husband. "Well, it's not gonna work."

"No," the two-headed preacher flung himself forward and grabbed her thick waist, "it's the truth. Brother Harman was sick abed and wanted to confess his sins. He told me how he was acquirin' the best farm land in Sulphur Lick Valley, infecting farmers' hogs with cholera so's to bankrupt them and get their farms dirt cheap. And, in the case of Farmer Johnson, caused this girl's granddaddy to commit suicide."

Loveda's freckled face turned gray.

"Told me about unnatural acts with children," the preacher said. "How he defiled and desecrated them in the Lord's name."

"My brother would do no such a thing," Aunt Big Bertha said. "Snakebite's demented you. My own husband, a lying sack of snake venom."

"It's what he told me. As the spiritual leader of this Holiness Christian flock, I had to put an end to his defilement. It was my God-given duty. I took some of Mildred Garnet's Destroying Angel mushrooms and fed them to Harman Cornelius. Told him they were sacramental wafers. I left him reading the Good Book."

I put Pink in Millie Faye's hands. "Take Pink and crawl into the woods. Hurry."

"I ain't going without you."

Aunt Big Bertha swung the shotgun to the two-headed preacher.

The two-headed preacher leaned back, supporting himself with both hands against the hood of the Dodge. "No, Bertha Sue!"

The shotgun blast and a scream carried out over the whole valley. Like'd to burst my ears.

The preacher's snakebite head imploded into pulp, and he catapulted backwards over the hood. His feet and arms jerked and thumped a few seconds, legs vibrated, then he lay still. Blood splattered the snow in a jagged circle.

Crows sprang out of the surrounding trees and filled the sky with flapping wings and cawing beaks. A red bird flew to a tree and, for once, didn't have nothin' to say.

Aunt Big Bertha froze, one shotgun barrel smoking, still aiming her weapon at her husband's body.

"Stay behind the car door," I said to Loveda and Millie Faye. I reached in the back seat ashtray and retrieved my magnet. Warm to the touch and fitting favorably in my hand, like when I used it to clobber the Postlewaite brothers. Magnetic powers at full tilt.

I thought about smacking Aunt Big Bertha in the back of the head as she cogitated over shooting her own husband, but she turned too quick. And, I could tell by the way she swiveled the shotgun in our direction, she was through with talking.

I faced the last out of the ninth inning. The only moving target I'd ever hit before with my good pitching arm was the banty rooster for Mama's ceremonial sanctifying of our farmhouse, but that was no life and death situation. Well, maybe for the rooster.

I didn't have no windup time so's I just concentrated on that flaming red head and said an incantation to one of Mama's favorite pagan witches:

"Oh, gentle Charra, I will always love you,
if my pitching arm be quick and true."

I let fly.

I watched the magic magnet twirl toward Aunt Big Bertha's elongated head. Alas, the metal disc took a steep nosedive slightly short of its target.

I had failed. I closed my eyes. I'd failed not only myself, but Millie Faye, Loveda and Pink. I waited for my chest to be torn apart with buckshot. Instead I heard a distinct clink.

My eyes popped open.

The flat of the magnet had stuck positive to the end of the shotgun barrel, sealing both exit holes.

Oh, if only a St. Louis Cardinals talent scout could see me now! I'd just thrown the greatest sinker in the history of baseball. 'Course the magic magnet's natural attraction to steel didn't hurt none.

Aunt Big Bertha pulled the trigger, and the gun exploded in her face. Her big red wig hurled over the Dodge like a fiery tumbleweed. Her face and bald head were blackened, eyebrows singed to match. Give her a set of horns and you'd think she was the Devil incarnate.

She staggered backwards, still holding the shotgun.

"I'm gonna tackle her before she can reload," I said. "Only chance we've got."

"Two tacklers are better'n one," Loveda said.

"I'll keep Pink safe," Millie Faye chimed in.

Before I could say yay or nay, Loveda took off. My feet sped after her.

We didn't get much past Uncle Harm's coffin.

A flock of crows followed a fast-moving object coming up the bog road. A heavy galloping, like a plow horse unshackled, shook snow off tree limbs in its wake.

Aunt Big Bertha heard it, too. Her charcoal head cocked sideways—the shotgun, belching smoke out both ends, drooped on her hip.

CHAPTER 41

Steamrollering Death
and Ripe Persimmon

Ol' Slasher topped the ridge, breath billowing on either side of his head like a steam engine. His livid pig eyes spotted me, his slavering snout let out a satisfied grunt and, without slowing down, plowed snow in my direction.

So awesome was Ol' Slasher that, for a split second, given my choices, I considered jumping over the bluff again. But then me and Loveda, as if tuned in to each other's mind, swerved behind Aunt Big Bertha, putting my step aunt and the smoking gun between us and the snorting hog.

Nothing like steamrollering death to focus the concentration. Aunt Big Bertha come'd out of her daze and, quick-like, swung the butt end of the shotgun at the rushing hog. Hit him square between his beady eyes.

Alas, Ol' Slasher hadn't slashed his last. A hog the size of him has a forehead plate three-quarters of an inch thick. That steel gun may have slowed him down a mite and given him a hog-sized headache, but it wouldn't stop him for long.

He did stop plowing snow. He leveled his bloody head at Aunt Big Bertha, who fumbled in her pocket for more shotgun shells. Her hand shook so bad she dropped the ones she pulled out. Didn't matter much. That shotgun, way it bent from the inward explosion, didn't look fit for shooting.

Ol' Slasher wheezed, wobbled sideways first to the left, then to the right and then, averaging things out, charged straight in the middle.

Aunt Big Bertha moved so quick, she runned right out from under her shotgun. It plopped to the ground, and Ol' Slasher galloped right over it.

Aunt Big Bertha, availing herself of the only high ground in her immediate vicinity, plowed toward the red Chevrolet, pulled herself up on top of Uncle Harm's coffin and straddled it with her log legs.

Ol' Slasher smacked the coffin so hard the whole car shook. Hard tusks and soft pine collided.

He jerked his head around and, had not a 250-pound woman been sitting on that coffin, the hell hog would've yanked it right out of the car. The box, as it was, bounced around so turbulent, Aunt Big Bertha flailed her arms and legs—a rider of a bucking bronco. Uncle Harm thumped and rattled inside.

The red Chevrolet lurched forward again. Snow squished. Rock gnashed. Metal groaned.

When the boar backed off, I saw he'd gored a gash in the coffin the size of a watermelon. Rancid air gushed out. The giant hog jerked away and rubbed his nose back and forth in the snow.

Ol' Slasher lunged again. Tried climbing over the bumper at her and got a cloven foot stuck. Shoved the car ahead another yard. A scraping sounded in the wheel well. Brakes protesting. Only two car lengths separated the red Chevrolet from the edge.

Behind me, the two-headed preacher groaned and stumbled to his feet, not dead like I'd thought. He'd just lost his spare head. His shoulder was a mangled mess. He lunged toward the driver's side of the red Chevrolet.

"What's he up to?" Loveda said.

"No telling. He's insane with pain," I said.

The two-headed preacher's feet dangled out the driver's side door, his hands on the gearshift and emergency brake. He struggled to pivot himself, and then put his foot on the brakes.

The hog bucked, caused the car to roll in fits and starts closer to the bluff's edge.

The two-headed preacher slumped over the wheel. Aunt Big Bertha tried to swing her leg over her brother's coffin but fell back and plowed her right foot in the watermelon-sized hole in it. Leg wedged firm up to her shin. She cussed and leaned over and reached in the hole, grabbed and jerked. Sure enough, her hands came away with a leg, but not the leg she was pulling on: Uncle Harm's skeletal big toe had hooked onto her shirtsleeve.

Aunt Big Bertha bellowed, "Abomination!" She near to shook her arm loose from the shoulder, trying to get shed of that foul thing.

"Shoot the hog," Aunt Big Bertha said, pointing at the shotgun and shells on the ground.

"Don't shoot Ol' Slasher. He needs our help." Millie Faye clutched Pink to her neck. "Do something to get him unstuck."

"What?" Loveda said. "He's tried to kill us twice now."

I picked up the shotgun, leaving the shells in the muck. Pulled my magic magnet off the gun barrels. I palmed the metal disc, hot and heavy, still doing its polarity work. My skin felt the suck energy stronger than ever.

I dashed round the rear end of the bucking hog. Reached the furthest lip of limestone and wedged the magic magnet up between two stout rocks, suck side having a clear shot at that red Chevrolet.

A metallic clunk sounded within the car's steel framework. The brakes letting go. The red Chevrolet crept onward.

I ran back to Loveda, grabbed her hand and pulled her with me whilst I rounded the hog once more. Ol' Slasher quit jerking and cocked his great head to peer at me with eyes big as ripe persimmons.

"Gab his tail and pull," I told Loveda, "and I'll pry on his hoof."

She didn't question, just grabbed a'hold and pulled on that grungy tail for all she was worth.

I slid the shotgun barrel over a bumper bracket and under Ol' Slasher's hoof. Then fell on the stock for leverage.

Aunt Big Bertha pounded me on the head with a fist. "What the hell you doin'? Shoot the fucking hog!"

The car tilted, pulled by the magnet's force.

Ol' Slasher's leg popped out.

Without the hog's ballast, the car plunged forward.

The two-headed preacher tromped brakes that wouldn't brake.

Aunt Bertha's mouth twisted into a curse.

Front wheels slid over the edge of Luella's Leap.

The red Chevrolet tipped at a 90-degree angle, high centered on its frame for a second, then the whole lot slid forward, separating from the earth.

The two-headed preacher drove that red Chevrolet through the Pearly Gates. Aunt Big Bertha rode it into Hades, her big legs wrapped around her brother's coffin. Just before she disappeared into the thick, blue mist, she looked up with eyes like onyx gravestones and waved Uncle Harm's leg bone at us. Her last words echoed throughout Sulphur Lick Valley: "I'll come back to haunt you, you little bastard, and your retarded sister, too."

Millie Faye, clutching Pink to her chest, stretched her pencil-thin neck over the cliff. "I ain't retarded," she shouted, "I'm just puny!"

CHAPTER 42

They Just Don't Make Cars
Like They Used To

We stood at the edge of the bluff for several minutes, staring down into the Blue Bog.

Loveda elbowed me and whispered, "There's a giant hog beside you, and he don't look any friendlier than before."

Ol' Slasher snorted and pawed loose rock with his injured leg. Must've had a splitting headache from the shotgun butt, too.

Ol' Slasher leveled his beady eyes at me.

We two-legged folks backed away. I still had the shotgun, but with its crooked barrels it weren't no use. 'Sides, Ol' Slasher had just saved us, and we him in return. Figured that made us even. Just hoped Ol' Slasher was equally willin' to let bygones by bygones and forgive us stealin' a tusk tip.

As we continued our backwards shuffle, Sheriff Starkey's black and white Mercury pulled up behind the Dodge coupe. Mama and Freeman Joe sat in the back seat.

The sheriff got out and reached under his seat. Pulled out a high caliber rifle. I heard him shuffle a shell in the chamber. "Don't move, Mo Grady, so's I can get a clear shot."

I moved. Moved in between the sheriff and the hog. I stood not five feet from Ol' Slasher, keeping eye contact. "No, Sheriff," I hollered over my shoulder, "don't shoot! Give him a chance to go back to the bog. He saved our lives."

"Get away from there, Mo Grady," Mama said.

"Nothin' doin'. I've had enough death for one day."

"Listen to him, Mildred Garnet," Freeman Joe said. "Give Mo Grady a chance to do what he needs to do."

Millie Faye broke the standoff. She handed Pink to Loveda and walked right over to Ol' Slasher. Nose to tusk. Goblins got guts—even puny goblins.

Ol' Slasher raised his great head.

My twin's dreamy eyes met his, and I heard thoughts going back and forth between them. Pain. Loneliness. Heartache. Two misfits finding each other.

Millie Faye wrapped her tiny fingers 'round his sharp tusk and took her other hand and rubbed the blunt one, like soothing a wound. She lay her head on his massive forehead.

"Do somethin', Freeman Joe," Mama said.

Freeman Joe shook his head. "Them twins got a plan. I got confidence in 'em. They come by it honestly, you know."

I lowered the shotgun. Strained to hear Millie Faye and the great hog talk—a jumble of words, gaacks and images gliding along so fast, I just caught some here and some there.

Millie Faye crooked her head and said, "I think I understand what he's sayin': humans—with their predictably unpredictable ways—sure do get teedjus. He wants to be done with us. He's tired of it all. Just wants to go back to his cave in the Blue Bog and heal his wounds. Please, everybody, let him go home." Her voice was soft but clear.

Millie Faye's fingers grabbed a'hold of Ol' Slasher's blunt tusk and tugged him toward the forest. He limped after. Waddled and gimped. His stout tail laying on the ground. No longer the fearsome beast.

I kept pace, my body in line with Sheriff Starkey's rifle.

Freeman Joe reached a hand out and tilted the sheriff's gun barrel up in the air.

Me and Millie Faye entered the trees, and Ol' Slasher's tail sprang straight up. He lumbered ahead, disappearing into the woods.

Hogs may not forget, but they do forgive.

I felt Mama's cuff upside my head. I turned and saw tears in her eyes. She hugged me to her breast. "That was for keepin' awful secrets from me, son. Why didn't you tell me about Harman Cornelius doing wrong by you and Millie Faye? Now I'm sorry it wasn't me that killed him."

Millie Faye wrapped herself around Mama's legs, "Mama! Mama, you're not going to the 'lectric chair!"

Mama's tears flowed freely. She pulled Millie Faye up in her arms. "How could I have been so blind," she said, "and put my chillun in such jeopardy? I wouldn't blame you if you hated me the rest of your life."

"We don't hate you, Mama. We missed you," Millie Faye said. "We missed you somethin' awful."

As usual, Millie Faye said it all.

Freeman Joe came up to me and stuck out his hand for a real man-of-the-house handshake. He smiled a rare, uncrazy smile. Eyes clear.

My hand got lost in his big paw, but I squeezed real hard and the next thing I knew, I'm being hugged to his barrel chest, just like he might do if he was my real daddy, the sonsa ... Wait. I didn't have to call my real daddy a sonsa-you-know-what, anymore.

I knew better. I wasn't raised that way.

"How'd y'all know to find us here?" I said.

Sheriff Starkey thumbed his gun belt. "My phone's been ringing off the hook 'cause of you. Got a call from Mr. Postlewaite, said his boys claimed Bertha Sue Waywater done tried to kill you and then took their car. Got a call from Widow Johnson, said her granddaughter done run off with you. Said you left your scarf by their telephone. Got a call from Doc Abernathy, said you and your sick sister never showed up, and he worried you might've had trouble on the way."

Sheriff Starkey drew in a deep breath and released it unhurried. "And got a call from Widow Atkins, said the Reverend and Bertha Sue stopped by her place in this here stolen Dodge, askin' if they'd seen the red Chevrolet. She said the Reverend blessed her new fruit hat and handed her his very own Bible. He'd stuck a note in it for me, next to a circled Bible passage in Psalms 91, Chapter 10. His note confessed to the murder of Harman Cornelius Claggett. The last Widow Atkins seen the Waywaters, they were headed up the main road to Luella's Leap. Well, I put two and two together, and I ain't the Sheriff of Stonecrop

County for nothin'." He shifted his gut around his belt and looked at me. "By the way, where's the reverend and his wife?"

Me, Millie Faye and Loveda all pointed at the cliff.

"Look here," the sheriff said. "There's tire tracks leading over the cliff."

Freeman Joe stiffened: "Psalm 91, Chapter 10 says 'no evil shall be allowed to befall you, no plague come near your tent. For he will command his angels concerning you to guard you in all ways.'"

He gently pushed me away. He and Sheriff Starkey peered over the edge. The distant cry of a red bird "good cheer, good cheer" floated around us. Way down there, a glubb sounded.

The sheriff put a hand on my shoulder. "What happened here?"

I told him what we kids had witnessed, then I took another few minutes in the telling of how it came to pass. I no sooner got done than Freeman Joe fell down on his knees and bowed his big head.

I plumb forgot that Aunt Big Bertha and Uncle Harm were his kin. We let him mourn in peace.

Millie Faye separated from Mama. "So, what about the farm?"

"Freeman Joe did a fine, uncrazy job in court," Mama said. "The farm's ours—fair and square."

Mama reached up and pulled on Millie Faye's straw hair. "Oh, chillun, I don't know how I'll ever be able to make thangs up to you."

Loveda sidled up next to me and slipped her hand into mine, still clutching Pink to her breast.

"Ain't this Loveda," Mama said, "Alma Belle Johnson's grand-daughter with a strange haircut? And making so freely with my boy's hand?"

"Yes, ma'am," Loveda smiled wide as the valley below. "And I'm gonna marry your son."

"Marry?" Mama said. "I can see by the blush on your cheeks and the moon pie look in Mo Grady's eyes, you two got a hankerin' for each other. But you'll just have to tone it down a bit—thirteen years old is a couple years too soon to think about getting' hitched."

"Same age you were when you had Rose Phoebe," Millie Faye said, reaching out to Loveda for Pink.

"I surely didn't miss your aggravatin' truth-telling mouth," Mama grabbed the puppy first. Brought it to her face for a look-see. Pink yipped, eyes still closed, tiny tail wagging.

"Mama," I said, "I know you hate dogs, but that pup's mama saved our lives. This pup deserves a chance. And now we got us a working farm, we need us a working dog."

"'Sides," Millie Faye said, "I feel a fit coming on if you don't let us keep Pink."

"Pink?" Mama held the pup over her head, away from Millie Faye's clawing hands. "Moses Grady Witt, I wonder at you and your notions. I don't hate dogs. I just hate men with dogs, who take off and leave me their hungry hounds to feed. You can keep this pup on one condition: you get that school paper writ for Miss Haige right away and 'pologize to the class."

Mama handed the pup to Millie Faye, reached over to caress my cheek. "He's a good boy," she said, like I wasn't there, "but he spends too much time studyin' on other folks' things." Her trigger finger traced across my forehead. "But you know, I see a grown-upness in him—he's gotten so tall—wasn't there before I went to jail."

"Those are his skate-feet, Mama," Millie Faye said.

I closed my eyes and let my skin enjoy Mama's touch.

Loveda's hand turned me loose. When I opened my eyes, she, Mama and Millie Faye stood off aways, all talking at once. Mama petted Pink, then handed her to Millie Faye and took out an embroidered handkerchief. She stooped down and got some snow on it and scrubbed Loveda's face.

Loveda's chicory blue eyes looked at me over Mama's shoulder.

No doubt about it, I still wanted Widow Johnson's granddaughter in the worst way. Well, maybe not the worst way. I wanted her, but didn't feel driven to own her. I knew she'd be going back to school in Springfield. And that was okay. I had things to do myself, like go to my own school. If I was ever to keep a girl like Loveda interested in me, I had to get more of an education than the eighth grade and set my sights high—be the first Witt boy to ever graduate from high school. Maybe even college.

I also had to watch over Millie Faye. Keep her alive. I didn't care what Doc said about other little people in these Ozark hills only living to eighteen. He thought my sister was already a goner when she had her Number 4 fit. Maybe he was wrong about her expiration date as well.

Somehow, watching out for Millie Faye didn't seem like such a burden anymore.

Sheriff Starkey, craning over the bluff, called to me. "You most likely got better eyesight than me, Mo Grady. What you reckon that shiny thing is, down there about ten feet on that ledge."

My eyes didn't want to see what they were seeing.

My magic magnet.

Somehow it must've dislodged before the red Chevrolet plunged into the Blue Bog. It lay suck side up, pulling on me, wanting me to climb down there and get it.

Well, for all I cared, it could be there till hell froze over. I dug my heels into the earth atop Luella's Leap. "Looks like a piece of car bumper got peeled off," I said. "You know, they just don't make cars like they used to."

I turned and helped Freeman Joe away from the bluff.

"Someone needs to drive this Dodge down the ridge," Sheriff Starkey said.

Mama started to get in the driver's side, stopped and got the keys out of the ignition. Dangled them out to me. "I reckon you drove up here, why don't you drive us on home, and then we'll get this car to the Postlewaites?"

Loveda got in the back seat with Freeman Joe, her scrubbed eyes watching me. Millie Faye sat in the front seat, cooing at Pink.

"These shoes are killing me, Mama," I said. "I'd just as soon get in the back seat and give my pretty feet a rest."

I climbed over Loveda and sat between her and my daddy.

"Your what feet?" Mama said.

"His pretty feet," Loveda said. "Your son has got the prettiest feet in Sulphur Lick Valley, maybe in the whole great state of Missouri."

Mama snorted. "I got a lot of catchin' up to do. Can't even go to jail for a spell without all polarity gettin' out of whack."

We rolled away from Luella's Leap.

I felt glad to be going back home. That ridgetop road with the broken sign leading away from Sulphur Lick Valley would have to wait.

I turned to Mama. "I'm eager to get started on my essay. I got so much to say, I don't see how I'm gonna keep it to a thousand words. Maybe it'll be one of those novels with little Heidi and Huck Finn travelin' on a journey down the Mississippi."

"If'n you do," Millie Faye popped up and said, "put me in it. Call it *Holy Roller Heart*."

I hunkered around for a last look out the rear window. My mind replayed the image of that beat-up, bran'-spankin'-new, red '55 Chevrolet diving over the bluff—a bloody, black-clad figure hunched over the steering wheel; a righteous, charcoal-faced, bald-headed woman cussing a blue streak on her way down; and the last thing to disappear, a coffin. So long, Uncle Harm.

It was then I recollected: last time I saw the two-headed preacher, the two-headed preacher only had one head.

BIOGRAPHY

MITCH LUCKETT spent the first 12 years of his life on a hard-scrabble farm in the hills of ol' Missouri. He did a stint in the Navy during the Vietnam era and returned to Missouri to get a BA in English Literature from Truman University. He then headed west to Oregon and settled on the Olympic Peninsula in Washington. He has been a hod-carrier, pre-school teacher, landscaper, school bus driver, and Portland Audubon Nature Sanctuaries Director.

Mitch enjoys storytelling, songwriting, and playing old-timey music. Mitch's flair for storytelling and music came together in a CD, *Tall Tales and Blue Grass*. As a freelance writer for 35 years, he has written dozens of articles and short stories for regional magazines and newspapers. Mitch combines two art forms, music and storytelling, into humorous and sometimes poignant stage performances. Whether Ozark Mountain tall tales, narrative songs, Olympic Mountain parables, Native American myths or a book-length yarn, Mitch has a gift for the ancient art of storytelling.

Holy Roller Heart is Mitch's third novel. *To Kill a Common Loon* was Mitch's first novel, followed by a sequel, *The Man in the Loon*.

You can contact Mitch at mluckett43@gmail.com or visit his website: www.mitchluckett.com.

ACKNOWLEDGMENTS

I'd like to thank General Motors for inspiring this story. The first time I laid eyes on my step uncle Hiram's 1955 red Chevrolet Bel Air, it was lust at first sight. I was eleven, living on a hog farm outside Hawk Point, Missouri, when I locked sights on that fiery juggernaut coming from beyond the corn field. Coveting came naturally. A lifetime later, I had no choice but to memorialize that blazing chariot in a novel.

I also thank Celeste Bennett, my intrepid publisher, who was forced by a world-wide pandemic to detour from our original plan to publish *Holy Roller Heart* in 2020. Thankfully, its publishing time has come around again. Her talented editor, Adam Finlay, gave my story a skillful tune-up, tightening the nuts and bolts. Another driving force who helped overhaul this yarn, was Janet Anthony (a nit-picky Virgo)—who better to have behind the wheel?

Finally, I want to acknowledge my Portland, Oregon writing critique group for steering me in the right direction in the early stages of story development.